Praise for *Return to Exile*

"Compelling. *Return to Exile* took me to a time period that I had never been that interested in and built a sympathetic heart in me for the horrific things Christians had to face in that area and time. Because Lynne Gentry's characters are so well developed, they took up residence in my thoughts and have lingered there for over a week after I finished reading the book. Of course, I can hardly wait until the next book comes out. I believe every Christian should read these books to give them an awareness of how blessed we are to be able to live our beliefs without fearing for our lives."

—Lena Nelson Dooley, author of the double-award-winning *Catherine's Pursuit*

"*Return to Exile,* Lynne Gentry's sweeping saga of lost dreams, epic struggles, sinister passions, and unrequited love—all playing out against the stunning backdrop of third-century Rome—returns to enthrall readers of her earlier *Healer of Carthage.* With surprising twists readers won't see coming, Gentry has created an inspiring story few will be able to put down until the final page. I am a huge fan of the Carthage Chronicles series, and of author Lynne Gentry. Can hardly wait for the final installment to see how everything turns out for Dr. Lisbeth Hastings!"

—Kellie Coates Gilbert, author of *A Woman of Fortune*

"Gentry has done it again! Book Two in the Carthage Chronicles had me weeping and cheering right along with the main characters, Lisbeth and Cyprian. Their struggle to forge a life from the ashes of Carthage's diseased city made my heart pound, and as the peril facing them ratchetted, so did my pulse rate. Add Gentry's enviable talent for wordsmithing, and *Return to Exile* makes for an incredibly entertaining read."

—Elizabeth Ludwig, author of *Tide and Tempest*

"In *Return to Exile,* Lynne Gentry takes readers on another breathtaking journey as they are transported with Lisbeth from the twenty-first century back to third-century Carthage. But this time, while Lisbeth thinks she's prepared for what awaits her on the other side of the Cave of the Swimmers, there's no way for her to anticipate the frightening reality, as she is thrown into an impossible situation that will leave readers begging for more."

—Lisa Harris, author of the Christy Award–winning novel *Dangerous Passage*

"Author Lynne Gentry has done it again! *Return to Exile* is a high-stakes adventure filled with unforgettable characters and amazing historical details. Gentry doesn't just write with boldness and authenticity but delivers powerful messages in the midst of the plot twists and turns. Turn the page to return to ancient Carthage and join Dr. Lisbeth Hastings in this time-traveling journey!"

—Elizabeth Byler Younts, author of *Promise to Return*

More from Lynne Gentry

THE CARTHAGE CHRONICLES

A Perfect Fit: An eShort Prequel to Healer of Carthage

Healer of Carthage

Shades of Surrender: An eShort Prequel to Return to Exile

Valley of Decision (coming Summer 2015!)

RETURN *to* EXILE

A NOVEL

Lynne Gentry

HOWARD BOOKS
A Division of Simon & Schuster, Inc.
New York Nashville London Toronto Sydney New Delhi

Howard Books
A Division of Simon & Schuster, Inc.
1230 Avenue of the Americas
New York, NY 10020

This book is a work of fiction. Any references to historical events, real people, or real places are used fictitiously. Other names, characters, places, and events are products of the author's imagination, and any resemblance to actual events or places or persons, living or dead, is entirely coincidental.

First Howard Books trade paperback edition January 2015

HOWARD and colophon are trademarks of Simon & Schuster, Inc.

Cover design by Dogeared Design
Front cover photographs by Kirk Douponce, Thinkstock, and iStock Images

Manufactured in the United States of America

10 9 8 7 6 5 4 3 2

Library of Congress Cataloging-in-Publication Data

Gentry, Lynne.
Return to exile : a novel / Lynne Gentry.
pages cm.—(The Carthage Chronicles ; 2)
ISBN 978-1-4767-4636-4 (paperback)
1. Women physicians—Fiction. 2. Time travel—Fiction. 3. Carthage (Extinct city)—Fiction. 4. Christian fiction. 5. Love stories. I. Title.
PS3607.E57R48 2014
813'.6—dc23

2014006722

ISBN 978-1-4767-4636-4
ISBN 978-1-4767-4640-1 (ebook)

For Lonnie

A man of extraordinary courage.

A man of unshakable faith.

A man who inspires me to cast aside fear.

"Perfect love casts out fear."

—1 JOHN 4:18 NASB

RETURN *to* EXILE

Prologue

Carthage

"MASTER, YOU'RE IN NO shape for today's Senate session." Pytros bustled into the council chambers laden with all of his writing supplies and a pitcher of water. "You should have canceled."

"Your lack of forward thinking is why you will live and die a lowly scribe." Aspasius limped to his place at the *curule* seat.

Pytros carefully spread his utensils. "I don't know what you hope to achieve. The order has been issued." With a peevish look upon his face, he poured a cup of water and held it out.

"But has word of Valerian's edict reached the ears of the Senate? That is what I must know." Ignoring Pytros's pout, Aspasius took the cup and plopped onto the ivory chair with curved bronze legs. He wanted to be well situated on the bowl-shaped stool before he allowed the chamber doors opened. These days his physical comfort was hard to come by. He was either in desperate need of a drink of water or access to a chamber pot. And most disturbing of all, the feeling had disappeared from his foot. A fact the power-hungry vultures waiting to take his place must never discover.

He downed the water, then gave his slave the empty cup. "Knowledge is power, and I intend to make certain I always possess the bulk of it."

Pytros sighed. "Very well. I'll light the braziers and double the incense, but I can't guarantee it will cover the stink of your secret."

If Aspasius hoped to control the manner and level of his compliance to the new imperial order, he did not have the luxury of rearranging the affairs of state to suit his health. In preparation for today's council meeting, he'd sent his scribe in search of a medical remedy for the increasing pain in his foot. Pytros procured a concoction of myrrh, citron pips, northern cypress flowers, and gazelle droppings from a crusty arena surgeon who conducted experiments on the bodies of dying gladiators. Aspasius had soaked his foot in the slimy potion until his flesh nearly fell off. No sensation was restored, and the foul odor of decay continued to trail him everywhere he went. He'd even tried slathering the rotting appendage with an expensive nard purchased from an Egyptian perfume dealer . . . all to no avail. Unfortunately, chilly weather had forced the chamber's windows closed today. Without a sea breeze, it was much more likely someone would notice the proconsul of Carthage had the reek of a stagnant pond.

If the pungent incense wasn't strong enough to conceal his declining health, there would be no stopping the rumors of his imminent demise among the patricians.

He laid the blame for his mounting maladies squarely at the feet of the Christians. From the moment the insubordinate Magdalena's attractive daughter had appeared out of nowhere, aiding the church in its interests, the gods had not been happy. First, some sort of pestilence had struck the tenements and toppled his workforce faster than Roman road builders could fell a forest. Next, his shriveled foot began to rot. And now, as if the gods intended to rub salt into his wounds, Valerian's victories on the battlefield had given the new emperor a false sense of security.

Thus the reason for Valerian's order. Aspasius was to bring home the very man he hated most, Cyprianus Thascius.

The idea of the smug, young rabble-rouser coming back to Carthage stank worse than his own foot. Maybe between now and when the weather changed enough to send a ship, Valerian would suffer a defeat that would wipe out this unprecedented generosity, and Cyprian would remain in exile. After all, the rapid succession of emperors these past few years had proved the empire's rulers weren't really the immortals they believed themselves to be. But just in case, Aspasius intended to keep the son of his sworn enemy from gaining support in his province.

Exhausted and short of breath, Aspasius waved Pytros to him. "Undo the laces, and make certain only the tips of my shoes show."

Pytros filled his water glass again and proceeded to arrange the excessive folds of Aspasius's snowy white tunic until the band of purple trim brushed the tops of Aspasius's blood-red boots. "This is a bad idea."

Aspasius guzzled every last drop. "Close your mouth and open the doors, or I'll sell you to the next camel caravan."

His scribe set the empty glass upon his recording desk, then stalked to the heavy cedar panels and pressed them open.

The chatter in the outer hall stopped. Aspasius sucked in his stomach and steeled himself for the decisive click of red shoes upon marble. One by one the senators swept into the chamber, an air of aloof indifference swirling about their silky robes. Aspasius had known most of these men since they were boys together. He'd grown up going to school with the likes of the gangly Titus Cicero, the wealthiest landowner in his province. Aspasius could recall word for word the taunts of Titus and his pimpled friends.

Gimp. Shrimp. Dung beetle.

Because of Aspasius's uneven legs, he'd never been chosen for their rowdy games of *paganica* ball or swordplay. So he'd concentrated on loftier pursuits. While Titus and his admirers flexed their muscles, Aspasius had slowly climbed the political ladder, determined his tormentors would one day beg to be chosen for his team.

Today was that day.

Casting furtive glances at Aspasius, the patricians took their seats.

Aspasius let them stew for a moment, quietly basking in their growing discomfort. After his term as consul ended in Rome, Emperor Decius had granted him a one-year term ruling over his home province, which he'd managed to extend to nearly twenty. Unheard of. As unheard of as the redesign of his council chambers. He'd had the hard, straight rows replaced with a less structured half curve that forced the council members to remain within a manageable reach. Which was especially prudent now that Decius had gone to his grave and left him at the mercy of the shortsighted and foolhardy Valerian.

Aspasius cleared his throat and addressed the room of nervous senators. "My fellow Carthaginians." He loved how the hard surfaces of the stone walls added power to his voice. "Plague is raging through the slums. The gods must be appeased."

Silence hung in the sickly sweet air.

Titus cleared his throat and rose slowly in a bold attempt to use his height to his advantage. "Perhaps the gods wait upon you to remove the filth. It's creating such an awful stench and putting all of us at risk. Our servants come and go in the slum markets. How long before they carry the sickness to our doors?"

"Shall I raise your taxes to pay the workers needed to finish the aqueducts and clear the streets?" Disgruntled murmurings rippled through the assembly.

"If you persist in this egregious lack of due diligence, then I will take my family to the mountains and wait out this sickness in the safety of my summer estate."

"You always were a coward, Titus," Aspasius replied condescendingly, easily bringing the meeting back under his control. "If you do not have the courage to stay and make our prosperity happen, I shall declare you guilty of treason." A collective gasp echoed in the chamber. Aspasius paused, letting the threat sink in. "Should any of you choose to join him—put your tails between your legs and flee to the hills—I will confiscate your properties as well." He directed his glare toward Titus. "And don't think I don't know the location of every one of your secret holdings."

"You can't do that. Not without a majority vote," Titus countered, his confidence sure.

"It was also said I couldn't send a senatorial candidate to Curubis, especially one whose father had so many loyal friends." He waved his arm over the wide-eyed senators. "And yet, do you see Cyprianus Thascius seated in our chambers?"

Slack-jawed, Titus returned to his seat.

Aspasius chuckled. Growing up with these bullies might have been painful, but pain had brought its reward. He knew all of their weaknesses and how to exploit them. A few of the wealthy merchants may escape, but the ruling class would not be closing their villas in the city and setting out for summer homes in the country. Not until he'd secured enough loyal support—coerced or not—to guarantee his eventual acquisition of all Cyprian held dear. He would take from the young noble the same way Cyprian's father, Julius Thascius, had taken from him. He would never forget that Cyprian's mother, the beautiful and well-positioned Numeria, was to have been his wife.

A ship could not be sent to fetch Cyprian until spring. This gave Aspasius plenty of time to do what he considered most important: restore the favor of the gods. After his province was returned to its previous splendor, he'd take over everything Thascius and have his revenge. Then he wouldn't cry if the whole lot of his

Senate council packed their litters and left town. He would even pay for the movers from his personal accounts.

He held up his hand for silence. "In the past Rome has allowed its conquered peoples to maintain their traditions and their gods. This is no longer the case. Now everyone is required to sacrifice to the gods of Rome. Achieving religious conformity, especially from the Christians, is a daunting task, but a task I intend to accomplish."

"And how will the sacrifice of heretics secure our holdings?" Titus asked with a bit more contrition.

"It's really quite simple. Each of you has a covey of clients who must answer to you. All I'm asking is that you convince your clients to sacrifice to the gods."

"How will you determine if our clients' sacrifices are sufficient?" another senator asked.

"When the sickness goes away."

Titus adjusted his toga. "And if it doesn't?"

"It will, once the gods are appeased. Until then, you and all your clients are required to purchase certificates of *libellus* as proof of sacrifice and loyalty to our gods. Any found to be without one will be executed as a traitor."

Aspasius savored the senators' shocked looks. It mattered not whether they liked him, as long as they feared him.

"Now, is there anything else the Senate would like to discuss with Carthage's proconsul?" He waited, patient as a mongoose at a viper's nest. The senators kept their eyes to the floor and their mouths closed. No one, not even Titus, brought up the possibility that such an imposition upon religious freedoms would be debated with fervor when the former solicitor of Carthage returned. "Then you are dismissed."

After they had all filed out of the room, Aspasius grinned and poured himself another glass of water. "They do not know."

"It's only a matter of time." Pytros closed his tablet. "News of the bishop's recall is probably tucked inside letters dispatched to every province."

"Right now, my council is too concerned for themselves to care about the return of a man convicted of conspiracy against the deities of the throne." Aspasius downed his water. "By the time they know, it will be too late for them to grow a spine. Cyprian and his church will be dead."

"What will you do if Cyprian has had a change of heart and recants upon his return? His father's friends won't let you murder one of their own, then turn around and steal his wealth."

"The fair-haired noble was ready to lose everything to stubbornly hold to his new beliefs. He won't recant."

"He might to save his wife."

"Either way, I win. For as long as he thinks I hold the power over his wife's life, I hold the power over him."

"But we don't know where she is."

"Cyprian doesn't know that. And he won't." Aspasius smiled. "When people are afraid, they are far easier to control." He reached up and squeezed his slave's cheeks. "Isn't that so, Pytros?"

1

Curubis

THE SALTY BREEZE TASTED of chum left to rot in the African sun.

Cyprian tugged at his damp tunic. The coarse wool sanded his sun-burned flesh. Chapped skin was only one of many indignities he'd suffered since a Roman freighter dumped him in this dank little fishing village. Twelve long months of exile had given him ample time to consider how far removed he was from Carthage and his former life.

While his friend and fellow exile Pontius penned angry protests to Rome in the shade of the crude lean-to they'd constructed from scavenged deadfall and fishing nets, Cyprian paced the endless stretch of sand. To think, only a year ago Aspasius, the ruler of Carthage, had reclined at Cyprian's wedding table. The heavy-jawed proconsul had sipped imported wines, debated the merits of slum renewal, and plotted treachery behind Cyprian's back.

How smug the foul proconsul would be if he could see the solicitor of Carthage now. A flea-bitten pleb. Forced to live in conditions far worse than those of the city's poorest tenement dweller. Disgraced. Banished from friends. Separated from his new bride.

Jade swells tumbled ashore, gobbling up large chunks of beach the way Aspasius devoured anyone who got in his way. Cyprian waded in and scooped water into his cupped hands. His eyes and face stung with the splash of salt. What had become of his wife? The worry was eating him alive.

Lisbeth had proven his equal. Smart as he in every way and far brighter when it came to healing. But did she have the cunning required to free herself from Aspasius? The thought of Aspasius dragging her into his lair haunted his dreams and drove his plans to escape.

Come spring a ship would sail into the harbor, and when it did, he intended to slip aboard, return to Carthage, and rescue his wife from the clutches of Aspasius Paternus.

"That's enough for today, Pontius." Cyprian rolled the papyrus his resourceful secretary had woven from reedy dune grasses. "We'd better work on catching our supper."

"I'm determined to finish your petition, along with your response to the note from Felicissimus, before the next freighter comes." Pontius dragged a whittled stick through the soot of last night's cooking fire, a poor substitute for the expensive octopus ink turning rancid in the gold-trimmed ram's horn in Cyprian's old office. "Rome will not survive if it continues to allow injustice in its provinces."

"We haven't seen a ship port in this rat's hole for months."

"Today could be the day of our salvation."

"I pray you are right." Cyprian scanned the empty horizon. "Last night, my dreams once again revisited Carthage. Lisbeth stood on the proconsul's balcony, crying my name, but before I could get to her . . . I awoke to the truth that Aspasius now rapes my wife."

"A wrong your appeal will right." Pontius took the scroll.

Cyprian clasped Pontius's bronzed and sturdy shoulder. "Friend, even if I am released, I'll need help to rescue my wife, and there is only one way to squelch the ugly rumor floating around Carthage that I hide in Curubis out of fear. Find the man who told

Aspasius where my wife would be that day the soldiers took her and Ruth. Find him, and expose what he's done, why we're stuck on this godforsaken beach."

His thoughts returned to his argument with Lisbeth, a moment in time he remembered with absolute clarity.

"I'm not about to let Aspasius keep me from doing my job. I need those supplies," she had argued.

"Let me or Barek run your errand."

"You're still convalescing. And Barek wouldn't know a eucalyptus leaf from a mustard seed."

"At least take Barek with you."

"If it will help you sleep better."

"No heroics. Promise."

"Straight to the herbalist and back. I promise."

Cyprian rubbed the throbbing scar on his upper arm. He'd let a little injury hinder his judgment that day. And his weakness had changed all of their lives.

Could he have stopped her? Doubtful.

They'd only been married a few weeks, but the one thing he knew for certain about his wife . . . nothing altered her path. Once Lisbeth set her jaw she would not be deterred. Perhaps women from her time counted bullheaded determination as admirable, but failing to heed wise counsel was a dangerous gamble in the world of Roman Carthage.

Her time?

Would the ludicrous idea that his wife came from another time and place always leave him so unsettled? Months of having nothing to do but contemplate the impossibility of falling in love with a woman from the future had brought him no closer to understanding his destiny. No closer to how or why their different paths had crossed. Or why he'd failed to make the most of such a miraculous blessing.

Although his regrets included the years he'd wasted serving pagan gods, failing to keep his wife from harm topped his shame. She hadn't fully understood his sacrifice. He'd seen in her eyes the possibility she'd even hated him for the choice he'd made that day to stand firm rather than deny his faith, to give up the power and standing that would have kept him from exile and her from Aspasius's grip.

"Who could have tipped the proconsul to Lisbeth's plans?" Pontius's question tugged him from the horrors of that day.

"I don't know, but I intend to find out."

"I would be no friend to you or our dearly departed bishop if I didn't remind you that vengeance belongs to the Lord and—" Pontius abandoned his preaching in midsentence and charged past him. "Look! A scarlet topsail." He directed Cyprian's gaze seaward. In the distance a tiny blood spot smudged the cerulean horizon. "Who would dare travel the seas this time of year?"

"Someone with no choice."

Without another word, Cyprian and Pontius snatched up their letters and raced toward the imperial frigate drifting into the lagoon. Water lapped the dock's warped planks beneath Cyprian's bare feet. Word of an approaching ship spread quickly among the villagers. Soon a host of neglected savages pushed them toward the water. Every man rank with the odors of outdoor living and desperate for a crock of wine and a few handfuls of grain.

The teakwood ship creaked into the substandard quay. The boat's lofty goosenecked stern, decorated with an intricate carving of the bearded face of Neptune, blocked the sun. In the shadow of the fierce-eyed god, Cyprian muscled to the front of the crowd, anxious for the advantage of being recognized for the powerful man he was . . . used to be.

"Stand back." The port's lone stevedore pressed the crowd from the gangplank landing.

Upturned faces, every one of them as scraggly and sunken-cheeked as Cyprian's, searched the ship's deck. Instead of the usual hustle of a crew eager to make landfall, not a soul stirred onboard. Murmurs rippled through the crowd. What was taking so long? Why weren't the slaves lowering the gangplank? Where was the security detail that accompanied every vessel commissioned for Rome's service? An eerie quiet settled over the dock.

A heavy rope sailed over the ship's railing. The crowd cheered and swelled forward. Cyprian grabbed a pylon to steady himself against the surge of filthy bodies. The grating slide of iron bolts signaled the release of the gangplank. Before all could get clear, the bridge crashed upon the dock, forcing some to dive into the water or be crushed. A ragged boy appeared at the ship's opening. He planted his red-speckled legs and raised a sword twice the size of his scrawny body to block the entrance.

"Unclean!" he shouted. "We carry plague. We've only ported to rid ourselves of the dying."

Howls of horror erupted. Men pushed and shoved in the opposite direction.

Cyprian caught sight of a Roman captain's crested helmet near the bow. Desperate for news as the others were to escape possible contamination, he knew what he had to do. Cyprian pushed through panicked men, forcing his way along the dock until he reached the front of the ship. He cupped his hands to his lips. "Captain!"

A square-shouldered man came to the railing. Several days' growth on his chin made him appear uncharacteristically disheveled and unkempt for a Roman officer. He did, however, still possess that unmistakable air of Roman authority.

Cyprian shouted, "Any correspondence for Cyprianus Thascius, solicitor of Carthage?" Unsure if he'd been heard over the thundering retreat of frightened men, he shouted his question again.

When the captain spotted Cyprian a scowl wrinkled his brow. "What if there was?"

"Even exiles are entitled to send and receive mail," Cyprian demanded in his most forceful barrister voice. The voice that had once bellowed with power in the imperial courts. The voice he had once used to instill fear in his adversaries. The voice he barely recognized anymore. "If you refuse to hand it over, I shall appeal this abhorrent treatment to Decius."

"Not if he's dead."

"Dead?" The word rang with a hope almost impossible to believe. A new emperor on the throne could possibly end the persecution that had sent him into the abyss. "When? How?"

"Killed in battle against the Goths. Nearly a year ago." The captain stooped, retrieved a bag, and threw it at Cyprian's feet. "Traitors! The lot of you. Unfit to live on Roman soil."

"He's got food!" one of the retreating exiles shouted. The others quickly forsook their fear of disease and swarmed in Cyprian's direction.

"Pontius! Run!" Cyprian grabbed the bag and leaped from the dock. His bare feet hit the sand hard. Pontius landed right behind him.

Legs pumping, they scrambled down the beach, cutting through the dune scrubs, sand flying. They sped toward the marshes and plunged into knee-deep water. Cyprian tossed the mail sack over his shoulder and sloshed after Pontius. Deeper and deeper they trudged into the shadows of the cypress trees. A startled marsh bird took flight, signaling their location to the ensuing mob.

"This way." Pontius ducked behind a large root, and Cyprian followed. Backs to the smooth bark, they panted. Listening. Nothing but the sound of their own hearts thundering in their ears.

"Think we lost them?" Pontius whispered several minutes after the sounds of wildlife returned.

"Not for long." Cyprian held the bag tight. "Powers of action always equal a man's desires. The outcast hunger for news as much as food." He slowly peeked around the tree. "Keep a sharp eye out, Pontius." He tore through the mail sack.

"What are you looking for?"

"Proof that Aspasius has lost Rome's backing."

Pontius checked for pursuers. "Would a new emperor be more sympathetic to our plight?"

"If there is any justice in this life."

At the bottom of the mailbag, Cyprian found a small parchment addressed to him, folded and sealed with wax. "It's from Ruth."

"What does she say?"

Cyprian broke the seal and began reading the scratchings from Ruth's hurried hand. "Plague. Persecution. Struggles to keep both the hospital and the church going." He scanned the rest of the letter. "Valerian is the new emperor and"—he couldn't believe what he was reading—"and rumor has it that the proconsul has been ordered to summon us home."

"Yes!" Pontius pumped his fist. "God has not forgotten us." He wrapped Cyprian in a bear hug, then pulled away when Cyprian failed to embrace him. "Why are you not pleased, my lord?"

"If Aspasius is still in power, our return will not be without challenge. He will dispatch an escort to see us safely delivered to his court." Cyprian folded the letter. "Mark my words, no matter what I do, that eel will still find a way to see me martyred in the arena."

Pontius swallowed. "And Lisbeth? What news does Ruth give of your wife?"

Cyprian read the widow's words one more time, praying he'd missed something in his haste the first time through, then shook his head. "Not one word."

2

Dallas, Texas

TIME IS NOT THE *healer of all things.*

Dr. Lisbeth Hastings did not need this latest lab report to confirm what she already feared. Measles.

How had the thirty-five-year-old she'd just moved to intensive care circumvented routine vaccinations? Almost every child born during the immunization initiative of the late seventies had gone to school with their shot records current.

The hospital's intercom crackled. "Code Blue. ICU. Room six."

Lisbeth dropped the chart, grabbed her stethoscope, and sprinted through the halls. The patient in room six was her patient, and she wasn't leaving until she had taken care of her.

Out of breath and in a cold sweat, Lisbeth skidded around the corner. Her patient's worried husband paced outside the room from which medical personnel silently filed out. He jostled a crying toddler. "Dr. Hastings, what's going on?"

"I promise I'll get back to you as soon as I can." Lisbeth shot past him and burst into the silence that consumes a room where death is the victor. "What happened, Nelda?"

"Convulsions." The charge nurse handed Lisbeth fresh gloves, then quietly started closing drawers on the red crash cart.

Lisbeth plowed through the litter left by the team of airway specialists, nurses, and ICU attendings. During her residency, she'd assisted on hundreds of Code Blues. Heroic measures to prolong a life always inflicted unavoidable trauma on the crashing patient. Yet, when she reached the still body lying on the bed, she couldn't help but gasp at her patient's total loss of dignity.

Damp, blond strands stuck to the woman's face. Red-rimmed eyes. Blue lips. Fiery pustules that made her look like some kind of distorted monster. Her hands limp as if life had slipped through her fingers. Lines of all sorts tethered her rigid frame to silent machines. And most disconcerting of all: she reeked of an odor similar to plucked chicken feathers.

Two days ago, this perfectly healthy woman, her beautiful two-year-old, and her handsome husband were enjoying Disney World when she suddenly spiked a fever. A measles diagnosis meant this young mother was contagious the day her family flew home from Orlando, the three days they were in the theme park before her rash appeared, and on the initial trip to their vacation destination. Lisbeth could not let herself think about how many lives this woman had touched between Dallas and Florida in the past six days or she'd lose what was left of the sandwich she'd choked down ten hours ago.

Lisbeth brushed a strand of hair from the woman's forehead. Body still warm but slowly cooling. She pulled a penlight from her pocket and flicked the beam across glassy eyes. Foolish, she knew, but she wanted a reaction, needed this young wife and mother to wake up and prove her theory wrong. Any trace of the former eye color had been pushed away by the large, black holes of pupils blown beyond repair. Lisbeth clicked off the pen.

"Dr. Hastings?" Nelda maneuvered around the equipment and handed her the chart. "You want to tell the husband?"

"Tell him what? 'Merry Christmas, and oh, by the way, you're a single father now'?" Powerlessness shook her insides. "It's hard enough to tell someone their spouse died, but when it might have been prevented, what do you say?"

Two decades without a single case of measles reported in Texas. Now this was the third death presenting similar symptoms in the past twenty-four hours. The first two had been kids. Their deaths she could attribute to the increasing fear surrounding the safety of vaccinations or the possibility they had medical conditions that prevented inoculations. But how had this woman slipped through the immunization cracks?

"I'm sorry, Nelda. It's not your fault." She took a step back from the bed. "Drop your gown and gloves on the floor. Cordon off this room."

"Do we need to quarantine the father and daughter?"

Lisbeth nodded. "And get their shot records, including those of the deceased." Her mind double-timed a new plan. "And contact the CDC." The tiled walls seemed to be closing in, squeezing the breath from her chest. She would not let this happen again. "We could have an outbreak on our hands."

LISBETH WHIPPED her rusty, old Toyota into the parking garage of her downtown loft apartment. She killed the engine, but its usual hiss and bang continued. She dropped her head onto the steering wheel. She was only a year younger than the mother who'd died, but failing to prevent these senseless deaths made her feel fifty. Six years ago, she believed she'd been sent back to the twenty-first century for a reason. At least that was the pep talk she gave herself late at night when her longing for the man she'd left in the third century made it impossible to breathe. But now she was painfully aware that if she had stayed in Carthage and seen this virus put to bed, that mother on the morgue slab would be home hugging her baby tonight.

In the tomblike darkness, fingers of cold snaked through the vehicle's broken window seals. A guilty shudder ripped through Lisbeth's exhausted body. Despite her best efforts, the past had caught up with the future.

Lisbeth grabbed the sanitizer out of the console and scrubbed her hands. Even though she'd showered and disposed of her scrubs before she left the hospital, she reeked of failure.

Determined not to be undone by the pain, she squirted an extra glob of sanitizer into her hand and glanced at her cell phone: 3:00 a.m. If she was lucky, she'd have time to see Maggie before the CDC's chartered jet arrived. Prompt action by public health officials was essential in addressing emerging outbreaks. The governmental investigators would expect every local infectious disease specialist to be front and center until they'd contained the danger.

Lisbeth yanked the phone from the charger and dragged herself from the car.

The elevator dinged. She trudged the dingy apartment corridor. A glass of milk and a plate of homemade cookies waited on the welcome mat. She bent to read a note written in red crayon.

Dear Santa,
I want my daddy.
Maggie

Beneath her five-year-old daughter's signature were three red stick figures. A mom. A dad. And, in between them, a child with outstretched arms.

Yearning clenched Lisbeth's empty belly. She and Papa had done their best to piece together a family for Maggie. Grateful as she was for Papa's help, returning to this century meant Maggie would never know her own incredible father. Santa could more easily give her daughter the moon.

Lisbeth folded the paper and stuffed it, along with her regret, into her pocket. She scooped up the cookies, drank the milk, then slid the key into the front door lock.

Inside the quiet apartment, oatmeal and cinnamon lingered in the air. Lisbeth inhaled deeply, letting the sweet scent carry her back to the makeshift ICU she'd thrown together in Cyprian's third-century villa and what it'd been like awakening to Cyprian standing over her, a steaming mug of warm wine laced with spices in his outstretched hand. She'd begun falling in love that morning, and nothing had been the same since.

Lisbeth quietly dropped her keys on the kitchen table and draped her white coat over a chair.

Papa snored on the couch, an afghan snugged tightly beneath his chin. White lights twinkled on the spindly spruce leaning against the TV. Under the tree was Maggie's new Little Mermaid doll. Lisbeth was relieved her father had remembered her instructions to get the red-headed mermaid out of the closet.

"Papa?" She pressed two fingers into his sinewy shoulders.

He roused with a start and opened one eye. "Home already?"

Life with her father had been like growing up with Indiana Jones. She was only five years old when Mama fell through the time portal at the Cave of the Swimmers and disappeared from their lives. For the next thirteen years, she and Papa traveled the world, leapfrogging from one archaeological dig to another. Roman baths in England. A long-buried, first-century villa in Artena. A crumbling, midempire amphitheater in northern Libya. They'd probably still be digging together if Papa hadn't insisted she go to school in the States and become a doctor . . . to be more like Mama. The four years she spent in college had been her first experience of staying in one place longer than a digging season. That's when she realized that while Papa loved every moment of their vagabond travels, she longed for a more controlled environment. Stability. A normal life of school, ballet lessons, and friends.

She patted her father's hand. "Got to go back when the CDC calls."

"So it's measles?"

"Yes," she hesitated. "Can't let it get worse."

"Worse?" Papa pushed himself upright, his white hair wild and restless as a desert wind. He eyed her carefully. "How can it get worse?"

"A virus must mutate to survive. Epidemic is its ultimate goal. This is a virus that could easily gallop out of control."

"Sounds like you're going to need your strength to fight this one." Papa wrestled his lanky frame from the afghan. "How about I fix you something hot and solid to eat?"

"How about some more of those cookies you made?" It took everything she had not to throw herself into his arms and tell him just how frightened she was. What if she couldn't keep this virus in check before someone else died? "Thanks for taking such good care of Maggie."

"A real corker, that one. Got your beauty and my brains." Papa winked and swung his legs off the couch. "We had to set up Santa's snack by the front door. In Miss Magdalena's opinion, the man in the red suit's way too fat and way too smart to try comin' in through this fake gas fireplace." Papa refused to call Maggie by anything other than her proper name, the name that had belonged to Mama. It kept the extraordinary woman alive for both of them. "That girl won't be put off much longer. You're going to have to let me teach her more than her daddy's language."

"Learning Latin won't hurt her." Lisbeth pulled Maggie's note out of her pocket. "But finding out about the cave before she's old enough to understand could. I thought I made it clear that I would decide when to tell her about what happened in the desert."

He held up his palms. "Haven't said a word."

"Then why did she draw this?"

Papa fished his glasses from his pocket. "It's a family. Every kid wants one, right?" He lightly tapped her forehead. "Anyone smart enough to write notes to Santa is smart enough to ask why he didn't deliver."

"She's not ready to hear that her father is never coming here."

"You were five when I had to tell you your mother wasn't coming back. We managed."

Managed? Yes. But she'd had to deal with the hurt her whole life. "This is different. You didn't know what happened to Mama."

"And you know where to find your little girl's father."

"Going there's too risky."

"Keeping her from him is a bigger risk."

"I turned out okay."

He nodded. "As long as you're in control."

"What's wrong with being able to take care of yourself?"

"Nothin'. But sooner or later the day will come when something bigger than you can handle will come along, and you just might have to let go and trust someone again."

"Don't preach." Except for Papa, it felt like everyone she'd ever trusted had abandoned her. Including Cyprian. Some days she found it hard to trust the God she'd come to love not to do the same. "What good will it do to tell Maggie about a father she can never meet?"

"I don't have all the answers, Beetle Bug. Just make sure your plans line up with God's." From his expression she could tell he knew he'd lost this battle, but the set of his jaw told her they would have this discussion again. "Should we wake Magdalena now? Give her a good Christmas before you get called out?"

"Let her sleep a little longer. The CDC team has to come from Atlanta. That gives me a few hours before I have to go back."

"You could also use a little shut-eye."

"I can't let measles win this time."

"The future's a heavy burden when you can't let go of the past. I know." Papa drew her into his arms, forcing her to relax a little. Six years since their return to Dallas and he still smelled of the desert right before the rain. He kissed the top of her head, his scraggly beard sanding a few of the splinters from her ragged thoughts.

Lisbeth pulled back, checking his eyes for clarity, a habit she couldn't seem to break since she'd brought him back to the States. "Go on to bed, Papa."

"It's already Christmas in the Middle East. Think I'll catch CNN. See if Santa left *me* a little present." Unlike her, he hadn't given up on the Egyptian government granting access to the cave that had changed everything.

Lisbeth patted his shoulder. "You think Santa has any pull in Egypt?"

"No." He grinned. "But God and Nigel do. And Magdalena would get her Christmas wish."

"I'm not letting that bald Irishman smuggle my daughter into Egypt."

"Well, you sure couldn't leave her with Queenie. I know she's the only friend you've got, but her call schedule keeps her at the hospital sixty to eighty hours a week. Plus, I took *you* all over the world."

"I'm not you."

Papa paused. "Who is it you're really protecting, Beetle Bug?"

"I don't know why we're arguing about this. It's a moot point. Even if I wanted to go back, which I don't, the cave is closed to archaeological exploration."

"Why do you think I've been praying?" He winked. "Now go check on our girl."

Lisbeth headed toward Maggie's room, contemplating the

changes in Papa since he'd hauled her from the secret shaft at the Cave of the Swimmers.

Not only had Papa's mind cleared, his sole reliance upon science had shifted to a strong conviction in a higher power. According to her father's new way of thinking, the same God who'd created the unknown dimensions of time had also created scientific minds determined to unravel its mysteries. He was convinced God would provide a way for him to fling himself down the time portal and bring Mama home.

Light from the Little Mermaid lamp next to Maggie's twin-size bed cast a blue glow over the Mediterranean wall mural Lisbeth had commissioned when she finally finished her fellowship and got a real paying job. Even with her increased income, hiring an artist was a splurge on a hospitalist's salary. But Maggie loved art. The other three walls of her room were covered with her watercolors and sketches of animals. Living in an apartment didn't mean they couldn't put down roots.

Lisbeth thought about Papa's earlier words. The truth was she really wasn't afraid of hauling Maggie around the world, but she also believed her daughter deserved a normal life . . . if a child conceived from a cross-temporal marriage could ever be considered normal.

Maggie's pale legs were sprawled atop the covers, her latest crayon creation clutched in her hand. Lisbeth resisted the urge to cover her. Instead she bent and removed the drawing of a reindeer, then lifted a strand of hair stuck to Maggie's angelic face. Her daughter had inherited silky blond tresses, blue eyes, and a perfect forehead from her aristocratic father. Her claustrophobia, unfortunately, had come directly from her mother's genes. No matter what they tried, Maggie refused anything that could possibly pin her arms and legs down. Lisbeth found it easier to wait until her daughter was sound asleep before attempting a proper tucking in.

Even then, she proceeded with caution. She was certain Maggie had some sort of built-in sensor capable of detecting confinement . . . the very reason Lisbeth could never take her down that tight time portal shaft.

Lisbeth kicked off her shoes and freed the blanket from beneath Maggie's legs. She slid in next to the perfect little body, careful not to crowd her.

Maggie roused. "Mommy?" Her hand found Lisbeth's face. "Is he here?" she asked without opening her eyes.

"Who, baby?"

"My daddy." Her solid expectation was a balled fist to Lisbeth's stomach.

Lisbeth brought Maggie's hand to her lips. Cinnamon tainted her fingers. Fighting tears, Lisbeth kissed each chubby digit. "Not yet, baby."

"Santa will bring him, right?"

Maggie's vaccinations would fend off measles, but Lisbeth knew for certain the shot had not been invented that would protect her daughter from a broken heart. Inhaling the scent of tear-free shampoo, Lisbeth wished she could seal her baby inside a sterile bubble. A place where nothing bad ever happened to children or their mothers. A place where little girls didn't wish for parents who couldn't or wouldn't return. A place where families were never separated. No such place existed. Past or present.

Lisbeth pulled Maggie close. Her tiny, fist-sized heart beat steadily beneath her thin gown. Lisbeth held her breath waiting for her daughter to launch her usual struggle for freedom. When she didn't, Lisbeth drew her closer. Maybe Papa was right. It wasn't Maggie she was protecting, but herself. She'd crack if she couldn't hang on to the reason she'd given up both her mother and the love of her life to stay in the twenty-first century.

Any explanation she could offer for Santa's inability to bring

Maggie's daddy from his world and put him under their tree would break Maggie's tender heart. What kind of a mother gives her kid heartache for Christmas? But Maggie was a smart kid. Perhaps the time *had* come to start working through Maggie's need for a father. She could tell her a little about him and save the rest of the impossibly-difficult-to-believe story for when she was older.

"Daddy lives far away. If he could, I know he would come to you." Lisbeth swallowed the lie stuck in her throat. "Somehow. Some way."

"If Santa can't bring him, I'll ask God."

She'd tried prayer. A million times. So far God hadn't reunited her family. The silence had drilled holes in the rookie faith she'd brought back with her from the third century. No doubt about that. But prayer was the only hope she had to offer. "Good idea."

Maggie wiggled free. "Too tight, Mommy."

"Sorry." Lisbeth eased her grip, and Maggie's tiny body relaxed. "'Night, baby."

Maggie drifted back to sleep. Lisbeth waited until she was out soundly; then she carefully tucked little arms and legs inside the blanket. Cyprian's exile had carried him miles from the portal. He couldn't come to them, even if he knew his daughter existed. And until Egypt opened access to the cave, going to him was impossible.

In the glow of the Little Mermaid lamp, Lisbeth traced the outline of Maggie's perfect little face. Mama's words drifted into her thoughts. *"You can't possibly know how much I love you until you become a mother."*

She was right. The moment the nurse placed the swaddled baby in her arms, Lisbeth had known instinctively why small animals charge predators twice their size to protect their young. She could do it. Fight to save her child, even against something as difficult to pin down as the unpredictable consequences of parental loss.

Lisbeth couldn't help snuggling in beside Maggie. She held her breath, waiting to be pushed away. When Maggie didn't move, she inhaled the sweet scent of her, savoring each breath as if she'd just surfaced from being underwater too long.

For now, she'd focus on what she *could* do for her child: get this current measles outbreak under control. There had to be a simple explanation for the patients she'd lost in the past few days. Compromised immune systems. Weakened hearts. Something. Until she had autopsy reports, though, speculating on the connection was borrowing trouble and wasting valuable time and energy.

Lisbeth gave in to the exhaustion, allowing her heavy eyelids to close and shut off the nagging feeling that she'd missed something important. Gradually, her own respirations synced with the peaceful in and out of Maggie's slumber.

But the sudden vibration of her phone jerked Lisbeth alert. One arm around Maggie, she struggled to fish the cell from her pocket.

A text from Nelda glowed on the screen.

Five new cases. Help.

3

Curubis

CYPRIAN PULLED OFF THE humiliating garment of a man stripped of everything. He would have agreed to spend the rest of his days as an outcast in exchange for Lisbeth's freedom ten times over if need be.

His life for his wife's.

But if something unspeakable had happened to Lisbeth that Ruth was hesitant to mention in her letter, then neither his legal skills nor this one God for whom he'd forsaken his Roman upbringing had been enough to save her from Aspasius. Perhaps he should have known better than to trust a god he couldn't see or touch.

Cyprian waded into choppy waters the exact color of his wife's eyes, intent on washing the disgraceful stench of lingering doubt from his body. What was happening to him? He'd meant every word of the declaration of faith he'd so boldly made that day before his accuser. Now he questioned the wisdom of that choice. Had his rejection of his Roman heritage condemned not just himself but also Lisbeth?

Scrub as hard as he might, nothing could purge the torture from his soul. The failure to protect Lisbeth belonged on his shoulders. Not God's. He was the one who had entered into a marriage for political gain. He was the one who'd put her life in danger by allowing her to cast her lot with Caecilianus's little band of believers. And he was the one who'd let her go to the market without him. Saving her from a fate worse than death was his responsibility.

But how? Aspasius had reduced him to a man without title or influence. His father's supporters had turned their backs in disgust when he denounced the gods of Rome. The average citizen had no idea what had really happened in the proconsul's private chambers. And most painful of all, according to Felicissimus's earlier letter, the majority of those in the church now considered him a deserter, one intent on saving his own skin rather than finishing the fight alongside Caecilianus.

Return to Carthage now, and he would be bereft of support. No one would follow a coward. What could he do without an army behind him? Storming the palace of the proconsul alone was suicide.

Cyprian waded deeper into the pounding surf. Every day spent here was one more day those he loved suffered. Not only must he rescue Lisbeth, Ruth had written that the church and hospital also needed his help.

He would no longer play by the rules of Rome and act the dutiful citizen forced to wait for the ships of Aspasius to haul him before the Senate. No, he would return to Carthage on his own terms. At the moon's first light, he and Pontius would pack their meager provisions and set out on foot. The rational course, the one Aspasius would expect once he discovered his enemy had slipped through his fingers, was to follow the sticky web of highway that hugged the North African coastline. The paved roads were the easier land route for two men used to wheeled vehicles, a retinue of servants to attend their every need, and a proper lodging every ten to fifteen miles.

He and Pontius were no longer those same coddled men.

In case the envoys of Aspasius marched the cobblestones

promoting the expansion of Roman commerce, he and Pontius would take a path only bandits dared to travel . . . they would cross the sparsely populated plains of the Cap Bon peninsula. Fewer farms and villages meant scant opportunities for restocking their supplies, but it also meant less chance of detection. If they moved at night, he figured, they could reach his country estate in two or three hard days. From the shadows of rural obscurity he would regroup. Once he assembled those still willing to believe in him, he would march to the city and take back what was his.

Cyprian shook the salty water from his hair and strode ashore. In the shade of the lean-to, he and Pontius ate a small portion of a fire-blackened cod. Their hunger only partially satiated, Pontius wrapped the flaky remains in a broad leaf and hid their rations inside the mail sack. While they awaited nightfall, Cyprian stowed the bag under his head and settled down for a short nap.

A few hours later, Pontius shook Cyprian awake. "It's just a dream."

Cyprian stopped his thrashing and worked to shake off the acute sense of fear the ghostly images had left in his head. "What time is it?"

"The moon has crested. Gather your wits, and let's be off."

Cyprian pushed up on his elbows, hoping the change in his position would stop the world from spinning. "A storm is coming." Sweat trickled down Cyprian's neck despite the cool fall breeze pushing the waves ashore.

Pontius lifted his eyes to the twinkling stars. "I don't see any clouds."

"God has revealed my future." Cyprian swiped his mouth.

"From your lack of color, I take it what awaits you is bleak?"

Cyprian nodded. "A spear, a sword, and an executioner."

Pontius helped Cyprian to his feet. "Your work on behalf of

the believers stirred a flurry of conflict among the togas of Carthage, but I'm sure things have calmed by now."

"This time I won't escape." Cyprian let the words sink in. "You don't have to go with me, Pontius."

If marching to his possible death had in any way unseated his faithful deacon, Pontius gave no indication. "From the day I followed you into faith, I knew there would be consequences." He lifted the mail sack and stuffed in the scrolls that recorded the true story of their exile.

"This struggle will not be like the last."

Pontius turned his gaze to the blaze of moonlight dancing on the dark waters. "Since it has pleased God to forewarn you, then it seems to me he's giving you a choice. Go or stay?"

Cyprian had only told his friend a portion of his dream. His steadfast and loyal friend. The one person he could count on to follow him through the gates of the proconsul's palace with or without an army. A loyalty that meant everything to him.

Cyprian took the bag from Pontius and hoisted the sack over his shoulder. "To Carthage we go."

THEY WALKED for what seemed like hours. By the time the sky began to pink, their strength was spent, but they pressed onward. Until the eastern coast and its swarms of mosquitoes were far behind, they couldn't afford to rest. As the morning's first rays crested the horizon, Cyprian was pleased to see that the landscape had changed. They'd reached the peninsula's fertile plains, the breadbasket of the empire.

Soaked with sweat, Cyprian pushed on. "Fields up ahead. We'll seek cover in the stalks."

They forded a dried streambed and set out across the parched earth. Knee-high wheat stalks succumbed to their passing and crunched beneath their blistered feet. Tender shoots of winter green would have replaced these dried husks had the normal seasonal rains fallen. Two years of drought had carved big cracks in the once productive soil. If Rome's grain supply dried up, hunger would carve an even bigger hole in the bellies of the ravenous empire. Someone would pay for the emperor's displeasure at the gods' withholding of blessings. And Cyprian knew exactly upon whom the ax would fall.

In the distance the rhythmic march of Roman scavenging parties beat a warning. Cyprian glanced over his shoulder. "Not enough cover here."

"I see a cave up ahead." Pontius nodded toward a small outcropping of limestone at the field's far edge. "Hurry."

They raced through the stalks. When they reached a small indention in the rock, they dove headfirst into a space just big enough for the two of them. Hunkered down with their backs pressed against the jagged stone, they worked to slow their breathing as they watched the mouth of the shelter and waited. Cyprian's eyes darted past the cave entry and on to the distant two-horned rim of Mount Bou Kornine, his home away from home. How could something so desired be so close and yet so far away?

The sounds of a lone horseman crashing through the stalks came closer and closer. Neither man dared breathe. Less than a stone's throw from where they hid, the soldier reined his mount. Hooves pawed the sandy soil, nervous and wary. Clouds of vapor huffed from the animal's lowered nose as if he smelled the cornered prey that they were.

"Easy." The captain patted the horse's neck, scanning the area with a trained eye.

Booted footfalls approached the rider at a brisk pace. "These fields have already been plundered, sir," one of the troops reported, his breath coming in short spurts. "There's nothing for us here."

"Move out." The captain wheeled his horse and cantered from the field with the entire patrol trotting after him.

Not until the soldiers' footfalls receded did Barek dare suck in air freely. Without a word, Pontius unwrapped their leftover cod. They devoured the cold fish and guzzled the last of the water from their hollowed gourd canteen.

"Today the Lord has provided food, shelter, and safety." Pontius dragged the back of his hand across his mouth. "With at least another night of hard travel ahead of us, we've no choice but to trust our tomorrow to him as well." Prayers on his lips, Pontius curled into a ball and fell asleep with his back to the cave opening.

Cyprian envied a faith that would allow a man to sleep with his back to possible danger. His own trust in God's justice and ability to rectify the sorry state of his affairs wavered like the weak flames he and Pontius had huddled around in the swamps of Curubis. Cyprian scooted across the dusty cave floor. He inched his back as close to the stone walls as possible and kept his eyes on the mountains of home as he drifted to sleep.

Several hours later, he awoke shivering and disoriented. Late afternoon shadows had lowered the cave's temperature several degrees and turned his mountain a dark purple. Neck taut from his refusal to assume a relaxed position, his thoughts floated upon an angry sea of emotion.

He'd been gone nearly a year. In that space of time, more than Lisbeth's well-being could have changed. Did he still own his country estate? Aspasius had wanted more than Cyprian's wife and good reputation. The proconsul needed Cyprian's wealth to erase his lavish and foolish spending before Rome conducted an audit and removed him from office.

Cyprian roused Pontius. In hungry silence they waited for the last golden rays of light to bleed from the day. Stiff from cramped quarters, they trudged through the night, bellies empty of nourishment and hearts full of worry. If Aspasius had used Cyprian's time away to discover the many layers to Cyprian's holdings they could be walking into a trap.

"Lights." Cyprian held out his arm to halt Pontius, his senses on high alert. "Could be trouble."

They ducked into the dry creekbed across from the wall surrounding a large country house and peered over its banks. Except for the wind sweeping down the mountain, the night was quiet. In the past, his country house had always seemed small and cramped, especially compared to his expansive city villa with its wide marbled terraces overlooking the port of Carthage. Now, as Cyprian struggled to take in the sight of his favorite rustic retreat, he realized the days he'd spent living in a small lean-to had magically transformed this modest stone house into a palace. A flicker of an oil lamp breached the shutter slats of a second-floor window.

"Who occupies Bou Kornine this time of year?" Pontius whispered.

"Probably just the caretaker." Cyprian snagged a broken branch.

"Generous with your oil, don't you think?" Pontius found a stick, too. "Why would Silas be awake at this hour?"

Two shadows crossed the shutters. "Only one way to find out." Cyprian crept from their hiding place clutching his makeshift club.

They climbed the stone wall to avoid the squeak of rusty gate hinges and landed feetfirst on the courtyard's hard-packed earth. Growling came from the shadows. Clubs poised and ready, Cyprian and Pontius prepared for battle. Two dogs sprang from the shadows and quickly surrounded them, howling and nipping at their scratched and bruised legs. The door of the villa opened a crack. A faint shaft of light slit the darkness.

"Who's there?" The woman's voice sounded more tired than frightened.

"Travelers." Cyprian shook a dog from the frayed hem of his tunic. "In need of food and lodging."

"We're not allowed to offer assistance, sir. Be on your way."

"By whose orders?" Cyprian demanded.

"The proconsul of Carthage." The woman's bold reply had the ring of familiarity.

The dogs objected to Cyprian's attempted advance, forcing him to shout toward the eyes peering out at him. "Since when does the proconsul control the larders of private citizens?"

"Cyprian? Is that you?" The door swung open, and a small woman flew at him, her arms around his neck before he had time to withdraw. "I prayed for your return."

"Magdalena?" Cyprian dropped his stick and held his sobbing mother-in-law, hope blossoming in his chest despite himself. "What are you doing here? Are you all right? Is Lisbeth with you?"

She released her hold on him and wiped at her tears. "Come. You must not be seen, especially not with me." She took his hand and led him toward the house.

"I hate to break up this touching reunion"—Pontius shook his leg—"but could someone call off these dogs?"

Magdalena whistled, and the dogs charged inside. Once the healer had everyone safely behind closed doors she quickly went to work preparing a fire in the hearth. "No need to worry. Aspasius doesn't know about this place." Flickering light revealed pink scars across her face.

"What are you doing here?" Cyprian surveyed the kitchen where he'd once spent so much time watching the cooks prepare meat pies and wondered who had used Magdalena's face as a cutting board. "Where's Lisbeth?"

"When my master learned what I'd done, he beat me." She cracked a piece of kindling over her knee. "Before he could sentence me to die in the arena, I took what was mine and left through the tunnels." She waved to the person hiding in the shadows.

Cyprian's gaze eagerly swung in the same direction. "Lisbeth?"

Magdalena shook her head. "You can come out, Laurentius. It's safe." Her son, a slump-shouldered young man with thinning tufts of hair and clubbed fingers, shuffled into the room. Even with the boy's chin resting upon his chest, Cyprian recognized Lisbeth's simpleminded half brother. Laurentius had won his heart as well as Lisbeth's with his sunny smile and gift for art, but Cyprian couldn't help deflating with disappointment.

"You remember Cyprian. Don't you, Laurentius?"

"Thyprian and Lithbutt." The boy raised his chin long enough to give Cyprian a brief peek into his almond-shaped eyes. "My favorith."

Cyprian wrapped him in a hug. "Good to see you, my man."

Magdalena relieved Pontius of the long stick he still clutched and gave it to Laurentius. "Can you tend the fire for me, son?" Once Laurentius was occupied, she turned her attention back to Cyprian. "Laurentius and I managed to make it to your villa. If we'd stayed in Carthage, Aspasius would have found us, and I didn't want to endanger Ruth and Barek. Ruth gave us two of the bishop's dogs and suggested we hide in your summer home in the mountains." She tossed him a guarded look. "I hope you don't mind."

"No. This is the perfect place for you."

"Not really." Magdalena brushed wood shavings from her hands and set to work removing the gauzy cloth from a round of cheese. "Ruth needs me, especially since she grieves the death of Caecilianus. Barek's there to help her with the hospital Lisbeth set up, but the plague is spreading so fast they can't possibly meet the demands."

The stench of bodies in the tenements had been one of the

reasons for Cyprian's attempt to remove Aspasius from office. Without a healthy workforce, Carthage would never be restored to the commanding port it had once been. It appeared that Aspasius's rejection of his proposals to at least repair the aqueducts and restore running water to every home in the city had facilitated an unstoppable spread of a sickness. If the ship that had limped into Curubis was any indication of what was to come, the sickness could destroy more than just Carthage. The entire empire was at risk because of one man's folly.

"And Lisbeth?" Her name hung in his throat. "Did she manage to escape Aspasius as well?"

Magdalena took his hand. "Sit."

Something about her tone immediately unsettled him, but Cyprian did as she commanded. "These long months have been almost more than I can bear. Tell me."

Magdalena carefully poured a cup of wine for him and another for Pontius. It seemed her effort to seal the crock took longer than necessary. Just when Cyprian thought he could stand her silence no longer, she wiped her hands on her woolen tunic and looked him straight in the eye. "My daughter is free."

"Thank God!" Cyprian picked Magdalena up and spun her around.

Pontius raised his glass. "How did you manage it?"

"It wasn't easy," Magdalena admitted.

"What matters is my wife's safety." Cyprian couldn't quit grinning. "You took her to Ruth, right? She'll be a great help to Ruth, I'm sure."

"She would be, if she were there . . . but . . ."

Cyprian set her down. He took a step back, bracing for whatever the year apart had dealt his beloved. "Tell me."

"I sent Lisbeth home."

4

THROUGH THE SWIRL OF disbelief, Cyprian could see that time travel had cost Magdalena everything. Stranded for years in his world, she'd made the best of her situation, yet she'd never truly become one of them. She was a foreigner, a stranger held in place by the thin root of a sickly son. The increased stoop in her once proud shoulders indicated that the healer carried wounds deeper than the scars on her face. Lost freedom. A lost marriage. And now, the unbearable loss of a daughter after an all-too-brief reunion. Cyprian had no intention of inflicting more pain, yet the shock of what she'd just told him stung. Rang in his ears.

His wife was gone. Shipped off to a world he could never reach. Dead to him forever.

Magdalena would not have dispatched Lisbeth without good reason. He'd watched with great admiration the joy Magdalena took in working to rebuild the years she'd lost with her daughter. At first, Lisbeth had resisted any kind of reconciliation, too angry to forgive her mother's abandonment. But once Lisbeth learned of Laurentius and understood Magdalena's reason for staying, mother and daughter quickly became one in purpose. Working together so closely it seemed they'd been chiseled from the same piece of exquisite marble. Same hands. Same strength and determination. Same ability to care for others. He had no doubt that sending Lisbeth back to the place she'd be safe had cost Magdalena the last piece of her soul.

Small consolation for his shattered heart.

"We can't stay here." Magdalena touched his hand lightly, apology in her tone. "Aspasius claims the drought is the retribution of the gods, due punishment upon Romans willing to allow the nonsensical belief of the one God to spread and pollute their cities. For the most part, the Roman doctors have abandoned their wealthy charges. Some slaves have begun to flee to the country estates of their masters, taking disease with them." She gazed at the sputtering oil lamp. "I thought you were someone seeking refuge in an abandoned estate."

"Where shall we go?" Pontius's face flushed with concern.

Without Lisbeth waiting for him in Carthage, where *would* Cyprian go? Whatever was left of his estate meant little to him now, and even if his fortune was somehow intact, no amount of gold could ever take his wife's place. She'd quickly become everything to him in the short time they'd been together, and now there was nothing he could do to bring her back. . . . But he could avenge her loss.

Cyprian rose. "The last place Aspasius will look: home."

IT WAS late afternoon before they eventually reached the hewn cobblestones of one of Rome's finest highways. The breeze sweeping off the sea had turned brisk and salty. Cyprian had tucked Laurentius beneath the tarp covering their cart. He worried jolting across the frozen ruts cut by the farm wagons would elicit protests from the boy. So far, though, he'd not heard a peep. Lisbeth's younger brother was a tough little man.

With each stone highway mile marker passed, Cyprian's chest tightened. The paved road had been laid with the most direct path in mind, so it was not the added distance bothering him but the unusually high volume of traffic hurrying away from the city. Men and women loaded with bedrolls, clothing, and strings of dried vegetables hanging around their necks.

If things were getting worse in Carthage, where were the litters and slave entourages of the rich? Cyprian considered stopping someone to ask about the conditions they'd left behind, but then he decided against stirring suspicion.

The closer they came to the city, the more congested the road. At this rate they would not arrive at the city until dusk. Then they would be forced to wait for the gates to open with the other wheeled traffic banned from the urban streets during daylight hours. Milling among the traders increased their risk of being recognized. Although Cyprian's exile had seemed an eternity to him, it wasn't that long ago that he'd had a sketched likeness of himself commissioned. His face had decorated campaign banners hanging from every lamppost along the colonnade. He could not count on his unkempt hair, beard, and weight loss to prevent his being easily recognized.

But even riskier than his discovery was the fact that someone might recognize Magdalena. For years, this striking woman had been a regular in the private arena and theater boxes of the city's most hated man. Though she'd secretly carried out her work among the poor and sick in the tenements, the curative powers of the healer's unusual methods had become legendary. People talked. Magdalena Hastings was far more apt to be recognized than a disgraced politician, a fact that made Cyprian both proud and determined to be even more careful to conceal the precarious plan forming in his head. For Lisbeth's sake, he could not allow harm to come to Magdalena.

Lisbeth. Gone.

Of all the unspeakable things he'd dreamed could have happened to his beloved wife, returning to her time had never occurred to him. Of course, Magdalena was right to send her back. Lisbeth had to go home. In truth, he'd known of that possibility from the moment she'd shared her identity. Much as Lisbeth had tried to fit in, her destiny rested in the future, not in the past, the past to which he was forever bound. If only he had a way of contacting his wife in the future, of letting her know her family was safe and would be well cared for, then perhaps Lisbeth could go on, free to live a full and happy life, in her time, in her different world. Go on to become the doctor she was destined to be without worry or regret.

Once he'd recovered from the initial shock of losing Lisbeth forever, Magdalena had tried to reassure him that he would still go on to walk the path God had set before him. But how? A life of sorrow was no life. Bitterness spread a poisonous ache through his tired limbs.

"Soldiers," Pontius warned under his breath. "We'll be required to pay tribute at the customs station."

A soldier flicking the reins of a fine black horse with the legion's brand seared into its flank spurred his beast close enough to trample their feet. "Fall out and pay your tax."

Cyprian dropped his head to avoid recognition, his temperature rising at the injustice of having to sneak back into the city that had once embraced him. In the space of a year he'd lost his position, his wife, and the last of his self-respect. He joined the line waiting at the official tent erected to fleece anyone brave enough to enter the diseased city.

"State your business in Carthage." The government agent's seal ring flashed on his left hand as he used his right to press numbers into a wax slate with a sharp stylus.

"Commerce."

The agent scribbled down the answer without looking up. "And what do you intend to sell?"

"Grain."

The agent raised his stylus. "Who has grain left to sell?"

Cyprian recalled the parched fields of the Cap Bon peninsula. The few sacks of grain he'd brought from his country estate would scarcely put a dent in the needs of Carthage. "To the east the rains have been generous." God forgive him, but now he'd lost his integrity, too.

"Increased harvest?" The agent's eyes slid from Cyprian's head to the money pouch Cyprian had purposefully attached to the outside of his belt. "Increased tariff."

Cyprian put his hand to his belt, struggling to maintain his cool facade. "Shall you tax my virtue as well?"

"Smart-mouthed cur." The agent dropped his stylus and reared back to strike. "You'll pay more than coin."

Pontius appeared from nowhere and leaped between them, his palms raised to show himself unarmed. "Sir, our only wish is to fill the empty bellies of the empire." He slipped the man a few extra coins, then pulled Cyprian back to their wagon. "What were you thinking, angering the agent? We have no papers, nothing granting us safe passage. The spies of Aspasius are everywhere."

Cyprian broke free of Pontius's grasp. "It's not right." The source of his fury was not really that he'd been denied respect; rather, it was his struggle to reconcile the life that now was with the life he'd once hoped to have. "But you're right, Pontius. We've trouble enough." Cyprian stomped to the wagon and busied himself tightening the straps on the load.

In the thickening gray dusk, they waited with the wagon handlers, tillers of soil, and tradesmen milling outside the massive stone walls. Fear-tinged murmurs echoed Cyprian's own thoughts. What would they find once they entered the city? Would Aspasius wait with an executioner's sword? Was he a fool to go in while others rushed out? Especially now that Lisbeth was gone. If Caecilianus were here, he'd second Pontius's lectures on the futility of vengeance.

Magdalena appeared at his side. Her anxious breath formed pale clouds in the gathering dark. She held out a strip of cloth. "Cover your nose and mouth. Touch nothing, especially the dead."

Faces covered, they watched linkboys carrying torches along the wall's thick ledge, lighting lamps that circled the city in an eerie yellow halo. Amid the growing buzz of anxiety, wagon handlers took their places at the reins, trying to calm the animals that stamped and pulled against the yokes to get on with whatever awaited them in the city. A groan from inside the massive gates signaled the lifting of the large wooden beam from the metal locking arms.

The gates swung open. A putrid plume of air swooshed over the waiting crowd.

"Death!" someone shouted. "Death!"

Women gasped. Mules shied, backing into the carts behind them. Burly oxen drivers grabbed their noses, tears streaming down their faces like babies. A few drivers vomited upon the cobblestones. Though ten wagons stood between Cyprian and the open gates, he caught a glimpse of the horror awaiting his return. He reached to steady Magdalena, but it was he who needed steadying.

"Move out!" Soldiers from the customs tent spurred their horses. "Move it, plebs."

One by one the wagons lurched into motion.

Cyprian's bare feet trod the stones worn smooth by those who'd come and gone through this gate for centuries. Abandoned water jugs, torn pieces of garments, and smashed baskets littered the boulevard flanked with a bevy of inns, taverns, and brothels. Large arched doorways extended the full width of each business and opened straight onto the street. Instead of the usual flurry of ruffians and men bent on satisfying themselves with the boldly dressed prostitutes, folding wooden shutters were drawn across the windows and thresholds, bolted tight. Carthage was no longer the shiny jewel in the empire's crown.

Bloated bodies stacked two and three high blocked most of the doors. Ravenous maggots, undeterred by the cooler temperatures, plundered the carcasses with the intensity of an invading army. Cyprian wondered if there were any patrons left to navigate the putrid mess. Why would Aspasius allow the stink of rotting flesh to defile his city, or more importantly, to shut down the lucrative trades of a shipping port?

Several wagons back, Cyprian could hear someone slap the reins. A nervous team of mules shot forward, trampling any carts in the way and coming straight at them. In an instant, Cyprian grabbed Magdalena and pressed her into the nearest doorway. The bar's door was not completely shut. Together, they stumbled inside, tripping across what felt like a stiffened body. The stench they'd endured outside paled compared to the overwhelming odor of death trapped inside these walls.

"Let's get out of here." Cyprian latched onto Magdalena's elbow.

They heard a whimper and froze. Straining to hear it again, they listened with every nerve on high alert. Then it came again. No louder than the mewing of a stable kitten.

"The sleeping loft." Magdalena started toward a rickety ladder that led to a stone ledge.

"Stay here." Cyprian wove through the racks of dried herbs and empty wine casks and climbed to the loft. He peered over the dusty floorboards. A small child huddled on a filthy sleeping mat with his knees pulled to his chest. "What's your name, boy?"

"Horace."

"What has happened here, Horace?"

"Sickness." The boy coughed as though his insides were trying to escape.

Cyprian backed two steps down the ladder. "He has the rash."

"We can't leave him." Magdalena blocked his retreat. "Let me get him."

A sick child was not what they needed, but he couldn't leave him. "Be quick."

They traded places, and Magdalena motioned the boy to her. "It's all right, Horace. Take my hand." Pretty soon Horace's legs dangled over the ledge. Magdalena gathered him into her arms and backed down the stairs. "Whatever you do, Cyprian, don't come closer."

Boy in tow, they quickly withdrew.

Cyprian burst onto the street and pulled down his mask, gasping for fresh air and finding none out on the street. "Lisbeth would not have gone if she knew how bad things would get."

"I gave her no choice." Magdalena motioned for him to bring his mask to his nose. She lifted a corner of the tarp on the opposite side of the cart from where Laurentius hid and slid the boy inside. She told the child to say nothing, then covered his splotchy red face. "We should cut through the tenements."

At the first side street they encountered, Pontius led them off the main thoroughfare. Progress was slow through the narrow alleys. Since few in the slums could afford the luxury of lamp oil, the streets were black as the sea on a moonless night. Cyprian would have abandoned the cart were it not for his concern that Laurentius and their new charge would be unable to finish the journey on foot.

Near the heart of the ghetto, they encountered a small group of people huddled around a fire pit. Dressed in rags, the peasants warmed their hands near glowing embers. Only one woman turned to see who dared come this way. Her face drawn and eyes blank, she clutched a bundle in her arms.

Cyprian halted the wagon. Pontius and Magdalena exchanged worried looks. The dogs flanked Cyprian, low growls in the backs of their throats.

"She has a child." Cyprian reached under the tarp.

Magdalena stayed his hand before he could withdraw a sack of grain. "What are you doing?"

"They're starving."

She lowered her chin and moved close. "They'll storm the wagon."

His eyes darted from the tarp to the group huddled around the fire. "But her child—"

"I'll come back tomorrow," Magdalena said. "Bring only the bread I can carry. When it's gone, it's gone."

"Same as you couldn't leave the boy, I can't leave them," Cyprian argued.

"Save a few? Or save many?"

Magdalena was right. He must not forget why he had returned. A riot in the slums would bring the soldiers. Aspasius would have him nailed to a cross before the sun came up.

Cyprian clicked the reins, and they moved on. The tenement dwellers gathered around the fire didn't even bother to pursue them.

Thirty minutes later, the wrought-iron gates to Cyprian's villa came into view. He couldn't help but pick up the pace. It was foolish to think Lisbeth had somehow returned, yet he burst through the front door calling her name as he had done in his dreams.

A small lamp burned in the atrium, illuminating the pallets that surrounded the fountain. Every bed was full.

"Cyprian?" A petite blond woman who'd been resting beside one of the beds scrambled to her feet. "It is you! I prayed you would come. Thank God you're home." Ruth flew into his arms.

He held her sobbing frame. She was much thinner than he remembered, but then so was he. This past year had been hard on everyone. "Where's Barek? Is he safe?"

She wiped her cheeks, but the dark circles remained under her eyes. "We've run out of room, so we had to set up our living quarters in the gardener's cottage." She assured those who'd roused from their beds that it was safe to go back to sleep. Then she noticed Magdalena. "Oh, my friend. I thought we'd lost you forever."

The two women hugged.

"You shouldn't have returned, but I'm so glad you have." Ruth waved at the line of beds stretching the full length of the hall. "Sometimes I don't know what to do for them."

"I should never have left you." Magdalena wrapped her arm around Ruth's shoulders. "You look as though you could use a bit of rest yourself."

"My feet are nearly as worn as my heart. So much death and sorrow." Ruth turned to Cyprian. "I pray you don't mind that I took over your home. After my husband's death, we didn't know where else to go, and the sick just kept coming."

"My home will always be your home, just as I promised our dear Caecilianus."

A guarded look passed over Ruth's face, one that warned of trouble. "Your home may not be yours for long. I've heard rumors that the moment your exile ship cleared our harbor the proconsul set to work securing the senatorial votes needed to confiscate your property. Once he finally forces your father's powerful friends to give in, he will bring an army crashing through your door."

"Let him come. I intend to be ready." Cyprian peeled off his dirty cloak. "Until then, no one must know of my return."

5

Dallas, Texas

LISBETH SAT IN THE blue glow of a hospital computer, staring at the CDC's spreadsheet. The latest entry on the growing list of victims was a boy about Maggie's age. If she couldn't figure out how this child fit into her mathematical model, she couldn't pinpoint the source of his infection or calculate how many potentially infected people had yet to present themselves for treatment. In a highly mobile world, one person could easily come in contact with several people who, for a multitude of possible reasons, had not been vaccinated.

Effective control was what the Centers for Disease Control and Prevention team considered themselves . . . the cavalry charging in to save the day.

Less than forty-eight hours after the first official measles death, the CDC had swooped in with their black gear bags loaded with Kevlar-reinforced gloves and Tyvek body bags. They'd set up a fully operational command center in the hospital's emergency room, taken over the morgue and the postmortems, and declared a state of voluntary quarantine for every unvaccinated person who'd come in contact with the dead or the ill still in isolation. Medical personnel were included in this sequester, which meant adding folding cots in the break rooms and on-call suites. If the viral samples, urine specimens, and throat swabs sent off to the national labs confirmed a measles outbreak, which Lisbeth felt certain they would, dealing with a mandatory quarantine would keep her away from Maggie for days.

Lisbeth gulped down the dregs of cold coffee. The CDC hadn't been in camp twenty-four hours, and they'd already created a landfill of paperwork. After a bitter run-in with the team's arrogant leader, she'd been denied access to the autopsies and tasked with the tedious job of digging through the statistics. She took a file from the top of the heap and began inputting the extensive immunization histories and chains of contact information she'd collected from the five new admissions in isolation.

A rumbling down the hall alerted her to her chance to get back into the action.

"Dr. Pruda?"

The CDC's chief of infectious diseases stopped before her desk and gazed over the top of his glasses. "Dr. Hastings?"

She wasn't necessarily expecting a Roman noble, but every time the government's self-assured epidemiologist with the intense bedroom eyes and broad shoulders entered her space, her mind automatically dressed the hunk in a toga, despite how off-putting his manners were. She quickly blinked away the image. Since her return to the twenty-first century, she'd begrudgingly agreed to a couple of blind dates her old roommate Queenie had arranged, but she'd never let any progress to a second date. In her heart, she was still married, even if her spouse was technically long gone.

"Have you had time to review my case notes?" she asked.

He remained on the opposite side of the counter, keeping a safe distance between him and anything that might be contaminated. Including her. His triple-gloved hands clutched a stack of charts. "Measles are extremely rare in the United States. Most clinicians have never seen measles, especially people our age. What led you to make this particular diagnosis?"

"I've seen measles before."

"Really?" His dark brows rose. "Where?"

Dr. Pruda wouldn't believe the horrors of third-century Carthage even if she could find the right words to describe the suffering she'd witnessed in that place. If it wasn't for the charcoal brazier scar on her wrist and the pregnancy stretch marks on her belly, she wouldn't believe the impossible story either.

Lisbeth tugged her white coat sleeve over the fading mark just above her watch band. "North Africa."

"When and where exactly?"

"My father's an archaeologist. I grew up traveling from one desert hole to the next. I'm not sure exactly where. Why?"

"The lab results are back." He offered a piece of paper for her review. "Seems your diagnosis was correct." Dr. Pruda leaned in. A hint of something powerful and musky penetrated her own mask and hit her nose. "Measles is the most highly infectious virus known to man, aerosolized with a simple cough. It's easy for an infected person who's not yet covered in the telltale rash to get past airport security. Put one hundred unvaccinated people on a plane, let that infected person cough, and ninety people onboard will contract the disease."

Lisbeth's racing mind surpassed her galloping heart. "Are you ordering mandatory vaccinations?" It was what she would do to control the possibility of a few cases becoming an epidemic, but she was just a novice infectious disease specialist. Dr. Pruda, though no more than five years her senior, was the only one with the clout to sound that governmental alarm.

He straightened, his expression condescending. "What is rule number one of outbreak management?"

"Avoid full-scale panic."

"Fear spreads faster than fevers." His charcoal eyes turned hard and drilled into her over his mask. "Communicable diseases are never entirely absent from the community. There will always be sporadic cases and minor outbreaks like what we have now. We've not nearly enough information yet to jump to conclusions." Dr. Pruda tapped the back of her computer screen. "I shouldn't have to explain to someone with your brilliant reputation the importance of managing this situation to avoid a fluke transmission becoming a large-scale panic that leads to an epidemic when the public tries to flee the area. Isolation, quarantine, and making sure the press doesn't catch wind of this will be our first lines of defense." He'd spoken precisely—every word sifted through a filter, stripped of any contaminants before released into the atmosphere.

"Wait a minute. That's it? Keeping this out of the news is the best you've got?" Lisbeth pushed away from the computer, unwilling to have the urgency of this situation dismissed because of politics. "You might as well toss us into the third century with nothing more than a homemade vaporizer and a few eucalyptus leaves."

"Excuse me?"

"Improving herd immunity by upping the numbers who've received viable vaccinations *is* our only line of defense. Trust me. I've tried every stopgap control you've suggested, and it didn't work."

Suspicion hung in the disinfected silence, a knotted noose awaiting her neck. "Dr. Hastings, exactly *when* did *you* try this methodology?"

How had she let something so stupid slip? Lisbeth clenched her jaw, fuming that she'd lost control, and lost it to this pompous weasel. "I meant, I've read several historical attempts at isolation and quarantine. You're right. Those protocols reduced the transmission rates, but they didn't stop them."

"But you have no *practical* experience managing even a small outbreak?"

Sharing the details of how badly she'd handled being thrown into the terrifying experience of a third-century plague would do nothing for her credibility. Lisbeth swallowed and gave a slight shake of her head.

"Well, Doctor, I do. And what I'm saying is this." He took back his report. "We will work to achieve complete containment within forty-eight hours by sticking to our current protocol. Observe the quarantine, and treat our isolated patients as best we can." He raised himself to his full six-foot-one height. "Do I make myself clear?"

"Yes, sir."

Lisbeth slumped into the desk chair and buried her face in her hands. Her mind traveled back eighteen hundred years to an exquisite villa by the Mediterranean Sea. The stench of fear and desperation filled the marbled halls. Twigs draped with strips of fabric, eucalyptus leaves floating in boiling water, and homemade hydration solutions had saved a few. But she'd been forced to leave long before she knew the true effectiveness of her efforts. She'd left the frightened people of Carthage to fend off an invading virus with nothing but their prayers. Was she overthinking things now out of guilt over the past? Was she making an outbreak into an epidemic in her mind because she'd been unable to forgive herself for deserting the people she'd grown to love?

"Dr. Hastings?" The tap to Lisbeth's shoulder startled her upright.

"What is it, Nelda?"

"Your father just tried to get past the command center."

"Oh, no."

"I hustled him outside and told him to wait there until you could come to him."

"Thanks." After shedding her contaminated clothes, Lisbeth scrubbed her hands and arms with the vigilance of a surgeon headed into the OR, then suited up in a fresh paper gown, mask, cap, and gloves. She stuck a couple of extra masks in her scrub pocket, waited until the cop on door duty left for a bathroom break, then quickly slipped outside for the first time in days. A cold mist stung her eyes.

"Maggie?" She fought the urge to run to her daughter. "Papa, you shouldn't have brought my baby here."

"Wasn't about to leave her home alone."

Maggie scooted behind Papa. "Stranger!" She clutched her Christmas doll with one hand and Papa's legs with the other. "Stranger danger!"

"Maggie, it's me, Mommy."

Maggie peered around Papa's leg. "Let me see your face."

A man with an umbrella hurried along the sidewalk, coughing as he passed their little huddle.

"Hey, buddy, cover your mouth." The man ignored Lisbeth's direction and scurried inside the hospital without looking back. Lisbeth held out a mask to Maggie. "I can't take my mask off, baby. In fact, you and G-Pa need to put these on."

"Why?" Maggie backed away, fear flashing in her saucer-wide eyes.

"We're playing a game." Lisbeth hated lying, but the truth would rip the scab off the dark hole Maggie wasn't ready for. "Hide-and-seek. Only with doctors' masks."

"No."

"Look, Miss Magdalena. I've got mine on." Papa danced around like a circus clown trying to coerce a smile, but his gyrations were getting nowhere. "Let me help you." He quickly slipped the strap of the pleated paper over Maggie's head.

Her little limbs immediately tensed. "It's too tight." Maggie clawed at the mask and tried to wiggle free at the same time. "I can't breathe."

"Loosen the metal clip across her nose, Papa."

"That's the best I can do," Papa said.

Maggie took evasive action and squirmed out of Papa's grasp. "I can't." She ripped off the mask. "I won't."

"Baby, it's just paper. Air can pass straight through. Watch." Lisbeth demonstrated breathing in and out. "Want to try again, baby?"

"No." Maggie threw the mask on the ground. "I can't."

"What if we get a mask for your baby doll, too?" Papa bent to retrieve the soiled mask.

"Take her home, Papa."

"She'll be fine. Give her a minute." Papa put an arm around Maggie. "She's got to learn to face her fears."

"Not today, she doesn't." Lisbeth waved them away. "Get her out of here!"

"Okay. Calm down." Papa scooped Maggie up and started for the parking lot. Then he stopped, turned around, and handed Lisbeth a thick manila envelope he'd pulled from beneath his coat. "Almost forgot why we came. You need to see this."

"Mail? You put my child at risk to bring me mail?" *The Vatican Apostolic Library* was stamped in the upper left-hand corner. "Your early-church research can wait until I get home."

"When's that gonna happen?"

"I don't know."

"Then no, this can't wait." Papa lifted Maggie's hood over her head. "Promise you'll read that as soon as you can." He thumped the envelope in Lisbeth's hand. "That paragraph I marked changes everything."

6

Carthage

WINTER REFUSED TO GIVE way to spring. The sun hid behind clouds as heavy as Cyprian's mood these long, dark days since his return from exile. Nothing was coming together like he planned.

The boy he and Magdalena rescued from the herb shop had died within hours of their homecoming. Cyprian had wanted to bury the lad in the back corner of the garden, but before he could dig a proper grave, several of the others who lined the mats in his halls had died as well. His gardens, while exceptionally large for a city property, did not have the space needed for multiple graves. The best he could do for the deceased was to wait until nightfall, put a cloak over his head, drag them out of the neighborhood, and place their bodies upon the growing heaps in the slums.

"You really should let Barek do that," Ruth had said, insisting he take her place in the gardener's cottage. "We've both had the measles. I don't want you exposed."

"Who took care of you?"

"Those we'd helped." She had a pleased smile, one he couldn't understand. "It was as if the hand of God put the cooling cloths upon our heads."

Her ability to forgive was a root that ran deep, an anchor that shamed him. "Lisbeth declared me immune after my run-in with that infected sailor. I'm not worried about catching measles."

The reminder had satisfied her, and they'd all quickly settled into the new arrangement of Barek and Laurentius bunking with him in the cottage while Ruth, Junia, and Magdalena shared his master suite in the villa.

Daily more and more ill arrived on his doorstep, their faces flush with fever and their eyes wild with desperation. Magdalena and Ruth had done their best to tend the people, to offer them peace and comfort in their last hours, but without Lisbeth to share the load, the sick were dying faster than they could stock the vaporizer pots. At night, after he finished his accounts, Cyprian added a body or two to the rotting pile.

Tonight he stood at the tiny window of his groundskeeper's cottage watching another northern gale toss anchored ships. Spotty reports came by way of the daily addition of sick. Foul weather had delayed the launch of the ship meant to fetch him. But once the waters warmed and his escape was discovered, Aspasius's soldiers would tear the province apart searching for him. If he had not managed to rally his father's old supporters by then, he would die in the arena. And the proconsul of Carthage would not only be free to steal Cyprian's wealth, he would never have to answer for his dirty deeds.

Cyprian had used these days of lying low to get his finances in order and prepare for the possibility of the confiscation of his estate. He'd done as much as he could without an outside agent acting on his behalf, one who could secretly convert the sale of his properties into the cash required to transport Ruth and Magdalena beyond the proconsul's reach. Pontius could do the foreign sales without risk of exposing their early return, but for Cyprian's local holdings Ruth had suggested he use Felicissimus. Someone no one would suspect.

Turning over something this important to a former client bothered him. It wasn't that he didn't trust the pudgy little slave trader. In fact, over the years, this particular client had proven exceptionally trustworthy. He and Felicissimus had conducted several secret and very successful business transactions after Cyprian's conversion to Christianity.

They'd been introduced by their mutual friend Caecilianus. The old bishop believed if Felicissimus and Cyprian worked together, not only could Felicissimus be rehabilitated from the lying cheat he'd been before he became a believer, but together they could curtail Aspasius's ability to acquire slaves. As one of the city's shrewdest slave traders, Felicissimus knew of Rome's latest conquests and what merchandise would appear on the block long before even the most prominent buyers. It was, after all, Felicissimus who'd alerted Cyprian to Lisbeth's arrival. That he'd been allowed the opportunity to spare her from Aspasius, if only for a brief season, was a debt Cyprian could never repay.

Rescuing slaves with a slave trader did not make him uncomfortable. What bothered him was the blurring of well-defined lines of social standing. Caecilianus had encouraged him to let his patrician prejudices go. While his mentor was close at hand, Cyprian had to confess that he'd made progress. After all, hadn't he married a slave? But he found it unsettling to see women doing men's work, masters caring for slaves, and Felicissimus an appointed church deacon. If Caecilianus had lived, he would have relished the dissolution of the walls that separated the church into distinct classes. But Cyprian was not Caecilianus in more ways than that. The whole idea of "neither slave nor free" felt like shifting sand beneath his feet.

Wishing things were different would change nothing. He had no better ideas. If Ruth believed Felicissimus a suitable agent, she would not let the idea go until he gave it serious consideration.

An urgent rap at the door drew Cyprian from his brooding thoughts. "Ruth?" Water gushed from the eaves and soaked her head covering. The dogs rushed inside and began to shake water everywhere. "You'll catch your death getting out in this storm."

"We need the rain." She swept into the room. From the basket upon her arm came the enticing scent of freshly baked bread. "You need dinner and a haircut."

Ruth handed Cyprian the basket. She removed her black scarf and shook out the water. Since her husband's death, Ruth had abandoned her elaborately styled hair in favor of a simple sunshine-colored braid that hung to her waist. She'd also taken to wearing bland, serviceable cotton tunics stained with her hacking patients' phlegm. She turned down offers to purchase something better, claiming tailored silk *stolas* could be put to far better use ripped apart and converted into vaporizer tents.

Ruth looked up to find him staring at her. "I'm glad you're here. Barek has been missing the companionship of a father . . . a man."

Though she tried to lace her voice with cheer, sorrow had etched its deep, dull pain into the sunken eyes of Caecilianus's young widow. A widow at thirty-four. Still beautiful, yet stripped of the vivacious sparkle that had always turned a lackluster gathering into a party, Ruth stood before him in her loose-fitting dress, brave on the outside, so vulnerable and lost on the inside. An alabaster jar whose seal had been broken, the priceless perfume poured out and wasted.

Guilt closed his throat. He'd failed to save his friend. He would not fail to save his friend's family. If wealth could restore the luster to Ruth's eyes, he would give his fortune. "Barek is a fine young man. You've done well raising him."

"Kind of you to say, but he can certainly benefit from a man's influence right now."

Neither dared venture into the deeper truths they'd once sat around in his library sharing with Caecilianus. Since Cyprian's return, they'd perfected the art of keeping their private griefs concealed beneath the surface of small talk. Admitting their bereavement risked the possibility of breaching the walls protecting their hearts and overwhelming them both with sadness. Instead they focused on the tasks at hand.

The business of surviving one more day.

In his absence, Ruth had thrown herself into caring for the sick and was continuing to do an admirable job. But Cyprian couldn't help but see Lisbeth's face in every vaporizer tent, every pot of boiling water carried in for proper hand washing, and in every cup of pomegranate juice spilled upon his expensive carpets.

Cyprian set the basket on a small, low table surrounded by plump cushions. "Barek isn't here."

Ruth rubbed warmth into her crossed arms. "I told him he could meet his friend Natalis for a few hours of fishing."

"In this weather?" Cyprian noticed her shivering and draped a blanket around her shoulders. "Can't have either one of you getting sick."

"Barek doesn't really fish anymore. Natalis is such a fine young man. I was hoping he could help cheer Barek." Her hand grazed his as she reached to clasp the wrap.

An unexpected jolt of longing sparked through him. He stepped back. "The lad has suffered a great loss."

"He's always struggled to find joy. The darkness has worsened since his father . . ." She turned from him, as if she'd felt the same desolate ache, and lifted the basket's covering. "I encourage his love of water in hopes that the roar of the sea will drown out the failure pounding in his head." Hands trembling, she removed the food and also a pair of shears and a comb.

"Maybe if I talk to him?"

"Will he even look at you?"

"No."

"Me neither." She uncorked a wine flask and filled a cup. The dogs whined, and she tossed them each a scrap of bread. "My son feels that if he'd done more to defend me his father would still be alive."

"That's not true. The blame is mine."

"If truth and blame could erase pain, the Roman temples and arenas would be empty." She offered Cyprian a drink. Water trickled from the wisps of hair plastered to her forehead. "Pain is the way of this life, but that doesn't make our wait for heaven any easier, does it?"

"Do you ever question the promise of a better life?"

"I'd be lying if I said no. Everyone questions. My son's questions keep him from taking his father's place as bishop."

Cyprian took the cup. "He's young. Give him time. He'll grow into it."

Rain splattered the windows. The drops, no bigger than tears, merged into sad, pathetic little streams that cut through the foggy film obscuring the garden view.

"The church does not have time for Barek to mature into his heritage, Cyprian." Ruth motioned for him to sit. "Enough of my troubles. Let me see if I can restore order to those curls."

"I don't see the point. No one even sees me."

"I do."

He sighed. "If you think a haircut will make me human, have at it." He sank upon the stool.

"I'll be glad when you can make your presence known in the church." She draped a towel around his neck, her hands skimming his shoulders.

"I don't think the church will be anxious to welcome someone into their midst that they believe to be a coward."

The word, sharp with accusation, stuck in his throat. If there were those who didn't believe he'd run from trouble, they would find it disappointing to learn he was now hiding in his gardener's cottage while a widow continued the brave work of Caecilianus. Cyprian told himself his plans must be protected, kept secret until everything was in place. He knew proceeding without the support of the Senate was foolishness. But was he wise or simply too frightened to take bolder, brasher steps? He thought of the story of Peter, how the apostle of Christ had sworn he'd follow his savior into battle. But when the day of reckoning arrived, he ran. How could a man lop off ears one moment, then turn tail and hide the next? Cyprian remembered sitting at the feet of Caecilianus listening to the tale and judging Peter's desertion rather harshly.

Now he couldn't help but wonder. Had disappointment and fear similarly softened his own resolve?

"I was there the day you offered your life in exchange for ours," Ruth said, as if she could read between the lines of his conflicted thoughts. "I'll tell them you are the bravest man I know, next to my Caecilianus." She reached for the shears and dropped them.

Cyprian bent and picked them up. "I have not been nor will I ever be half the man your husband was." He steadied her hand. "You're shaking."

She withdrew her fingers and took up the comb, her eyes large and weary. "The believers will need help if we are going to save the movement."

"I've turned over my house for their use. I'm depleting my accounts. What more can I do?"

Clip. Clip. Clip. The cool iron slid across the base of his neck in a forceful line. "I've spared you the worst of it, Cyprian."

"Why?"

"You've needed the opportunity to grieve Lisbeth's loss."

"Will it bring her back? Spare me no more, Ruth."

She removed the towel from his shoulder, careful to catch the locks that had not fallen upon the floor. She retrieved a small hand mirror from her basket and passed it to Cyprian.

He held the polished side down. It had been more than a year since he'd looked at himself, and it would take more than a haircut to clean up the nasty unruliness that had sprouted deep within his soul.

Ruth came and stood in front of him, her head cocked to the side. Her thoughtful perusal gave him the feeling she was checking for more than the accuracy of her work. "As the persecution and plague worsen, it has become difficult for the church to assemble. They're less likely to risk coming together for worship when there's no bishop to explain the Scriptures. Without regular fellowship and encouragement, I fear, some believers will recant, desert their faith, and flee the city to protect their families."

"I can't say as I blame them." Cyprian considered his reflection in Ruth's huge blue eyes. He didn't like what he saw. A broken and tired man who questioned the validity of a faith that required so much suffering in addition to the weighty sacrifice he'd already made—or, for that matter, that Caecilianus had made. Where was the just and loving God the bishop had introduced him to? The path they'd chosen that day in the proconsul's chamber had changed everything. Were he given the choice today, would he do the same? Would he look Aspasius in the eye and boldly proclaim himself a follower of Christ? Or would he do everything he could—including deny his God—to retain the leverage to free his wife? How foolish his bravery seemed now.

He didn't need a mirror to know that the man he'd been was no more. "Tell me what you want me to do, woman, for I have no answers of my own."

"Help the church."

"Isn't that what I'm doing if I ask Felicissimus to take over the liquidation of my properties?"

"No one knows better than I what you have already done and intend to do for the cause of Christ." She lifted the mirror to his face. The hardened features staring back at him were not a shock. "But I think God is asking for more."

"More?"

"You should assume your rightful position as head of the church."

Cyprian placed the mirror facedown upon the table. "No."

"Barek may have grown taller in stature since his father's execution, but with each passing day he seems to grow smaller in confidence." She took in a sharp breath. "You are the bishop they need. The one to share the Scriptures and offer words of hope. The one to lead them through their fear."

Cyprian pulled away, the empty space in his soul bigger than ever. "I agree that Barek may not be up to the task, but there must be someone better suited to provide the spiritual guidance these people need."

"Who else but you?" The reluctance in her voice, no more than the faint flapping of a bird with an injured wing, drew him to her side. Before he could stop himself, he wrapped an arm around her shoulder. She leaned into him, as if his support were the only thing keeping her upright. "Caecilianus adored you. You trained at his feet. Did you not proclaim yourself the future bishop of the church that day in Aspasius's office?"

"It was the proclamation of a desperate and foolish man." Cyprian backed away.

Ruth took Cyprian's hands, pressing her need into his. "My husband confidently gave his family into your care." Her voice hiccupped, but she kept going, determined despite the sudden flow of tears. "He would be more than confident that the church should be in the hands of no one else." The request had taxed the last of her strength, but she managed to sob out the only thing that did not need to be said. "Oh, Cyprian. I miss him so."

"As do I." Cyprian gathered her into his arms once again. "Your grief is one more reason Aspasius must pay."

"Promise me you will let the Lord deal with Aspasius."

He could not bring himself to confess the vengeance in his heart. "Ruth, I . . ."

"Know this, Cyprianus Thascius: I shall die if I should lose you twice." She melted against him. Months of bottled anguish poured forth.

When she'd cried herself out, she pulled away silently. She slowly lifted her tearstained cheeks. Red-rimmed eyes took him in, but he could not be sure if she saw him or Caecilianus. Before he could speak reassurance, she threaded her arms around his neck, drew him close, and kissed his lips.

Pull away.

His hands found her waist, thin and easily grasped. He tried to push free, but the solidity of her existence caused his own grief to slowly unravel. He pulled her tight and returned her kiss with the passion of a man tired of exile.

God forgive him; while his arms held Ruth, his mind held only Lisbeth.

7

CYPRIAN PACED THE GARDENER'S cottage, alternating between wringing his hands and readjusting the folds of his old election toga. His attempt to wear the simple homespun tunic of his exile had resulted in Ruth burning the rag, declaring it beyond redemption. She'd dug through one of his many storage chests and produced what she called a more respectable garment.

To prevent rumors of his return reaching the ears of Aspasius, she'd cleaned and pressed his electoral swag herself with the same efficiency and perfection of the professional laundry houses. When he'd stepped out from behind the dressing screen, Ruth had proclaimed him restored to his old self.

For the first time since his return, she'd smiled. "The church will be so glad to see you."

"I wish I could say the same." The garment felt heavy and awkward upon his shoulders, but he was done arguing with her. This meeting was going to happen. The sooner he got it over with, the better.

He was grateful that Ruth's preparations had distracted her from probing into the blackness of his soul. His discomfort stemmed not from the weight of the wool but rather from the anger he wore like a soldier's breastplate. Even Ruth's eternal optimism had failed to penetrate the armor around his heart. He was not his former self. Before the exile, he'd been a man of ambitious views. A man comfortable in gold, jewels, embroidered garments, and the possibility of leading a radical movement from obscurity into victory. But since those long days adrift and his discovery of the loss of Lisbeth, he'd become a man of plain apparel, shattered heart, and depleted faith. A man uncertain of where to place his feet.

As per his promise, he'd taken in the widow of Caecilianus. Kissing her was a mistake they'd silently agreed never to mention, in exchange for his agreement to gather the church for encouragement. He would put to death the feelings her nearness stirred in him and treat her with the respect his promise deserved.

Cyprian had spent hours poring over Caecilianus's Scripture parchments and personal notes, searching for the perfect words to say to the believers. Words to comfort, restore, and unite the frightened flock against this blight of plague and persecution. Words he could deliver to pacify Ruth without choking on his own hypocrisy. He glanced at the notes he'd carefully crafted. His stomach had not been this knotted since his first day in court.

Ruth's gentle rap on the cottage door cinched the knot tighter. "The sun has set. It's finally safe for the believers to make their way here. We haven't met in weeks. I'm so excited to have everyone together. I think it best if I go first and break the news of your return and my reason for calling this special assembly." She smoothed a fabric fold at his shoulder. "After you deliver your message of encouragement, I think you should move among them."

Cyprian felt himself flinch. "Move among them?"

"Speak to them. Touch them. Reassure them. Like Caecilianus used to do." Ruth snapped her fingers, and the dogs leaped to their feet and followed her.

"I'm not Caecilianus."

Ruth was so excited he doubted she'd heard his reply. Which was just as well. It wouldn't take her long to see what a mistake this had been.

Cyprian waited outside the door to the garden, notes twisting in his hands.

Quiet murmurings of sickness, death, and persecution filtered out. The somber mood did not match his memories of the joyous gatherings that used to fill his gardens. Judging from the believers' concerned whispers, he was not the only one suffering disillusionment. When he could stand the suspense no longer, he peeked around the door. Ruth was right. Between deaths and desertions, the number of believers had definitely dwindled.

He spotted Felicissimus sitting next to Ruth and sighed. Ruth would find a way to bring up Cyprian's need for a local agent. Given his circumstances, partnering with his former client didn't look so bad.

Ruth welcomed everyone, then gave a quick update on the sick. "I thank those who have aided my struggle to fill the shoes of my late husband. I know each of you has sacrificed time and supplies to help me keep the hospital running." She waited for the murmurs of approval to die down. "However, as the plague worsens, my duties to the sick increase, and the time I have left to care for the church lessens. Before his death, my husband chose one man to take his place as your spiritual leader. I'm excited to say, today that one man is here." Felicissimus shot to his feet with a self-satisfied expression, but before he could say anything Ruth pointed to the door. "Cyprianus Thascius!"

A collective gasp held Cyprian stationary as he watched expressions turn into a mixture of confusion, doubt, and hostility.

Ruth called again. Cyprian wiped the light sheen of perspiration from his forehead. What had she done? He had agreed to encourage the church. He had not agreed to assume the role of bishop. Tightening his belt, Cyprian stepped out into the chilly, torch-lit evening.

Shocked faces communicated everything from disgust to distrust. He could almost feel the crowd physically shrinking back, as if he were covered in the dreaded red blotches of plague. The respect his entrance would have commanded a year ago had sailed with his exile ship.

Ruth beckoned him to the dais, Felicissimus at her side, his eyes bulging in disbelief.

Cyprian followed the dogs as they cleared the path to Ruth. He forced himself to stop and apply Ruth's admonition to speak to as many as possible. By the time he reached the center of the garden, all he could say for the effort was that the distance between him and the church was greater now than when he was living on a beach in Curubis.

"Felicissimus!" Cyprian lightened his voice and opened his arms. Surely the man who'd helped him rescue many from bondage would recognize his current entrapment.

"My *patronus*. I had no idea you had returned." Obviously Ruth had kept Cyprian's return a secret from Felicissimus. He seemed completely taken off guard, but he adjusted his surprise with the speed of a man skilled at culling the most profitable flesh from a slave freighter. He accepted Cyprian's embrace and quickly shored up his sagging confidence with a hearty greeting. "Welcome home."

Cyprian patted him on the back. "Ruth tells me your efforts to aid the church have earned your election as deacon."

Red flushed Felicissimus's cheeks. "I did what I could."

Cyprian leaned in and whispered, "Truth be told, I think Ruth should be bishop."

"But she has chosen you." Felicissimus folded his arms over his stomach. "And a fine choice she has made." His sincerity did not match his words.

Before Cyprian could reply, Ruth told everyone he had a few words of encouragement to share.

Cyprian pulled his gaze from Felicissimus and removed his notes from his pocket. Fear of omitting a single word of his well-planned speech kept his eyes glued to the parchment. "Friends, I—"

"Friends don't desert their friends," said a man in the shadows.

An older woman stood, a baby in her arms. "You left us to suffer alone. My daughter and son-in-law died covered in the pox. Who will raise their child when the pox takes me?"

"Quinta, you know we're all pitching in," Ruth said. "Didn't Lydia send you a basket of freshly laundered wrappers and two skins of goat's milk?" Ruth's smile softened the pointed edge of her rebuke, and the woman gave a reluctant nod.

"He tossed us a few crumbs and fled to the mountains like the rich in summer." The man in the shadows stepped into the light of the torches, holding tightly to a small walking stick.

"You saw me board the exile ship in chains." Cyprian could not believe how quickly they'd forgotten all he'd done for them . . . all he continued to do. "You eat my bread, drink my wine, and enjoy the safety of my walls. What more do you want from me?"

"Giving us bread does not give you the right to lead us." The bent-over old man waved his cane.

"Metras!" Ruth chided. "You have no idea what this man has given for the sake of Christ."

"I did not come back to be your bishop. I only came back because—" Cyprian's explanation was cut off.

"If we don't leave, soon there will be no one left to bury the dead!" shouted another.

"Brothers and sisters!" Felicissimus held up his hands, and order was immediately restored. "This is what matters: our brother Cyprian has come home." He put a hand on Cyprian's shoulder.

"He had the means to go anywhere in the empire, and he returned to us."

Cyprian had done what Ruth wanted him to do: he'd appeared to the church. Yet the effort had not encouraged them or diminished the rumors of his cowardice.

He glanced at the dogs resting at Ruth's feet. Their eyes were closed, and their paws were crossed over their large ears. Even the old bishop's dogs doubted him capable of leading these people anywhere.

8

Dallas, Texas

LISBETH SAT ALONE IN a quiet corner of the hospital cafeteria, terror pounding a warning in her chest. Reshaping fate would not be easy. Time had an uncanny way of refusing to deviate from the path of least resistance.

She struggled to focus on the papers spread across the table. On the slim chance the emergency plan forming in her head was simply career suicide and complete foolishness, she reread the highlighted paragraph in the article.

> *Relevant evidence of a significant disease load has been preserved in the human bodies discovered in the mass graves of Carthage. Contrary to previous conclusions, these children were not the victims of some sort of religious sacrifice. More likely they died as the result of a deadly plague. These new facts support the writings of Pontius. This third-century church deacon and onetime exile claims that were it not for the valiant efforts of one man, Cyprianus Thascius, a wealthy Roman Christian whose head was struck off on the 14th of September, AD 258, the loss of human life would have ended the Roman Empire.*

Beheaded.

Nausea flooded Lisbeth's grave of white-hot memories. That

deepest part of her where painful memories resided no matter how hard she tried to forget. She could almost smell the dust rising in the sultry Mediterranean air. Hear the jeering crowds stomp their feet upon the Colosseum's marbled seats. Taste the mob's thirst for blood. Feel the pressure of the evil proconsul's crushing grip upon her wrist. See the iron gates rise with the simple wave of her captor's sausage-shaped index finger. But instead of the wild beasts the crowd expected, soldiers decked in pageant finery had marched into the arena dragging an old man with a lion's mane of white hair. Trailing the entourage was a dour-faced, black-cloaked priest wearing a leather skullcap. Gray smoke snaked from the brass incense burner the priest swung back and forth. As the soldiers tightened the prisoner's chains, Lisbeth had increased her own efforts to break free. Once she realized all she could do was scream, she did. At the top of her lungs. Until the entire arena stilled. The old bishop's hooded eyes had searched the crowd. When his gaze found hers, he flashed a forgiving smile, then dropped to his knees. He folded his hands in prayer and lifted his face toward the shaft of light that had broken through the clouds. The executioner raised his blade and swung. In one horrifying, slow-motion stroke, the sharp mind of Ruth's husband was forever severed from his oversized and forgiving heart.

Lisbeth wiped the sweat from her forehead.

When she first returned to the twenty-first century, she'd spent hours trying to make sense of her experience. She read the accounts of prominent Roman historians. Livy, Cicero, Varro. The bloody transformation of a rugged frontier turned world-power franchise fascinated her. She'd picked Papa's brain. Memorized the list of emperors. Studied the judicial system. Pored over the records of a society based on good behavior, trust, and a sense of duty undergirded by a strict standard of public service. She'd been surprised to learn that in the empire's beginning, the haves cared for the have-nots. But as centuries of social evolution destroyed their founding qualities, only a handful of third-century Romans possessed any desire to care for others. The hungry masses and the sick had been left to die alone, and the stench lingered in her nostrils even these six years later.

If this obscure paragraph she'd never seen before were true, Cyprian faced the same fate as her old friend Caecilianus. Her strong, proud husband would be forced to bow before the executioner's sword. If she did nothing, she'd be no better than those people in the Colosseum who'd turned their backs on the dying. She must act quickly.

Hands shaking, Lisbeth reached for her cold coffee.

Going after him was the right thing to do.

This time she would enter the situation better prepared than when she took that initial accidental tumble. She would go to the third century not as a green, first-year medical resident but as an experienced internist with a specialty in epidemiology. She'd pack everything she needed to beat back measles and reunite her family. This time everything would be different, including Cyprian's fate. She would convince him to come home with her.

Then why this knot in her belly?

Maggie, that's why. Maggie was a child who hated tight spaces even more than she. What if they were zipping down the time portal hole and Maggie panicked? Any child who would claw her way out of a surgical mask could never withstand miles of confinement in a solid rock waterslide.

These concerns didn't even include what would happen when Maggie found out her father was a third-century Roman noble. Where does one start explaining such impossibilities? She'd been so careful with what she told Maggie about her heritage. She'd allowed Papa's Latin lessons and Roman history quizzes as games, not survival tools in case her daughter happened to fall into a different world.

And then there was Papa. Even if she wanted to give him the slip, which she didn't, no way would he miss his chance to see Mama. His desire to reconnect with his wife was as great as her hunger to reunite with Cyprian. Papa would be the first one down the hole.

The whole idea of going back to the Cave of the Swimmers and purposely launching an old man and a little girl through a time portal was crazy thinking. How could she even consider risking the health and safety of the two people she loved more than her own life? Especially when a trip into the past was such a gamble? Say, by some miracle, the current-day political climate suddenly changed in Egypt and they were allowed back into the country. Say they even gained access to the cave. She still didn't know exactly how to return to the exact moment in time that would save Cyprian.

Jumping blindly into an underground aquifer with nothing to steer her direction or keep her on track meant she might not land anywhere close to where she was needed. Maybe not even in the exact same location. Miss the date of Cyprian's death by even a day, and she would be too late. Miss her hoped-for destination, and she might never reach him. Although she hadn't fully explored the possibility of Cyprian's life being recorded in history until now, she *had* studied everything she could get her hands on about time travel. Isaac Newton. Albert Einstein. Even modern-day philosophers and physicists. All of their theories were either sheer speculation or just plain fiction. Nobody could say definitively how time worked, and none of the endless rhetoric was the least bit reassuring.

Since her return to the twenty-first century, almost six years had passed. So much had changed for her in that amount of time. She'd given birth. Finished her medical education. And, most importantly, fully embraced the faith she'd seen demonstrated so many lifetimes ago.

If time proceeded at the same rate and linear progression in Cyprian's life, going to him with her newfound faith now would be useless; she would not arrive in time to save her husband from an execution that happened less than two years after his return from exile.

But, then again, who knew how the time portal worked for certain? Should she still try? Even if she could arrive in third-century Carthage today, was there enough time to find Cyprian, rescue her mother and half brother, *and* save the world from further attacks of this virus? She didn't know. But if she didn't at least try, there was one thing she knew for certain: her family would remain fragmented this side of heaven.

She thought she'd chosen her future based on her experience in the past, but now it seemed her past had been a preparation for the future . . . in the past. Lisbeth dug her phone from her pocket.

Her father answered on the first ring. "So you read the research?"

"Yes."

"Well?"

"I think I should go."

"You mean *we* should go."

"No, I'm going after him myself."

"I'm not missing an opportunity to find Magdalena, and you know your daughter is not going to miss a chance to find her father." Papa paused, letting the thought of Maggie crying her eyes out at Queenie's sink in. "You and I have traveled all over the world and lived to tell about it. Don't you think it's time Maggie got a little sand under her nails?"

Maggie. That was the first time her father had dared to separate his granddaughter from the memory of his wife. *Lord, what should*

I do? Leave Papa behind and dash his hope that their family could be reunited? Take him and Maggie and run the risk of losing everything that mattered to her?

Lisbeth gathered the papers from the Vatican. "Find Nigel."

"Done."

"Papa," she hesitated, the lump in her throat strangling her words.

"Anything else, Beetle Bug?"

"Tell me I'm not crazy."

9

DESPITE THE FEAR CLAWING her stomach, Lisbeth went online and ordered Maggie an expedited passport. She finished inputting the CDC's final analysis of the outbreak that had thankfully been contained, discharged the last measles patient, then turned off her phone. She spent the next few days holed up with a stack of Papa's Roman history textbooks and the assortment of early-church history articles she found in the Vatican's online library. If she was going to do this, she wasn't going in blind.

Every page she read stung like rubbing alcohol poured on an open sore. The last day she'd spent in third-century Carthage, she'd stood on her captor's balcony and screamed as her husband's ship sailed into exile. When her mother sent her tumbling back through the time portal, back to life in the twenty-first century, Lisbeth had planned to return. But a difficult pregnancy had made international travel impossible and time travel totally out of the question. Once Maggie was born, she knew giving her daughter the normal, stable life she'd wanted as a child meant she and Cyprian were destined to die apart. Her husband would fade into the rugged African frontier, and eighteen hundred years later she would probably die of natural causes in some metropolitan nursing home.

She could kick herself now, but it had never occurred to her that Cyprian would be recalled to Carthage, make an indelible mark upon history, and leave a trail of extensive writings. So far she'd dug up at least eighty letters and fifteen treatises Cyprian had written during his exile and his subsequent return to Carthage. She'd pored over his work, intent on reading every word and carefully excavating the layers, no matter how painful.

Digging through the research confirmed her husband's impressive rhetorical skills. She could almost see him pacing the carpets in his quiet library, his aristocratic forehead lined in concentration while Pontius frantically scratched his master's frustration upon a scroll. What she didn't see in the collection of missives to the church was the depth of kindness and compassion that had drawn her to Cyprian in the first place. Each carefully crafted entry touted a firm, legal perspective that obliterated any sign of the charity she'd always associated with him. Detailed accounts of the barbaric incursions upon the frontier borders, food shortages, and even the Christian persecutions were assessed against the empire's volatile political climate.

Facts. Not feelings.

Even Cyprian's tract *De Mortalitate*, the most expansive record of the plague she'd found to date, was little more than a stone-cold list of numbers and symptoms.

When her eyes became too bleary to read any more, she contemplated the reason for the abrupt change. Perhaps the death of Cyprian's old mentor and friend Caecilianus had hardened his heart. She could understand how the time he spent wasting away in banishment could have soured him. What she didn't want to consider was the possibility that her unexplained disappearance had also somehow played a part in this shift.

Lisbeth flipped the page of her notepad and scribbled down the plague symptoms on Cyprian's list.

Red eyes. Inflamed and ulcerated throat. Burning fever. Unquenchable thirst. Rash over the entire body. Loss of sight for those who survived.

All of these symptoms she'd seen firsthand and would never forget, but it was good to reaffirm their fit with her original measles diagnosis. She studied the entry again. The mention of gangrene of the extremities and continual vomiting and diarrhea had her stumped. She reminded herself that Cyprian wasn't a doctor. The queasy pallor his face took on every time he'd assisted her was the very reason she'd often spared him the gritty details. It wouldn't surprise her if a few of his medical specifics were incorrect.

However, the variation made her wonder if this brief entry described one disease or two. An additional pathogen, maybe one even more sinister, that could have arrived after her departure? Bacterial infections loved to piggyback upon the weakened immune systems left in the wake of a virus attack. A double and unnecessary whammy. Like mowing down half-starved concentration camp survivors with an AK-47.

She skimmed the medical entry again. No mention of buboes or swellings. Bubonic plague could be eliminated. So what else could lay waste to a population in such a short amount of time? She jotted a question mark in a margin and circled it in red. *Hmmm, troubling.*

If the plague or plagues were seasonal, planning her arrival during the winter months, assuming she could target an arrival time, might allow her an opportunity to get in front of the virus with an effective containment plan. She'd already given her resignation at the hospital and couldn't afford to sit around Dallas for several months. Besides, Papa and Maggie were already packed and ready to go.

Finding Cyprian would be her first priority when she returned to Carthage. Next, she'd rescue Mama and Laurentius from Aspasius. Then she would make sure Cyprian and her half brother were vaccinated. Once the family was together again, they could regroup and do whatever it took to wipe this sickness from the pages of history before they all jumped back into the twenty-first century.

She flipped through some more brittle pages, stopping at a biography reportedly written by Pontius, Cyprian's truest friend. She'd always admired the church deacon who willingly left a life of privileged service behind and boldly followed Cyprian into disgrace. This man had probably risked his neck by immortalizing the truth of the man he served. His devotion touched a raw place in her core. Over and over again, she'd witnessed Christians expressing extreme devotion, even to the point of exchanging their lives for another's. Acts of lunacy, it seemed . . . until she became a recipient of this kindness. Selfless lunacy that changed her life forever.

What the church deacon lacked in eloquence, he made up for in bombastic fervor. Pontius wrote of his fury that some had accused his friend of cowardice, of fleeing the persecution in Carthage to save his own neck.

Cowardice?

Indignation straightened Lisbeth's back. Who would make such an unfair and unjustified charge? Maybe Cyprian wasn't the saint Pontius claimed, but he certainly was *not* a coward. Her husband had his faults, hardheadedness and single-mindedness to name two. But in the end, he'd sacrificed his life without reservation. Everyone in the proconsul's chambers that day knew the truth: Cyprianus Thascius was no coward.

Lisbeth wiped her wet cheeks. She scanned the rest of the account, desperate to know what Pontius said of her and the impact her marriage to Cyprian had made on his heart.

Not one word.

Incredulity bolted through Lisbeth. Hands trembling, she searched the document again, word for disheartening word. She slammed the book closed and shut her eyes. Reality seeped into her veins.

She might as well have never existed.

10

Tunis, Tunisia

UNTIL A WEEK AGO, Lisbeth had only dreamed of returning to Carthage. From the safety of her lonely bed, she imagined growing old in Cyprian's arms, probably in much the same way Mama had dreamed of coming back home to Papa one day. And, like her mother, each time Lisbeth had woken drenched in sweat, she told herself she'd done the right thing to stay put.

Yet here she was.

Back in Africa. Hurrying across an abandoned Tunisian airstrip with ten precious MMR vials tucked in an isotherm cooler. Tugging her daughter and father toward a grisly bootlegger waiting to smuggle them into a war-torn country. And all of this adventure only a few days after she'd shut down a measles outbreak in the States.

When she first told Maggie they were going to look for her father, Maggie had immediately pulled her Little Mermaid suitcase from the closet and begged for more details.

What's Daddy's favorite color? Does he like to draw? What does my daddy look like?

Papa suggested Lisbeth show Maggie the medieval portrait she'd found in one of his history books. To Lisbeth, the sad-eyed, bearded man looked more like the old bishop Caecilianus than the rich, young nobleman who'd swept her into his arms and carried her across the threshold of their bridal chamber.

In the end, she'd settled on "Your daddy loves the color green, like my eyes. Knows a boy who loves to draw. And best of all, your father has a handsome face with a kind smile and blue eyes just like yours, baby."

"You have to get in the plane if you want to see your daddy," Papa bargained.

Maggie peered inside Nigel's Cessna where Aisa, Papa's beloved camp cook, waited with his tire iron and a toothless smile. Maggie shook her head. "I won't be able to breathe in there."

"We'll be at the cave before you know it." Lisbeth lifted Maggie's stiff body into the seat. "Here, hold your doll so she can see out the window." When the tears started, Lisbeth looked to her father. "Maybe I should have given her something to calm her nerves."

"You can't control everything, Lisbeth." Papa climbed into his seat. "Long as she's screaming, we'll know she's breathing."

Lisbeth slid in next to Maggie and handed her fussing daughter some paper and crayons. Maggie immediately settled. While her daughter happily worked on her art, Lisbeth took in the wind-sculpted spine of the desert. The closer they came to the cave, the more her excitement grew. So many unanswered questions lingered in the third century.

What had happened to Mama and Laurentius topped her list. The last she'd seen them was at the tenement well, captured by the soldiers of Aspasius before they could escape with her. If they were still alive, she needed some sort of plan to free them.

Also, what had become of Junia, the orphan she'd rescued? Especially if Ruth had . . .

Lisbeth could barely allow herself to think of Ruth. In the short time she and Ruth had been together, the bishop's beautiful wife had taught her so much: How to act like a lady. How to make guests feel welcome. How to love with selfless abandon. After Caecilianus was beheaded, Lisbeth wanted desperately to comfort her dear friend, but Aspasius had forbidden any contact. This was her chance to let Ruth know she'd listened and learned. She couldn't wait for Ruth to meet Maggie.

And then there was Cyprian.

If she let herself dwell on whether Cyprian was still alive or whether his marriage to her had cost more than she dared imagine, she wouldn't be able to breathe. Instead she preferred to ponder happier things, such as whether he'd missed her as much as she'd missed him. What would he think when he met their daughter? Would he adore Maggie enough to follow her home, to safety?

"Look, baby." Lisbeth pointed at the granite rising in the distance. "It's the Cave of the Swimmers."

"It looks like a birthday hat." Maggie got a new piece of paper. "I want to draw it for you, Mommy."

Lisbeth couldn't help but smile. Maybe this jumping-down-a-narrow-shaft idea was going to go better than she thought.

The plane dropped sharply, leaving their stomachs suspended several hundred feet above them before Nigel finally set them down on a bumpy strip of sand that separated the cave from rugged basalt cliffs.

Lisbeth was the first out of the plane. She reached in and quickly freed Maggie from her seat belt. As she set Maggie's feet upon desert sand for the first time, she watched her daughter's face shift. "Want to explore the cave with me, baby?"

Maggie glanced at the dark cave opening several hundred yards away. Doll clutched close to her chest, she backed toward the plane. "No."

Papa unfolded his lanky frame and exited the cockpit. "There are drawings all over the walls." He stretched the kinks from his arms and legs.

"Animals?" Maggie asked.

"Some."

Maggie's eyes darted between the plane she hated and the cave she suspected wouldn't be any better. "Is that the only way to see my daddy?"

"Yep," Papa said. "Choice is yours."

Jaw clenched, Maggie took Lisbeth's hand and braved a cautious advance. The moment Maggie stepped through the cave's mouth, her respirations increased. She gave the paintings only a cursory glance. "I don't see him. You said I'd see my daddy."

"We have to go down the hole to see him." Lisbeth was about to point out the swimmer triplets, a prehistoric family Papa had named the Hastings years ago, but Maggie wiggled free and shot from the cave. She'd nearly made it back to the plane before Lisbeth caught up.

"No, I can't. I can't."

"It's okay, baby." Lisbeth rocked her back and forth. "We don't have to go down the hole today."

Maggie broke free. "Why can't my daddy come to me?" she panted.

Images of Cyprian bowed before the executioner's sword flashed in Lisbeth's mind. "I'm sorry, baby. He would if he could. That's why we need to go. To help him come home." She offered Maggie her hand. "Let's set up our tent."

Nightfall rode in on a chilly gust and whipped sand over the secrets buried beneath the desert floor. Sitting cross-legged before the campfire, Lisbeth stroked Maggie's hair while Nigel, Aisa, and Papa tried to douse Maggie's growing concerns with crazy tales of lost treasures. Lisbeth had hoped seeing the openness of the cave would eliminate Maggie's anxiety. Instead her little girl had had a full-blown panic attack and refused to climb into the confines of her sleeping bag.

Thirty minutes later, Maggie's head finally lolled. Lisbeth checked to see if she'd fallen asleep. No such luck. Tongues of fire danced across the crystal seas of Maggie's wide eyes. The same blazing determination to outlast the opposition had flashed in Cyprian's eyes when he'd boldly exchanged his life for hers. Nothing Lisbeth said or did during their last moments together had changed his mind. Nothing she could say or do now would convince Maggie to sleep before she was ready. If Lisbeth couldn't convince her daughter to risk the enclosure of a sleeping bag, how would she persuade her to hurl herself into the narrow, dark tunnel?

Lisbeth gave in and handed Maggie one of the extra tent stakes. "Why don't you try drawing in the sand?"

An hour later, Papa nudged Lisbeth's shoulder. "She's finally a goner." He scooped Maggie into his arms. "Let me carry her to the tent."

Lisbeth sprinted ahead and held back the canvas flap. Papa ducked inside with his precious cargo. She watched him gently settle Maggie on top of her sleeping bag. Even in her sleep, Maggie's face twitched with anxiety.

Papa took Lisbeth by the elbow and whispered, "Better get some sleep. Tomorrow's a big day."

"Do all children inherit their parents' fears?" she whispered back.

"I don't like snakes." He pointed at his extra pair of digging boots positioned neatly at the foot of his bed, a sock pulled tightly over the top of each. Then he pointed at the boots thrown haphazardly beside Lisbeth's duffel. "But they don't seem to bother you."

"Thanks for making me feel worse than I already do." She kissed his cheek, then bent and brushed a blond curl from Maggie's face. "Much as I dislike my own claustrophobia, I hate seeing my daughter struggle with it."

"Parental guilt is one of the immutable laws of nature." Papa sat on his cot. He rubbed his knees as if massaging some courage into what he had to say next. "After your mother left, I saw the twinkle drain from your eyes." His palms ironed his faded dungarees. "My fear of never making anything of myself played a big part in your sorrow. Knowing my selfishness had hurt you pained me more than losing Magdalena." In the yellow glow of the kerosene lantern he appeared to have aged ten years since they arrived. "I've devoted my life to rekindling your spark. Tried everything I could think of, even sending you to the States for an education." He nodded in Maggie's direction. "But it wasn't until the doc put that little one in your arms that the light finally snapped back on." He lifted a leg and tugged at his boot. "Whatever is down that hole is worth saving. Not just for her, but for you."

Lisbeth watched Papa climb into his sleeping bag and waited until his snores rattled the tent. Then she rose from her cot, fished his Bible from his rucksack, and searched the lined pages one last time for a definitive stance on meddling with the past.

Second Peter mentioned that to God a day was like a thousand years and a thousand years like a day. The book of Luke had a *story* of Moses and Elijah transfigured from the past to stand beside Jesus in the present. But as far as something exact, the best she could find was the Gospel of John's reference to God's presence from the beginning. Obviously God operated in a realm of great complexity when it came to time. Eternity, for example, was one of those complexities. Time without end was a difficult concept to grasp. Especially when everything in humanity's known realm had an expiration date. Milk. Medicine. Men.

But what if it was possible to delay Cyprian's untimely end? What if there wasn't some kind of supernatural force that prohibited such an action? What were the risks if she once again succeeded in crossing the time barrier? Rerouting pivotal events could have far-reaching ramifications. If the bishop of Carthage died of natural causes rather than a martyr's death, would Christianity advance? Cyprian's selfless example had rallied a scruffy little band of misfits to look death in the eye. If the movement died because Christians chose to bail rather than sacrifice, history's entire course would be altered.

Even worse, if by chance Lisbeth found that changing the past *was* possible, would she then return to the same future she'd left? Would Papa and Mama marry in an altered world? If her parents had never married, she would never have been born. And if she'd never existed, as the pages of Pontius's work suggested, she couldn't have gone to the third century, and her precious Maggie wouldn't even be a twinkle in Cyprian's eye.

She peered into the drug cooler, checking the calibrated thermometer. Forty-two degrees. The ice was melting. At forty-six degrees the vaccine would begin to suffer a rapid deterioration. Her descent through the time portal could not wait for Maggie to warm up to the idea.

Hands shaking, Lisbeth turned down the lantern's wick and blew across the top of the glass chimney. She crawled in beside Maggie. In the darkness, she listened to her daughter's peaceful respirations, willing her own breaths to slow to an even match.

Nothing about her plan to leap into the underground darkness had even the slightest degree of reliability. If, for some reason, she pierced some unknown artery in time, no telling where they would end up. She was being forced to simply rely on the slim hope that if God wanted her back in the third century, then God would get her there. And trusting her life to anyone or anything beyond her control did not come easily.

A fretful sleep settled upon her. Dreams of losing Papa and Maggie in the waterslide caused her to bolt upright more than once in the night. Each time, she checked on Maggie, adjusted a thin blanket over her bare legs, and willed herself back to bed. She fell asleep remembering the last time she and Cyprian were together . . . walking the beach below his villa, holding hands, and making love in the shadows of the vine-clad pergola. Safe. Satisfied. Secure. Yet, somewhere deep inside her, she knew their time together was short. That her time in his world mattered. That even though history believed her never actually there, it was not the truth. Or was it?

When morning finally came, Lisbeth woke with a guilty start. Guilty that she had no better control of her emotions. Guilty that she loved this man so much she was willing to put her family at risk to save him.

Pinholes of morning light salted the tent seams. Soon the sun would turn what now served as their protection from the elements into an Easy-Bake oven. Lisbeth slowly became aware of an arm wrapped around her neck. She lightly stroked the baby-soft skin of Maggie's arm. Lisbeth had always been such a tomboy; she'd never played with dolls. So it had surprised her how easily she could love a child and how that love would push her to become the mother she never had. The weight of her daughter's safety and security rested heavily across her throat.

Going to Carthage was the only way to stop another measles outbreak and save Cyprian, but what kind of a mother willingly, and with forethought, places her child in harm's way? This had gone far enough.

Lisbeth kissed her daughter's forehead, then extracted herself from Maggie's tight grip.

"Papa," she whispered, pressing his shoulder until he stirred, "there's been a change of plans."

"Huh?"

"I can't send Maggie through the portal."

He slowly opened one eye. "Why not?"

"It's too risky." Lisbeth slipped on her boots. "And the confinement will scare her to death. Bringing her here was a bad idea."

He pushed up on his elbows, blinking to bring her into focus. His eyebrows furrowed. "You go then."

"Without her? I can't."

"You've always done what had to be done for her. This is one of those jobs." He swung his long, bony legs off his cot. "It may have seemed to you like you were gone months last time, but from my side of things you were only missing a few hours."

"What if this time it's not the same?"

"Who do you think watches Miss Magdalena when you're at the hospital? I can entertain our girl for a day or two. You know I've been dying to get back to that cave and poke around. Maybe while I'm at it, I can convince my granddaughter to become an archaeologist."

"She wants to be a painter."

"No reason she can't do both." He yanked the socks off the top of his boots and checked for snakes. "She's a bit more girly than you were, but I bet I can have her digging in the sand by the time you come sailing out of that hole."

"But what about Mama? I know you wanted to see—"

"Go." He waved her on. "Find your mother, then bring her and your brother back, along with that saint you're always thinking about."

Lisbeth fingered the ring that hung from the leather cord around her neck. Papa's suggestions had merit. She could secure Maggie's safety and proceed with her plan to bring everyone home. She lifted the necklace and placed it in Papa's palm. "When I bring Mama home, *you* can give this back to her yourself."

He slid the necklace over his head and kissed her cheek. Papa suggested she slip out before Maggie woke, but Lisbeth remembered her own terror, wondering what had happened to her mother all those years ago. No way would she leave her baby with the same questions. No more buried secrets. Maggie deserved a proper goodbye, a tangible reassurance that her mother would come back, and as much of the truth as a five-year-old could understand.

After breakfast, Maggie perched on the cot, combing her doll's hair as she watched Lisbeth seal plastic bags filled with as many emergency medical supplies as she could single-handedly transport into the third century. Acetaminophen. Vitamin A. Syringes. Penlight. Latex gloves. Surgical masks. A new scalpel, a small bone saw, and some decent suture needles for Mama. The three rounds of antibiotics her friend Queenie had called in for each of them. She'd hoped for more, to make more of a dent in the plague, but she'd barely had time to get those prescriptions filled. And the most important piece of equipment, Mama's stethoscope. She waited until the last possible minute to remove the box of MMR vials from the cooler. Once they hit the desert air, she had less than eight hours to travel through time and inoculate her loved ones.

Maggie tugged a comb through her doll's ponytail. "After you jump in the hole, will you see my daddy?"

"That's the plan." Lisbeth stuffed the plastic bags in a big backpack, dug out a pair of nose plugs, and slid the band over her head. "You can help Aisa cook while I'm gone, right?"

Maggie shrugged.

Lisbeth zipped the backpack. "G-Pa might need some help digging up buried treasure."

Maggie wrinkled her nose, then returned to styling her doll's hair. "Will you bring my daddy home?"

"I'm sure going to try, baby."

Papa paced the tent, adding to the growing unease in the stuffy space. Lisbeth slipped the pack's straps over her shoulder and clicked the belly straps securely into place. "You don't have to go inside the cave, Maggie, but I think you'll feel better about my trip if you stand at the entrance and see me go down the hole."

"And then you'll come right back?"

"Fast as I can."

Maggie tucked her doll under one arm and took Lisbeth's hand. "Promise I don't have to go inside."

"Promise."

The closer they got to the cave, the tighter Maggie's little hand squeezed. At the opening, Lisbeth squatted before her daughter. Maggie clutched her doll. Tear-filled eyes searched Lisbeth's for one last reassurance.

Lisbeth cupped Maggie's face and ran her thumb over the slope of Maggie's upturned nose, willing time to stop as she memorized every perfect feature. "Mommy has to go." She drew Maggie into a tight embrace. Instead of trying to wiggle free, Maggie hooked an arm around Lisbeth's neck. Lisbeth soaked in the touch, pulling away only after Papa tapped her shoulder.

She stroked Maggie's hair. "You be a brave girl for your g-pa."

"It's dark in there." Maggie's wide eyes searched the cave's interior. "Don't go."

Lisbeth looked to Papa to bail her out. Instead he said, "This is something your mother's got to do."

Lisbeth kissed Maggie one last time, saying a silent prayer for the Lord to keep this part of her family safe while she went for the rest of them. She clamped her nose plugs in place, then went to stand before the location on the cave wall where the Neolithic swimmer family waited.

A mom. A dad. And in between the parents, a child with outstretched arms. Frozen in a moment of pure bliss. She intended to re-create the same joy for her family.

Lisbeth checked the straps on her backpack, positioned her feet, then blew Maggie a kiss. "I'll be back before you even have time to miss me." Lisbeth placed her hand on the picture-perfect child standing in the middle of the swimmer family.

"That's the family I asked Santa to bring!" Maggie tugged against Papa's grasp. "I want my daddy!"

Sizzling heat radiated through Lisbeth's body. "Stay there, Maggie."

The ground trembled, no more than a tremor in the soles of Lisbeth's feet at first, and then a familiar rumble transmitted from the center of the earth and shook her bones. Sand shifted beneath her boots, slipping out from under her.

"I want my daddy!" Maggie broke loose and took a step toward her.

"Go back, baby!" A vacuum-cleaner-strength pull sucked at Lisbeth's feet, tugging her through a plate-size hole.

"Magdalena!" Papa yelled. "Come to G-Pa!"

"Mommy!" Maggie ignored him and ran. "Wait!"

The portal suddenly opened, and Lisbeth dropped. She stopped her plummet into the abyss by catching the side of the hole with one hand. Her feet pedaled nothing but cool, dank air as she worked to bring her other hand around.

"Go back!" Lisbeth clawed desperately at the crumbling sand. "Papa! Get her."

"Don't leave me, Mommy!" Maggie screeched to a halt at the edge of the opening, her face frozen in terror.

"Go back, Maggie!" The chasm groaned, splitting the hole wider.

Maggie teetered on the edge, her eyes wide. "Take me."

"No, baby!" Chunks of damp sand broke away and pummeled Lisbeth.

Just as she lost her grip, Maggie screamed, "Mommy!" She dropped her doll and leaped into Lisbeth's arms.

End over end they tumbled through the darkness, a speeding bullet ricocheting off the stone walls. The roar of rushing water grew louder and closer.

Lisbeth held Maggie tightly and shouted, "Hold your breath!"

They hit feetfirst.

The force parted the water. Raging currents sucked them deep into the cold river.

Before Lisbeth could think of what to do, a burst of turbulence ripped Maggie away.

11

The Cave of the Swimmers

CASCADING WATER SCOURED LISBETH'S empty arms and sent her body keeling through a dark tunnel.

Maggie.

Lisbeth thrashed against the angry swells. For every stroke of progress, she was pushed several hundred yards farther downstream. Strength draining, the last of her composure dissolved. Raw awareness tingled in every cell of her body.

I've lost Maggie!

She screamed as she felt her body slip deeper into the depths.

Cool liquid swamped her gaping mouth and muted her terror. She tried to close her lips, but her activated cough reflexes forbade it. Within seconds, a viselike pressure crushed her chest and threatened to snap her sternum and spinal column. She was drowning. If she was drowning, so was Maggie.

I can't let my baby drown alone.

Desperate for air, Lisbeth fought to stop the spinning. Arms flailing, she kicked frantically. Her hands struck rock. She thrashed the sandstone, searching for rungs of a nonexistent ladder. Just as she latched onto a jutting shard a sharp slice across her palm caused her to quickly release her grip. In an instant, she was sucked deeper into the cramped darkness.

Faster and faster she twirled, a pebble tossed about in a polishing tumbler. Excruciating force ripped at the straps tethering the heavy weight of the pack to her back and tore her boots from her feet.

Her waterlogged lungs swelled with unexchanged gases. Her brain felt hot. She knew if her body's demands for oxygen were not met in minutes, her chest would explode.

Maggie!

Entombed in darkness, Lisbeth gave up her fight to regain her wits. In the fog settling over her, memories of Maggie floated before her like a desert mirage. Not the terrified Maggie who hated tight spaces, but the towheaded, round-faced two-year-old toddler afraid of nothing. A child too young to fear the things parents teach them to fear. Phantom Maggie peered into a toilet, her tiny hand on the flushing lever, her white hair floating around her like a dandelion blowball.

Ariel swim, Mommy. She tugged on the handle at the exact same moment "Nooooo," left Lisbeth's mouth. Ariel's plastic fin swirled around the ceramic bowl, then disappeared from sight.

Maggie's pleased face vanished. *Noooo! Come back, baby!*

Incredible energy flushed Lisbeth's exhausted body. As she kicked against the current and struggled to lift her arms, a sudden trajectory change whirled her around and hurled her toward a shimmering beam of light.

A few seconds later, Lisbeth broke the water's surface, sputtering and frantic. "Maggie!" Her shredded voice echoed off the well's towering sandstone walls. High above her, a full moon poured out a circle of light.

Her eyes quickly cast about the coal-black liquid for blond curls. "Maggie!"

Nothing.

Oh, God! Oh, God!

Sucking in small gulps of dank air, Lisbeth filled her lungs and dove. Her outstretched arms pawed at the zero visibility. On one of her crazed sweeps, her fingers brushed tiny, cold fingers. She snatched Maggie's hand and kicked desperately toward the surface.

"Maggie!" Her daughter's beautiful little face had been bleached of healthy color. "Hang on, baby. I've got you." Lisbeth hooked her arm under Maggie's chin and swam to a two-foot-wide ledge jutting from the smooth cylinder of hewn stone. She hauled Maggie from the water and placed her limp body stomach-down on the slippery outcropping.

Oh, God! Help me!

How long had they been submerged? Time was everything when it came to near drownings. Four to five minutes without oxygen, and her daughter could have suffered permanent brain damage. Longer and . . . no! She couldn't let her mind go there.

Unsure whether Maggie had sustained other injuries, Lisbeth opted to risk moving her and gently rolled Maggie onto her back. "Maggie!"

No response.

She heaved herself out of the water and perched on the slippery edge. She ripped the nose plugs from her nose. Palm to her daughter's forehead, she tilted Maggie's chin toward the moonlight. With Maggie's airway open, Lisbeth lowered her ear close to the tiny blue lips. No escaping air warmed her wet cheek. She pinched Maggie's nose and blew two rescue breaths into her child's mouth. She lifted Maggie's T-shirt. No chest movement. She pressed two fingers against the artery in Maggie's neck. As the seconds ticked by, she prayed for a pulse.

Finally, a faint beat rippled beneath her touch. "There you are, baby. Stay with me." Lisbeth delivered ten more rescue breaths with a five-second-eternity wait between each.

Maggie's body jerked, and she suddenly began coughing.

Water spewed from her mouth. Her eyes fluttered open, and she gave an irritated shake of the head.

"Thank you, God!" Lisbeth rolled Maggie on her side and patted her back. "Spit it all out, baby."

After a few seconds of productive coughing, Maggie's lips and cheeks began to pink. "That was scary," she sputtered. "But I was brave."

Lisbeth laughed, relieved Maggie's response sounded so clearheaded. "Yes. You were very brave, kiddo." Even though all she wanted to do was hold Maggie's quivering body forever, she instead began checking her extremities. "Are you hurt?"

Maggie shook her head, her eyes growing wider as she took in their surroundings. "Where's my daddy?" Maggie lifted her chin toward the light streaming in from above. "Daddy!"

"Brave and a one-track mind." Lisbeth tugged Maggie's T-shirt down over her belly. "You *are* your father's daughter."

"I want my daddy."

"Me, too." Lisbeth kissed Maggie's cheek. "Let's go get him."

Her gaze scrambled up cement-covered walls. Ancient trowel marks gave her hope they'd arrived at the same Phoenician cistern Mama had pushed her down six years ago. Protruding stones every few feet offered a way of escape, but she doubted she could manage Maggie's weight and a ten-foot climb. At the same time, she couldn't stay here and do nothing.

"Help!" Lisbeth's plea bounced around the cylindrical tunnel. "Somebody, please help us!" Her eyes sought the rim and a plan B. "Help!"

Nothing . . . but the echo of her own regret and stupidity for allowing her daughter anywhere near the Cave of the Swimmers.

If no one came for them, what would she do? They'd freeze to death down here. It would take a miracle to convince Maggie to brave that wild water ride again and try for a return to Papa.

"What if my daddy doesn't come for us? It's tight in here." Maggie threw her arms around Lisbeth's neck, knocking them both from the ledge. Lisbeth frantically treaded water to keep Maggie's struggles from forcing them under again. "Mommy, I can't breathe."

"You're breathing, baby. Hang on." Clutching the ledge with one hand, Lisbeth wrestled Maggie back onto it. "Try to sit still for a minute."

For the first time since their traumatic arrival, she felt the extra weight on her back and remembered the backpack. Thankfully, she'd not lost her medical supplies. Once they climbed out of here, she'd figure out a way to pump all of the dirty water from Maggie's lungs and start her on a serious round of broad-spectrum antibiotics to ward off pneumonia and kill Lord only knew what other bacteria were swimming around in her waterlogged lungs. But between the waterlogged backpack and Maggie's weight hanging from her neck, Lisbeth didn't know how much longer she could tread water.

"Baby, I need you to try to stay calm while I get us out of here."

"I can't breathe." Maggie thrashed her legs.

"Baby, we need to make some noise. Remember how G-Pa taught you to say help in Latin?

"Adiuva."

"Good. When I count to three, yell *Adiuva*!"

Maggie nodded, her teeth chattering. "I'll try."

"One. Two. Three. *Adiuva*!"

Muted voices sounded above.

"Mommy, someone's coming." Maggie squeezed tighter. "It worked."

"I think you're right." Lisbeth scanned the well's rim. "Help!"

"It's *adiuva*, Mater," Maggie said matter-of-factly.

"Fetch some fresh water, but we must be swift about it," a male voice ordered in Latin.

A dark object hurtled toward them and whacked Lisbeth's arm before she could get out of the way.

"Owww!" Lisbeth's scream echoed in the tunnel. Whatever had splashed beside her disappeared below the rippling surface.

Someone peered over the well's rim. "Who's down there?"

Lisbeth couldn't make out the details of the person backlit by moonlight. "*Adiuva*," she croaked.

The woman disappeared, but Lisbeth could hear her distant summons. "Come quickly." Two heads appeared in the opening.

"Stand back," a male voice ordered. He tossed a heavy log across the shaft opening and secured a rope to the beam. Without wasting another minute, he gathered the loops of twisted hemp in one hand and threw a shoeless foot over the side. Lisbeth and Maggie watched two bare, muscular legs support his easy rappel down the wall.

He stopped a few feet above them, tawny arms effortlessly supporting his weight as he held tightly to the rope. "Do you have sores?"

"Barek?" Lisbeth answered. "I'm so glad I found you."

His dark eyes worked to adjust to the poor light. "Lisbeth?"

"I didn't know where we'd land. If we'd be too late. Tell me we're not too late."

"Too late for what?"

"To save Cyprian."

He lifted his chin and shouted to the woman peering down at them. "Clear the crowd before I bring her up."

Lisbeth felt Maggie's arms cinch her neck. "I have a child with me."

Barek searched below him. When he spotted Maggie he grumbled something that sounded like *Foolish woman*. He pulled off his sash. "Make a sling for her."

Maggie put her cupped hands up to Lisbeth's ear. "Mommy, why is that boy wearing a dress?"

Lisbeth fumbled with the long strip of fabric. "It's a tunic. I'll explain all about tunics later." Once she had the sash knotted, she looped it around her waist, and Barek hung the sling off his shoulder.

"Load the child into the sling and hold on." With one large hand, he latched on to Lisbeth's bruised arm. She held on to Maggie. Barek hauled them out of the water with a single tug. In the time that she'd been gone the boy had definitely grown in size, but he still seemed pretty stunted in the maturity department.

Hand over hand he silently scaled the cistern walls, panting as he hauled their combined weight on his back. Seconds later, they burst into brilliant moonlight and were greeted by a female gasp.

"Lisbeth?" The woman who'd tossed the gourd wrapped her in a hug. "We thought you were never coming back."

Lisbeth had spent days preparing for the mental shift that occurred in one's equilibrium after passing through the time portal, but once again, the physical changes that come with rearranging your place in history buckled her legs. Maggie went down with her.

Lisbeth rubbed her eyes and tried to focus on the person standing over her. "Naomi?" She couldn't believe how Cyprian's mousy house slave had blossomed into an attractive young woman, a woman who eyed Barek like he was Liam Hemsworth or Ryan Gosling. Time had moved forward here. But at what pace? Teenagers changed so rapidly it was hard to tell if the passing years matched hers.

"What were you doing in the cistern?" Naomi asked.

"Hiding."

"From Aspasius?"

Lisbeth realized Naomi had no idea this water source was a time portal. Ruth and Mama must not have told anyone how she'd been sent home. "Well, sort of."

Naomi's eyes darted to Maggie. "Who's this?"

Precious seconds ticked by as Lisbeth debated when to explain the unexplainable. "I pray I have not returned too late. Tell me of my husband. Has he returned from exile?"

"Time stands still for no one." Time may have moved forward in Carthage, but she recognized that Barek's opinion of her remained stuck where they'd left off. The young man who'd hauled her from the bowels of the earth had also retrieved his old dislike of her.

She followed his line of vision to the bodies stacked nearby, and she could tell he had assumed the worst about her. That she had willingly abandoned them in their greatest time of need. That her cowardice would never be forgiven.

12

Carthage

BAREK GAVE THEM LESS than a minute to get their third-century legs under them. "We must not be found here." He cut off any more of Lisbeth's questions about Cyprian and fought his way through a cloud of buzzing flies, setting a brisk pace down one of the dark tenement alleys.

"Why is that boy wearing a dress?" Maggie's whisper was anything but subtle.

"We'll talk about it later." Explaining the reason Barek wore a dress would be easy compared to answering questions about bloated corpses. More corpses than when she'd left.

Lisbeth shielded Maggie's eyes as they skirted the bodies blocking the tenements' entrance. "Don't look, baby."

Maggie parted Lisbeth's fingers. "What are those?"

"I'll explain everything later. For now, I need you to keep quiet and"—Lisbeth swatted insects from Maggie's hair—"try to keep up with Daddy's friends."

"I lost my shoes," Maggie huffed. "And I'm cold."

Lisbeth fought tears, not from sadness but from the realization of how close she'd come to losing more than Maggie's shoes. She scooped her up. "Hang on to me, and you'll warm up." She settled Maggie on her hip.

"Your shirt is torn." Maggie slipped her arms around Lisbeth's neck. "It's okay, Mommy. My daddy will buy us new clothes."

"How do you know?"

"Because he'll love me."

Lisbeth laughed. "From the first moment he sees you." She smiled at the thought of Maggie wrapping Cyprian around her little finger.

"Quit dawdling." Barek's face was set in a grim line.

They followed Naomi and Barek through the slums, as if they were superheroes in crusader capes.

Right before they reached the market at the center of town, Barek snatched two tunics from a line stretched between the apartment buildings. "Cover yourselves."

"He's cranky." Maggie gave Barek the fish eye while Lisbeth set her down and unfastened her backpack. "I think he needs a nap."

"Quiet, girl." Still the same grisly teenager who'd refused to let her treat his arrow wound.

"You don't need to snap at her." Lisbeth quickly tugged one of the garments over what remained of her shredded twenty-first-century pants and shirt. Maggie was too wide-eyed and distracted by Barek's pacing to complain about the tight fit of the coarse brown wool. "What errand brought you and Naomi so far from Cyprian's villa?"

Something about Barek's excessive agitation compelled Lisbeth to conduct her own search for trouble. The city that appeared strangely familiar, yet totally foreign, also seemed eerily quiet. Lisbeth surveyed the deserted streets, remembering them full of children kicking balls made of animal skins and old men gathered around beer crocks. These streets were vacant of the fish vendors, vegetable growers, and beggars. It was so quiet she could hear the surf several blocks away.

Barek's eyes scanned the area. "People are afraid to leave their homes."

She hadn't lost her footing. She'd lost her mind bringing her child to Carthage.

The moment she and Maggie were dressed, Barek had them moving again. The cadence of Lisbeth's bare feet upon the hewn cobblestones arranged in a cunning jigsaw pattern had taken some getting used to her first time navigating this world. Despite her growing reservations about being here now, having the ancient pavers beneath her feet felt right. Based on the fact that Barek and Naomi would neither confirm nor deny her questions about Cyprian, Lisbeth was choosing to believe her husband was still alive. Maybe even still in Curubis.

They passed through some open gates, and Lisbeth gasped. Broken shop awnings flapped in the breeze. Despite the coolness of the night, maggot-speckled carcasses of fowl, sheep, and even a cow rotted on lines strung across vendor booths. Baskets of raw fish guts had turned rancid. Acrid smells burned her nostrils.

Lisbeth drew two scarves from her backpack. She covered the lower half of her face and helped Maggie do the same. "Pinch your nose, and don't touch a thing."

Missing were the greasy olive oil merchants who pranced before colorfully decorated booths bragging about how their superior inventory had kept the lamps of Rome burning night and day for a hundred years. *"Warms the body. Protects from the cold. And calms a fever in the head,"* they'd boasted to the rich patrician women who entertained themselves with shopping the same way modern women cruised the mall. These retail experts could take one sniff of an oil salesman's product and know whether it had been purified properly.

Dusty were the long shelves of African red slip, exquisite thin-walled vases whose usual sparkle rivaled decorative potteries produced in the Italian Arezzo. Where were the quiet men who eyed the silk pocketbooks of the wealthy and shooed beggar children with sticky fingers away from their priceless wares?

Shuttered were the tax-collection booths everyone hated.

This wasn't the bustling market awaiting nighttime deliveries. Throw in a couple of tumbleweeds blowing across the avenues normally crawling with people, and Carthage would have become an ancient version of an American Wild West ghost town. Something was terribly wrong. If this desolation had been the result of conquest, anything of value would have been looted. Instead the vendor booths were fully stocked and deserted, as if the proprietors had abandoned their goods and left town in a hurry. Or worse. Died before they could settle their business affairs. Lisbeth couldn't be sure, but she suspected the latter. If she was right, she was looking at the aftermath of an outbreak turned epidemic. She tightened the straps on her backpack. She'd underestimated everything. With the few supplies in her bag, she'd be lucky to save her family.

Maggie's face was ashen. "What is this place?"

"It's kind of like a superstore."

"You sure my daddy lives in this town?" Maggie's brow puckered. "It stinks."

"Shhh."

Until she could confirm they'd landed in the right time, she couldn't offer the solid reassurance Maggie needed. There were far more bodies stacked at the crossroads than when she'd helped the frantic Numidicus drag his dead wife to the street. She couldn't put an exact estimate on how much time had passed, but if she and Maggie had overshot their target by even a day, Cyprian's headless body could be buried in one of the city's smoldering garbage heaps.

Lisbeth pushed the gruesome thought from her mind and took Maggie's hand. "Come on, baby. Let's go."

By the time they reached the affluent climes of the city, the brisk, salty sea breeze had scrubbed the stink of the market from the air. Lisbeth clung to the hope that maybe the epidemic hadn't spread as far as she first feared. They hurried down a broad avenue lined with large houses where climbing vines circled the balconies that overlooked the harbor's turquoise waters. This was their street, the place where she'd spent some of the most exhausting yet happiest days of her life.

Anxious anticipation pumped Lisbeth's legs. She was home. Hope surged toward her heart. Maggie had to run to keep up. While Barek fumbled with the gate latch, Lisbeth wished she'd added a mirror and a comb to the essentials in her bag.

She licked her fingers and wiped dirt smudges from Maggie's face.

"Mommy."

"Hold still, baby." She tried to finger-comb some order into her daughter's damp curls.

The gate squeaked open.

Maggie broke loose and shot around Barek. Lisbeth hurried after her.

The courtyard had the same deserted feel of the marketplace. Dry fountain. No exotic fish. Unruly vines obscuring the stone pillars. Dried leaves skittering over the garden pavers. Varnish peeling off the front doors in jagged little pieces. No barking dogs.

"Where is everyone, Barek?" Lisbeth's knees turned soft. "Please tell me they're alive."

Barek planted his body between her and the door. "Wait here."

"No." She tried to push past him. "This is my home. I don't even have to knock."

"You've been gone awhile." He held her at arm's length. "I think it's best if I prepare them."

"Them?"

"Wait." He wheeled, slipped inside the house, and shut the door in her face.

"What's wrong, Mommy?"

"I don't know. . . ." Lisbeth noticed Naomi watching from the shadows, an expression of impending doom on her face. *What's happened here? Has the plague swept through and killed* . . . Lisbeth captured her fears. If they were too late and Cyprian had already returned and been executed, her sorrow would only escalate Maggie's disappointment. Until she had more information, she would tuck Maggie in the safest place she could find. She glanced around the empty courtyard. "Let's play a game, baby. You hide behind the fountain, and stay there. Don't come out until you hear me say . . . *child.* Then you can jump out and yell 'Surprise!' Understand?"

Maggie didn't seem too keen on being stuck out of sight, but for once she played along and crouched behind the empty fountain.

The door flew open, and Cyprian rushed out. "Lisbeth!" He stopped, only a couple of feet short of embracing her. Except for the slight drooping of his shoulders, Cyprian was the same handsome, square-jawed man she remembered. Movie-star sex appeal infused with irresistible kindness and charm.

For a moment, his eyes said what his mouth could not. "Lisbeth." He opened his arms, and she fell into his embrace.

"You're home and safe." She buried her nose in his clean, familiar scent, holding on to him as hungrily as he held on to her. The substance of the words gushing from his lips was lost in Lisbeth's pure joy at seeing her husband again.

At first she thought her inability to understand what he was saying was her shock of hearing him speak her name after so many years, but she soon realized it was the way he drew out the syllables. Sad and . . . hard. She pressed her ear to his chest. Something had changed. Lisbeth pulled back. She kissed his lips to reassure herself that her imagination was simply playing tricks, that Cyprianus Thascius was still the strong and compassionate person she remembered, but he immediately pulled back. Shock, no doubt.

Her eyes sought his. "I'm not too late."

His mouth opened and closed. Finally, he managed, "Lisbeth, I . . ."

"Lisbeth?" Ruth stood in the open doorway, lamplight framing her in a hazy glow. "You're back?"

"My friend!" Lisbeth started for Ruth, but Cyprian snagged her arm.

"Lisbeth . . . I . . . Ruth is . . ." Cyprian's words hung in his throat, his eyes darting hopelessly between the two women.

"His wife." Barek stepped from behind his mother, his expression smug. "And she carries his child."

"Surprise!" Maggie shouted in perfect Latin as she scrambled out from behind the fountain. "Daddy! It's me, Maggie!" She barreled across the courtyard and threw her arms around Cyprian's legs, looking up at him with her big, blue eyes.

Lisbeth glanced from Ruth's ashen face to her swollen belly, then back to Cyprian. For what seemed an eternity, they stood face-to-face. No one moving. Each of them stunned into silence.

"Daddy?"

Maggie's pleas yanked Lisbeth from her stupor. "Funny, I thought Barek just said Ruth is your wife."

Cyprian swallowed. "She is."

Lisbeth didn't know what to say or which language to say it in. Her mind sorted the jagged pieces, laying them down one at a time. She had given birth to Cyprian's child alone. Risked her normal, stable life to return for him. And then discovered her husband had married another.

Slowly, an unexpected picture formed. An image of betrayal.

The baby her best friend carried belonged to Cyprian.

Where did that leave the claustrophobic child clinging to Cyprian's legs?

Or the lost, bent, and broken piece of this convoluted puzzle . . . her?

Where did her marriage to a man she no longer knew belong? She couldn't have crammed this piece into her plan if she'd tried.

13

THE CLATTER OF FARM wagons rolling through the city roused Aspasius from a fitful slumber. Through the fog of his hangover, he struggled to organize the slatted patterns of moonlight on the ceiling into some kind of tangible recollection. Celebrating his success at keeping secret the order for Cyprian's recall may have been a bit premature.

Aspasius shoved his girth upright in the bed and wrestled his plump arms into a silk robe. He would make his regular appearance at the temple of Juno after he popped into the public baths to check on the progress of his senators. If filling the temples with sacrificing plebeians failed to appease the gods, he would have no choice but to return to pressuring those who flatly refused to give his gods their due respect. People like the Christians. He should never have listened to the complaints of a few narrow-minded senators' wives who thought it beyond good taste when he allowed the arena cats to shred a defenseless believer's child. If Christians refused to bow, no matter their age or status, he would toss them into the ring and laugh at their screams.

He grabbed the massive bedpost and pulled himself to a standing position. Hot streaks of pain shot from his toes to his groin. Curse Magdalena. Curse her diabolical salves and bandages. Curse her ability to cure plebs of anything while his sores continued to fester. Most of all, curse the woman who'd slipped through his fingers and taken her attractive daughter with her. Aspasius forced his swollen feet into a pair of fox-lined red slippers.

What if Magdalena's creams and tonics were as lethal as the concoctions she'd mixed for him to drink? What if her plan had been for him to rot from the inside out? More than once, he'd downed the wine she'd proffered for his aching legs only to sleep for hours and awake disoriented and in more pain. He could only guess at the full extent of the treachery she'd accomplished during his long periods of incapacitation. He'd been a fool to submit to her ministrations and even more foolish to believe she might one day come to care about him. In the end, Magdalena had been as deceitful as Numeria and as willing to leave him.

Magdalena had been his slave for more than two decades, and somehow she'd managed to keep her dalliances with the Christians a secret. How could he have been so stupid? How could he have overlooked her treachery? Somehow, in some way, he would make every treasonous heretic who'd received her help pay for what rightfully belonged to him.

With a pleased chuckle, Aspasius drew his robe closed and shuffled to the double doors leading to his marble balcony. He stepped into the clear, crisp night. To view his city from a god's perspective was a privilege and an obligation he took seriously.

He would not lament Magdalena's unexpected disappearance. No matter how much it angered him. No matter how betrayed and alone he felt. He did not miss her far-too-thin body in his bed any more than he missed her sharp tongue and the eternal judgment smoldering in her eyes. Being rid of her was actually a relief. No longer would her observations about his inability to rule the unsettled masses make him feel the fool.

If anyone inquired of her whereabouts, he would say she and her high-strung daughter had died at their own hands.

In the meantime, he would secretly have them both found, returned to him, and Magdalena put to death for separating him from Lisbeth Thascius. He considered Cyprian's wife the spoils of war. As ruler of this province, he had the right to claim the property of any convicted war criminal. He intended to claim it all. First, Cyprian's vast estate, and then his wife.

A voice broke through his thoughts. "Master, you'll catch your death out here." Pytros came to him and draped a fur across his shoulders. "Come in and warm yourself."

"Tell me again what Felicissimus said." Aspasius turned to look at his scribe. "Is Cyprian's estate still occupied?"

"I had to remind him of his obligations before he was forthcoming with information." Pytros brushed lint from his robe. "Sick plebs from the tenements have flooded the nobleman's villa."

"It's been more than a year. Why do the masses still flock to his halls?" he demanded. "What could possibly still draw them there? Are you sure Cyprian has not returned home? Perhaps slipped in behind my back?"

"Felicissimus would neither confirm nor deny my inquiry."

"What other explanation could there be for the stream of plebs who go in and out? Someone is accessing the money that keeps them fed."

"I do know the poor go to the home of Cyprian for medical care as well."

"Healing?" It infuriated him to think Cyprian could have been under his nose all this time, but the possibility that Magdalena and her daughter might have been hiding in plain sight as well made him want to hit someone. He turned to Pytros. "Is Magdalena acting as their healer?"

"I don't think so." His scribe shrugged. "Felicissimus pleads ignorance, and you know he has no love lost for her. He'd be only too happy to tell you of her whereabouts if he knew."

"Ignorance is something the slave trader does not have to plead."

"It took me a while, but I finally persuaded Cyprian's neighbor to talk."

Aspasius cast a pleased smile at his scribe. "And?"

"He said the pretty widow of that Christian bishop you beheaded returned to Cyprian's villa the very next day. Perhaps she is the reason sick plebeians come and go all through the night."

"Why was this neighbor willing to speak against the house of Thascius?"

"He fears having the slum sickness in his part of town."

"Are any of these plebs Christians?"

"So far, the neighbor denies any knowledge of Cyprian's presence or of seeing Christians meeting in the home."

"Did you remind him that aiding Christians and heretics is punishable by death?"

"I did. Yet he had no proof that Caecilianus's wife is teaching her husband's treasonous ways. For all we know, the bishop's widow is a bored and lonely squatter."

"No one renders charitable aid for their own entertainment." He wagged his finger before Pytros's nose. "Treating the poor with the same respect due the wealthy smacks of Christianity."

"What are you going to do? If Cyprian is already home, he could be gathering supporters as we speak. Waiting for the perfect time to attack."

"If he overthrows my rule, whether I followed Valerian's edict will be a moot point." Aspasius thought a moment. "I've been extraordinarily patient about taking what is lawfully mine. I can't afford to lose what's left of my plebeian workforce if they switch their loyalties to some woman curing their fevers in the house of a noble flaunting his misplaced allegiance. This traitor and his healer will have to die."

"Crucify the widow giving desperate citizens a respite from death, and you'll have riots." Pytros clutched his robe. "Martyr the man most call a saint, and it will be political suicide."

Aspasius peered over the balcony railing. Silvery light illuminated the decks of the empty ships moored in his glorious harbor. In the past, he'd always found the moment the winter winds changed direction intoxicating. He loved standing on his terrace and issuing the command that unfurled a fleet of scarlet sails that would carry the wealth of Africa to the far reaches of the empire. Wealth his leadership and vision had amassed. Wealth sure to bring him the attention and affirmation of the emperor. Wealth that would allow the entire Mediterranean to be shaped to his will. He would not allow a little group of rabble-rousers to take this right from him.

A ring of fire still glowed along his city's walls. But to his dismay, inside the walls, darkened brothels lined the port streets. Before the harbor closed for the winter, he'd stationed soldiers at the gangplanks to push any arriving sailors hot with fever into the sea. The efforts had done little to slow the spread of the wicked red rash killing the prostitutes. To the west, large portions of the city, including most of the slums, suffered in darkness.

Just as Cyprian had predicted, a fact that only served to irritate Aspasius more, half of the city's workforce was either dead or too weak to work. Restoration of the aqueducts had nearly halted. Without proper sanitation, Cyprian's neighbor was right. The sickness might very well crawl out of the slums and make its way into the homes of the wealthy.

Aspasius rubbed his chin. He could not afford to lose a single coin from the higher-income tax bracket. Every denarius was needed if he was to fulfill his destiny.

Truth was, at his feet lay a poor, torn, and wounded Carthage—he would not desert her now.

If Magdalena were here, she would tell him what to do. Offer treatments that would help him stop the siege laying waste to his city. Sometimes late at night he could hear her voice echoing through the corridors, an apparition sent by the gods to haunt him. Once he even raced room to room searching for her, only to find her lamp dark and her bed cold.

No! He would stop this foolish remembering and think for himself, for even after she was found he would not take her into his confidence ever again. For all his blustering threats to confiscate senatorial properties, the best diplomatic course of action by which he could seize Cyprian's estate had not presented itself . . . until now.

"If Cyprian has laid low this long, he must not know that I am obligated to send a ship for his recall. I believe I'll let him think it is not safe to show his face in Carthage a while longer."

"So you're going to allow your enemy the freedom to rally his followers into an army?"

"I must not do anything that would alert Cyprian's supporters in the Senate. I don't need his father's old friends siding with him." Aspasius steepled his fingers and thought. "Rather than attack the widow's little group from the outside and cause unnecessary hostilities, what if I destroy the movement from the inside?"

"Divide and conquer."

"Yes." Excitement pulsed in Aspasius's veins. "Once those sickly little Christians scatter like rats, Cyprian will have to go deeper into hiding to regroup. Then I can move in and claim his property officially deserted, and there isn't a thing any of Cyprian's old friends can do to stop me."

"And how do you intend to accomplish this division?"

"Fetch Felicissimus."

14

As REUNIONS GO, THE painful and uncomfortable silence crowding the courtyard was not the heartwarming welcome Lisbeth had envisioned. Tension crackled in the sooty smoke of the single lamp. Ruth, whom Lisbeth had never seen go more than two minutes without saying something, stood mute, her hands woven into a shield over her soccer-ball-size belly. Cyprian's hands hung limp at his side. His feet refused to take even the smallest step in Lisbeth's direction. Only his gaze registered any movement, and it was the wild-eyed dart of an animal caught in a trap.

"Daddy! It's me." Maggie tugged on Cyprian's sleeve. "Say something."

Maggie's pleas cut through the rapid heart rhythm pounding in Lisbeth's ears. Struggling to shake off the shock, she looked from Cyprian to Ruth and back to Cyprian.

Her husband had given up on her and married her best friend. All this time, she'd imagined him wasting away in exile, fighting to return, and then bravely kneeling before the executioner. When she'd discovered her name missing from the historical records, it never occurred to her that Cyprian had cut his losses and moved on.

"Daddy?" Maggie pulled on Cyprian's hand. "Please," she croaked, tears gathering behind her lashes. "We have the same eyes." Any minute, the dam would break, and once Maggie lost it, there would be no stemming the tide.

For Maggie's sake, Lisbeth knew she'd have to get past the roadblock of Ruth's pregnancy and the conflicted look on Cyprian's face. She could fix this. Somehow. Some way. "Let's give Daddy a minute, Maggie." Lisbeth peeled her off.

"I want my daddy!" Maggie wailed.

"So do I." Lisbeth picked her up. "Don't cry, baby. Daddy and I will work this out."

"A daughter?" Cyprian whispered. "I didn't know."

Of course he didn't know. How could he know she would return with his five-year-old in tow? He hadn't even known she was pregnant. She hadn't discovered her pregnancy until she began throwing up in the twenty-first century. It wasn't like she could send him a text or an Instagram shot of the first ultrasound. The fair thing would be to let him off the hook. To say it was perfectly natural for him to go on with his life. But in her heart, she'd harbored the foolish notion that somehow he would have known his love grew inside her. The same way he would have known she'd find a way to come back. That he, of all people, would never give up on her.

"Lisbeth!" Mama emerged from the house. Lisbeth gasped, immediately aware of what her mother's decision to stay behind had cost her. Aspasius had carved a permanent jokerlike smile on Magdalena's face. "Lisbeth!" Mama pushed her way between Cyprian and Ruth. "I prayed I'd see my daughter again."

"Mama!" She set Maggie on the ground and ran to her mother's open arms. "You're alive!" She let her relief tumble out. "I saw the soldiers come and take you and Laurentius away from the well. I was afraid . . ."

"Your brother's fine."

"Thank God."

"Mommy?" Maggie tugged on her sleeve. "Who's this?"

"The woman you were named after. Your grandmother." Lisbeth noticed the deep lines around her mother's eyes soften, and suddenly her disfiguration didn't seem so hideous. "Mama, this is Maggie. Your granddaughter."

Mama's lips quivered. "A grandchild?" She dropped to her knees and framed Maggie's face with her work-worn hands. "The Lord has blessed me beyond what I deserve."

Maggie stepped back warily. "What happened to her face?"

"Love." Mama answered before Lisbeth could think of an age-appropriate way to describe the horrors her mother had suffered on her behalf. "Love so deep for you and your mama I will never quit smiling." Mama looked up at Lisbeth, tears streaming down her cheeks. "I see your courage in her beautiful eyes." She lightly touched Maggie's hair. "You are a brave one, aren't you, Maggie?"

"No. But I want to be."

"Then we shall learn together."

Maggie stepped forward and lightly traced Mama's scar with her fingers. "I think your smile is pretty."

Years melted from Mama's face. She kissed Maggie's forehead. "Tell me what you like to do for fun, my little one."

"Draw!"

Mama's laughter hadn't aged a bit. "Of course you do." Mama stood and offered her hand. Maggie eagerly grabbed hold. "You'll want to meet your uncle Laurentius. He has plenty of paper and ink." Mama turned and instantly triaged the tension of the situation. "Ruth, why don't you help me scrounge up some bread and cheese to celebrate? Naomi, I know you and Barek will want to help me welcome Maggie."

In Mama's effective, take-charge way she cleared the courtyard, leaving Lisbeth and Cyprian alone to sort through their situation.

Lisbeth and Cyprian stood there staring at each other, frozen in this gut-wrenching moment. Neither making a move to close the distance. A cold gust swept through the courtyard, bending the lamp's small flame so low to the bowl it nearly sputtered out.

Cyprian was the first to break the silence. "Magdalena said she sent you home."

If she had fought harder to stay or refused to go, none of this would be happening. "Against my will."

"She didn't say you could come back."

"Then I guess I should have called before I dropped in." The bite in her voice was a slap to his face she regretted.

"Called?" Tolerance for her twenty-first-century sayings was gone, along with the ease they'd once shared.

"Never mind." Lisbeth hoped her rusty Latin meant she'd misunderstood Barek's claim that Cyprian and Ruth were married. That all of this was some glitch in her calculations and that somehow Ruth had been pregnant with Caecilianus's baby before he died and Cyprian had done the chivalrous thing and taken her in. She'd guess Ruth to be five or six months pregnant at the most. "So when did you get back?"

"In the fall."

She couldn't be sure of the current month, but judging from the chill, spring hadn't made its appearance. She didn't need the calculator app on her phone to know this baby was his. Cyprian must have married Ruth only a short while after his return from exile. Lisbeth felt her lip quiver. Had their marriage meant nothing to him? Had he always had secret feelings for Ruth, and now that she and Caecilianus were out of the way, seized his opportunity? No matter the reason, what he and Ruth had done hurt her feelings. Even worse, she'd put their daughter at risk for nothing, for a father who'd moved on, and that was harder to forgive than his betrayal.

Lisbeth silently nursed the sting while waiting for Cyprian to explain why he hadn't waited for her return.

"I thought you were lost to me forever." He reached for her

hand, then changed his mind midextension and let his hand return to his side. "I'm sorry. I never intended this."

Of course, the man who'd given his life for hers would never hurt her on purpose. She knew that. He'd proven himself more than honorable. The Cyprian she'd married was the most loving, giving man she'd ever known. And she wanted to take that man back to the twenty-first century. Not this man who could only offer excuses. The constricting walls of her chest had made it impossible for her to do more than whisper, "Me either."

He started to speak, then retreated into the void. They stood there, listening to the mournful howl of the wind and watching the last bit of life hemorrhage from their relationship.

What was left to discuss? History had not mentioned either woman in the accounts of Cyprian's life. Some scholars even reported him celibate. Fighting over who was Cyprian's real wife was foolish. Especially if his marriage to the bishop's widow had somehow altered the timeline of political tensions and Carthage no longer had need of a selfless hero. Something had calmed Aspasius. Otherwise, why would the proconsul leave Cyprian alone after his return from exile? If this reprieve meant Cyprian had been spared a martyr's death, one of her most important reasons for being here had been eliminated.

Cyprian's marriage to Ruth had ended the second. She, Maggie, and Cyprian would never be the put-down-roots, stable kind of family she'd dreamed of. How his relationship with Maggie was going to look going forward would depend a lot on him.

That just left eradicating this plague and taking Mama and Laurentius home. Okay, maybe an eradication plan was too grandiose when comparing her limited vaccination supply with the destruction she'd seen. But she wasn't ready to concede that the virus may have multiplied beyond her ability to implement focused surveillance and mandatory quarantine. She could also increase survival rates by improving supportive care. The good thing about measles, if there was a good thing, was that survivors gained lifetime immunity. The faster she could reduce the number of viable hosts, the faster the virus would flame out. Lessening the plague duration would save many lives in the third century and eliminate heartaches for future centuries. She could only pray that her efforts this time around would somehow make up for having left these people the first time.

She'd vaccinate whoever she could and get the hospital going again; then she'd gather Mama and Laurentius and shake the dust of Carthage from her shoes forever.

"I brought medicine." Lisbeth adjusted the weight of the backpack. "I guess I should go check on Maggie, then get started on the reason I came."

"Maggie" slipped from Cyprian's lips. "After your mother." In her dreams, Lisbeth had heard him say their daughter's name many times. But never in a million years could she have predicted how the actual sound of his approval would tug at her heart. He smiled and whispered "Maggie" again. "Perfect."

She swallowed the lump in her throat and gave a slight nod. "The best work either of us will ever do."

He took a step toward her, his quick breaths forming heavy clouds in the night air. "She's a masterpiece."

Lisbeth stepped toward him, drawn until her breath mingled with his. "The best of you and the best of me."

Had he touched Ruth in the same places he'd touched her? Sent her soaring into the blissful worlds they'd promised to share with no one else? Lisbeth blinked away hot tears. Of course he had. A person didn't have to be a doctor to know how Ruth's child took up residence in her womb.

He reached up and tucked a strand of her hair behind her ear. "A beautiful legacy I do not deserve." His fingers traced the outline of her jaw, and she felt her flesh melting into his.

She pulled away before the fire consumed her. "No, you don't."

15

STARING INTO THE EYES of Lisbeth had been like looking at a ghost. It wasn't until he held her, until he felt the heat of her flesh and tasted the sweet tang of her lips, that he knew his dream had come true. His love had returned to him, complete with his exquisite child in tow. He'd give anything to take back the hurt he'd seen in Lisbeth's eyes when she realized he'd given up on her and married Ruth.

Two wives.

Impossibly complicated. Truth was he could more easily sort this mess than keep either of them safe. If he could not unseat Aspasius before he discovered that Lisbeth was within easy reach, the proconsul would unleash his full wrath. He would haul Cyprian into the arena to face certain death. Both Ruth and Lisbeth would become grieving widows.

Difficult as these new developments seemed, it was the good-bye in Lisbeth's voice twisting his gut. Their discussion had ended with Lisbeth saying she would leave the medicine she'd brought to stop the plague. Then she'd take their daughter and her mother and brother back to Texas.

Texas.

How far away was Texas? Was Lisbeth's strange world far enough away to keep her and Maggie safe? "Maggie." The name felt foreign in his mouth. An acquired taste he could quickly come to love.

The sound of scuffling feet right outside the gate drew Cyprian back to his unsettled present. Soldiers of Aspasius? Coming for him?

He quickly doused the lamp and listened. Voices, thin and anxious, argued outside his walls. He eased toward the commotion.

A desperate rap, rap, rap rattled the gate hinges.

"Hello," a raspy, male voice whispered. "Anyone home?"

Cyprian peeked through a chink in the wall. Two hooded forms labored to support a third stretched out between them. More sick. He was in no mood for more surprises or doling out more charity. "We've retired for the night."

"We need help," the man insisted. "I can pay."

In his absence, Ruth had continued offering the hospital care Lisbeth had started. This might please Lisbeth. It wouldn't lessen her hurt to know the demand had grown so great Ruth and Magdalena could barely keep up with the constant stream of poor seeking help. Ruth insisted that the comings and goings of plebs shouldn't worry him. He argued that increased foot traffic also increased the risk of Aspasius learning of his return. She felt certain the destitute wouldn't out the man who'd given them shelter when no one else cared. And even if word of his return spread outside the tenements, patricians rarely put much stock in the words of plebs.

But this man offering payment for medical services was obviously not the average plebeian beggar.

Cyprian listened to the desperate groans of the visitors struggling with their load on the other side of his gate. The numbness caused by Lisbeth's return quickly reorganized into alarm. Lisbeth's presence had put them all at risk. If he granted entrance to someone of means, Aspasius would surely discover her whereabouts. As much as the proconsul wanted Cyprian . . . he wanted Lisbeth more.

Cyprian plastered his cheek against the chink. "Come back tomorrow."

"Cyprian," the man said, loud enough to rouse the neighbor's dogs, "I'll report you to Aspasius."

He couldn't place the voice, but Cyprian recognized the razor-sharp edge of patrician condescension when he heard it. Ruth had been wrong about the influence of the plebs. If word of his return had already climbed this far up the social ladder, it was only a matter of time before the news reached the top rung.

He'd misjudged the power of gossip as surely as he had misjudged Lisbeth's love and loyalty. His wife had returned on her own volition and at her own peril. No one held a knife to her throat. Lisbeth hadn't given the reasons for her return, but the threat to her life had precipitated Magdalena's need to send her home. And yet here she was. Bolder and more beautiful than he remembered.

For certain, Aspasius would take Lisbeth should he discover her living under Cyprian's roof. When that day came, how could he protect her?

"Let us in, man. Please."

Cyprian shoved his fear aside, undid the latch, and opened the gate. Two people stumbled in, nearly dropping their load. The man supported the arms of a limp girl. The woman carried the girl's feet.

"Titus?" In the moonlight, Cyprian could tell that the second-wealthiest man in Carthage had come begging at his door.

"Our driver refused to bring us," the man huffed. "We've had to carry our daughter all the way up your hill."

"You brought Diona here?" He remembered the spoiled waif

from a brief encounter at her home a few weeks before everything had turned upside down. "Why?"

"She has slum sickness." Titus's back bowed at the deadweight of his burden. "One of our slaves told us you have a healer."

Cyprian's mind raced back to the day he had stood before the Senate begging for the life of his wife. Titus Cicero had remained silent when Cyprian needed help from a longtime family friend and received none. The land baron's vote of exile should not have surprised him.

Titus had blamed him for Diona's embarrassment at their broken engagement. But Cyprian had not been the one to call it off. It was Titus who'd believed the rumors of Aspasius and set out to ruin Cyprian's political career.

No. Titus Cicero was not on his list of loyal senators he hoped to rally against Aspasius. Nor was he on the list of people he intended to befriend. "You know how untrustworthy a rumor can be, Titus."

"I obviously received false information concerning your health, Cyprian."

"You believed lies."

"I'm sorry. I know I have no right to ask for your help." Titus shifted his weight, barely able to keep Diona's damp, unbound hair from dragging on the pavers. "My daughter's been feeling poorly for more than a week."

"We'd been very careful to keep her away from the sickness," his wife, Vivia, explained. "But just to be safe, we decided to risk losing our city properties to the hands of Aspasius and leave town." Vivia's shoulders sagged under the weight of lifting anything heavier than a ruby ring. "Before we could set out for our mountain villa, Diona doubled over in pain. Now she's burning with fever and mumbling things we can't understand."

"Please," Titus begged. "In the name of your god, help us."

"Where are *your* gods?"

"I've done all the temple priests have asked, and still my gods do not answer me."

"Nor will they." With this declaration, Cyprian felt a sudden surge of . . . he wasn't sure what. Conviction seemed too strong a word, but he had no other name for the swelling in his chest.

"Then will your Christian friends help us?"

Cyprian surveyed the face of the delirious young woman. Sweat beads glistened on Diona's forehead. Skin, once velvety as a lamb's ear, hung loosely from her aristocratic features. Her plump, rosy cheeks had turned sallow and sunken. Her snowy blond curls were a matted tangle unbefitting a self-respecting lady of her standing.

He wouldn't wish her condition on any man—save Aspasius Paternus, the tool of Satan who'd manipulated Titus Cicero into becoming an enemy.

Cyprian closed the gate. "Come." He took hold of Diona's ankles and relieved her mother. "But no one must know."

16

LISBETH LEFT CYPRIAN STEWING in the havoc of his hasty remarriage. Searing tingles radiated from the shock to her system. Her husband had married another woman. How could she explain to Maggie what she didn't understand herself? She took a few breaths, pressed her hand to the throb at her temple, and stepped inside the villa.

The atrium was lit by two wall torches. Simmering eucalyptus and the fevered stench of measles combined into a nauseating aroma similar to wet chicken feathers. Add another surprise to the list of things she never expected in the third century: Ruth had kept the hospital going.

Multiple rows of woven sleeping mats lined the great hall. Most were equipped with the vaporizer tents Lisbeth had designed on her first foray into the third century. She remembered the long days she and Ruth had spent converting Cyprian's home into a makeshift hospital ward. Difficult, rewarding work that had forged a bond beyond friendship. Until today, she'd thought Ruth felt the same way.

Lisbeth bent beside the nearest vapor pot and lightly touched the side. Temperature perfect. She hadn't really expected Ruth to continue offering supportive care after Cyprian went into exile and Aspasius sequestered her and Mama in his palace. From the organized precision of added vaporizer tents and steaming water pots, Ruth had taken over Lisbeth's hospital as skillfully as she had taken over Lisbeth's house and husband.

Maggie's laughter floated from the kitchen. Ruth was not getting her daughter, too. Lisbeth set off for the back side of the house. She pushed open the kitchen door unnoticed.

Laughter galloped from the table where Maggie, Laurentius, and Junia had their heads pressed together over pieces of parchment.

Mama perched on a nearby stool, enjoying every minute of the touching reunion. Barek leaned against the wall, a scowl on his face and his arms crossed belligerently over his chest. Obviously he wasn't any happier about this than she. For once, she felt an affinity with the teen. Naomi stoked the oven fire, cutting her eyes at Barek like a lovesick schoolgirl who thought no one was looking.

Ruth stood on the other side of the table, her head bent in concentration on her task. Her long, slender fingers split open the violet skins of fresh figs with the same grace and enthusiasm she had poured into Lisbeth and Cyprian's wedding day six years ago. From Lisbeth's custom-designed dress to the exquisite table decorations, every detail had been executed with Ruth's unmatched perfection.

"Here, Maggie. Try this." Ruth held out a section with the amber jelly of the fruit exposed.

"Yum." Juice dripped from the corner of Maggie's lips as she stared at Ruth with undeniable admiration, like she was looking at a Disney princess or something.

Lisbeth remembered when she'd first met Ruth a lifetime ago and thought her far too elegant, well-spoken, and witty for the grandfatherly Caecilianus. But never had she considered her old friend the mesmerizing vision she was now, peeling figs in the glow of yellow lamplight.

Ruth's thick braid shimmered with golden highlights women

in Dallas mortgaged their houses to acquire. The usual black line of kohl was missing from above Ruth's thick lashes. Despite her pregnancy, she'd lost so much weight that a pale, loose sheath of skin revealed her cheekbones, yet her eyes sparkled with the intoxicating contentment of an expectant mother. A playful smile tugged her perfect pink lips as she watched the children enjoying each other. No wonder Cyprian had fallen in love. Ruth was an angel.

Lisbeth worked to smooth the kinks the wild waterslide ride had left in her mane. "What have we here?"

Junia threw down her stylus and ran across the kitchen. "Lisbeth!"

The malnourished orphan had grown a couple of inches, and her missing teeth had come in perfectly straight. And from the twinkle in her eyes, this victim of so many tragedies had found healing. No doubt Ruth deserved the credit for the healthy girl standing before her now. Lisbeth's blood boiled.

"Lithbutt!" Laurentius jumped up and joined in the giving of big hugs. "You're home." Laurentius, only six years younger than Lisbeth, buried his head in her shoulder like a three-year-old. Her half brother had aged, but thankfully his childlike mind meant he would never have to deal with adult heartaches. "Thyprian came home. Ruth thaid if we prayed my whole family would come home . . . and they did!"

"Look, Mommy." Maggie held up a scrap of paper. "Larry is teaching me to draw mice."

"Larry?" Lisbeth released her half brother, giving him a closer examination. His almond-shaped eyes were watery, and he'd lost a few pounds, but not his endearing, saw-toothed smile. "My brother's name is Laurentius, Maggie."

"My *jaddah* said I could call him Larry."

"Jaddah?" Lisbeth smiled.

"It was what you would have called my mother had she lived."

Mama motioned her in, a pleased glow on her face. "We've all become fast friends."

Barek snorted.

"Except for him, Mommy. He's cranky." Maggie nodded toward Barek and then quickly turned her attention back to her art. "Larry, show me how to do ears without smearing." She blew on the parchment. "Junia, come sit by me."

"You taught her our language?" Mama's question was really more a pleased statement.

"And how to be bossy," Barek muttered.

"Barek," Ruth scolded. "That's enough."

Lisbeth started to say something to Barek, but Mama's shake of the head indicated she should let this one go. "Papa deserves the credit. He thought Maggie should know her heritage."

Mama's face brightened at the mention of Papa. "I was afraid to ask if Lawrence came with you, in case he didn't want to."

"He wanted to. More than anything." Lisbeth hated crushing her mother's hope. "At the last minute, we decided he should stay with Maggie. But she jumped in after me, and there wasn't time for him."

"Oh, no, I messed up again." Maggie waved Laurentius over. "I need your help, Larry. I want to draw my daddy."

Laurentius grinned and ducked his chin. Lisbeth loved how her half brother stroked her arm, hanging on to her like he never wanted to let her go. She prayed his great capacity to love had helped ease Mama's guilt for choosing to stay in his world. The animosity she'd once felt for her mother's choice had long since vanished. She couldn't even leave Maggie with Queenie for a few days; she didn't know how her mother had borne the thought of leaving her with Papa forever.

"Larry!"

"Maggie needeth me."

"We all do." She kissed the top of Laurentius's head.

He released her arm, returned to his seat, and picked up a writing quill. "Watch." He held the stylus between clubbed fingers. "Firth you dip the tip, then you drag it thlowly along the horn rim so it won't drip."

Of all the ways she'd imagined this scene, she hadn't prepared herself for the overwhelming emotions of having nearly everyone she loved in the same place. Giving up the dream of having Cyprian as the head of their family would not be easy. Maggie would be crushed.

"Hungry?" Ruth offered Lisbeth an opened fig.

Lisbeth locked eyes with Ruth. The knife of betrayal stabbed her again. "Not really."

"Oh." Ruth placed the fruit on a plate and wiped her hands on a towel. "Thirsty, then?"

Face-to-face, they stood on opposite sides of the table, silently staring at each other. Best friends who hadn't seen each other in years. Each of them hanging on to the friendship they remembered. Neither of them knowing how or where to start the sticky conversation likely to end their treasured relationship once and for all.

Lisbeth opened her mouth to say—to say what? *"How could you marry my husband?"*—but it was Ruth who once again made the first move.

"Barek, fetch one of our best wines from the cellar," Ruth said.

He frowned. "Mother, I'm no longer a child who needs to be sent out of earshot."

"Go," Ruth said pointedly.

Once Barek left the room, Ruth glanced at Maggie and then back at Lisbeth. "I'm sure you'll tell us all about what's happened in your life when you're ready." Ruth had mustered her old familiar tone, the one that said they could fix this. Forgive one another and be friends again. "If I'd known Cyprian had a daughter," she whispered.

"You knew he had a wife." Lisbeth didn't hide her hurt. "And you married him anyway."

Sadness flickered across Ruth's face. Her hand flew protectively to her belly. "If we'd known you would come—"

"I wasn't dead."

"We didn't know that."

"You saw me go down the cistern."

"But I didn't know what happened to you."

"You could have waited to find out."

"How long?"

"Long enough to at least mourn the death of *your* husband. Did you even cry over Caecilianus?" Lisbeth instantly regretted the verbal shot and Ruth's stunned recoil. They'd been friends; Ruth deserved a civil conversation and a chance to voice her point of view. "I'm sorry." Her weak apology didn't stanch the tears flowing from Ruth's eyes. The damage had been done.

"Mommy?" Black ink smudged Maggie's cheeks. "Why are you fighting with the nice lady?"

In less than ten minutes, Maggie had done exactly what Lisbeth had done upon her first meeting with Ruth, become completely taken with the strong, compassionate woman. Is that what had happened to Cyprian? He'd come home to an empty bed and the warm smile of the enchanting blonde running his household. Who could blame him? Every life Ruth touched was instantly infused with her unconditional love. "I'm not fighting, baby. I'm—"

Mama pulled Lisbeth aside and whispered out of Maggie's hearing. "This misunderstanding is my fault. I sent you home for a reason. I expected you to stay there. It's too dangerous here. Aspasius is a constant threat."

"Me? What about you? I couldn't let that jerk hurt you anymore, Mama."

"Is that why you came back? To get me?"

"And Laurentius. And . . ."

"Cyprian?" Ruth's voice quivered. "You came to get Maggie's father, right?"

Maggie's head snapped up, the quill dripping ink on her design. "Right, Mommy?"

Lisbeth could feel her daughter waiting for her answer. Now was not the time to hash this out. Now was the time to make the unhappy trip back to the twenty-first century without Maggie's father as easy as possible on her child.

"I came to help fight the measles." Lisbeth reached into her backpack, praying Maggie would let this one go until she had some sort of explanation figured out. "I brought vaccines." When she presented her treasured box of MMR vials and another box of the diluents, she was relieved Maggie had returned to her art for now. "Since there's no way to maintain the proper temperatures to ensure viability, I've got to use them up fast."

"Is it still a two-dose protocol?" Mama asked.

Lisbeth nodded. "Two rounds would be ideal, but the recipients have to wait four weeks between doses. Without a fridge that's not happening. So I'm hoping one shot is better than nothing."

Mama came and stood by Laurentius. "Start with your brother."

Inoculating someone with Down's made her nervous. "Any signs of leukemia?"

"No." Mama immediately dismissed the possibility that Laurentius's genetic mutation increased his odds of contracting a cancer. Vaccinating him was extremely dangerous. "And he for sure has never had chemo. It's safe," Mama desperately insisted.

Without a battery of blood work to confirm or deny Laurentius's health, Lisbeth would have to rely on visuals. Laurentius did not seem overly tired. Nor did he suffer any unusual bruising. Other than a little weight loss, which could be explained by the lack of good nutrition available, he seemed fine. She'd never forgive herself if he contracted measles and died because she'd withheld the one thing that could save him. "Roll up his sleeve."

Mama set to work preparing Laurentius while Lisbeth turned her back and loaded the syringe.

When she faced Laurentius with the needle, his eyes grew wide, and he backed into Mama. "Will it hurt?"

"Don't worry, Larry." Maggie continued drawing. "Shots only sting for a second. I know. Mommy made Queenie give me lots of them before we got on the plane."

"Who's Queenie?" Laurentius asked.

"She's my aunt in Texas." Maggie blew on the parchment. "Ruth's my aunt here." Maggie had already made them all into one big, happy family.

"Laurentius, can you keep your eyes on Maggie's mice?" Lisbeth flicked the side of the syringe. "Look, I think I see them moving." The moment Laurentius was distracted she inserted the needle at a forty-five-degree angle into the posterolateral fat of his upper arm.

Laurentius flinched. "Ow!" His face scrunched. "I don't like thots."

"You were a brave boy." Mama rubbed his arm and unrolled his sleeve, relief on her face. "Thank you, Lisbeth."

"Who's next?" Lisbeth looked at Naomi. The girl needed a nudge from Mama, but she took her shot without complaint. "Next?"

Ruth stepped forward, rolling up her sleeve. "I'll go."

"Sorry, this shot is best given *before* pregnancy." The old Lisbeth, the one who only thought about herself, would have thought leaving Ruth unprotected served her right for stealing her husband. This new Lisbeth, the one with the Holy Spirit constantly perched on her shoulders, felt sick to her stomach. She tried to soften her response. "If you haven't gotten measles yet, then I suspect you're already immune."

"Barek and I have had the measles."

"When?"

"Right after you left."

"Who cared for you?"

"Those we'd cared for—"

"Help!" Cyprian's shout rang through the whole house and cut Ruth off.

Ruth dropped the towel and raced from the kitchen.

"Do *not* leave this room, Maggie." Lisbeth scrambled after Ruth, tripping over mats while Ruth moved more with the ease of a gazelle than a very pregnant woman. "Ruth!" She caught up and took Ruth by the shoulders. "For the baby's sake, I can't let you go in there."

"And who do you think has been in there in your absence?" Ruth pushed past her and began directing the new arrivals to the vacant mat in the last free corner.

Barek emerged from the wine cellar. "What's going on?"

"More sick." Ruth took the crock from him. "Naomi, fetch my herb box." Ruth dished out orders with the ease of a charge nurse. "Barek, more hot water." Ruth motioned to Cyprian. "Over here."

"The floor?" A tall man with his arms hooked under the limp arms of a young woman had his back to them. Cyprian was on the opposite end, supporting the girl's ankles. Standing beside the sick girl was a woman Lisbeth guessed to be the girl's mother. She was an exact replica of the younger one, except for the scowl on her face, and she had her hands tucked inside the folds of the very expensive stola draped around her graceful figure. The impressive shimmer and rustle of Coan silk accompanied her slightest movement.

"We'll make her comfort—" Ruth looked up from her preparations and gasped.

Lisbeth's gaze followed the bead of Ruth's focus: The man holding the beautiful girl with light blond hair, perfectly chiseled features, and flaming red spots scattered across her neck and chin was the same man who'd been there that horrible day she and Ruth were hauled before the council. The man who had voted to kill Caecilianus and exile Cyprian. Anger boiled inside Lisbeth, and it was all she could do not to charge headfirst into the man.

The man's bloodshot eyes assessed the crowded villa halls, his nose wrinkling slightly at the hacking patients rousing from their mats. "The daughter of Titus Cicero does not sleep on the floor with plebs."

"Patricians are nothing but trouble," Barek said.

"Hush, son," Ruth scolded. "We'll do our best to make her as comfortable as possible."

"She'll have a bed away from plebs," Titus demanded.

"Hold your tongue, Cicero," Cyprian said. "After what you did to Ruth's husband, it is only by the grace of God that she'll help you at all."

Titus looked shocked, like he had no recollection of Ruth or the man she loved. "I don't know what you're talking about."

"The old bishop you had beheaded!" Cyprian snapped.

"What?" Barek lunged for Titus.

"It's all right, son." Ruth snatched Barek back. "I'm sure Titus is just worried about his daughter. Any parent would be. She's obviously very sick."

"He had my father killed!" Barek pulled against her hold. "I'll kill him."

"He was not the only one who voted that day," Ruth soothed.

"I'll kill him."

"I don't blame you, Barek, but you're not killing anybody tonight." Lisbeth stepped between Barek and Titus. "Your daughter can either receive treatment on the floor or die in your arms. The choice is yours."

The man bristled at their unified front. His eyes conjured the image of a wildcat sizing up prey. Arresting. The eyes of a dangerous man. "Who are you?"

Lisbeth kept her gaze steady. "I am the woman whose husband you sent into exile."

"Titus?" Vivia's hands churned beneath the yards of fabric draped across her shoulder. "What are these strange people talking about?"

"Coming here was a mistake." Titus started to back out, stretching Diona between him and Cyprian.

"Titus, what have you done?"

"It was business, Vivia. Just business."

"Tell that to the people whose lives you ruined," Cyprian said.

Lisbeth could see the patient deteriorating. "You can hold him down, and I'll punch him later, Cyprian. That girl needs help." She put her hands on her hips. "You want the bed or not, mister?" She waited, giving Titus little time to weigh his options. "If not, I'm sure we can find someone who will. Might even be you in a few days."

Titus struggled under the weight of the girl's limp body obviously growing heavier and heavier in his arms.

"Do it, Titus," the woman with him ordered. "Now!"

"Very well, Vivia. But don't blame me when they murder our daughter on that filthy mat."

17

LISBETH STOOD ON THE balcony watching the moon slowly slide into morning. Ruth had handled the shock of seeing Titus with the enviable maturity of the saint she was. Forgiving those who'd betrayed her like they'd simply stolen a piece of bread rather than murdered her husband. If mature faith could grant someone that kind of peace, then Lisbeth had a long way to go. Not only did she have to fight back the urge to slap Titus, this impossible mess with Ruth and Cyprian still made her fume.

By the time Lisbeth and Mama had the Ciceros settled to Titus's satisfaction, the MMR vaccine she'd brought had warmed beyond the recommended safety margin. She hated that Ruth and Barek had suffered through measles without her, but she was grateful the church had nursed them. Laurentius was now safely vaccinated, and Junia was immune since she'd had measles before, too.

That just left Cyprian. So far it seemed he had some kind of natural immunity, because as much as he'd been around measles, he should have contracted them by now. She regretted the need to dispose of the unused vaccine vials before she could inoculate him as an added precaution. The vaccinations may not have gone like she'd planned, but after seeing the relief on Mama's face when she vaccinated Laurentius, she would plunge through the portal again just to save her half brother.

Mama had convinced her to put Maggie and Junia to bed and to try to get some rest herself. Mama would take the first shift with Diona.

Thankfully, Maggie's preoccupation with her new friend had spared them a long discussion as to why her daddy had two wives. Lisbeth tossed and turned for an hour, but between the continual coughing of patients in the hall and her replaying the events of this long day, sleep would not come. She could not close her eyes without thinking of Cyprian and Ruth sleeping side by side in the gardener's cottage, his hand upon Ruth's belly, their child stirring beneath his touch.

A biting chill seeped deep into Lisbeth's bones. She drew her shawl. Spring would not be put off forever. Soon warming winds would blow in from the desert, stir Aspasius from his den, and awaken his fury. A ship would be sent to fetch Cyprian home. And when the proconsul learned he'd been bested yet again, there would be no corner of the empire where Cyprian would be safe.

Lisbeth's eyes traced the outline of the coast. Not far from the trodden path that led from Cyprian's villa down to the water was the vine-clad pergola where she and Cyprian had made love for the last time. For six years she'd grieved the eighteen centuries and thousands of miles that separated them. Now here she was, not a stone's throw from where he slept, and it dawned on her that she'd felt closer to her husband then than she did now.

To be fair, how could Cyprian possibly have known she would return? He couldn't. He *should* have gone on with his life.

She had. Maggie hadn't given her much choice. Infants don't care for themselves. She'd moved forward, but she hadn't remarried. She'd believed what they had together, although brief, was real. True. Something worth risking everything to keep. Replacing him wouldn't have felt right.

Beyond the pergola's deserted columns, linkboys snuffed the

swan lamps of the ships docked in the doughnut-shaped harbor. Once the weather turned predictable, Aspasius would open the harbor gates and launch this life-snuffing sickness throughout the Roman world. Someone had to stop him.

"Lisbeth!" Mama's summons drew her attention to the door. "You better come see this."

"Is it Diona?"

"She's not presenting like the others."

Lisbeth grabbed her backpack. "Brief me on the way." They set off in a sprint.

"Abdominal pain. Pea soup diarrhea."

Lisbeth's stomach lurched. "Does she smell like freshly baked bread?"

"How did you know?"

"Bad hunch."

They zigzagged through the maze of mats until they got to the corner Diona's family had claimed.

"Why is she getting worse?" Vivia's hands thrashed beneath her stola.

"Do something, please," Titus said.

"I need you to hold the lamp." Lisbeth dropped beside Diona. "Can you do that?"

Titus nodded.

Lisbeth dug her stethoscope out of her bag. The yeasty smell emanating from Diona's glistening skin was nauseating. In the flickering light, she did her best to conduct a cursory exam. Fever. Rash. Dry cough. Abdomen tender. "Looks like typhoid."

"Are you sure?" Mama squatted on the opposite side of the mat.

"Without blood tests it's hard to be certain, but waterborne diseases thrive in nasty environments. Bacteria love to set up house in the ruins of a virus. From what I've seen and smelled of the city's current state, I'm guessing Aspasius still hasn't completed those aqueducts."

Mama shook her head. "His workforce is too depleted."

"Without proper sanitation support, sewage backs up. Bacteria can infiltrate the city's water source and spread through the supply system faster than an army on steroids." Lisbeth sighed. "And before you know it, every tap in town is contaminated." Lisbeth's gut liquidized. "I only brought a limited supply of antibiotics. We'll have to find a place to quarantine their entire family, start the girl on some serious oral rehydration solutions, and disinfect anything she's touched."

Mama agreed. "I'm guessing your expertise is not an accident."

"I did an infectious disease fellowship."

"So you went home, had a baby, finished your residency, *and* tackled a fellowship?" Pride beamed on Mama's face. "Admirable."

"More selfish really."

"Selfish?"

"I wanted to come back and save our futures."

"Wait. Where are you going?"

"I need to get Maggie out of here."

"Didn't you have her inoculated?"

"Of course I did. But typhoid vaccinations are still only fifty percent effective in kids."

"I was hoping something more reliable had been developed."

"You mean like the common sense I seem to be lacking?"

18

"ANOTHER BAD DREAM?" RUTH pushed up in bed. The wooden frame creaked with her movements.

"The same dream." Cyprian turned from the tiny window, his neck stiff from peering into the darkness.

He'd spent the night pacing the tiny cottage while asking God questions bigger than the universe. How was he supposed to fix this? Especially now. Titus Cicero had discovered not only his whereabouts, but Lisbeth and Magdalena's as well. The news was sure to reach the ears of Aspasius before Cyprian had the chance to get everything in place.

No matter what he did, these precious women were going to get hurt. And what about the children? If Lisbeth took Maggie back to Texas, how could he be in two places at once: a father to the child of his time, and a father to the child of the future?

So far the dissonant howl of the wind had been his answer. The old closeness he'd felt to the Lord in those early days after his conversion had disappeared into a dark chasm. Perhaps his mummified emotions had made it impossible to detect God's presence. Or worse, perhaps God had grown as weary as he of his anger and had officially deserted him.

"I didn't mean to wake you, Ruth."

Thunder rumbled in the distance. "This one was as restless as his father last night."

"He?"

Her eyes twinkled. "I think so." One hand rubbed her belly, the other patted the bed. "Tell me why you spent the night wearing out the floorboards."

Living with Ruth these past six months had proven as difficult as he had anticipated. Not because she was hard to live with. She'd done everything she could to make this arrangement work. Their union was her suggestion, after all. A federation of weakened states joining together for the good of the Lord's kingdom. Marriage would give him credibility with the senators, and Barek would provide the suitable heir necessary to contest Aspasius's seizure of Cyprian's vast wealth should the unfortunate need arise. But they both knew that he was not the man to fill Caecilianus's shoes . . . or his bed.

Late at night, after their physical attempts to fill the emptiness, grief's fog would creep between them. Cyprian would roll to his side, and Ruth would turn to hers. As her silent sobs shook their downy tick, icy fingers reached inside his chest and squeezed the breath from his lungs. Unable to bear her tears or his own hypocrisy, he would rise and pace the cliffs. For hours, he'd stare at the dance of moonbeams upon the restless sea. Somewhere across the span of ocean and time Lisbeth might have been looking at the same moon. Did she know how much he had loved her and always would?

"Cyprian? You're scaring me."

He turned and took her outstretched hand. "It was only a dream."

"And was *she* in your dream?" Ruth's question lacked the edge he deserved. Instead it was kind and forgiving, like her, and asked with the same genuine concern she lavished upon all the strays, including the ungrateful Titus Cicero.

His hasty decision to jump into another marriage had done enough damage. Why hurt this wonderful woman with words that should never be thought, let alone spoken? He shook his head, unable to voice a lie, and changed the subject. "I'm sorry about Titus."

"I'm not. It will give me a chance to demonstrate to Barek how to forgive those who wrong you." She looked at him in that disarming way of hers that meant she had more to say. "Back to your dream. Under the circumstances, how could you help but dream of Lisbeth?" Ruth smoothed the tousled strands of her braid. "I feel I've aged a hundred years in the time she's been gone. Yet she hasn't changed a bit. She's still so determined and certain of her convictions." Ruth let her hand slide from her hair to his arm. "And even more breathtakingly beautiful, don't you think?"

"Ruth, I—"

She laid a stick-straight finger across his lips. "She was your wife . . . *is* your wife . . . and my friend. We must talk about her. I want to talk about her."

"And say what? Persecution. Plague. Exile. And now two wives. *'Why this, too, God?'*"

"He's big enough for our questions."

"Then why doesn't he answer?"

"Why would you say such a thing?"

"Caecilianus prayed all the way to his death." He saw her stiffen a little at the mention of her first husband.

"It was not for his own life my husband prayed. It was for the future of the church. God has answered that prayer. We are still here."

He stood. "Why didn't he save Lisbeth from Aspasius?"

"He did," she said with a reassuring smile. "He sent her home."

"Then why did he wait to bring her back until it was too late?"

Ruth recoiled, and he immediately wished he could return his misery to the dark recesses of his soul. "You'll have to ask God," she whispered. "His timing is seldom our own."

"I'm sorry, but I've tried. Truly I have. But I can't hear him, Ruth." He pulled up a stool and faced her, the bravest thing he'd done since his return. "When Caecilianus first told me of his one God, the one more powerful than the totality of my false gods, I could hear that God. His voice rang in my ears the day he told me to trade my life for Lisbeth's." He lowered his head into his hands, then slowly raised his eyes. "And now . . . I hear nothing, nothing but the infernal howl of the wind."

Ruth considered him for a moment, her eyes watery. "After Caecilianus died, I felt like you do now. Angry. Lost. Afraid." She flung back the covers and lifted his chin. "If there's one thing I know"—she leaned forward, cupped Cyprian's face with her hands, and lightly kissed his lips—"loving others is the only way back to him. Don't be afraid to love again, Cyprian. No matter how daunting the task may seem."

The saltiness of her tears lingered, along with his shame at letting her down. "You must give up the church, Ruth."

"What?"

"It's only a matter of time until Aspasius learns I am back. And when he does, he'll come after me, and then he'll come after the church." He picked up her hand and kissed her roughened knuckles. "I don't want to give him any more reason to target you and the baby."

"How do you know what tomorrow will bring?"

"Titus."

Her brow furrowed. "What does Titus Cicero have to do with us or the church?"

"If Diona dies in my house, who else will Titus have to blame but the Christians tending her?"

She put her hand on his shoulder and stood. "Giving up the

church would be giving up on everything Caecilianus believed in, everything I believe in. Everything I know you still believe in."

"I'm not asking you to give up your leadership forever. Just until things settle down."

"But who'll guide and care for the people in the meantime? No one else cares for them. They're frightened little sheep easily scattered in these shaky times."

"Felicissimus." Cyprian took her hand. "Have you not encouraged me to relinquish my affairs to him?"

"The church is not a business to be managed."

"You said he rallied the believers after Caecilianus's death. Isn't that why you rewarded him with the appointment of deacon? If anyone can weather these hard times, it is our brother Felicissimus." Cyprian gave her a worried, provisional expression. "Ruth, until we've sorted what it means that Lisbeth has returned, neither you nor I have any business trying to tell other people how to live." He let the embarrassment of their situation sink in before issuing his summation. "We must turn the church over to Felicissimus."

"Caecilianus wanted *you* to lead the church."

"But, apparently, God did not."

19

RAIN USHERED IN THE gray light of dawn. Not as little drops, but as great walls of cold water sent to snap the world from its lethargy.

Lisbeth and Mama huddled under the eaves. The moment one clay jar filled, they grabbed it; dumped the clear, fresh contents into a barrel; and set the crock out to fill again.

To avoid setting off a full-scale panic, Lisbeth had agreed to wait until she had a chance to reexamine Diona in better light. Not one Koplik spot could be found inside the girl's mouth, and the rash on her upper torso was limited to only five lesions. Add those findings to the continual diarrhea and severe stomach cramps, and Lisbeth felt certain typhoid was the correct diagnosis.

She left Maggie and Junia sleeping soundly in the master suite. She would move them to the gardener's cottage once they woke. She closed the door and went to wake everyone else. All hands would be needed to scrub every inch of Cyprian's home with fresh, uncontaminated water.

Soaked to the skin, she and Mama joined those gathered for the emergency meeting in the kitchen.

Lisbeth decided the best way to get through the necessary details of what must be done was to focus on Naomi, Barek, and Mama. She purposefully avoided making eye contact with Cyprian or Ruth, who'd answered her frantic summons wearing their bedclothes. Ruth's belly was even more pronounced in the thin, wet undertunic that clung to her curves. "This piggyback bacteria we're facing has symptoms similar to measles: Fever. Cough. Headache. Sparse, pinkish rash."

"Bacteria?" Naomi asked.

"Another kind of sickness," Mama patiently explained.

"How will we know the difference?" Barek asked.

"Smell." Lisbeth kept her eyes off Cyprian and the tender way he wrapped the shivering Ruth in his cloak. "Typhoid patients have an infection in their intestinal tracts that produces a yeasty, baking-bread odor on their breath and skin." She let that disgusting detail sink in before moving on with the worst. "They also tend to have a white coating on their tongues, severe abdominal pains, and a soupy diarrhea."

Ruth didn't even flinch. "Can we touch them?"

"Not a good idea," Mama said.

"You should have let me kill them when I had the chance. Patricians are nothing but trouble," Barek said.

Ruth placed her hand on Barek's arm. "Son, please. That's not helping."

"These bacteria thrive in water," Lisbeth continued. "Eating or drinking anything contaminated could be fatal. Sweat, urine, wet cough, blood . . . coming into contact with any excreted bodily fluids is extremely dangerous."

"Then how are we going to care for these people?" Ruth asked.

"I've started Diona on a pretty strong antibiotic. We'll have to move things around and create a quarantine ward in one hall and a measles ward in the other. After we get everything settled, it will be important to keep her hydrated. We'll add some herbal remedies. Cool drinks of boiled cloves and honey, some dried echinacea flowers steeped like a tea, and mixtures of boiled pomegranate skins and raisins. Once she's able to hold down fluids, we'll introduce some carrot soup laced with crushed peppercorns and eventually get her back on solids." When Lisbeth realized she'd flown through her list, she paused to give everyone time to catch up. "Ruth, how are our herbal supplies?"

"I think we've got enough to get started."

"Good." Lisbeth passed out latex gloves. "These will protect your hands. I could only bring a couple of boxes, so use them sparingly. Unless you're working with the Cicero family . . . then double-glove." She demonstrated the proper technique for removing contaminated gloves, then stowed the box inside her bag. "All soiled linens must be burned. All drinking water, boiled.

"To eliminate flies, we'll toss sawdust or ashes down the latrines after every use, and we'll bury Diona's waste far from any water source." Lisbeth thought of all the flies crawling over the meat in the market. This thing could spread fast. She swallowed hard. "We need to spread the word through the tenements . . . no more tossing the contents of any chamber pots onto the streets. And most important of all, every one of you will wash your hands with soap and hot water, even if you wore gloves. No exceptions. Are we clear?"

Everyone nodded.

"What can I do?" Cyprian asked.

"Gather the church," Lisbeth said. "Anyone who's immune to measles. We are going to need a lot of help."

20

"FORGIVE ME, RUTH." CYPRIAN slung his wet tunic into a basket. "My return has brought destruction upon your head. First, the threat of Aspasius. Then the ill-mannered Titus Cicero. And now another plague."

"Lisbeth's right." Ruth handed him a towel. "We are going to need the help of the church."

He could see that the task at hand was greater than the smattering of healthy people left on his estate could manage. At the same time, he could also recall the disgusted faces of the weary believers who'd risked their lives to meet in his garden for a bit of encouragement a few months ago. When they'd learned Ruth had chosen him as their spiritual leader, they'd made their positions quite clear. They were unwilling to follow a man they believed to be a coward and a traitor.

Sending him to gather the church would be a catastrophe.

Of course, when Lisbeth asked this of him, there was no way she could have known of his earlier failing. He should have told her the truth the moment she asked. But when her tired eyes sought him for help, his lips had remained sealed. She still thought him the brazen noble who'd boldly stood before a roomful of senators and declared himself the new bishop of the Lord's church. If only he was that man.

So much had changed during their exiles. Much more than a child he never knew about and a marriage Lisbeth never expected. It was something deep within him that he wanted desperately to change back.

Cyprian scrubbed his dripping head. "I should not have allowed Titus Cicero to set foot into my home. Not after what he did to us."

"It was the right thing to do."

"Then why is every good I do rewarded with evil?"

Ruth placed her hand upon her stomach and smiled. "Not everything."

"You know I didn't mean . . ."

"No one is expecting you to be perfect." She paused. "No one except you."

He took her by the shoulders and kissed her forehead. "Promise me you'll stay out of the typhoid hall while I'm gone."

"If you'll promise me that you will take Felicissimus with you."

"Then you agree he should lead the church?"

She silenced him with a finger to his lips. "Just in case you run into trouble."

"You mean in case no one will follow me."

21

THE COLD, SOUR FEELING in Lisbeth's belly had nothing to do with typhoid.

Lisbeth had seen them together . . . Cyprian and Ruth . . . when she went to the cottage to ask if Maggie could stay there. Out of harm's way. They were hunched over a scroll spread across the low dining table. Their shoulders touching. Their faces intent upon the Scriptures. They were a team, an intricate relationship bound by more than vows spoken before a priest. Cyprian and Ruth's shared understanding of what was at stake and comfortable familiarity with the same time period required no long explanations. No raised brows. No fights.

The weight of Lisbeth's loneliness bore down heavily on her steps. No matter how much she'd hoped Maggie would bridge the gap, she and Cyprian would never be so united. They were two different people who saw the world from two different vantage points.

His eyes looked ahead.

Hers always looked behind.

The twenty-twenty hindsight was killing her. The thought of him dying such a horrendous, senseless death made her blood curdle. History didn't have to follow the course written in some musty old books. If she thought Cyprian would choose her, she would beg him to come back with her to her time. But he was far too noble to desert his pregnant wife, and to tell the truth, she loved him all the more for it. At the very least, perhaps she could persuade him to take Ruth and Barek and flee Carthage until this turmoil settled. Anything rather than face Aspasius. Her heart would remain forever broken, but at least Cyprian would have a shot at a future.

"Mommy?" Maggie tugged on Lisbeth's sleeve, pulling her back to the task of getting Maggie to safety. "I don't know how to flush." She pinched her nose and peered into a small oblong hole carved into the marble latrine.

"You don't flush." Lisbeth shoveled ash into the hole. "You just go, toss in a little of this, and leave it."

Maggie scowled at the idea of letting things lie where they fell. She reached for the long stick with a sponge tied on the end resting in a communal bucket of salt water.

"No!" Lisbeth grabbed her hand. "Don't touch that filthy thing."

"But Junia says that's how you wipe in Carthage." She pointed at her new friend washing her hands at the basin. "Right, Junia?"

Lisbeth ripped the hem from her tunic. "Not now. Not ever for you. Or you either, Junia."

This world had so many different mediums for passing typhoid and other assorted diseases. Keeping Maggie safe required full-time attention, which, thankfully, Ruth had agreed to provide. She hated being indebted to Ruth, especially since they hadn't been able to sit down and work things out, but for now she didn't have a choice.

Lisbeth instructed Maggie to join Junia at the bowl of freshly boiled water cooling on the counter.

Maggie moved her hand through the diminishing steam. "It's too hot."

Lisbeth stuck her hand in to test. It wouldn't burn. "I'm sorry, baby, but it has to be a little warmer than you're used to in order to kill the germs. Stick your hands in and out as quickly as you can."

"Watch me." Junia plunged her hands into the bowl, then held them up for Maggie's inspection. "See? Not even pink."

Maggie examined Junia's hands. "It didn't hurt?"

"Not if you do it fast."

Maggie closed her eyes and cautiously slipped her hands beneath the water. She scrunched her face, swished her hands for less than a second, then yanked them out. Her eyes flew open, and a big smile lit her face. "I did it, too."

Lisbeth kissed her forehead. "You are becoming such a brave girl."

"Not all the time." Maggie dried her palms on her tunic. "I'm scared to live with my daddy. He doesn't know me."

"Not yet. But he already loves you."

"Why do I have to move into the cottage?"

"I told you why." Lisbeth herded Maggie and Junia out the door. "There's a really sick girl in this house, and I don't want you and Junia catching the bug she has."

"But you said all those mean shots Queenie gave me would keep away bugs."

"Unfortunately, vaccinations are not always a hundred percent effective. I'm not taking any chances. Besides, aren't you the girl who asked for a daddy for Christmas?"

"And a doll."

"Maggie."

She sighed. "He doesn't like me."

"Baby, that's not true."

"He likes me." Junia skipped ahead. "He'll like you."

Maggie flashed Lisbeth a doubtful look.

In all fairness, Cyprian had a lot on his mind. His first wife's unexpected return. An evil man hunting him down. A new health crisis. Plus, having to navigate fatherhood in two different centuries.

"If there's anything I know about your daddy, it's this: Cyprianus Thascius will do anything in the world for you."

"But will he love me?"

"Baby"—Lisbeth knocked on the cottage door—"he already does."

Ruth answered. Her normally sunny smile graced her tired face, and from what Lisbeth could tell, her joy at being able to take Maggie in was genuine. "Here you are."

Junia flung her arms around Ruth's thickened middle for a quick hug, then marched on in.

"Maggie?" Ruth peered around Lisbeth. "I've made some sweets."

Maggie pressed a stack of parchment to her chest and scooted closer to Lisbeth.

"Baby, you need to go in."

Maggie shook her head.

Ruth offered her hand. "Barek and I have rearranged and made a pallet for you next to your uncle Laurentius."

"Maggie!" Lisbeth's half brother sat cross-legged on a small mat. "You brought paper?" A crooked smile split his face. He waved her over. "Leth draw."

Maggie shook her head. "I don't want to draw mice."

Laurentius nodded and patted the mat. "Okay."

"We can play doctor or house," Junia offered.

Maggie only had to consider the offer for a second. "'Bye, Mommy." She dropped Lisbeth's hand and went in without looking back.

Papa would pop the buttons on his chambray shirt if he could see how independent and brave Maggie had become. Lisbeth, on the other hand, would love to have her father's bony shoulder to lean on right now, to reassure her that letting go of the person she loved the most was a good thing.

"Where's Cyprian?" Lisbeth asked Ruth. "I'd hoped he'd be here to help his daughter settle in."

"He and Felicissimus are rounding up the church."

"Felicissimus?"

Lisbeth hadn't seen the sleazy little slave trader since her return. She'd just assumed he'd taken his two-timing, deceitful self and either left town or publicly joined forces with Aspasius. It hadn't occurred to her that he would dare to hang around the very man he'd betrayed. What was he? Some kind of vulture waiting for his chance to pick at the bones of the church? But, when she thought about it, he really wasn't risking much to stick around. When Mama pushed her back into the twenty-first century, Lisbeth had taken the truth of what she'd seen in Aspasius's palace with her. With Cyprian out of the way and Lisbeth reported as dead, Felicissimus must have felt it safe to swoop in and take what he'd wanted all along. In the chaos of her return she hadn't thought to mention Felicissimus to anyone.

She started to tell Ruth what she knew about the little traitor, but she caught a glimpse of Maggie eyeing her, waiting to see if she and Ruth would get into it again. Her daughter had enough uncertainty to deal with; she didn't need controversy.

Now was the time to make peace, gain allies; for when the time came to deal with Felicissimus, she would need a friend she could count on, someone who would back her insistence that the little snake not be allowed anywhere near Cyprian or his family. "Ruth, about Cyprian. I'm sure we can work something out so that he doesn't—"

Ruth laid a finger across Lisbeth's trembling lips. "We both love him."

"Ruth, I—"

"Two are always better than one"—she squeezed Lisbeth's hand—"for when one falls down, there's a friend to help them up." She smiled. "We'll sort this out. Together."

How could they possibly sort this out? Cyprian had two wives. One of them would have to go, and Lisbeth knew she was the logical choice. She glanced past Ruth. Maggie lay sprawled on her belly between Junia and Laurentius demonstrating the proper way to draw a family. A mom. A dad. And, in the middle, a child. Taking Maggie away from her father would crush her dreams. Staying and watching Cyprian love another woman would break Lisbeth's heart.

"Sorting this out may be easier said than done, Ruth."

22

CYPRIAN WRAPPED A CLOTH around his face and then stuffed his hands into the tight blue gloves Lisbeth had demonstrated to the workers he'd gathered. The air in the villa crackled with excitement rather than the fear he'd expected from such a dangerous task. All around him, people hurried. Clearing the hall of measles victims, toting heavy pots of hot water, scrubbing walls and floors, comforting those too ill to help, or carrying food to the sick. Even Quinta, the forty-year-old grandmother who'd taken over the care of her grandson after she lost her daughter and son-in-law, had strapped the infant to her back, rolled up her sleeves, and started washing dishes.

On his own, he'd asked for help from the church. And, to his surprise, the believers came. Leaving their beds and loved ones, they'd slipped into the pouring rain and made their way to his villa without complaint. Everyone but Felicissimus. When Cyprian made the dangerous venture to the docks in search of the slave trader, he was not only disappointed when his client claimed a prior obligation, but also worried that his attempt to rally the church would be for naught.

"Where do you want me to set up this little tent?" Metras leaned on his cane, a wad of silk and sticks crammed under his other arm and his lips pulled in a determined line across his toothless gums.

It had taken the better part of the night to locate the apartment of the man who'd accused him of tossing the believers crumbs and fleeing to the mountains. He would have crossed Metras off the list were it not for Ruth's insistence that a big heart beat beneath the shriveled exterior of the injured carpenter. The moment the old man opened his door, Cyprian was glad he'd changed his mind.

"I'd invite you in," Metras had said, "but ain't enough room in here for a blade of grass."

Rain running down his back, Cyprian had peeked around the weathered plank. The old bachelor's flat was filled with beggar women and children. Those who weren't coughing or covered in a rash were caring for the others the best they could. All of them were starving.

"Metras, is your family ill?"

"They ain't exactly blood kin." He'd stepped outside and closed the door. "They're just some folks who had no place to go."

"So you took them in?"

"I couldn't very well tell them about Jesus and then let them sleep on the street." His face screwed into worry. "Why is a patrician in my part of town? I'm not one of your clients." His eyes widened. "Something wrong with Ruth?"

The man's generosity and genuine concern humbled him. Here he was thinking he'd given so much. But he had much, and what he'd given financially so far hadn't even made a dent in his huge coffers. This man had only his humble abode and his life left to give. "She's fine, but a new sickness has been brought to the hospital and Ruth needs our help."

"Let me get my cane." Metras had followed without a moment's hesitation and hadn't stopped working since he'd arrived.

Cyprian held out his gloved hands. "Metras, you look like you could use a rest."

"This bum leg makes it hard for me to do the liftin' and totin' of the sick, but I can cobble these things together. I'll find Lisbeth and ask her where she wants this one."

"You're a good man, Metras."

"You're not so bad yourself, Bishop."

"Bishop?"

"Someone's got to do it."

The title grated on his ears every time it had been spoken in the past several hours. He'd be the first to admit watching the church work together and putting their lives at risk for others stirred embers he feared had grown cold. But bishop? No. He was not their bishop.

"I need some help moving Diona Cicero," Cyprian announced after everyone had finished their lunches.

"She's a patrician," Quinta pointed out.

"She's a sick girl," Lisbeth replied.

"But they're the ones signing our death warrants." Quinta raised her hands. "And I've got a bad back."

"You said Ruth was in trouble." Metras looked to Cyprian. "You didn't mention the trouble was a patrician."

"Like me?"

"I'll do it." Pontius gave his plate to Naomi and brushed the crumbs from his hands.

Cyprian knelt at the head of Diona's mat and motioned for Pontius to take the foot of her flaxen bed.

"Careful." Titus fluttered back and forth. "She's in a great deal of pain."

"We're doing our best here, Titus."

"I don't mean to seem ungrateful; it's just—"

"Which way are we going with her?" Pontius asked Cyprian.

"To the bedroom by the master suite. Lisbeth and Magdalena want to stay close as they can." He looked at Vivia and Titus, who stood apart from the church, watching helplessly. "You two are going into quarantine with her. You should be fairly comfortable. It's a rather large room."

"Why are you helping us?" Vivia asked once they were safely inside the room. "I don't think your plebeian friends approve."

Cyprian let a few answers cycle through his head, including the one where he agreed with Quinta that he'd rather eat sand than help the likes of Titus Cicero. "I couldn't tell you about Jesus and then let you sleep on the street."

"What of him?" Titus asked.

"It will wait."

After all the measles victims and the Ciceros were settled to Lisbeth's satisfaction, she called an important meeting of all the church volunteers in the kitchen. Cyprian crowded in with Ruth, Pontius, and Magdalena.

"Thanks for all your hard work." Lisbeth dragged her hand across her brow. "Before you return to your homes, I've got a few more instructions. To eliminate flies, toss sawdust or ashes down the latrines after every use. When you work your shift here, bury Diona's waste far from any water source. In the meantime, I need you to spread the word through the tenements . . . no more tossing the contents of any chamber pots onto the streets. And most important of all, every one of you will wash your hands with soap and hot water, even if you wear gloves. No exceptions. Are we clear?"

Everyone nodded.

"Collect as much of this rainwater for your personal consumption as you can," Lisbeth said. "Keep it separate. For all other water usage, the water must be boiled.

"I suspect the contamination is coming from your part of town. So our next workday will concentrate on cleaning up the gutters, removing the bodies, and rerouting all sewage away from the water supply."

"That's a bigger job than we've got the manpower for," Metras said.

"Perhaps I could hire any healthy and unemployed men we can find to carry the bodies to the cemeteries outside the city." Cyprian turned to Lisbeth. "These men can help us alleviate the problem while earning a wage that will allow them to feed their families."

"Great. And while you're hiring, we could also use a corps of transportation carts and medical attendants to police the streets and quickly transport anyone who's sick to us here, to one centralized place. Separate and isolate quickly is the best way to maximize the quarantine."

Cyprian noticed Lisbeth seemed to be holding back. "What? What else can we do?"

"I don't know how we could do this, but I wish there was some way to cut Carthage off from the rest of the world. Give these pathogens a chance to flame out."

"We can erect barricades on the highways," Barek offered.

"That might help," Lisbeth agreed.

"Until the soldiers knock them down," Cyprian said.

"It's the ships I'm most worried about. Since it takes seven to twenty-one days for measles or typhoid to appear, vessels can leave here with what they think is a healthy crew. But by the time they know they carry the sicknesses, they've exposed every port of call along the way. In less than six months the entire empire could be very sick."

Everyone gasped. Murmurs of the impossibility of such a thing happening buzzed around the table.

"She's right." Cyprian's raised voice silenced the group. "The ship that ported in Curubis had lost most of its crew to measles. I'm not sure where it was going, but I know it transported mail from here. If one ship carried the plague from our harbor, there's a high possibility the others will, too. We can scrub our hands raw, but it won't stop the onslaught when the rest of the world ships the sickness right back to us."

"Closing the harbor will require someone to go before the Senate." Magdalena's calm did not diffuse the tension building in the room.

"And Aspasius," Ruth whispered.

Cyprian kept his eyes on Lisbeth, the muscle in his jaw twitching. Wooing senatorial support to remove Aspasius from office would take finesse, money, and every minute between now and spring. Gathering enough votes to shut down the empire's most lucrative ports would take a miracle. "How long must the city stand still?"

"Two months at least." Lisbeth's eyes suddenly widened. "Oh, no, you wouldn't."

"Consider it done."

"No!" Ruth and Lisbeth shouted at the same time.

Lisbeth started for him, but Ruth's quick movement to his side cut her off. "Aspasius will kill you."

"If we don't do everything we can to make certain Diona Cicero and the rest of the ruling class lives, Aspasius will make certain we do not. My father still has friends in high places." Cyprian gently grasped Ruth's shoulders. "You've been telling me God has a plan for me. I've been a fool to be so fearful."

"Must his plan include losing your head as well?" Tears spilled onto Ruth's cheeks. For him or for Caecilianus, he could not be certain. "Promise me you won't go to the Senate unless you know for certain that you've gathered enough support."

"She's right, Cyprian," Metras said. "We can't afford to lose another bishop."

23

BAREK SNATCHED THE WATER pot near the cottage door. He'd spent the past thirty minutes watching the men, including his friend Natalis, slip through the back gate to begin their jobs of tossing ash down the public latrines. He did not appreciate how Cyprian had quashed his idea of a road barricade in front of everyone and then later relegated him to women's work.

He turned to his mother. "That woman has only been here a week, and once again everything has come undone." He started for the door. The dogs scrambled to their feet, anxious for the opportunity to stretch their legs.

"I, for one, appreciate your help fetching water. I don't think I could lift another jug." His mother sat on a cushion teaching Maggie and Junia how to sort dried herbs and crumble the leaves and stems into different-colored muslin bags. "Wait until dark to search for firewood along the beach. It will be safer."

Slaving in the measles ward had caused his mother's feet to swell and darkened the sagging circles beneath her eyes. She had grown old and tired doing her part, while it seemed Lisbeth's time away had granted her the luxury of growing more beautiful.

He'd seen how quickly the attractive interloper had brought Cyprian back to life and spurred him into action. "How can you sit there so calmly?"

"Would you rather I rant and rave like you?"

"The sudden return of Cyprian's faith could cost him his life."

"He promised he'd start with his most trustworthy connections in the Senate."

"There *are* no trustworthy connections. Aspasius's reach is great. He will come and take Cyprian and this estate. Then who will hear the moaning of your precious church?"

"God," Maggie said, looking up from arranging herb bags in a basket. "My g-pa says God hears *everything*."

He snorted disapproval. "What is a g-pa?"

"Barek, leave her alone," his mother scolded.

He let his perturbed gaze linger on Maggie in hopes of putting her in her place. Instead of backing down, the little chit lifted her chin with the same irritating manner of her mother. He didn't care how badly his mother hoped he and this miniature beauty could form some type of family bond; it would never happen. She was not, nor would he ever consider her, his sister.

"At least the poor appreciate what we do for them. Your good deeds won't make a speck of difference among the likes of Titus and Vivia Cicero. They will take our shelter, our bread, and our medical care"—Barek waved the empty jug in the direction of the villa, and the dogs jumped like he'd waved a bone—"but the rich of Carthage will never want the religion my father was selling."

"Cyprian did."

He had no answer. After all, the very home he was concerned about losing belonged to a man raised in the patrician class he despised.

"What the pagans do or do not want is not what matters." His mother straightened her back, and he knew he was in for a lecture. "In the end, service changes not those who are served but those doing the serving. Now do your chores."

"I no longer want to be treated as a child."

"Then stop acting like one."

RUTH REGRETTED letting Barek goad her into losing her temper.

"I'm sorry, Barek. I shouldn't have been so cross. These are hard times, no doubt."

Tempting as it was to blame her lack of control on her pregnancy or Lisbeth's unexpected return, the real worry was Barek's appetite for vengeance. Deep in the secret corners of her heart she knew the source of his anger.

Her.

She hadn't meant for the consequences of her choices to heap such an inordinate amount of stress on her son. Faithfulness to the cause of Christ had cost more than her husband's life. The resentment simmering in Barek's eyes spoke of the price. It wouldn't take much to fan the embers of his father's senseless death into angry flames.

The decision she and Caecilianus made years ago to follow the Lord was theirs and theirs alone. Barek would have to make his own choices. One day his unruly bush of black hair would transform into the great white mane of his father. There the resemblance would stop. Unless he sought his own faith. When the day came for her son to make his decision, she could only pray that somehow, in some way, his father's wisdom had miraculously taken up residence in his impetuous skull.

"Do not be fooled, Mother. The Ciceros will never regret what they did to us. They don't have to."

Ruth struggled to her feet. "In an instant, even the confidence of the rich can be swept away." She stretched her hand toward the stubbled face that towered over her. He may think himself a man, but she saw the same frightened little boy who'd sobbed in her arms after his father's beheading. "You may not be able to forgive them, but you will be kind."

Barek pulled free. "I've work to do."

"Can I come?" Maggie asked, brushing bits of dried herbs from her tunic.

"No!" He stormed from the cottage and slammed the door.

"You need a nap!" Maggie shouted after him.

24

Cyprian had not waited for the cover of darkness before he and Pontius went in search of Felicissimus. After a few close brushes with several soldier patrols, Cyprian had reconsidered the wisdom of that decision and waited for nightfall before attempting a return to the villa.

They'd located the slave trader in his holding cell near the docks. The plan they worked out was simple. Cyprian gave Felicissimus a sizable sum of money for hiring extra men to help clear the streets. After that venture was successfully under way, they would commission medical carts to patrol the slums. Meanwhile, Cyprian planned to do the hardest job alone: find enough of his father's friends in the Senate to propose a shutdown of the trade routes and to hold the majority when Aspasius threw a fit.

He'd confessed to no one that using up favors owed him to close the port rather than oust the current proconsul made him weak-kneed. But having Felicissimus shut down his personal shipping lines would not be enough. Every highway, cart rut, and footpath needed to be closed as well. Actions this drastic required government support and approval.

A fortunate cloudburst had given Pontius and Cyprian the cover necessary to make their way back to his estate undetected. Cyprian stood under the eaves of the cottage, brushing water from his sleeves. "Pontius, no need to hurry off to the stables. Stay and share a meal in the warmth of the cottage."

"I'd rather bunk with the broodmares than watch two women fight over the destiny of one man."

Until the issue of having two wives was resolved, he had to admit, moving in with the horses held a great deal of appeal. "Coward."

As his friend's lantern disappeared into an enviable night of freedom, Cyprian shook water from his cloak and stepped inside. The warmth and coziness that followed Ruth wherever she went enveloped him. As she had every night since their marriage, she sat at the low table mixing herbs into healing remedies. The dogs rested at her feet.

"You were gone for hours. I've been worried." Ruth seemed exceptionally tired by the pregnancy tonight. There was no point in mentioning this again. Nothing he said so far had convinced the woman to stay off her feet or give up even a portion of her caregiving duties, especially now that Lisbeth had returned. In fact, Ruth seemed more determined than ever to keep up the rigorous schedule. He suspected that this behavior would continue until they figured out their future.

"There were many patrols out," Cyprian told Ruth as he dried his hair with a towel and then scrubbed his hands with hot water and soap.

She handed him a bowl of figs poached in wine and pointed to the stool near the fire burning in the brass brazier. "Did you find Felicissimus?"

"Yes. He's going to start with hiring help to get the streets cleaned."

Ruth gave a nervous nod. "That should speed things along."

He wished he could tell her everything would be fine, but the truth was he couldn't make that promise. The men his father trusted had been strangely silent when Aspasius sentenced him to exile. If he couldn't persuade a majority to get behind him now, appearing before the Senate would end him. He pushed the memory of his haunting dreams aside, determined to prepare the best future he could for his families. Both of them.

Cyprian stuffed a spoonful of the mushy sweetness into his mouth. While he was out Ruth had managed to bring tranquillity to the chaos of the day. Across the tiny room, Barek and Naomi sat huddled over bone dice. From the pout on Barek's lips he hadn't forgiven being assigned to help his mother. In the opposite corner, Junia, Laurentius, and the girl with Lisbeth's spirit and his blond curls were deep into a game of playacting.

He regretted that the arrival of the Ciceros and typhoid had left him little time to get to know his daughter. For her to know him. He ate his figs while studying her intently.

The tiny, blue-eyed blonde bustled around the cottage bossing Junia, telling her how to rearrange glass vials of cosmetics on the windowsill. She didn't seem the least bit deterred by the fact that Junia was older and nearly a finger-length taller.

The mother-daughter resemblance between Lisbeth and Maggie was undeniable. Maggie's voice had the same clipped inflections, the same never-take-no-for-an-answer directness, and the same need to have everything in the order she thought best. Her eyes were fierce, determined, and not easily distracted from whatever they had locked in their sights. She had Lisbeth's perfect face, beautiful complexion, and that upturned nose capable of snubbing royalty.

But there the resemblances stopped.

Where Lisbeth had a mane of silky raven hair, this child's face was framed by the same unruly curls he'd fought his entire life. White as the dunes baking in the afternoon sun, Maggie's tresses had not taken on the darkened stain of struggle his hair had acquired, but there was no denying his part in this child's creation. Warmth spread in his chest.

He shoveled another spoonful of mush into his mouth as he observed the young girls playing their game. Both of them were dressed in silk stolas. According to Ruth, they'd spent hours dressing themselves in the few remaining pieces of her fine clothes and clomping around the cottage in strappy shoes several sizes too large.

Maggie gave Junia another curt instruction, then turned her attention on her uncle. "Larry, I can't take your temperature if you won't open your mouth." Maggie waved the handle of a wooden spoon under Laurentius's nose as he sat cross-legged on his sleeping mat staring up at his niece with adoring eyes. Tufts of his thinning hair had been tied up in different-colored ribbons, his cheeks sported bright red smudges of rouge, and one of Ruth's heavy gold earrings dangled from his left ear.

"But I'm not thick." Laurentius pursed his lips, refusing the spoon's insertion.

"You said you were tired, and my mommy says that's a typhoon symptom."

"I'm tired of being the baby."

Maggie put her hand on Laurentius's forehead. "Junia, this baby has fever."

"Why don't you leave the guy alone?" Barek let his dice smack the wall. "He said he was tired of you ordering him around."

"Ruth!" Maggie tattled. "Barek's not being nice."

"Barek, please," Ruth corrected. "Don't worry about him, girls. Go on with your game."

Junia clicked over to where Laurentius sat and placed her hand on his forehead. "I believe you're right, doctor. What shall we do?"

"Shots!" Maggie produced a whittled stick. She flicked the sharp point. "Hold still, Larry."

"No!" Laurentius tried to get his feet under him. "No more thots."

Maggie pressed him back into place. "Shots only hurt for a second."

Laurentius rubbed his arm and shook his head. "I'm tired of being the baby." He crossed his arms over his round belly. "When can I be the mommy?"

Maggie crammed her hands upon her hips and gave Laurentius the same determined look Cyprian had seen on Lisbeth's face when she proclaimed war on the new scourge. "I told you, we don't have a doll. You have to be our baby."

"There's a doll at my house." Junia placed her index finger over the opening of Ruth's expensive perfume and tipped it sideways.

Maggie cocked her head. "What kind of doll?"

"Perpetua."

"Is that like an Ariel doll?"

Junia looked confused, then shrugged. "My Perpetua has a delicate clay face, a soft rag body, and she was named after the beautiful martyr who died in the arena."

"What's a martyr?" Maggie asked.

Barek snorted. "You don't know anything."

"I do, too." Maggie said. "I know how to dial nine-one-one. I can work the remote control. And I can download games on my mommy's phone. Do you know how to do that?"

Barek scowled. "What?"

Cyprian chuckled to himself. The girl had spunk, and he knew exactly from whom she'd inherited that equally irritating and irresistible trait.

Maggie squared her shoulders and turned to Ruth, who was pouring mustard seeds into a mortar bowl. "Ruth, what's a martyr?"

Ruth's glance shot to Cyprian. "Someone willing to give their life for what they believe. Perpetua was a brave Christian woman who refused to renounce our Lord. Standing up for her faith cost her life."

Maggie smiled. "Let's go get her."

"The doll's probably not even there anymore," Barek said.

Ruth ground the pestle. "Barek, please."

"I hid her under the bed." Junia dabbed perfume behind Laurentius's ear.

"Thyprian, pleath let them get the doll." Laurentius tugged ribbons from his hair. "I don't want any more thots. I want to draw."

Ruth glanced at Cyprian. "What do you think?"

Keenly aware of how easily he could destroy Ruth's hard work to bring peace, Cyprian waded in cautiously. "It's not a good idea to go anywhere right now."

"You went somewhere." Maggie pointed at Cyprian's head. "You're wet."

"My errand was a necessity."

"Perpetua is all alone," Maggie declared gravely. "Saving her is a necessity."

"The tenements are especially dangerous right now."

"Hold this, Larry." Maggie gave Laurentius the spoon. Then she clicked across the tiles. She pulled up a stool opposite Cyprian, climbed aboard, and spun around until her knees nearly touched his. She smelled of Ruth's perfume, and wild clover honey stuck to the curly lock falling across the pained expression on her face. Cyprian reached toward her silky head, hungry to touch his own flesh and blood. To wrap her in his arms and keep her safe forever. As his hand neared her head, she wiggled out of reach, bending to free the gown's hem from the heel of her shoe.

"Here, let me help." Cyprian released the snagged fabric.

As he straightened, his hand brushed hers. Warm. Real. Part Lisbeth's . . . part his.

There was a pause, a moment when neither of them knew what to do next.

How to proceed deserved some serious consideration, especially if seeking senatorial support alerted Aspasius and cut his time with his daughter short. He slid back on the stool, dropped his elbows to his knees, and placed his hands on his chin.

Maggie observed him carefully and quietly. After a few moments she scooted to the edge of the stool, shrinking the distance between them until her knees were in full contact with his. She slowly lowered her elbows to her lap and plopped her chin into her cupped hands. Her posture and serious consideration matched his perfectly. Nose to nose, they were two thinkers contemplating the same deep chasm.

Maggie spoke first. "Mommy says you're my daddy."

He admired her directness. "Yes, Maggie. I'm your father."

She stared straight into his eyes. "And that you love me."

"We don't know each other very well, but I knew I loved you the moment I saw you."

She smiled. "Mommy says we'll be a family, because you're gonna come home with me."

Rain rattled the tiled roof of the cottage. Cyprian broke eye contact with Maggie and let his gaze slide around the room. Barek fisted the dice, his jaw clenching back obvious anger. Laurentius's mouth hung open. Junia held the perfume bottle in one hand, the stopper in the other. Ruth's white-knuckle grip ground the pestle against the bowl. Her eyes were misty, and he could tell she was holding her breath, waiting for his answer.

Cyprian turned his gaze back to the wide-eyed and hopeful little blonde. "Wouldn't you like to live *here* forever?"

She thought for a moment. "Okay. But if I'm going to live here, I need a doll. Daddy, can you please go get Perpetua?" Her eyes were the color of his, but they had the enticing clarity of purpose of her mother's. "Larry's a good baby, but he's cranky as Barek when he doesn't get his nap."

Cyprian laughed out loud.

Barek glared from the corner and slung the dice against the wall again. *"Stulte!"*

"I'm *not* an idiot." Maggie returned the full intensity of Barek's glare. "I have a plan."

"A plan?" Barek scoffed.

Cyprian held up his hand. "I want to hear what she has to say."

"Junia can run in, grab Perpetua, and then run back out." Maggie presented the details as if her way of thinking made perfect sense.

"That's crazy."

"Barek, please," Cyprian said. "Going back to the tenements isn't a good idea right now, Maggie."

"I can do it, Cyprian." Junia returned the stopper to the perfume vial. "I promise I won't touch anything else."

"Tell you what, girls." Cyprian shuffled through the options, looking for one that provided a way for everyone to save face. "Get some rest, and first thing in the morning, we'll figure out how Laurentius can go back to his drawings and you and Junia can have a real doll . . . even if I have to send Felicissimus out to buy one."

"I told Mommy my daddy would fix everything." She threw her arms around his neck. "Can she live here forever, too?"

Cyprian held her close, his tangled emotions lodged in his throat. How could he fix this without breaking his daughter's heart? He couldn't divorce Ruth and leave Barek and his unborn child without a father. And he couldn't bear to send Lisbeth and Maggie back to Dallas. Letting them go had the added benefit of ensuring their safety, but the idea of losing Lisbeth a second time was a sinking stone in the pit of his belly.

He dared not glance at Ruth, or he would lose his composure

for sure. "Your mother can do whatever she thinks best." He stood and carried Maggie to her mat. Her body weighed nothing, yet his arms ached as if he carried the weight of the future. He'd expected burdens to accompany fatherhood, but this taxing desire to protect his child no matter the cost was a surprise. He gently removed Ruth's heels from Maggie's small feet and kissed her forehead. "Good night, little one."

"Daddy, wait." She grabbed his neck and pulled him close. "Mommy's not here to help me say prayers."

"Your mother taught you prayers?"

"Of course."

"To whom do you pray?"

"Duh. God." Her brow wrinkled. "Who else?"

Had Lisbeth embraced the one God? "Ruth knows how to say children's prayers."

"No. I want you."

He risked a glance at Ruth. Surely she felt as tangled as he? His efforts to judge Ruth's frame of mind yielded nothing.

Ruth kept her eyes on the folds of fabric wrapped around Junia's tunic. She concentrated on removing them with the same gentle grace she demonstrated attending all the broken things under his roof. "We'll say them together." She helped Junia slide in next to Maggie.

"Like a family," Junia said, smiling.

"Like a family," Ruth said, allowing her eyes to drift to Cyprian.

"Family?" Barek stood, dice clattering to the floor. One of the dogs lifted his head to check on the commotion. "We're *not* one big, happy family."

"Barek, maybe you should step out into the rain and cool off," Cyprian said.

"Lisbeth of Dallas drops back into our lives after deserting us, and suddenly you're full of courage?" Ruth's son stalked from the cottage and slammed the door.

The accusation hit hard.

Ruth patted Cyprian's shoulder. "He'll come around."

"Barek's right. I have been hiding from my responsibilities, shirking my duties to you and the church." He brought Ruth's hand to his lips. "No more." There was no point in denying that the arrival of Lisbeth and Maggie had jolted him from the darkness. If they were brave enough to face the dangers of his world, surely he could muster the courage to face whatever the Lord had in store for him.

He rewarded Ruth's smile with a smile of his own, a real one that expressed the conviction that suddenly flooded him. He turned his attention back to the girls. "You first, Junia."

The child thanked the Lord for perfume and the chance to rescue Perpetua.

"Now you, Maggie."

Maggie clasped her hands and closed her eyes. "Dear God. It's me, Maggie. I'm a long way from home. But I like my new friend Junia, my uncle Larry, and my jaddah. Thank you for Ruth's baby. I hope it's a girl, because I have always wanted a sister." She opened one eye, catching Cyprian as he swallowed hard. "Most of all, thank you for my daddy. Help my mommy not to be mad at him anymore." She rubbed her nose. "And, God, *puhleeze* help Barek not to be so cranky. Love, Maggie." She opened her eyes. "Oh, I forgot one thing." She bowed her head again. "Make sure Perpetua is still under the bed."

25

A BREAK IN THE CLOUDS allowed the blood moon to shine gloriously upon Aspasius's palace. The first good sign of the return of the gods' favor he'd experienced in weeks.

He sat on the edge of his garden fountain, his feet unable to support him for any length of time, even with his declining weight. He tucked his bloated toes beneath the hem of his robe, then plucked fried snails and boiled peacock eggs from the small, boat-shaped dinner plates that floated above a tiled mosaic of a cobra striking a mongoose. The first architect he'd hired to remodel the gardens had counseled against the bloody design, offering samples of exotic fish and full-chested native women as a more peaceful alternative.

Aspasius slowly dragged his hand through the crystal waters. A dozen lacy-tailed fish imported from the East nibbled grease from his fingers. The feeding frenzy stirred ripples over the cobra and created the illusion of a snake rising to its full height, fangs poised to strike.

The image kept him sharp, reminded him that size didn't matter nearly as much as the venom of one's bite. A lesson he'd made certain that pompous architect he'd fired remembered right before the executioner's sword relieved him of his head.

Oh, how he longed for the day he would get even with

Cyprian for trying to make him appear the fool by sneaking back home.

Aspasius's gaze drifted over the luxurious outdoor space. He did not regret holding fast to his vision. This little oasis had turned out exactly as planned. Large palm trees. A raised stone stage for the naked dancers. Plenty of comfortable seating for his party guests. And a full-size altar that rivaled the granite monstrosity built in the great temple of Juno. Dire times such as these required more than a couple of household gods stuffed in a cupboard. Something much grander was needed.

He was the man Rome had charged with both the financial and spiritual responsibility of his province. Not Cyprian. An altar of his very own was not a luxury; appeasing Juno was a necessity.

Aspasius flicked water from his fingers and popped another rubbery egg into his mouth, thinking something sweet would better ease these cravings he'd had lately. Rattled bleating drew his attention toward the garden gate. "Finally."

Pytros backed through the opening, dragging a she-goat who'd been held in the temple's purification pen for the required days. The skittish animal bleated and fought the rope.

Scipios, the long-necked priest, pushed the goat with one hand and held his heavy black cloak closed at the throat with the other. Thin and in poor health, the old flamen signaled a pause, then coughed and doubled over as if he were expelling his lungs. His leather skullcap, with its chin strap and pointy wooden spindle, shifted forward and exposed the base of his pale, shaved head. When Scipios finished his hacking fit and righted himself, the apex spindle protruded from his forehead like the horn of a gemsbok, an exotic antelope imported from the southern plains to give the arena lions something to chase after he'd had to back off Christians.

"My friend." Aspasius held up a plate of snails. "Come. Have a bite to eat."

Scipios stepped around the goat and trudged across the garden. His cloak's heavy fringe dusted the pavers. He eyed Aspasius with slitted, feline eyes. "You should have called me sooner." He righted his cap.

Aspasius brushed his hands and stood. The priest towered over him by a hand's breadth, and the advantage irritated Aspasius greatly. But what was he to do? Until the gods removed their curse, the blasted pain in his feet made wearing his heeled shoes a discomfort he could no longer tolerate. "I appointed you to divine how the gods are feeling, not rule my province."

Scipios peered down his sharp nose. "It may or may not be evident what the gods will."

"Why must I suffer your vacillating pronunciations? Are the gods really so difficult to pin down? The Christians always seem so sure of *their* one God." Even as the wildcats sprang from the bowels of the arena, he'd seen beaten and bound believers offer their praise and trust to the one God. "Never in the history of the games have the arena attendees witnessed a single soul rescued from the jaws of a lion, yet the myth that true believers will be spared persists." His Roman gods were the ones who'd brought this much-needed rain. "Ours is not the strange practice. Ours is the way of truth." And Aspasius Paternus would never turn his back on what he knew worked. On the two things he trusted: himself and his gods.

"Do your work, Scipios," Aspasius commanded.

"I'll need help lifting the sacrifice to the altar."

"Well, Pytros. Don't just stand there. Help the man."

"Me?"

"Surely you don't expect your master to manhandle the animal?"

Pytros let out a disgusted sigh and circled the goat, not quite sure where to start. He wrinkled his nose and lowered himself close to the hooves. He grabbed hold of a hind leg, then a front leg, and flipped the animal on its side. The goat's flailing feet clipped the scribe's chest. Pytros let a string of curse words fly as he wrestled the animal atop the smooth altar stones. Quick as Pytros was with the stylus, he was a bit awkward securing the thin legs with the lead rope, but he finally managed the task.

"Step aside." Though Scipios appeared frail, his execution of the sacrifice was quick. His long, slender fingers wielded the knife with the skill of a field surgeon. Blood sprayed from the deep slit across the goat's throat and splattered Aspasius's robe. He lowered his chin to his chest and smiled at the redemptive sign. Scipios made another incision, and goat entrails spilled upon the altar.

The old priest clamped his buckteeth over his lower lip and reached inside the animal's warm cavity. He lifted out a gelatinous mass and brought it close for examination. A scowl drew his eyes in tightly.

"Tell me what you see," Aspasius demanded.

The priest laid the liver upon the red-hot altar. "A black spot."

"What does that mean?"

"The gods have aligned against you."

"Look again!"

Scipios stepped up to the altar. Tiny tongues of fire had charred the edges of the slick organ. He peered through the smoke. "An army of men, women, and children rising like mist from the sea and marching toward Carthage."

"Whose side are they on?" Aspasius pressed in until smoke stung his nose. He hated relying on others, especially when the margin for error was so great. "Mine or the Christians'?"

The priest looked back at him dumbly. "I don't know. They're covered in blood."

"I'm trying to save Carthage!" Aspasius bellowed. "I need more than mist and blood. I need something that will nail Christians to crosses." He jerked the priest from the altar. "I swear, if you're lying to me, I will see that you are the first to die." Aspasius stared at the curling liver, waiting for some sort of sign that the priest was wrong. "Make another offering."

"Huff all you want, Aspasius." The priest wriggled free. "It won't change the fact that the people of Carthage have turned from the gods. Religion commands their service but no longer endears their hearts. Juno has forsaken you."

"Bridge this chasm with Juno." He shook the priest. "Bridge it now, or I'll have your head."

"Your threats do not scare me." Scipios coughed, raising his bloody hands to support his chest. When the hacking fit stopped, he cleared his throat. "The gods have not granted me long life. My glory will not surpass my ancestors'."

Aspasius raised his hands to the priest's neck and clamped down hard. "Then I shall send you on your way with great speed."

"Master! No!" Pytros pulled him off. "Kill a holy flamen and you will bring protesters pounding at your doors, no matter how much they seem to disregard the gods."

The room was spinning as Aspasius backed away. "What do you suggest I do?"

Scipios held out his bloody knife grimly. "Say Scipios has succumbed to his cough. When I am out of the way, you can install a more effective mediator, one who says what you want to hear." Scipios waited, baiting Aspasius to end his miserable life. When Aspasius waved the knife away, the priest wiped his knife upon his cloak. "Or you could demand all of Carthage return to the gods."

"I've done that, you fool."

"Then make them listen this time."

"How?"

"Close the cemeteries outside the city. When they can no longer find a fresh breath of air, they will seek the gods." Although

Scipios tried to give the impression his own life mattered little to him, he beat a hasty exit, rubbing his neck on his way out the gate.

Aspasius turned and snarled at Pytros, who was trying to tidy up the altar. "Leave that."

"But the stench."

"We have more pressing business."

"Closing the cemeteries?"

"That and more." Aspasius went to the fountain and dipped his blood-splattered hands. "I want Christians afraid to leave their homes."

"How?"

"Scare them. Rough them up in the marketplace. Make them afraid to walk the streets. If Cyprian's army can't gather, they can't fight. If that doesn't work, we'll herd them into their hovels and do as Nero did: light the fires, burn them and the plague from our midst." Fish fanned the waters pinking beneath his fingers. "From the ashes of the heretics we shall raise a more solid populace. Mark my word, Pytros. Before spring my city shall once again be favored by the gods. And once it is, the friends of Cyprian's father will no longer be able to deny the danger of allowing the nobleman's son to live."

26

THE RANCID STINK OF certain death and dying hope fouled the west wing of Cyprian's villa.

So far, Diona's fever had followed the typical pattern of typhoid, rising as the sun lowered. In her fevered delirium, she mumbled constantly and picked at her bedclothes.

Diona's parents stayed close by her mat. Titus paced. Vivia's hands churned beneath the folds of her stola. Lisbeth thought the woman's behavior odd compared to most mothers of critically ill children. Usually they were so desperate to relieve their child's suffering they couldn't keep their hands off them.

But Vivia kept her hands hidden—as if she couldn't stomach any contact with things beneath her. The aristocrat's strange phobia might save her from the bad, but her unwillingness to reach out also kept her from experiencing anything good. The feel of a newborn's skin. The refreshment of cool water. The dying grip of her daughter, which was exactly where Diona was heading if something didn't turn around.

Lisbeth had no experience treating typhoid. But she knew two things: First, antibiotics and oral rehydration must take priority over other interventions. She'd already used up one of the three precious rounds of her oral antibiotic supply and poured every herbal remedy Mama mixed down the girl's throat. Yet, after nearly twelve hours of supportive treatment, Diona's condition had actually worsened. Apparently stopping typhoid's predictable progression would be very difficult without intravenous drugs. Second, she couldn't go back to the future and leave these people to suffer. At least not right away.

"Diona has always been so dramatic." Vivia watched as Lisbeth and Mama balanced on their knees, wrestling a bedpan out from under their patient. "Pouting over the many suitors her father turned away."

Titus looked up from his pacing. "It was always for her own good, Vivia."

"Diona didn't eat for nearly a week after you forbade her marriage."

"Don't blame me. You're the one who insisted Cyprian had the creeping pox."

Lisbeth's head snapped up, and she nearly spilled the foul-smelling bedpan. "Cyprian? Engaged to Diona?"

"Oh." Vivia tried to appear as if she'd made an accidental faux pas, but the jab felt intentionally placed. "I'm so sorry. I thought you knew."

"Lisbeth," Mama interrupted before Lisbeth could press the woman for details, "look." Her head tilted toward the bedpan. "Blood."

Satisfying her jealous curiosity would have to wait. "Vivia, how long have Diona's stools been bloody?" Lisbeth asked.

"Two, maybe three days." Vivia's hands twisted.

"Why would you delay your daughter's treatment?"

"You don't have to bark at my wife!"

"When Diona added blood to her complaints of belly pain, I thought she was whining about her monthly," Vivia explained.

"Her bowels could have perforated." Lisbeth conducted a quick exam. "Low pulse. Spleen swollen and tender. Abdomen distended."

"Sepsis." Mama stood. "I'll get my scalpel."

"Wait." Lisbeth's mind retraced the sketchy details of the ileal perforation surgery she'd observed in the OR as a medical student. "We don't have intravenous antibiotics, or a way to correct her electrolyte imbalance, or even an NG tube to suction her stomach."

"We'll have to improvise." Mama retrieved her tool satchel.

Improvising was Mama's go-to answer for every medical emergency. A broken arrow shaft had saved Laurentius. Elevating the head of a bed and pounding on a child's back had saved Junia. But Diona's rapidly deteriorating condition left little room for improvisation.

"Do you have any mandrake root in your bag of tricks?" Lisbeth asked.

Mama smiled. "Someone's done their homework."

She didn't consider herself anywhere near the expert herbalist that Mama had become, but she had devoted some serious study to the healing properties of natural remedies. "The least we can do is knock her out," Lisbeth said. "Any rue? We'll need to empty her stomach as best we can."

"Nothing makes a mother prouder than when her daughter knows how to induce emergency vomiting."

"You are a strange people." Vivia turned her head as if the whole subject was beneath her.

Mama and Lisbeth shared an amused glance as Mama poured rue oil into a cup of hot water and stirred until the contents turned a muddy brown. If the mixture tasted as bitter as it smelled, Diona's gag reflex would quickly accomplish what was needed. Mama added a hint of honey to make the emetic go down easier.

Lisbeth set about making the operating field as sterile as possible. She heard Ruth's voice in the kitchen. If Ruth was in the kitchen, who was watching Maggie? "Mama, I'm going to make sure someone's keeping an eye on Maggie while we knock out this surgery. I'll be right back."

Lisbeth hurried to the kitchen. "Where's Maggie?"

"In bed with Junia." Ruth chopped vegetables. "Poor Laurentius was ready for a break."

"Is Cyprian with them?"

"He, Barek, and Pontius are in the garden organizing the church into a more effective workforce."

Lisbeth couldn't drag her eyes up from the flawless movements of Ruth's hands. She hated the illogical resentment still simmering in her belly, the feelings she couldn't get a handle on, but simply by choosing not to do anything about the two-family situation for now, it was as if Cyprian had silently chosen Ruth. It seemed no matter how congenial they all tried to be, there was no going back. They'd each spent the day tending the assignments she'd made and sticking to their chosen areas of Cyprian's massive estate.

Which was just as well.

At least behind the safety of thick plaster walls, neither of them had to pretend they weren't stealing glances at the other. Lisbeth knew, coming back, that things might have changed a bit during her time away, but she had no idea she would feel so uncomfortable in her own home. She almost wished she'd stayed in Dallas rather than watch Cyprian dote on Ruth and her growing womb.

Jealousy burned in the place where her own child had developed within her womb. During those long, frightening months of waiting on Maggie's birth, she'd longed to have Cyprian's hand on her belly, to watch him smile when he felt Maggie's determined little fist pummel the walls of her watery cocoon.

Lisbeth started to reach for a vegetable but suddenly remembered they were raw, like her emotions. "Mama's doing an ileal perforation repair, and I'll be assisting. I'd appreciate it if you could keep an eye on Maggie. She likes to kick off the covers."

"I'm enjoying her. She's no trouble." Ruth scraped sliced vegetables into a large bowl. "Naomi's tending the fire close by, but if it will give you some peace, I'll sit with the girls as soon as the soup starts to simmer."

Enjoying my daughter? "Just keep an eye on her, that's all I ask."

Lisbeth returned to the typhoid hall, feeling guilty for her less than gracious response. Prickly as Lisbeth was now, she'd been even more caustic and difficult in the early days of her first visit to Carthage. Yet Ruth had patiently shared her clothes, her wisdom, and her love. Freely. Selflessly. With no strings attached to her offer of friendship. Lisbeth owed her old friend more than an apology. She owed her for introducing her to a whole new way of thinking, an introduction to Christ that had changed her life. She would find Ruth and offer an apology once they had Diona stabilized. A truce would make her time here bearable.

Lisbeth slipped back into their OR with her backpack. "I brought you something." She presented Mama with the new scalpel and suture needles she'd brought with her from the twenty-first century.

"Perfect." As Mama fingered the new equipment, her gaze traveled to a place Lisbeth could only guess at: her old operating rooms perhaps, maybe even Papa. She couldn't be sure.

Lisbeth dropped the new scalpel into the boiling water, then went around the hall, gathering lamps. She filled all three with oil and fresh wicks. After she placed a clean chamber pot within easy reach of Diona, she suggested to Vivia and Titus that they might be more comfortable waiting in the garden.

When Titus refused, Lisbeth rigged a blanket drape between Diona and her parents. "Whatever you do, stay on that side."

Titus lifted the blanket and marched to Diona. "If I'd wanted my daughter to be sliced up by a slave, I would have hired the quack who tends my horses."

Lisbeth bristled. "My mother is one of the best surgeons I've ever seen." She escorted Titus back to his chair. "If your daughter lives it will be because that wonderful *doctor* saved her life. Step around that blanket again, either of you, and I'll throw you out of here myself." She strode around the drape and lit the lamps.

"I hope you haven't made promises I can't keep," Mama whispered as she concocted an antibacterial solution of warm water, goldenseal, myrrh, and turmeric to wash the peritoneal cavity once she repaired the leak. "Ready?"

Not really. "When you are." Lisbeth dropped to her knees opposite Mama, gloved up, and lifted the girl's head.

Mama managed to pour a few sips of the rue down Diona's throat. Within seconds, the gut-wrenching results left their patient so weak she barely had the strength to chew on the dried mandrake root.

Once Diona's eyelids closed and her body went limp, Lisbeth removed the parsnip-shaped bark with the strong, earthy fragrance.

Mama stood ready with a stainless steel scalpel in one hand and a blunt bronze metal probe in the other. She swiped her brow on her sleeve. "Here we go." She leaned in and made a long, vertical incision.

Diona didn't flinch.

Mama used metal hooks to clasp the lip of the abdominal walls and expose the small intestine. "Hold these."

Lisbeth took over the hooks. "You know they have little cameras that can look around inside a person now."

"You don't say." Mama lifted healthy gray sections of bowel and carefully searched for the tear. "I'd rather trust my hands and eyes, but I'd give my right arm for some decent Kelly forceps."

"I'll keep that in mind next time I come." *Next time? There won't be a next time.* Lisbeth blinked back tears. How would she convince her mother to take Laurentius and leave with her when there were so many depending on her here? Was she going to lose Mama as well?

Mama poked around until she found the fiery ulceration on the intestine. A quick debridement of the perforation's ragged edges was quickly followed with some well-placed sutures. "We'll clean up the infection as best we can, then close."

Lisbeth plugged the earbuds of her stethoscope into her ears to check Diona's vitals.

"So much blood." Vivia peered over the draping.

"Lady, I said not to look over here." Lisbeth tilted her head to indicate Vivia should sit down.

"I hear singing. Do you?"

"It's impossible to hear anything with you jabbering."

"It is the water goddess." Vivia's wide eyes were locked on her daughter's open gut. "She comes from the sea to cry for the loss of her children."

"You've not lost your child." Lisbeth draped the stethoscope around her neck and handed Mama the antibacterial wash. "Titus, you better get her out of here."

"But I hear the water goddess—"

"I don't believe in your gods, Vivia." Lisbeth dabbed fluid from the open cavity.

"Then it must be the Christians singing."

Lisbeth and Mama glanced at each other over their masks.

"People talk, you know." Vivia clutched the lip of the drape. "Titus didn't want to come to the healer of the Christians, but I said we had no choice. Galen wanted to cut her wrists. Bleed her out a little. I said no." Her lips pursed, as if she might vomit. "And look . . . you've done worse."

Lisbeth and Mama kept working.

"Do you believe in the one God of these Christians?" Vivia asked.

This was one of those moments Lisbeth had considered since she first saw Christians ripped apart in the arena. Would she have the courage to stand up for her beliefs? Declare Jesus her Lord in the face of hatred?

Lisbeth slowly lifted her eyes to meet Vivia's earnest expression. "I do."

She noticed Mama's pleased smile, and she knew, for this moment at least, that her faith had passed its test. However, if there was a sword poised over her neck or a lion charging at her child, she wasn't sure she could trust her thin courage to remain so bold.

"Can this one God help Diona?" Vivia's voice quivered with more emotion than Lisbeth had seen or heard since her arrival.

"We're praying to him now," Mama said. "Now, Titus, you need to get her out of here."

Titus put his hands on Vivia's shoulders. "Come, my dear."

Lisbeth and Mama cast each other relieved glances.

Mama slowly irrigated the infection from the peritoneal cavity. "Apparently you didn't limit your studies to infectious diseases and herbal remedies."

How could she put into words how the selfless acts she'd witnessed on her last visit had changed her? Anything she could say would only be a clumsy attempt to explain something that just didn't make sense. She felt as naked as the first time she and Cyprian had made love, and strangely, just as happy.

"Lisbeth! Come quickly!" Ruth stood at the door of the typhoid hall, her face void of color. "Maggie's gone!"

27

LISBETH ABRUPTLY DROPPED THE surgical retractors into the bowl of hot water and rose from her squatting position beside the operating mat. "Are you sure she's gone, Ruth?"

"I've searched everywhere."

Maggie would never step out on her own, especially into the confines of the dark. She was afraid of everything . . . or at least she had been . . . until they came here. And that's what scared Lisbeth. Budding courage and a totally new and dangerous world could be a precarious combination. The scar on her own wrist was proof of the perils of fearlessness, and the scar on her heart, that of foolishness.

Lisbeth tore the gloves from her hands. "Where's Cyprian?"

"Still with the church. In the garden."

She raced from the typhoid hall. Fear thundered in her chest as she burst into the garden.

Twenty or thirty of the same people who'd come to help her reorganize the hospital had returned and were bunched around the fire, their arms outstretched over the flames and their faces intent on whatever was being said.

Lisbeth pushed through the crowd. Cyprian and Barek were seated on a stone bench. Between them sat Felicissimus. "What? Why is he here?"

Cyprian jumped to his feet. "Lisbeth?"

Part of her wanted to demand explanations for Felicissimus's presence, to expose his betrayal, but the swift retribution he deserved would have to wait. "Maggie"—tumbling from her lips—"is missing."

Cyprian rushed forward and put his hands on her shoulders. "Calm down. She's probably just hiding, playing one of her many games."

Before Lisbeth could reply, Ruth interrupted. "No. Junia is missing, too."

"They're together?" Lisbeth didn't know whether to be relieved or even more frightened. Maggie had grown much braver since she'd jumped into this world. No telling what she might do with an older friend to egg her on. "Where could they have gone?"

Barek stepped forward. "They must have gone to the tenements."

"How do you know?" Lisbeth demanded. Barek glanced from Cyprian to Ruth. Lisbeth grabbed the boy's arm. "Tell me."

"Maggie wanted a doll."

"I don't understand."

Cyprian shimmied into a cloak and tossed another to Pontius. "Junia left a doll under the bed in her old apartment." He added a small dagger to his belt. "Maggie asked me to get it for her."

"And you told her no, right?"

"Of course," Cyprian snapped. "But she has a will as strong as her mother's."

The knot in Lisbeth's lower abdomen told her what Barek and Cyprian had said was true. Maggie *would* risk everything to get her hands on a doll. "Let's go."

"You're not going. Barek, Pontius, and I will fetch the girls."

"Do you know where Junia used to live?" Lisbeth asked pointedly. "I do. I stayed there several days after her parents died."

"She's right, Cyprian," said Pontius. "The tenements are far too large to search blindly."

Cyprian reluctantly agreed. "Very well, but you will follow my instructions."

"Fine."

"Then we're all set to go," Ruth said.

"Whoa." Cyprian snagged Ruth's arm. "You have no reason to put yourself in danger."

Determination pushed Ruth's normally perfect features out of place. "Junia is like my own daughter." Refusing to entertain any further arguments, she ordered the dogs to stay and went to ask Naomi to keep an eye on Laurentius before leaving.

Lisbeth paced, furious they'd been forced to wait on Ruth to join their little entourage. Mama emerged from the typhoid hall, wiping her hands on a towel. Lisbeth quickly filled her in on what was going on and kissed her cheek.

Ruth hurried in, buttoning her clasp as she ran. "I'm ready."

"May the hand of God hide our babies from harm." Mama saw them to the door and collared the dogs. "I'll pray and keep a lamp burning."

28

"I'VE OFFERED THE SACRIFICES Scipios required." Aspasius sat on the edge of his bed, cursing the priest who'd attended him earlier. Why did his foot continue to rot? Because as long as Cyprianus Thascius was still alive, so was the threat to his gods.

Pinching the frayed tip of his leg bindings between his thumb and index finger, Aspasius slowly unwound the strips of cloth supporting his swollen ankle.

He never tended his own feet. The ugly ministrations were more suited to his mute slave, Iltani. Her lack of a tongue kept his secret safe. But tonight he needed privacy. He feared something sinister lurked beneath the green and yellow stains of his bandages. Until he knew exactly what he was dealing with, he could not risk the small chance that Iltani would grow a tongue and ruin him.

If Pytros managed to secure a competent physician tonight, Aspasius would be fit as a legionnaire for the day of Cyprian's execution.

Aspasius tugged on his bindings, glancing at the hourglass. Pytros had been gone for hours. Doctors were becoming harder and harder to find. As Carthage citizens continued to succumb in greater and greater numbers, most of the itinerant medical craftsmen had gathered their rusty tools and their little bags of herbs and set out for parts unknown. He'd done everything he could think of to keep as many doctors in town as possible, even reducing their tax liabilities to nearly nothing.

And yet, when he needed medical care, could a qualified man be found? He'd specifically instructed his scribe not to return with one of those quacks trained in Greece and seeking asylum in the provinces because of some unfortunate death they'd caused a nobleman's family.

He wanted a real healer. Someone like . . . no. He dare not say *her* name, for it would only serve to rub salt into his already festering wound. If Magdalena was indeed the healer the plebs sought in Cyprian's home, taking her now would tip Cyprian to his plan before he had everything in place.

Chills rattled his teeth. Aspasius peeled the final cloth strip stuck to the oozing sore on the ball of his foot. A foul smell, hot and sweet like fermenting fruit, stung his nostrils. He lifted his foot for a better look, wincing as he crossed his ankle over his knee. His toes were blood red and hot to the touch, and no wonder. The raw place had grown in size and more fiery in disposition. Oh, for the love of Juno, why had he allowed Magdalena to escape?

Aspasius cursed and threw the soiled bindings at the row of useless idols that lined his window ledge. Mercury. Juno. Jupiter. He snatched the flickering oil lamp and would have foolishly thrown it, too, had he not recognized Pytros's knock at his door. "What took you so long?" Aspasius growled as his scribe hurried in.

"Why is your foot not elevated?" Pytros closed the door behind him.

"You left me so long, I had to take things into my own hands."

"Finding a man who claims to be a doctor is not easy."

"But you found one?"

"Well, sort of." Pytros pushed a footrest within easy reach of Aspasius. "This man received his training in the service of the emperor."

Aspasius carefully lowered his foot upon the cushioned stool. "Serving him how?"

Pytros diverted his eyes and mumbled, "Keeping the army's mounts healthy."

"A horse doctor?"

"After he was dismissed from imperial service, he did find employment among the patricians."

Aspasius caught Pytros staring at his swollen foot. He tossed the edge of his robe across the grotesque appendage. "Has the situation really come to this? The wealthy treated no better than a soldier's mount? I blame the Christians for this indignity." He pinched the throb between his eyes. "Don't just stand there. Bring him in."

Pytros opened the bedroom door and motioned someone in. "This is Galen."

A serious man with haggard eyes and a blood-splattered cloak stepped cautiously into the room. He sniffed the air. "Infection." He wrinkled his nose. "Open the shutters."

"Good gods, man. Can't you see I have the chills?" The pungent odor of horse manure clung to the man's boots. Aspasius knew his fine carpets would be worthless if he allowed this man entrance. On the other hand, turning away the only available help would ensure his leg would suffer a worse fate. "Shouldn't you at least examine my wound before making pronouncements?"

Galen shifted the strap of the bag slung over his shoulder. "First, we shall discuss my price."

Aspasius raised his brows. "A horse doctor making demands. What next? Christians burning the temples of my gods?"

"Heal yourself then, consul." Galen wheeled and reached for the door.

"Name your price, pleb."

Galen peered over his shoulder, his expression wary. "I have a few outstanding gambling debts."

"Why am I not surprised?" Aspasius raised his hands in surrender when Galen once again started for the door. "Consider them paid."

"And . . ." Galen paused as if what he had to say next deserved Aspasius's full attention.

"And?"

"I no longer wish to peddle my services at the stables of the rich. I want a permanent place in your employ. A warm bed to call my own. Hot soup in my belly every night. And to never see the back end of a horse again."

"You want the respect the medical profession does not deserve."

"Very well. Heal your own foot."

Aspasius did not appreciate being robbed in his own home, but obviously it had come down to the fact that he had little choice. "Whom did you last serve? Anyone who can give you references?"

"The daughter of Titus Cicero. I was tending Titus's stable, but after the scum's personal physician fled, he had no one to bleed Diona's sickness from her veins."

"Cicero, you say?" Aspasius apprised the man anew. Perhaps he'd been a bit hasty in his judgment. "Titus owns most of the fields and granaries from here to Curubis."

"Yes," Galen agreed. "And the blackguard holds his silver tight as a green head of wheat."

Aspasius lightly drummed his fingers on his leg. "Did you say *bleed* Diona?"

"Weren't you listening, or do I need to mix a tonic to unstop your ears as well?" Galen dug through his bag. "Restoring your hearing will cost extra. I'll have to grind some earthworms—"

"My ears are fine." Aspasius worked to keep Galen on task. "Tell me what ailed the lovely girl."

"She has the slum sickness."

Aspasius's breath caught. When had the sickness made its way into the upper classes? "And you healed her, right?"

Galen gave a shrug. "I do not know."

"How can you not know, man? Either she's alive or she's dead."

"Titus and Vivia disappeared in the night, taking Diona with them, as well as my payment."

"How am I to keep this city afloat when patricians run like frightened rabbits to their mountain estates?"

"How am I to eat when the rich do not pay for services rendered?" Galen retorted with no thought to how easily Aspasius could order his head removed. "Titus did not go to the mountains."

"No?" Aspasius motioned him closer, suddenly very interested in this horse doctor. "Where, then?"

Galen shrugged again. "His servants say Titus sought your healer."

So it was true. Magdalena was hiding under his nose. "My healer? Where?"

"At the house of Thascius." Galen removed a long blade from his bag. "Why would your healer be at his house when you are obviously so ill?" He swiped the bloody tool on his tunic, then pointed the tip at Aspasius's foot. "I can bleed that out for you."

"No knives!" Aspasius yelled. "Tell me what you know of Cyprian!"

Galen held the blade over the lamp's flame. "You stand to lose your leg."

"If you wish to leave here without that knife brought across your tongue, you will answer me."

"Honest work deserves honest pay."

"I'll pay you for your information."

Galen considered the offer. "I went to the nobleman's back

gate hoping to sneak up on Titus. Not to hurt him. Just to scare him into giving me what he owed me. As I shimmied over the fence, I saw a man who resembled the one who boarded that exile ship more than a year ago. He's thinner, but I don't forget a face."

"What of him? Tell me everything."

"He had what looked to be a small army with him."

"Army? Were they armed?"

"Buckets, spades, brooms." Galen held out the heated blade. "I'll be quick. Won't even charge you extra."

"No one cuts me. Out!"

"What about my money?"

"Out!" The lamp flickered with the slamming of the door.

Pytros looked to Aspasius and shrugged. "He was all I could find. Do you want me to seek another?"

"No, fool." Aspasius threw a pillow squarely at Pytros's head. "I want you to round up a few soldiers and drag *my* healer and that underhanded coward Cyprian back to me!"

"You can't kill the man to whom the emperor has granted a reprieve. You'd risk immediate removal from office." Pytros rubbed his head. "Kill the woman who can heal you, and you risk your life."

"Continue to do nothing, and I'm a dead man either way."

"You've managed thus far without Magdalena. You still do not have the favor of the gods. What's a couple more days of letting her and Cyprian think they are safe?"

Aspasius glanced at his foot. "Tomorrow I'll visit the steam baths and boil the pus from my body." He carefully slid his feet into his fleecy slippers. "You will bring Felicissimus to my private chamber there."

29

"YOU SAID IT WASN'T far to your old house." Maggie pinched her nose as she hurried to keep up with Junia. The big orange moon disappeared behind the tall buildings when they turned down the alley where Junia used to live. "It's too dark." Maggie tried to calm her breathing and flicked on the flashlight she'd taken from her mother's backpack. She aimed the beam at Junia's head and giggled. "Your eyes are huge."

"What is that?"

"Flashlight. It's for seeing in the dark." Maggie waved the white light over stacks of bodies like the ones her mother wouldn't let her look at when Barek hauled them out of the well. "Why do dead people smell bad?"

Junia took the light from her. "Don't be a baby, Maggie."

"I'm not a baby." Her bare feet were cold. The sheet Junia had tied around her shoulders like a princess cape wasn't nearly as warm as the Little Mermaid hoodie Queenie had given her for her birthday. She'd left that jacket with her g-pa back at the desert camp. But she wasn't going to cry like a baby. "It stinks here."

"I wasn't the one who had to have the doll tonight." Junia turned around and around in the street like she wasn't sure which way to go. She shined the light up and down the tall buildings. "We should have waited on your father."

Maggie didn't appreciate being scolded. She was getting to know her daddy and she liked him well enough, but she didn't completely trust him to deliver on his promises. "Are you lost?"

"No," Junia said. "It's been a long time since I was here, that's all." But she looked lost to Maggie. "We should have asked Barek to bring us."

"He's too cranky."

"I know. I know." Junia sighed. "He needs a nap." She held out her arm. "Shhh. Do you hear that?"

"What is it?" Maggie's teeth chattered.

"Somebody's following us," Junia whispered, and clicked off the light.

Steps came closer. Maggie could hear men mumbling. She slipped her hand inside Junia's and peeked over her shoulder. Two dark forms hurried toward them.

Maggie cupped her mouth and whispered, "What should we do?"

Junia pulled her close. "When I say run, you run."

"Which way?"

"Follow me." Junia dropped the flashlight. "Run!"

They took off down the alley, their bare feet pounding the stones. Suddenly two other men jumped out in front of them.

Maggie screamed.

"This way." Junia jerked her around. They headed back in the direction they'd come from. The two men who were behind them earlier now blocked the alley. Maggie and Junia froze.

In the shaft of moonlight that sneaked between the buildings, Maggie could see the men better. They had hoods over their heads. Big white eyes shone from their sooty faces. They laughed—deep, growling laughs—and raised their hands.

Maggie whipped around. The other two men were doing the same thing. She inched her back against Junia's.

One of the men moved in. He circled them slowly. His smile was missing more teeth than G-Pa's cook. "Too young to sell." His breath smelled like the nasty fish sticks G-Pa cooked on nights Mommy stayed late at the hospital.

Another man stepped in close. "We could rent them out." He reached for Junia.

She slapped at his hand. "Don't touch me."

The man grabbed Maggie's wrist. He spun her around and pinned her arms to her side. "Or we could just eat you both."

"Stranger!" Maggie screamed at the top of her lungs. "Stranger danger!"

30

THE NIGHT AIR PRESSED against the urgency driving Lisbeth toward the tenements. The city was quiet except for the distant rumble of supply carts and the buzz of flies circling decomposing corpses. Rancid bran dumped in the streets for the roaming pigs and the tang of *garum*—the fermented fish sauce favored by the plebs who frequented the taverns and cheaper eating houses—added to the nauseating smells. But the dominating odor: urine.

Lisbeth tied a cloth across her nose. If they didn't get the sewage problem cleaned up and fast, typhoid would make the measles plague look like a bad cold.

"Stay close." Cyprian led the way.

He'd insisted on going without a torch to keep from attracting unwanted attention. Lisbeth followed Pontius. Ruth followed her. Barek brought up the rear, his hand on the hilt of a concealed dagger.

Once they passed the market, the broad avenues of the patrician neighborhoods narrowed into the slum district where meeting an oxcart would force a person to squeeze into the nearest doorway until the vehicle passed. Simmering onions, most likely scavenged outside the city walls to flavor watery broths, scented the darkened streets with a bitter hopelessness. Few could afford a carrot for their soup let alone meat, or oil for their lamps. The tenement buildings were black as the hole in the Cave of the Swimmers. Lisbeth wished she'd thought to bring the flashlight tucked in her backpack. If it weren't for the pale moon, they wouldn't be able to see their hands in front of their eyes.

A few men warmed themselves at a small fire ring. When the ruffians noticed the newcomers on their turf, they left the fire and started toward the little search party.

Lisbeth braced for an attempted mugging.

Nearby screams echoed off the cramped buildings. "Stranger danger!"

"That's Maggie!" Lisbeth sprinted past Cyprian at a dead run. "Maggie! Mommy's coming! Hang on, baby!"

Tracking Maggie's desperate pleas, Lisbeth vaulted over dead bodies. She could tell from the frantic pitch, her little girl was trapped. Lisbeth rounded a corner and skidded to a stop. Four men had Maggie and Junia surrounded.

"Maggie!" Without taking time to catch her breath, Lisbeth lowered her head and charged.

Her head smashed into the back of the nearest man and sent him sprawling onto the pavement. She wheeled and went for the bulbous nose of the man restraining Maggie by the shoulders.

"Let go of my daughter!" She thrashed him with her bare hands. "Let her go!"

In the middle of the struggle, Cyprian arrived, dagger drawn.

"Release them!" Cyprian raised the dagger. "Now!"

The man turned Maggie loose and drew a knife.

Maggie flew across the alley. "Daddy!"

Pontius and Barek arrived. Weapons drawn, they charged toward the scum choking Junia. The man saw them coming and shoved Junia toward them and ran. One after another, the other men, even the one with the knife, backed away and disappeared into the shadows.

Hot anger pumped through Lisbeth's veins. She didn't know whether to hug Maggie or chew her out. She opened her arms. "Maggie!" Maggie released her hold on Cyprian's legs and ran to her. "Are you okay, baby?"

"She's not a baby," Junia said. "She was kicking and biting and screaming like a madwoman."

"I remembered 'stranger danger,' Mommy." Maggie smiled, her lip bloody.

"Yes. Yes, you did." Lisbeth scooped her up and kissed her cheek again and again, amazed that her daughter was letting her hold her so tightly.

Ruth arrived, huffing and out of breath. "Junia!" The girl ran to her and began to sob. "It's all right. You're safe now."

"Let's get these spoiled brats out of here"—Barek waved his dagger—"before those plebeian scumbags come back with their friends."

"But what about Perpetua?" Maggie pleaded.

"Who?" Lisbeth asked.

"Junia's doll. We came for her, and we're so close we should get her. Right, Junia?"

"I guess." Junia wiped her nose. "I don't remember for sure where I lived."

Lisbeth quickly surveyed the surroundings. Six years ago, she'd spent several terrifying days in this apartment complex tending Junia. She would never forget the tiny room where both of Junia's parents had died or this very path that had led to the well where she'd fetched water for Junia's vaporizer. "That's Junia's old apartment there. But I don't want to risk any more trouble. Let's go."

"No, Mommy. Please."

"Pontius and I will stand guard," Cyprian said. "Barek, run and look under the bed."

"No. Someone could be living there."

"Barek, please," Ruth said. "We're here. What could it hurt to knock?"

"I could die for a doll; that's what it could hurt!" Ruth's son wheeled and stormed off.

Shortly, they heard a soft knock and then the careful creak of a door. A few minutes later Barek shot out of the apartment, a dirty-faced doll clutched in his hand. "Place was deserted, except for the rats." He crammed the doll into Maggie's arms. "Here, brat."

"Mommy, why did you bring the cranky one?"

"Let's go, Maggie."

"I'm tired."

Lisbeth attempted to lift Maggie to her hip, but with her adrenaline spent, her legs had turned to jelly.

"I've got her." Cyprian scooped up Maggie and her doll. He ran the back of his finger along Lisbeth's chin. "You've got a cut."

It felt good having Cyprian here, helping carry the burden of their daughter. Papa's help had been a godsend, but for the first time since Maggie was born she didn't feel so alone. Being a single parent was tough. She wouldn't wish the demands of it on anyone.

Lisbeth wiped at the blood. "I'm fine." She glanced at Ruth, who had watched the brief exchange between her and Cyprian with a strange expression, more of a longing for what she'd lost than what she now had. Lisbeth lowered her chin and stepped back. "Come on, Ruth. I'll help you get Junia home."

She and Ruth did their best to keep up as their party hurried through the narrow streets. As they neared the market the sound of supply carts clattering over the uneven pavers grew louder.

Somewhere ahead of them, the crack of an oxen whip sounded. The snap of chains and panicked shouts followed. Hooves thundered over the cobblestones. Lisbeth looked up to see a frightened ox. Horns down, he charged straight toward them.

"Run!" Lisbeth grabbed Ruth's hand, but Ruth's attempt to redistribute her bulk slowed her response. "Ruth! Move!"

The giant animal plowed into Ruth. The velocity ripped her from Lisbeth's grip. Ruth flew through the air. Lisbeth and Junia slammed into the wall.

Powerless to stop what happened next, Lisbeth watched Ruth hit the pavement directly in the ox's path. Hands clamped across her belly, she churned beneath a thousand pounds of thrashing, stumbling animal. A paper doll in a shredder. The ox failed to regain its forward momentum and went down hard, burying Ruth under its tawny hide.

Lisbeth snapped to her feet, screaming, "Ruth!"

"Mother!" Barek ran toward them with his weapon drawn.

Sharp, cloven hooves sliced the air. In an instant, the animal's powerful hind legs found footing in Ruth's middle. Agonizing screams ripped through the alley. The beast hauled his great weight upright, then spun in circles, searching for which way to go.

"Over here!" Cyprian waved his cloak like a matador.

Barek ripped his cloak off. "No, over here!"

The skittish ox bellowed and pawed the pavement. He cut right, then left, raising and lowering his massive horns. Cyprian moved in closer, his cape the only thing between him and the angry animal. He tossed his cloak. Before it could cover the ox's head, the bull turned on a dime and galloped off in the opposite direction, his head high and his freedom call echoing in the alleyway. The breathless cart driver arrived, screamed at the horror that was Ruth, and then raced after his property.

Lisbeth and Cyprian ran to the center of the street. Ruth lay like a crumpled bag of old clothes, her body crushed into a spreading pool of blood. Lisbeth's knees gave out.

"Help her," Cyprian begged Lisbeth as he dropped beside

Ruth. "I'm here, Ruth." He dug through the fabric of her bloody cloak and found her hand. "You're all right."

"Mother!" Barek peeled himself off the wall. "Oh, God! There's so much blood."

Lisbeth's breath came in panicked, gulping sobs. "Ruth!" A search for a carotid pulse produced a faint throb. "She's alive." She swept Ruth's hair away from her face. "Stay with me, Ruth."

"Mommy!"

Lisbeth whirled to see Maggie and Junia standing beside Barek, their faces white, eyes filled with terror. "Get the girls out of here, Barek." She ripped off her cape. Moving Ruth was irresponsible, but leaving her friend to die in the street was out of the question. She would need surgical help to save Ruth. "Tell Mama to prepare for an incoming C-section." Lisbeth wadded her cape in preparation for stanching a massive bleeder once she turned Ruth over. "Move it!"

"Go, Barek." Cyprian's raw voice rose above the thrum of fear in Lisbeth's ears. "Pontius and I will bring your mother home."

"Give me your cloak, Cyprian." Lisbeth checked for broken bones as Cyprian ran and retrieved the heavy cloth from where he'd dropped it in the street. "You take hold at her head. Careful with her neck."

Cyprian dropped to his knees at Ruth's head.

"I'll need yours, too, Pontius." Pontius kneeled at Ruth's feet.

Lisbeth spread Pontius's garment on the stones. She moved in beside Cyprian and placed her hands on either side of Ruth's head. Neck stabilized, she gave the order, and Cyprian and Pontius gently rolled Ruth onto the makeshift stretcher. Cyprian gasped. Blood quickly saturated the tunic stretched over Ruth's belly.

"Lift on three," Lisbeth ordered.

Cyprian and Pontius gently moved Ruth's battered body.

Her eyes fluttered open. "The baby."

"I'm here, Ruth." Lisbeth tucked Cyprian's cape around the bulge of Ruth's stomach.

Ruth caught Lisbeth's hand, her grip weak but sure. "Save my baby."

"I will, Ruth. I will." Lisbeth pushed down the fear pounding in her chest and ordered them to move out. "STAT!"

By the time they arrived at the villa, Barek had worked himself into a lather. He paced the courtyard with a torch. "This way," he said, and led them into the villa through a back entrance.

Mama had emptied Lisbeth's backpack. Combining their supplies, she'd turned the kitchen into a fairly sterile operating theater. Cyprian and Pontius hefted the cape and gently slid Ruth onto the clean, wooden table.

"Mother!" Barek pushed to Ruth's side.

"Get that torch out of my way, boy," Mama ordered.

Barek backed into a corner of the room, his face ghostly pale in the flickering light.

Cyprian's face had also drained of color. He gathered Ruth's hand into his and whispered, "Tell me what to do to help you."

"Pray." A tear trickled from Ruth's eye. "It's too early for the baby. I'm sorry, I should have listened to you."

"There's nothing for you to be sorry about." He kissed her hand.

"Our bodies disappoint us in this life." Ruth's breaths were labored and becoming more and more unproductive. "But in the next . . . we will be glorious. I'm sure of it."

"Don't talk." He kissed her lips lightly.

"Mother." Barek crammed the torch in a wall sconce and surged forward. "Don't leave me."

"I'm sorry this has all been so hard for you, my son." She

reached for him. "We'll see each other again." Ruth grimaced, and a gush of fluid spread between her legs. "Promise me you'll hold tightly to these people. They love you." She squeezed his hand. "And tighter to our hope."

"I think her water just broke," Lisbeth whispered to Mama.

"Cyprian, I'll need hot water . . . lots of it." Mama gently nudged him aside. "Go. Take Barek with you." The men each kissed Ruth one last time. As soon as they were out of the kitchen, Mama began issuing orders. "Administer the mandrake."

"What about a presurgery antibiotic?"

Mama shook her head. "You only have two rounds left."

"Ruth has to have a round." Lisbeth punched tablets from the Z-Pak. "Swallow these." After Ruth swallowed the pills, Lisbeth broke off a piece of the fetid bark. "Chew on this, Ruth."

Mama cut away Ruth's tunic. Lisbeth bit back a gasp. A huge gash had opened Ruth's middle from below the sternum to her belly button. Mama carefully swabbed around the jagged wound with a fresh batch of her homemade antiseptic wash.

Ruth weakly motioned for Lisbeth to remove the bark protruding from her mouth.

"What is it, Ruth?"

"You have been"—Ruth pulled Lisbeth close and spoke through the pain—"and will always be my friend."

"Oh, Ruth. I don't deserve—"

"Take care of my baby."

"I won't have to. You're going to be fine."

"There are many things you can control, Lisbeth of Dallas. Death is not one of them." Ruth smiled. "Promise you'll love my children."

"Ruth . . . I—"

"Promise."

"Of course. I promise."

"And that you'll bury me beside my Caecilianus." Ruth would not allow the bark slipped between her teeth until Lisbeth nodded her assent.

"Nobody's burying anyone today." Lisbeth placed her hand on Ruth's shoulder. "Please, Ruth, chew."

Ruth closed her eyes and made an effort to move her lips, but the analgesic was slow and ineffective. Her blood loss was already great, and she was hemorrhaging at an increasing rate.

Mama picked up the scalpel. "We can't wait any longer."

Find a loophole. Think of something. God, perform a miracle. Lisbeth grabbed Ruth's hand. There was no better course of treatment. "Hang on to me, Ruth."

The ox's horn had ripped open the peritoneal cavity but not the uterine wall. Once Mama was in, Lisbeth gently placed Ruth's hand on the table and picked up a pair of hooks to hold back the abdominal layers while Mama cut through the thin layers of the muscular sac protecting the baby. Ruth's torturous screams rattled the dishes stacked on the shelf.

Mama worked frantically to reach the baby. "The head."

Lisbeth swallowed bile rising in the back of her throat. The little skull had a deep, hoof-shaped indentation. Mama dropped her scalpel in a bowl of hot water and reached in and lifted out a tiny boy. Perfect, except for the massive injury to the back of his head.

Mama listened to his motionless chest with the stethoscope.

Lisbeth sucked in deep breaths to calm the panic spreading from her stomach. "Breathe, little fellow," she whispered.

Mama gave a useless shake of her head and handed the dead infant, no bigger than a small eggplant, off to Lisbeth. "We've got to save Ruth."

Lisbeth stared at the still body, silently counting tiny fingers and toes. Images of holding Maggie for the first time flashed in her mind. Pink. Alive. Kicking. A magical moment that had forever changed her world.

Lisbeth gently wrapped the miniature version of Cyprian in a blanket and carefully covered the boy's face. She placed him in a basket and returned to the operating table.

Between the shock from blood loss and the mandrake, Ruth was too loopy to ask after her son. *Thank God.* She did not want to be the one to deny Ruth a reason to live.

They worked through the night. Mama shouting orders and doing her best to repair damaged organs. Lisbeth digging through their scant supplies as fast as she could and praying.

It was astounding how much blood a woman could lose in childbirth, especially when things went wrong. And tonight, everything had gone wrong. What would have been a simple, easy delivery in a few weeks had turned into a nightmare.

Dawn crept through the shutter slats, shedding light on the truth. Despite everything they had tried, life was quickly ebbing from Ruth.

Mama wiped her brow with the back of her hand, then peeled off her gloves. "We have to let her go."

Lisbeth wrapped her fingers around Ruth's limp hand, wishing she could somehow will her own strength into her friend. She watched Ruth's chest, counting the expanding gap of seconds between the rise and fall of her respirations. Ruth gasped, went rigid, then slowly released her last breath.

Grief constricted Lisbeth's airways and shredded her protest. "No."

Mama gently closed Ruth's eyes and covered her face with a cloth. Drenched in blood and exhausted, she stepped back from the table, dropped her head into her hands, and wept.

Lisbeth stared at the damage her return had inflicted. The

kitchen was a mess of soiled rags and discarded medical instruments. Mama's strong resolve had dissolved into an emotional wreck. And despite the brightening of the sun, the room had the darkness that comes when pure light is snuffed out.

She had always heard that life passes before your eyes right before you die. What had Ruth thought when she looked up to see a thousand pounds of flailing hooves hurtling toward her? Had her eyes searched the alley for kind, old Caecilianus or for her handsome second husband? Or was Ruth so focused on saving the daughter of her dear friend that she'd not been thinking about herself at all? Lisbeth raced for an empty pot upon the shelf and retched.

"Are you okay?" Mama rubbed her back as Lisbeth continued purging the ugliness inside her.

Lisbeth nodded and wiped her mouth with the back of her hand.

As a doctor, she knew the mechanics of death. She could recite the sequential order of the devastating effects of trauma, organ failure, and the final shutting down of every system. But despite having watched more than her fair share of people expire, she wasn't prepared for the emotional destructiveness of losing the best friend she'd ever had.

31

LISBETH RINSED HER MOUTH, but the bitter taste lingered on her tongue. It took a few minutes before her trembling hands regained enough stability to help Mama prepare Ruth's body for viewing. While Mama sponged the blood from Ruth's battered limbs, Lisbeth undid her friend's thick blond braid. She brushed all the dirt and dried fluids from the golden waves, then arranged the shimmering cascade around Ruth's pale, bare shoulders. They crossed Ruth's stiffening arms to form a protective cradle around the bundled baby boy resting on her chest.

Mama raised a clean sheet to conceal the neat row of stitches she'd woven across the empty place in Ruth's belly. "We've done all we can."

"Did we?" In the sputtering light of the torch, Ruth looked peaceful. The beautiful mother, woman, and friend she had always been. "I shouldn't have let her go."

"Her Junia was lost, too." Mama tucked a strand of Lisbeth's hair behind her ear. "You're a mother. Could someone have stopped you?"

Lisbeth filled a wooden bucket with water and dropped to her knees. She dragged a rag over the tiles. The more she scrubbed, the wider the red circle grew. Cold, wet stains seeped through the fabric stretched across her knees. Her tunic would never be the same, and neither would she. How was she going to tell Cyprian?

The prospect of facing him turned Lisbeth's empty stomach. She'd had to announce deaths to family members before. It seemed like just yesterday when she had to tell that young father his wife had died of measles. Sad as it was to watch him sob, she'd been able to extricate herself, put distance between his grief and her failure. But this was different. Despite all that had transpired, Ruth was like the sister she never had. And hardest of all, Ruth would still be alive if she hadn't come back and screwed everything up.

Tough as Cyprian's grief would be to witness, telling Barek, Junia, Maggie, and Laurentius was the chore she most dreaded. She predicted inconsolable meltdowns. She was as ill-equipped as this ancient kitchen to handle the trauma of this awful news.

She hated the power of death. Wasn't that why she was here? To stop a plague from killing innocent people in the future and to prevent Cyprian's senseless death in the past? So far, not only had she failed to accomplish her tasks, she'd made things worse.

She kissed Mama's cheek. "I guess it's time to tell everyone." She prayed God would give her the perfect words. Something wise. Something reassuring. Something as comforting as Ruth would say to her.

She stepped into the garden where Cyprian and Barek paced.

"Lisbeth?" Cyprian asked hopefully.

She willed herself to look into their anxious faces. "The baby didn't make it."

Cyprian sank onto a bench. "And Ruth?"

Lisbeth shook her head. As the news lowered his shoulders, she longed to reach for him, to take him in her arms and absorb the brunt of his grief.

"You let my mother die?" Barek cursed, and hit the wall.

"What?"

Barek wheeled and shook his fist in her face. "You wanted her dead. Out of the way so you could have Cyprian to yourself!"

Had she? His accusation was more than that of a frightened and angry child who'd lost his mother and desperately wanted her back. Barek had put into words what she hadn't the courage to allow herself to consider. If Cyprian had chosen her, what would have happened to Ruth? To their child? To the home they'd built together?

"Your mother was my friend." Lisbeth tried to sidestep him. "We had a problem to solve, but she said we would work things out. And I believed her."

Barek grabbed her and slammed her against the wall. "You killed her!"

Cyprian snagged Barek's elbow and jerked him around. "Barek, she did not—"

"Don't defend her to me." He shook loose. "You made my mother an adulteress." He bolted from the garden.

Cyprian and Lisbeth stood there staring at each other. Neither knowing what to say next. In the tiny span of silence she watched Cyprian process.

"Cyprian . . . I didn't mean for her to die. . . ."

Finally, he spoke. "He's upset." Weariness weighted his voice. "I know you wouldn't hurt Ruth any more than she would hurt you. You loved each other." Cyprian's blue eyes pierced deep inside her soul.

Did he see how much she loved him, or did he see what she feared she'd become? A petty, jealous woman standing at the edge of a cliff, her feet slipping closer and closer to the perilous drop of all-consuming envy. Her attempts to manipulate the past into her version of a safe, happy future tumbled like rocks into an abyss.

"Cyprian . . . please . . . I . . ."

"I have a funeral to plan." He strode past her without another word.

32

ASPASIUS ADJUSTED THE LAUREL of bay leaves slipping down over his eyes. Pytros had insisted on weaving the fragrant wreath to protect him from contracting the plague during his trip to the public bathhouse. So far he'd heard no reports of plague from the wealthy patrons who frequented the upscale salon. But then, he'd also been the last to know about sickness in the house of Titus Cicero, the whereabouts of his slave, and the secretive return of Cyprian.

He tightened the sash on his robe, noting that achieving a good fit required him to pull the belt several notches tighter. Even though he couldn't seem to get enough sweets, weight had fallen off him these past few weeks. In his wasted state, he had to agree with Pytros: he could not be too careful with the little bit of health he had left.

Pytros sprinkled lavender oil over the new dressings binding his foot. "Ready?"

"You're sure none of the servants will talk?"

"I'll make certain their lips are sealed."

"The same way you made certain no one knew of Valerian's edict? Somehow Cyprian learned it was safe to come home, and look what it has cost me."

"That was not me. I swear." Pytros rang a bell, and six strong men matched in size and dressed in gorgeous liveries of royal blue entered the bedroom and hoisted Aspasius into his litter. One of the litter bearers caught a whiff of the nauseating odor and retched all over Aspasius's marble floor.

Pytros called for someone to clean up the mess. When Iltani appeared with a towel, Pytros yanked her aside and proceeded to parade Aspasius's speechless slave past the litter bearers. He pried her mouth open. "Should any of you breathe a word of what you see or hear tonight, your mouths will also be empty."

Satisfied with the men's obediently downcast eyes, Pytros climbed in beside Aspasius, closed the curtains, and with a tap to the frame, they were off.

Aspasius closed his eyes, contemplating how easily rumors of Valerian's edict had spread across the empire and how a convicted heretic known and recognized by many could have slipped back into town without a word from anyone. He rested his head on a cushion but did not allow the rhythmic patter of footmen toting him at top speed to lull his fury.

They arrived at the back entrance to the Baths of Antoninus, and Pytros directed the litter bearers to deposit them at the sauna. Once Aspasius limped inside his private compartment, slaves carefully removed his clothes.

Exhausted from the slight effort, Aspasius plopped his naked body on the mottled, marble bench inside the steam chamber. He tugged at the sagging skin where his rotund middle used to be.

He, and he alone, knew best how to save Carthage, and he intended to live long enough to see his scheme carried out.

"I'll fetch Felicissimus from the corridor." A chilly breeze cut the steam as Pytros exited.

Aspasius leaned back against the tiled wall mosaic of Neptune. He could feel the angry sea god cracking the whip over his chariot and mocking his decision to allow the horse doctor to return and botch the bloodletting. Galen's torturous procedure had not healed him. In fact, the moment the quack's blade slit his skin, Aspasius knew the wound had opened him up for the entrance of evil spirits. All through the night, fiery spasms rose past his knee, traveled beyond his thigh, and were now eating away at his core.

Aspasius signaled the wine attendant and snapped an order at the glistening slaves stoking the fire pit. "Hurry, fools."

Their black eyes cut curious glances at him as he waited for the wine to thin the sludge in his veins. He laid his head against Neptune's pronged fork, listening to the sounds of heavy stones being pushed across the tiles and shoved into the flames. When the stones were white-hot, two strong-armed men wearing long gloves and carrying giant metal tongs pulled the glowing rocks from the fire and doused them with water. A blast of hot fog filled the room.

Steam scalded Aspasius's skin. His gritted teeth nipped his scream. He willed his mind through the excruciating discomfort, which was more than twice the level of pain he'd suffered all these years from his ill-set leg.

Felicissimus poked his head in. "Aspasius?"

"Over here." Aspasius ordered the attendants out.

"Did something die in here?" Felicissimus appeared before him, bare-chested, a towel wrapped around his girth, two fingers pinching his nose. Obviously the slave trader had not only grown fat but also irritatingly sassy on the extra business Aspasius tossed his way as part of their previous agreement. Should Felicissimus forget his debt and try to weasel out of his obligations, Aspasius could think of any number of ways to collect what was due him. And he would not hesitate.

"Don't stand there gawking." Aspasius patted the seat. "How many writs of libellus have you sold to the Christians?"

"A few."

"Obviously destroying the church from the inside out is not working. No one is following you anywhere."

Felicissimus shifted in his towel. "If that foul odor is coming from you, you have a problem far more pressing than who does or does not follow me."

"My problems became your problems the moment you came to me with the promise of delivering Cyprianus Thascius and shifting the loyalties of these Christians. If you fail to hold up your end of our bargain, I will see to it that your hopes of leaving the slave trade to become my well-paid bishop with his own little kingdom of adoring subjects vanishes."

Felicissimus smiled. "You will need me come spring if you insist on bringing Cyprian before the masses and making him a martyr."

"Cyprian is already home! You know it, and so do I."

"I don't know what you're talking about."

"Don't lie to me, Felicissimus."

"What do you want?"

"I want to know why you're determined to keep Cyprian alive. From the beginning you have insisted he be spared."

"Once you execute Cyprian, the church won't be the only ones to hold him up as a martyr. You know how martyrs can make a movement grow. Look what happened after Perpetua." Felicissimus sipped his wine. "You do not want Cyprian turned into some kind of saint." The slave trader wiped sweat from his brow with the edge of his towel. "I said I'll sell those writs, and I will. I must wait for the right moment. For now, the church is happy with Cyprian's return and scurrying about doing his bidding."

"How is it a good thing for me to allow Cyprian to amass an army?"

"An army?" Felicissimus cackled. "They're a straggly little group who have rallied to Cyprian's call for help rearranging the sick in his house. They're making plans to clear the streets of bodies and take turns running their little home for the afflicted. Busywork that makes them feel righteous. But I know these people. They don't want to suffer."

"Are you saying my soldiers should go house to house?"

"Fear is our greatest weapon. When push comes to shove, even the most devout will wonder what has become of their one God. They will offer a pinch of incense to the gods of the emperor to save their own necks. If Cyprian has no one left to lead, then he will no longer be a leader in need of elimination. But remember, if you have Cyprian killed, you will make enemies."

Aspasius's laughter rang in the chamber. He stood and tossed his glass into the flames. "All the greats of history have inspired enemies. And I intend to make history."

33

FROM THE SHADOWS OF the colonnade, Lisbeth and Mama watched as hired musicians led the funeral procession from the kitchen to the *rogus* Cyprian had constructed in his garden. He'd laid the funeral pyre logs himself, refusing any help offered by the believers. In the hollow middle of the pyramid-shaped structure, he'd stuffed straw and kindling.

Aspasius had forbidden the Christians access to the cemetery outside the city walls. This edict meant Ruth could not be buried beside her beloved Caecilianus. Cyprian had furiously paced the garden, threatening to storm the proconsul's palace and demand the law be revoked. Ruth had always been the line of civilization that kept insanity at bay, the gentle voice that cooled hot heads. Lisbeth shouldn't have been surprised when her clumsy attempt to sway Cyprian toward another path had been met with hostility. Luckily, Pontius had intervened with two strong hands on Cyprian's shoulders and some in-your-face conversation Lisbeth couldn't quite make out. Whatever Pontius said, Cyprian eventually calmed enough to accept the idea of cremating his wife and baby son in the safety of his private property.

Lisbeth held her breath as Cyprian and Pontius gently placed Ruth's oil-anointed and properly shrouded body and that of her baby across the tepee-shaped chimney opening. The log funnel was designed to suck the intense heat to the upper tier and incinerate the corpses to ashes in a few hours.

Across the garden, Barek and Junia stood with their arms crossed over their chests, desperate as she to keep their hearts from leaping into the glowing embers. Lisbeth had purposely chosen to pay her respects from a distance. Not because giving Ruth's children space was the right thing to do, but because Mama had suggested it might be the best remedy for the hurt on their faces.

Neither of them would have anything to do with her or Maggie, which only added to Maggie's already bruised conscience. The child could not quit crying, saying she never wanted to play with dolls again. Lisbeth had put Maggie to bed early and patted her back for thirty minutes before she'd finally fallen asleep. When Mama asked Laurentius to stay in the cottage and keep an eye on his little niece, Laurentius cried, begging to go to the funeral. Mama diverted his attention with a fresh piece of paper and a full pot of ink. "Draw Ruth a picture."

Now, as Lisbeth watched Cyprian kiss Ruth's swaddled lips, she wished she could trade places with Laurentius. To live in his world of innocence, a world she hadn't known since she was five.

Cyprian ran his hand over Ruth's body, stopping at the bulge that was his child. His face contorted in tears. Lisbeth ached to go to him. To tell him she'd throw herself upon the smoldering logs if it would ease the pain on his face and erase the blame from his eyes.

Mama pointed at the back gate. "The church is beginning to arrive."

Naomi had spread news of the funeral details among the believers. Over the past hour, many of Ruth's surviving patients and their families streamed through the back entrance. Quinta. Metras. Natalis and his mother. They'd covered their bowed heads with dust to honor the woman they adored. To think, only a day ago they'd rallied around this woman with joy.

To Lisbeth's surprise, Felicissimus filed in among the mourners. She'd told herself after seeing him in the church meeting that if their paths ever crossed again she would give him the verbal lashing his betrayal deserved. Her eyes locked with his, and she knew Felicissimus understood their business was not finished.

Her breath caught; then she felt Mama's hand on her shoulder.

"What is it, Lisbeth?"

"A snake in the garden."

"It can wait."

"Not for long."

Lisbeth grudgingly joined Mama behind a pillar, but she couldn't help peeking around. The sleazy little slave trader waddled across the garden and offered Cyprian his condolences with a grave and sincere face. It appeared that Felicissimus had waltzed back into the life of the man he'd ruined, no questions asked, while here she was, standing on all too shaky ground.

Cyprian scattered a little grain on the stacked driftwood, sprinkled salt across Ruth's body, and lit the incense burner. Next, he withdrew the scroll tucked into his belt. "From the words of God's servant John." Cyprian unrolled the parchment. Collecting himself was taking longer than Lisbeth could bear. She took a step toward him, but Mama pulled her back with a stern shake of her head. Cyprian raised the scroll. He cleared his throat and began to read. "Blessed are those who die in the Lord." He paused, swallowed hard, and started again. "They are blessed indeed, for they will rest from all their toils and trials; for their good deeds follow them!"

"Amen" rippled through the crowd.

Cyprian slowly rolled the brittle parchment. "Ruth loved the Lord, and her toils on your behalf speak to how much she loved each of you. I, for one, will never let her good deeds be forgotten." His eyes canvassed the crowd. When his gaze met Lisbeth's, he stopped. "In the presence of these witnesses, I declare I will not rest, no matter the trials, until I am certain Carthage is safe from plague and Christians are free of persecution."

He moved back from the pyre, and Pontius stirred a long metal rod through the red-hot embers.

Hungry flames nibbled at the kindling and then quickly moved on to consume the grain. Scorching tongues licked the muslin and charred a black outline of a mother holding her child. The dry cloth caught fire with a whoosh. A pillar of angry smoke rose toward the setting sun.

Caecilianus's dogs loped into the garden and skidded to a stop inches from the pyre. Their forlorn howls rose above the foul smoke.

Lisbeth breathed in hot, acrid air that seared her throat. Despite the heat the burning pyre gave off, she shivered uncontrollably. Ruth had said everything was forgiven, but Lisbeth knew forgiving herself for making these past few days so difficult would not be so easy.

One by one, mourners filed by, wailing, dabbing their eyes, and pulling their hair. Some even stopped to scoop ashes from the fringe of the fire to add a smear to their faces. Once everyone had cleared but Cyprian and Pontius, Lisbeth made her way across the garden, her eyes stinging from a combination of smoke and tears. She slipped her hand into Cyprian's and squeezed. He stared straight into the flames, but to her relief, he squeezed back. The pressure created a fixed point in time, a place they had been and a place to which they would never return.

"I'm sorry," Lisbeth whispered.

"Ruth has exchanged the suffering of this world for a bright and eternal honor." Cyprian released her hand and turned to face her. "Go home, Lisbeth." His voice was tired and brittle. "Take our daughter to safety, and leave this place while you still can."

34

IT WAS THE LONELIEST part of the night. The time when the wind died down and the moon plummeted toward dawn. The time when Lisbeth's mind retraced her steps and tripped over her failures. The time she dreaded most.

Feeling broken and small, Lisbeth slipped out of bed and threw a robe over her shoulders.

The mouse scurrying across the bedroom floor stopped at the sputtering lamp to steal a few licks of the olive oil. She should send the sneaky thief scampering, but she didn't have the energy to waste on futile efforts. Hundreds of hungry, demanding mice waited behind the stone walls like the desperately ill waited at Cyprian's doors. The moment this little bugger was out of the way, another would quickly take his place . . . and then another . . . and another.

Lisbeth left the mouse to lap his fill and stepped onto the balcony. She pulled her robe closed and padded to the balustrade.

Needing a compass more than ever, she silently railed at the cloud cover obscuring her view of the stars. She had no answers as to why her good intentions to rescue everyone had gone so horribly awry. It was true she'd been upset with Ruth. But she'd never wanted her friend to die. And she'd never meant to trap Cyprian in the middle of such an impossible situation. She didn't know how to fix any of this. All she knew was that opening yourself to love was like opening your veins. The potential for serious harm was great. Everything that mattered could drain away before you knew it.

Torn between staying and going, she weighed her options. Clearly, meddling in the natural flow of events had set in motion unimaginable catastrophes. Cyprian had told her to go home. Obviously, he wanted nothing to do with her. If she went back through the portal now, their daughter would never truly know her father. Surely there had to be better a way. Something she could do.

"Maggie's had a bad dream." Mama came from behind and squeezed her shoulder. "I tried to calm her, but she's asking for you." She held out a steaming mug. "I've made my version of chamomile tea to help her sleep."

Lisbeth sighed, dragging her eyes from the distant sky, and took the cup. "I've spent ten years in the equivalent of indentured servitude trying to learn how to save lives, and when it mattered most . . . I had nothing."

Mama beckoned her to join her on the bench. "Sometimes the only thing a doctor can do after a loss like this is walk away, drink a cup of coffee, and reflect on how totally useless all of our efforts to fight death sometimes are."

"Why Ruth?" An apple-scented steam stung Lisbeth's nostrils. "Less than a foot in my direction, and that bull would have killed me."

"Things happen. Often with no explanation," Mama said. "Maybe this was God's way of protecting Ruth from the arena."

Lisbeth ran her finger around the mug's rim. "Who brings their child to a place where being trampled by a crazed ox is preferable to being forced to kneel before the executioner's sword?"

"I ask myself that question every time I look at you." Mama wrapped her arm around Lisbeth's shoulder. "Tell me the real reason you came back."

Lisbeth wanted to let go of the secret eating her insides, to be free of bearing sole responsibility for the futures of the people she loved so much. Sometimes she even imagined what it would look like to give up the stress of trying to fix everything and let things just happen. Then her instincts always kicked in. She could hear the familiar warnings . . . *Danger . . . Don't let go . . . No one else is coming along to save the day . . . God helps those who help themselves.*

She cleared her throat and changed the subject. "The first time Papa and I returned to the Cave of the Swimmers I found the portal because of you."

"Me?"

"You were there. You spoke to me, and I could see you. How is that possible?"

If Mama recognized her dodge, she chose to overlook it for now. "After we die, we dwell in a dimension not bound by time." Mama pulled away. "You know I'm going to die, right?"

She'd lost her mother twice now. Once when she was five and again when Mama sent her back to the twenty-first century. She couldn't bear the thought of losing Mama a third time to something as permanent as eternity. "How do you do it, stay in this trying place?"

"The same way anyone does anything: one day at a time." Mama stood and went to the railing. "When I first arrived, I was so afraid." She glanced back at Lisbeth. "Not for me, but for you."

"Me? I was safe with Papa."

"My heart knew that, but my head couldn't stop worrying. What would happen to my precious little daughter without her mother? What if your father couldn't fill in the gaps? You know how distracted he can be." Mama swallowed. "Once I realized I was stuck here, I fought hard. I refused to eat. Refused to submit. One night Aspasius locked me in his office." She stared at her extended hands. "I made my fingers bloody stubs trying to claw my way out.

But the harder I fought against my new reality, the more things spiraled out of control." Mama gripped the balustrade. "Then there was that painful, yet glorious moment of change. The moment I knew the only thing I could control in this world . . . or yours . . . was my attitude."

"What happened?"

"After I gave birth to Laurentius, Aspasius took one look at our baby's moon-pie face and beat me unconscious. I would have died were it not for the kindness of Iltani, a Christian slave who lost her tongue after a failed escape attempt." Mama's eyes scanned the horizon as if she searched for some sort of explanation for the unexplainable. "That precious little slave girl risked her life for me and Laurentius again and again. Iltani hid us in the subterranean tunnels beneath the palace and nursed me back to health with crumbs she stole from our master's table." An appreciative smile lit Mama's face. "By the time Aspasius asked for a healer, I was stronger and I'd made friends in the palace. I knew God. And I knew I'd been called to a purpose. I was no longer afraid, and I was no longer alone.

"Iltani and the other servants helped me work out a system. Laurentius was never left unattended . . . and neither was I." Tears glistened on Mama's cheeks. "God was with me." She took the cup from Lisbeth and set it on the bench. "I understand how difficult it is for you to let go. But as long as your hands are full, my precious girl, your heart will remain empty."

"I want to trust. Really I do."

"Then tell me the truth of why you risked everything to come back."

Lisbeth took a deep breath and plunged into the story, sparing none of the details. One by one, she purged the agonizing months of her pregnancy, her worries about Papa, and the fears of single parenting. She told Mama of her early-church history research, launching into the specifics of what was about to descend upon this struggling little group of people. By the time she finished, the tea had cooled considerably. "What is to come is far worse than measles or typhoid."

Mama's brows raised. "Go on."

"The church will soon lose its leader and the financier of their good works."

Understanding sobered Mama's face. "Cyprian?"

Lisbeth nodded.

"How?"

"Beheading." Lisbeth wiped the moisture from her cheeks and looked grimly into Mama's own brimming eyes. "And after what he just declared over Ruth's grave, I'm afraid I won't be able to stop it."

BY THE time Lisbeth reached the cottage to check on Maggie, surprisingly the child had fallen fast asleep curled up in Junia's arms. "Why can't adults forgive like children?" she whispered to herself, recalling the ice in Cyprian's tone when he'd told her to go home. Not that she didn't deserve his anger. His wife and baby son would be alive if she hadn't come back.

After carefully tucking Maggie's legs beneath the covers and raising a blanket over Junia's shoulders, she lifted the lamp and searched the cottage. Naomi slept on a mat in one corner, but Barek's pallet in the opposite corner was empty. While Barek pretended to be a man, he was really still a boy. He'd just lost his mother. He was probably still at the funeral pyre for some much-needed closure. She knew how lost and angry he must be feeling. All those years of not being able to find Mama's remains had left a bitter hole that she'd filled with blame. Mostly blaming herself. It would be a while before Barek would feel like talking to anyone.

Lisbeth's gaze moved on to the unmade bed, the one where Ruth and Cyprian had spent their last night.

Empty.

Her gut twisted. Maybe now was not the best time to work out some forgiveness between the two of them, but at the least she had to come clean. Tell Cyprian the truth about his future before it was too late.

She made her way back to the villa. From a Ziploc bag in her pack, she retrieved a photocopy of the historical account of Cyprian's fate. Tucking the paper in her pocket, she turned and went in search of her husband.

35

HEAT FROM THE BURIAL fire had singed Cyprian's brows and melted his anger and regret into an unbearable lump. His wife and son were dead, and he'd just told his first wife to take his daughter and leave. The losses were greater than anything Aspasius could ever take from him. Even his life.

Dreaming of a reunion with Lisbeth had kept him alive on that desolate beach. God had allowed her return. It was more than he deserved. Especially since he was the one who'd failed to wait upon God and taken things into his own hands. And, God forgive him, he was the one who longed to seek solace in her arms. To make amends for the hurt he'd caused.

It wasn't Lisbeth's fault that Ruth had died. More than once, he'd been privy to Lisbeth's ability to perform miraculous medical procedures. She'd saved patients Roman doctors would have left for dead. She would have saved her dear friend had there been any way.

And the accident wasn't Ruth's fault either. She was more than a concerned mother. She was a friend who would have thrown herself in front of that bull to save Lisbeth.

Snowflake-shaped bits of ash floated in the dwindling smoke. Cyprian rubbed his damaged brows. He wasn't mad at Lisbeth. He wasn't even angry at Ruth for insisting on accompanying their search for Maggie and Junia.

He was mad at himself.

He alone bore the responsibility of placing Ruth in harm's way. And he didn't mean the thundering hooves of a peddler's beast. He and Ruth should never have married. No matter how Ruth downplayed the danger and played up the advantages, the vision of his fate continually played in his head. The day was coming when he would stand before Aspasius and face the ultimate test of his faith. If he knew his death was to be the end of it, he could have rested easily. But the voice deep in his soul kept whispering that it was only a matter of time before Ruth's fate mirrored his. He'd tried to warn her, but she would hear none of it.

So, out of a misplaced desire to honor his word to Caecilianus, he'd pushed aside the hazards and made vulnerable those he'd grown to love, accomplishing, in fact, the exact opposite of what he'd sought to do. His poor judgment had not cost Ruth her life in a dirty tenement alleyway. No, Ruth lost her life the moment he agreed to their marriage. It was up to him to right this wrong. To make it up to her by securing the future of the church. Time was of the essence.

God, show me what to do.

Suddenly the northerly winds shifted. A gust of warmth blew in from the desert and shoved away the winter season. Tiny flecks of ash swirled in the moment of rebellion. Spring had arrived, and it would be put off no longer. The time for evading Aspasius had ended.

Cyprian passed through the wrought-iron gate and hurried toward the stables. He slid open the heavy barn door and stepped into the darkness. "Pontius!"

He'd always felt more at home amid the smell of parchment and ink than the manure of his father's stables. At the building's far end, his friend wept before one of his father's prize mares.

Pontius startled at his arrival and quickly wiped his eyes. "My lord, what brings you to the stables?"

Cyprian choked back the tears he'd yet to shed. "The good counsel of a good friend and the completion of a couple of important errands." He lifted the wooden scoop from a peg on the wall, loaded it with grain, and went to the stall.

"You've only to ask."

"Ruth's death has changed things. I'm afraid the morale of the believers will slip quickly." Cyprian emptied the grain into the trough.

"The church has suffered a great loss."

"We must do all we can to ease their suffering. Agreed?" Cyprian appreciated Pontius's brief nod. "First, I need you to send Lisbeth and Maggie home."

"I can understand your desire to spare them, especially after losing one wife and child, but you know Lisbeth won't go without her mother and brother. If you intend to end this plague, how can you do so without a healer?"

"Lisbeth has trained several women in the church in the ways of providing sufficient medical care."

"For those with measles. What of typhoid? We have no one who could do what she and Magdalena were able to do for Diona."

"That is where the next errand comes in. Shutting down the transportation systems is the fastest way to stop the spread of measles. The sooner we accomplish this, the sooner we end both plagues and the sooner the persecution ceases."

"A dangerous gamble without proper support."

"One that will require cash. Lots of it."

Pontius's brows shot up. "You intend to *buy* the senatorial support you need?"

"Yes." Cyprian charged ahead. "I need you to commission Felicissimus to move forward with great speed and liquidate my properties. Once the plague subsides, the senators will not have the patience to continue this war Aspasius has waged against Christians. They'll want things to return to normal. Back to the prosperous days when Rome let their conquests believe whatever they wanted as long as they remained peaceful and paid their taxes."

"If we plan well, we could end the plague and the persecution before Aspasius has a chance to end you."

"Either way, I'm ready to face the future."

36

THE DOGS WERE FAR too distracted by Ruth's funeral fire to notice Lisbeth. Neither Cyprian nor Barek were anywhere to be found. Barek had probably headed for his beloved ocean, and Cyprian for his devoted friend Pontius.

Lisbeth closed the cottage door, slipped through the back gate, and ducked into the night. Since Maggie had lost her flashlight, she was forced to rely on moonlight and memory to find the stables.

Gravel crunched beneath her feet. Several paces into the darkness, a twig snapped. She stopped, listened, then checked her surroundings one more time. Waves pounded the shore in the distance, but the crashing rhythm didn't camouflage the sound of fast-approaching footsteps. She blinked, hoping to force her eyes to adjust. Before she could get her bearings, someone grabbed her from behind. The thick arm wrapping her throat instantly cut off her ability to cry out for help. As she was pulled tightly against a heaving chest, a hand came down hard across her mouth, clamping it shut.

She struggled, clawing at her attacker's arms and hands.

The man dragged her from the path, his breath coming in short, labored huffs. "Scream, and I'll snap your neck."

Every muscle in her body tensed. The voice belonged to the same man who'd had his boot on her face when she'd awakened for the first time in this century.

Felicissimus.

She pounded her fists on his thick arms.

Once he had her completely concealed in the shadows, he whispered in her ear. "Ready to make a deal?"

Deal? What kind of deal? Fear ripped through her. Why hadn't she exposed him in the presence of witnesses? Hoping to outsmart him and make a run for it the moment he released her, she nodded.

"Remember, scream and you'll not be the only one to die." He kept his arm around her neck but slowly lifted his smelly fingers from her mouth. She sucked in air as best she could despite the pressure he kept on her windpipe. When she didn't scream, Felicissimus slowly released his hold on her neck. "Good girl."

She broke free and whirled. "What do you think you're doing?" She swung a fist in his direction.

He caught her wrist before her blow made contact with his jaw. "There are those who'd be only too happy to ask you the same question."

"Me? I'm not the traitor. I can't believe you have the guts to look Cyprian in the eye after what you did." She jerked her hand away and took a step back. "Let alone come to his church and then his wife's funeral and pretend to be his friend."

"Weren't you doing the same?"

"I . . . uh . . . no!"

"That wasn't you weeping in the shadows while Cyprian's second wife burned in the flames?"

She started toward the path. "I don't have to listen to—"

He snagged her arm. "There's obviously been a little misunderstanding between us. I want to clear it up before someone gets hurt."

"So you decided to assault me?"

"*Assault* is an ugly word. *Persuade* fits my purposes far better."

"Persuade me to do what? Forget what a snake in the grass you are? Good luck."

"I'm sure we can come to a workable agreement."

"Agreement?" Anger pent up for the past six years spewed forth. She hadn't liked him from the beginning. Cyprian had tried to convince her otherwise, but she should have followed her gut. "It was you who told Aspasius when and where Ruth and I would be that day the soldiers captured us in the market, wasn't it." Lisbeth poked his shoulder. "We were the bait to draw Caecilianus and Cyprian out, weren't we."

"Speculation at its worst." Felicissimus chuckled. "Difficult theory to prove at best."

"I saw you leave Aspasius's palace." Lisbeth felt her voice go up a notch.

"You saw a loyal Christian doing his part to bridge the gap between his Lord and his sovereign," Felicissimus countered.

"Don't think you can claim you were there trying to end persecution. Do you think I'm an idiot? You bragged about becoming the rightful bishop of Carthage!"

"Could it be possible that what you thought you heard was distorted by your overwrought emotions of the day? You have no idea what I've done to save Cyprian's life."

"No one would believe you."

"Oh, I think the church will."

"I don't know what you're up to or what you possibly hope to gain by taking over the church, but I know what I saw. And I plan to tell Cyprian."

"Well, now, that's the very reason I called our little meeting. I find *your* presence in Cyprian's home as surprising as you find *mine*." He leaned in. "I think there are those who would find it equally as disturbing to know you are *not* where you belong."

"Are you threatening me?"

"Merely reminding you."

"Of what? How despicable you are?"

The gloating smile in his voice made her cringe. "You're still officially the property of Aspasius Paternus." He had her there. He knew it. And the fact that she could tell he intended to use this piece of information drew her up short.

"So?"

He rubbed his palms together. "Since you have the most to lose, I think it'll make this situation simple."

"What do you want?"

"You forget what you saw in the palace of the proconsul, and I'll forget who I've seen in this house. Cyprian, you, your bewitching mother, and, most important of all, your beautiful little daughter."

Terror prickled Lisbeth's skin. "What do you know about Maggie?"

"I inquired around after your little search party set out. Word is how closely your little jewel resembles the exiled patrician evading justice . . . Christian to the core, dense as a gravestone, and yellow as a chicken egg."

She lunged for his throat. "Leave Maggie out of this!"

He pried her hands loose with a chuckle. "So can I assume we have a deal?"

"What about Cyprian?" Her entire body was shaking. "How do I know you won't turn him over to Aspasius just to get him out of your way?"

"You don't." Felicissimus laughed. "What you do know is that I obviously lack your sentimentality. Therefore, the best thing for you to do is tread very carefully and pray your *husband* never suspects a thing."

37

IN THE ANIMAL KINGDOM, unchecked herds can multiply and overwhelm their habitat. Disease is nature's way of eliminating the weak and less desirable. If plagues were meant to winnow the chaff from humanity, how did snakes like Felicissimus continue to thrive?

Lisbeth watched the slave trader slither into the shadows. How could someone who called himself a Christian act with such malice? She swiped angry tears from her cheeks. What was she going to do? Protecting Maggie meant she could say nothing. Saving Cyprian required she tell him everything. How could she do both at the same time and not get someone killed?

Still shaking from her unexpected encounter, Lisbeth prayed for wisdom as she stepped into the warmth of the barn. In the dim light her heightened senses worked to place the low, mournful sounds of someone wrestling with a huge sorrow. Once her eyes adjusted she spotted her husband standing before the stall of one of his father's prize Arabians. His face was buried in its mane, and his shoulders were shaking as he emptied his grief.

Of course, he'd loved Ruth and their child. He was a man capable of generosity beyond comprehension, a generosity that she prayed could somehow still include her once she told him what she knew.

She let out a slow, nervous breath. "I thought I'd find you here."

Startled, Cyprian jerked around. Moonlight silhouetted the lean lines of his body. "Then you've spoken with Pontius?"

"No. Why?"

"I sent him to look for you. He's going to help you take our daughter far from this trouble." His dull-edged pain sliced through her.

"Maggie and I aren't going anywhere until we talk." This conversation would have been so much easier before her encounter with Felicissimus robbed her of the luxury of transparency. "You deserve to know everything." She prayed her secret agreement with the slave trader hadn't tainted her voice.

"So if I let you finally speak your mind, you'll take Maggie to safety?" Cyprian's eyes held hers.

Lisbeth felt a constriction in her chest. "If that is what you want." Her hand went to her pocket, where she'd stuffed the carefully folded paragraph describing the separation of Cyprian's head from his shoulders. Was her job here double in purpose? Save Cyprian from those wishing him dead, and save him from throwing away a chance for their family to be together?

"This could take a while." She nodded toward the empty hay cart. "Mind if we sit?"

Cyprian's gaze danced between her and the wagon. He'd been through so much in the past twenty-four hours, and the strain of it all showed in his tightened jaw. How she wanted to touch him. To take some of his burden on herself. Instead she waited, keeping her quickened breaths shallow and the skirmish she'd just had with Felicissimus buried deeply.

Cyprian let out a reluctant breath, placed his hands on her waist, and lifted her onto the cart. Heat spread from beneath the span of his touch and ignited a fire in her belly. For what seemed like ages they stared into each other's eyes. His face, serious and determined, was inches from hers. So close she could have kissed the tear-streaked smudge above his right dimple.

Memories of him carrying her across the threshold on their wedding night rose from the ghostly traces of smoke lingering on his skin. Much like Ruth and Cyprian's marriage, theirs had also been a marriage of convenience neither of them had wanted. But both had agreed the arrangement was necessary to accomplish the greater good. The plan had been simple. Defeat Aspasius. In doing so, Cyprian would save Carthage and the church, and she would save Mama and Laurentius. Once each got what they wanted, they would shake hands, part company, and go their separate ways. Except things hadn't worked out quite that way. They had not defeated Aspasius. Neither had gotten what they wanted. And parting company wasn't an option for two people who'd unexpectedly fallen in love.

Lisbeth remembered standing in the middle of their honeymoon suite simultaneously searching for a way out and desperately clinging to this man. Similar conflicting messages plagued her now. She wanted to fall into Cyprian's arms and tell him about Felicissimus and his treachery. To be totally honest for the first time since her arrival. But for Maggie's sake, she had to stick to the facts in the history books.

"What is it that you must tell me?" Cyprian pulled back and stared directly at her.

She tore her gaze from his and forced her mind to concentrate on the controlled and methodical chewing of the midnight-colored horse emptying the feeding trough.

He seated himself beside her. "The time is short." His leg lightly brushed hers.

Lisbeth felt tiny hairs rise beneath the friction of his close proximity. Sparks, hot and jagged, swept through the dry tinder of her body. "What do you mean?"

"I mean it's best if you and Maggie travel to the cisterns in the dark."

Something about the way he hesitated didn't feel right. Maybe he was having second thoughts on sending her home.

She took a hopeful breath. "A few weeks ago, while I was still back in my time, a college girl from Dallas went to Africa on a mission trip with her church. She came home feeling like she had a cold. What she didn't know was that she had contracted measles. The girl, full of the invincibility of youth, blew off her mother's suggestion to spend a little time in bed. Instead she went to a church picnic. In less than an hour, this one carrier managed to infect every susceptible person there, including a young mother who unknowingly then took her family *and* the measles to Disney World."

"Disney World?"

"Uh, a big carnival." From the puzzled look on Cyprian's face, he was out of the habit of trying to comprehend her strange vernacular and the unbelievable things of her world, but he wasn't totally opposed to dusting off his rusty curiosity. "You know . . . silly shows, rides, lots of junk food?"

"Like the Festival of Lupercalia?" His sincerity elicited her first genuine laughter since her return. His brows crinkled, but his lips smiled at her. "Why is my question funny?"

"Modern theme parks don't usually have naked priests running around waving strips of goatskin, but I've heard that during spring break the crowds can be as crazy as a Roman holiday. Not to mention, places like Disney are always crazy expensive. I was saving up to take Maggie, but we came here instead."

"Maggie," he said softly. "You've done a fine job raising our daughter."

Lisbeth choked back tears. "If Maggie grows up to be half the person her father is, I will count my work as a parental success."

She wanted to throw her arms around his neck but reined in the urge and quickly returned her hands to her lap.

"What does a carnival have to do with me?"

"Right. Like I was saying, measles have the remarkable ability to find the susceptible. Without vaccinations, herd immunity drops. When the moat around the castle dries up, the infection can spread unchecked, leaping from host to host like a forest fire. There have been numerous outbreaks throughout the centuries. Some have even caused significant loss of human life. If we could stop measles now, think of all the lives we'd save in the future."

"So let me see if I have this straight." Sarcasm sharpened Cyprian's voice. "You not only know the past, but now you are claiming you can also predict your own future?" His eyes narrowed. "So you came back for the measles?"

"No." Lisbeth reached for his hand. "I came back for you."

He did not pull away, as she half expected him to do. "Maggie told me."

"She did? When?"

"One night while I tucked her in . . . before Ruth died." The sadness in his voice hung between them like a black curtain. They sat in silence, staring straight ahead, neither of them willing to pull back the veil and expose the depths of the other's grief.

After a few minutes, Lisbeth let out a slow breath and asked, "Do you want to come back with us?"

Cyprian lifted his eyes to hers. "I don't want to be separated from you ever again, but I can't go to your world and you can't stay here."

"Why not?"

He placed his straightened index finger over her lips. "For the second time in my life I have buried a wife." His feather-light touch burned with the intensity of the funeral pyre. "First you. And now Ruth." He removed his finger and moved in so close his breath became hers. "I cannot bear the thought of burying you again. And if you stay, that very well could happen."

She stared straight into his eyes, unwilling to let him see how frightened it made her to think she might have lost him forever.

When he finally spoke, it was with a surprising calm. "I know with absolute certainty that there is a spear, a sword, and an executioner waiting for me."

Lisbeth gasped. "How do you know about . . . that?"

"Dreams." He raked his hands through his hair and stood, pacing. "The same one. Every night since my exile to Curubis. I will not allow you or Maggie to suffer my fate."

"God warned you that everything was going to go south here, and still you came back?"

He cocked one dark brow inquisitively. "Go south?"

"Turn ugly. Fall apart. End in tragedy."

The corner of his lip rose in a half smile. He took a step toward her. "Isn't that why you're here?"

"I don't know what you're talking about."

"To keep everything from *going south*, as you say." He stepped so close his waist brushed her knees. His hand tilted her chin to his. "You went home and poked through your father's history books, didn't you?"

She was trapped between his solid chest and her flimsy plan. "Maybe."

"I don't know what you found, but I'm betting you discovered something so horrible in my future that you could not stay away."

Lisbeth's insides quivered, and tears gathered behind the curtain of her lashes. She needed his strength. His comfort. Hers was all used up. Did he want her as badly as she wanted to tell him everything and fall into his arms? Or was he too hurt and angry to feel the undeniable arch of her body, the magnetic draw pulling her toward him? She swallowed, unable to speak.

His breath, no more than a whisper, warmed her cheek. "And even though the historical accounts warned that things would end badly for me, you came back anyway?"

Lisbeth's chin trembled. Hot tears spilled onto her cheeks. "How did you know?"

He cupped her face with his hands. "I know you." He slowly dragged the pads of his thumbs over the wet streaks on her cheeks. He hovered over her, so close she could smell the musky scent of him, the intoxicating combination of strength and leather sealed deep within her sensory memory of their first meeting. "And I can think of no other reason you would risk our daughter's life."

A shiver rippled over her body. Her gaze dove into the desire swimming in his, and she felt herself being sucked into a vortex of tingling emotions. "I'm sorry," she whispered.

His thumb moved from her cheek and gently caressed the outline of her mouth. "Lisbeth . . ." Before she could answer, he lifted her chin and brought his lips to hers. Lightly at first, as if searching for familiar ground. Then again. The stubble around his mouth grazed her nose and sent her already heightened senses pulsing through her body. He tasted of tears and funeral smoke. He hauled her up against him. His lips pressed harder. Lisbeth could feel his heart beating beneath his tunic.

He pulled back but did not raise his gaze to hers. Instead he focused on his fingers gently tracing the curve of her collarbone before running along the slope of her neck and nudging her face up. When their eyes met, he smiled at her, and Lisbeth caught a glimpse of the man she remembered. A man capable of sweeping her into a time and place of their own making, a world where only their love existed.

Lisbeth twined her arms around his neck and drew him close. He growled low in his throat, and they fell back on the flatbed of the cart, his mouth fiery on hers. Cyprian's weight bore down hard on her. She could barely breathe, and she didn't care. She was his wife, and she was in his arms.

Suddenly, Cyprian let her go and broke away. "I'm sorry. I shouldn't have . . ." He quickly pushed himself off of her and stood.

Lisbeth sat up. "Why?"

His breaths were coming in short, rapid spurts. He straightened his shoulders and brushed the straw from his tunic. "I can no longer think only of my own needs."

"What?" She could feel her gown sliding down her chest, exposing her heart. "What do you mean?"

"Don't you see, Lisbeth? There is no one else who can do what the Lord needs done. He's called me for such a time as this."

He was choosing the path that would make him a martyr. How could she compete with such a noble undertaking?

Lisbeth felt as if she were coming apart inside. Bricks of control, ones she thought solidly cemented into place, crumbled. "What are you planning?"

"To do everything I can before Aspasius stops me."

"Let me help."

He shook his head. "Go home, Lisbeth."

38

THE MOON FADED FROM the sky while Barek waited for the embers to lose their red-hot glow. In the chilly, blue-gray of dawn, he approached his mother's burned-out funeral pyre. The sea air was heavy with the acrid scent of smoldering wood and incinerated flesh and bones. Cyprian had counted the chore complete and taken his leave after the wooden altar crumbled.

For Barek, the task of properly laying his mother to rest was just beginning. Twice he had failed to protect his mother in this life. He would not fail to keep her safe in the next.

Barek had prepared the bottom of an empty crock with a splash of goat's milk, half a chalice of Cyprian's finest wine, and the entire bottle of his mother's favorite perfume. Fighting nausea, he crouched before the mound of debris and set the crock beside his feet. He gently began to shovel bits of ash and bone fragments into the urn. The first shovelful hit the liquid mixture with a thunk. Each blackened scoop added thereafter was more than a painful reminder of his family's destruction; it was the end of life as he knew it. No longer was he bound to the one God of his parents or their needy little band of believers. He would honor their religious choices by placing his mother's remains beside those of his father, but then he would be done with their God. What would become of him after he completed this last chore for his mother was an itch he couldn't seem to scratch.

He'd always loved the water. Perhaps he would join the imperial navy and set sail for parts unknown. Once the skies cleared and the harbor reopened for the summer shipping season, the captains would need sailors to replace those who had died of the fever. Barek emptied another scoop of ash into the urn. A powdery, gray puff rose and filled his nostrils. Blinking away the stink, he continued gathering the remains of his mother.

"Whatcha doin'?" Maggie's voice came from somewhere behind him.

He didn't need the little chit poking around in his business. Barek glanced over his shoulder. There she stood. Tangled blond hair, wide blue eyes, and two bare feet. A spoiled princess used to bossing everyone around and getting her way. Well, not anymore. Without his mother here to scold him, he wouldn't bow to Maggie's demands. Without his mother . . .

Barek dug at his watery eyes. "None of your business."

"Are you crying, Barek?"

"No."

Maggie came and stood beside him. "My mommy says it's not safe to play with fire."

"Your mother says a lot of useless things." Barek blinked the traces of ash from his eyes and continued shoveling. "Go back to bed."

"I went to bed early. I'm not tired anymore." She put her hand on his arm. "I know why you're so cranky."

He wiped his forearm across his nose. "You don't know anything."

"I know your mother died." She tiptoed and whispered into his ear. "And I know it's my fault."

He stopped shoveling long enough to see a tear roll down

Maggie's cheek. "Where's that doll you had to have?" His jab deflated her face. He felt bad for being so cruel.

Maggie squatted on the other side of the urn. "I don't play with dolls anymore." She sniffed and took hold of a small stick where only the tip had burned.

Barek sighed. Much as Lisbeth's daughter irritated him, she was but a child, and he wasn't a barbarian. "It wasn't your fault the ox broke out of its harness."

Maggie shrugged. "Why did Cyprian burn Ruth and the baby?"

"How did you know that?"

"I heard people crying, so I peeked out the window."

He started to explain the battle between the Romans and people like his parents, people who thought there was a god somewhere who cared, but what did the religious bickering matter now? "Cyprian did what he had to do."

"Oh." Maggie eyed the blackened ruins. "Would my daddy burn me if I died?"

"You're too young to die."

"So was the baby." She chewed on the corner of her lip as she dragged her stick through the ashes. "Does it hurt?"

"What?"

She used her stick like a stylus and carved trenches in the dirt. "Getting burned up."

"No, fool. You're dead." Barek went back to his task, carefully raking through the debris, searching for anything that even slightly resembled his mother. When he had another sooty scoop ready for the urn, he looked down and found Maggie etching a design on the side of the crock with her charred stick. "What do you think you're doing?"

"Drawing a pretty picture for Ruth."

He dropped the shovel and snatched the urn away. "What is this?"

"It's your family." She pointed at the row of three black figures with potbelly waists. "The big one is your daddy. That one is your mommy." She wiped her nose with the back of her hand. "And the little one in the middle holding their hands is"—she raised her eyes to his—"you."

Memories of his family's old life, the happy one they'd had before his mother made room for these strangers, clogged the back of Barek's throat. His attempt to quickly clear them away failed, and they pushed up in a bittersweet rush. His parents had been so honored when Cyprian invited their family to move in after his conversion. Barek remembered that the new arrangement had made him happy, too. Cyprian's villa was so close to the sea, he could go fishing whenever he wanted. And his table always had more than enough food. Their little church grew. And Barek met his best friend, Natalis.

Barek had been young and starry-eyed then, and he'd looked up to the man who'd brought them into his home. Cyprian was an honorable noble who had influence in high places, the kind of influence Barek intended to have someday.

Barek finally managed to swallow, and when he did, he felt his dreams slip away as well. "Isn't there someone else you can bother?"

"No. Junia and Laurentius are asleep." Maggie watched as he filled the jar to the brim and carefully set the lid in place. "Now what do we do?"

"*We* don't do anything." Barek rose and tucked the urn under his arm. "*You* are going back to bed, and *I* am going to bury my mother beside my father."

"I'm coming with you."

"No, you aren't."

"I'll scream."

"So? Scream."

She parked her hands on her hips. "Cyprian will come running and tell you to stay home."

After what Cyprian had done to his mother, he didn't want Cyprian telling him anything anymore. "You are a bossy little tyrant."

"And you're cranky."

"All right. Fine. But no complaining."

BAREK AND Maggie hurried along the avenue. For someone with such short legs, Maggie was doing a fair job of matching his stride. If she could keep up their current pace, they would reach one of the more obscure city gates during the changing of the guard. Barek rehearsed his plan in his head. He would hide this little pain-in-his-backside behind the soldier's station, slip through the gate, bury his mother inside their family tomb, slip back inside the city, snatch the brat, and race home before anyone was the wiser.

As they neared the edge of the city, Barek spotted soldiers. "Quick. Follow me."

He turned onto the well-worn path that led to the Tophet, an ancient burial ground rumored to be the site where his Carthaginian ancestors sacrificed their children to the gods. His father had called the place a living hell, a sad monument to the ability of humans to inflict pain on one another in the name of religion, a black mark on Carthage's past. As far as he was concerned, humans didn't need a specific place to be ugly to each other. They could do it in the comfort of their own homes and churches and never blink an eye.

"Halt, plebs!" Behind them, hobnailed spikes scrambled over the cobblestones. Barek motioned for Maggie to step up her pace. "They went that way!" a soldier shouted.

Barek wove thorough grave markers. Some of the limestone

stelae had carvings of what looked like different versions of the drawing Maggie had made of a child with outstretched arms. He remembered the urn hidden beneath his cloak and ran faster.

"Wait for me." Maggie tripped. She fell headlong onto the pavers. Her bloodcurdling scream bounced off the rows of stone pediments.

"Hush." Barek scooped her up. "Or you'll lead them to us." Urn tucked under one arm and Maggie stuffed under the other, he ran toward an opening in the side of Sanctuary Hill. He ducked inside, his breath coming in short spurts, his arms burning from the weight of his load. He waited for his eyes to adjust to the dim light filtering through the door-sized arch opposite the one he'd entered.

Maggie squirmed and fussed, but he wouldn't let her down. "What is this place?" she whispered. "I can't breathe."

"Shhh." Barek looked around.

Above them, a barrel-like ceiling had been carved out of the rock. A few steps below them . . . crematory urns. Thousands of plain clay crocks just like the one he was holding stacked fifty to seventy-five high against the walls. Hundreds of piles were scattered across the vault's floor. Countless urns sat on little shelves carved into the walls.

Barek lowered Maggie to the ground.

"My ankle!" she screamed.

"Shhhhh."

"In here." Soldier's boots thundered down the Tophet's path.

"Now look what you've done." Barek searched their hiding spot for an exit. "We've got to get going."

"My ankle hurts." Maggie hopped like a one-footed flamingo. "I can't breathe."

"You're breathing."

She shook her head and waved her hands in front of her face. "No, I'm not."

He'd never seen anyone upset so quickly. No telling what would come out of her mouth next. Her panic was sure to give them away. He would have to carry her home and be quick about it. But they would never escape if he was carrying both Maggie *and* his mother's ashes. Barek carefully set his mother's urn at the base of the nearest pile of crocks, telling himself this was only a temporary solution.

He snatched up Maggie and flung her on his back. "Hang on, and keep quiet."

Her arms wrapped his neck in a terrified grip that crushed his throat as he picked his way across broken pots, scattered beaded amulets, and brittle bones.

When he reached the opposite exit, Barek did not stop to see how many soldiers had poured in the burial cavern in pursuit of them. Holding tightly to Maggie's thin legs, he leaped over a stack of urns.

They burst into daylight and smacked into Felicissimus.

"Stranger!" Maggie screamed.

39

"COME QUICKLY." FELICISSIMUS TOOK off at a surprisingly brisk pace.

The man had been a friend to his father. But Barek didn't trust him, any more than he trusted the man who'd married his mother and ruined their lives. Unfortunately, he didn't have a better plan. He tightened his grip on Maggie's waiflike legs. "Wait." He set out to keep up with the toad-shaped slave trader hopping from the cover of one grave marker to the next.

"What are you doing?" Maggie pounded his back. "He's a stranger!"

"You have a better idea?" Barek asked, hissing.

"No."

"Then hush."

Weaving their way clear of the Tophet had not shaken the soldiers chasing after them with their swords drawn. Felicissimus pointed to a thicket of thorny shrubs at the base of the hill. Barek ordered Maggie to duck her head and dove in after Felicissimus.

Once inside the briar, he pulled Maggie from his back and clamped his hand over her mouth. "Not a word" he whispered, and scooted them deep into the shadows. For once, she did what he said.

Through the leaves he could see the glint of armor. The frustrated guard captain shouted furious orders to search the perimeter.

Holding their breaths, Barek, Maggie, and Felicissimus waited until the crunch of hobnail boots on gravel subsided. The slave trader jerked his head, indicating Barek and Maggie should follow.

"No." Maggie tugged Barek back. "Stranger danger."

Barek warned her again with a silent finger to his lips. Thrashing through the brush as quietly as they could, they exited the thicket opposite the side they'd entered. Cross-hatched scratches bloodied Maggie's legs, but again she'd done what he'd asked and hadn't uttered a single complaint. Perhaps the girl was tougher than he gave her credit for.

Barek hefted Maggie onto his back. The threesome scampered through back alleys Roman troops seldom patrolled. The scent of fish alerted Barek that they had emerged deep in the warehouse district down by the docks. Spring's delay had kept the harbor closed longer than normal. But with the return of the warming winds, any surviving stevedores and military men would soon emerge from their winter dens and haul their pasty faces back to the ships.

"This way." Felicissimus led them past a large stone platform, stained dark by the blood of slaves forced to parade across the stage.

Barek's chest tightened. He'd been to the auction block only once . . . that horrible day he'd disobeyed his parents and followed Cyprian to the docks. He remembered hurrying to catch up and having to squeeze through the crowd. When he'd reached the staging area, he saw a large black man whipping chained captives into large, stone washbasins. Sour-faced plebeians stripped the filthy men and poured jugs of scalding water over their lice-infested bodies. Once the prisoners had been washed, they were forced to climb aboard the bidding platform. As they stood naked beneath the glaring sun, he could almost smell the pus oozing from their festering battle wounds. These once proud men, some not much older than he, had dared to raise their swords against Rome. Now, in their shame, they struggled to remain upright. Their bodies, thin and weak from days spent crammed inside the hold of a Roman slave freighter, were no longer their own.

Barek remembered wanting to punch the auctioneer who came to the podium and made a few jokes as he prodded the men with a long metal rod. But as his father had trained him, he had remained silent. *"Turn the other cheek,"* his father's voice rang in his head. In truth, he knew full well he was turning a blind eye to their suffering, and he hated how the teachings of the church had turned him into a coward.

The men with any strength left sold to the highest bidders. Those who crumpled or failed to secure a clean bill of health were speared through the heart and hauled to the arena to feed the lions.

If he'd learned anything that day, it was the high cost of losing to Rome. A price he vowed never to pay.

Felicissimus lumbered down some stone steps. When he reached the bottom, he withdrew a key from his pocket and opened a wooden door. A rank odor escaped a dank, dark cell. "It's not the luxury you're used to, but you'll be safe here until your trail grows cold and those bloodhounds give up." He stepped inside, lit a lamp, and motioned them in.

Barek felt Maggie's arms tighten around his throat.

"Don't go in there," she whispered in his ear. "I won't be able to breathe."

"You want the soldiers to find us?"

She shook her head.

"Then keep quiet." Barek descended the stairs and stepped inside.

Felicissimus closed the door. "Wait here." He crossed the little room, then kicked the sleeping man curled into the corner. "Metellus, you might want to cover yourself. We've got company."

Metellus stirred, pushed up from his mat, and stretched his sinewy, black arms. His hands and feet had the roughened appearance of a desert warrior. Jagged scars created a map of pale pink mountains and dark gray valleys across his bare chest. When he lifted his shaved head, his dark eyes swam in bloodshot pools.

Barek gasped and took a step back. This was the man he'd seen flog the skin off an unruly Syrian who'd refused to mount the slave platform.

Barek tightened his grip on Maggie's legs. "Don't say a word."

"It smells like pee in here." She pinched her nose with one hand and clutched his tunic in the other. "I can't breathe."

"You're breathing." Barek took in their surroundings, calculating how quickly he could get them out the door.

The buzzard's nest was feathered with the tools of the slave trade. In the corner opposite Metellus, chalky limestone covered the sides of an empty wooden bucket. Barek guessed the bucket held the dust used to mark the feet of slaves. Everyone in the province had been trained to recognize the familiar sign of bondage and to report anyone caught out and about without their master. Lisbeth's foot had been coated in the white substance when Cyprian brought her home. Barek remembered Cyprian and his parents cleaning Lisbeth up and trying to pass her off as a desert princess, but he knew from her chalky foot that she was no more than a slave, nowhere near the equal of his mother.

Above the chalk bucket, a flagellum hung from a peg in the stone wall. The whip's Elmwood handle looked as if it had been carved to fit the big hands of Metellus, and the three strips of rawhide laced with bits of bone still dripped blood from his most recent use.

"Hungry?" Felicissimus opened a dilapidated cupboard. Two little mice squealed. "Greedy little thieves. Scram." The slave trader flicked his wrist, and the mice jumped to the floor, dashed about the room in a crazed flurry, then scurried across Barek's boot.

Maggie screamed and nearly climbed atop Barek's shoulders as the furry little creatures circled the cell again. Their second lap around, one of the mice found a crack in the plaster, squeezed his plump body into the opening, and disappeared. The other creature hesitated a moment too long. Metellus snatched the whip from the peg. Leather strips slashed the air with a loud crack. The lashes lapped up the rodent's little gray body and hurled it against the opposite wall. Metellus grunted and returned the whip to the peg.

Felicissimus reached into the cupboard and retrieved a half-eaten round of bread. He brushed away the crumbs gnawed free by the mice as if nothing had happened. "Day old. But at least you won't starve." He broke the bread in half and offered Maggie a piece.

Barek could feel Maggie's fingernails digging through his tunic. "We're not hungry." He reached up, pried her loose, then pulled her off his back and set her down beside him. She immediately went into her flamingo imitation, tugging on Barek's sleeve to keep her balance.

"Suit yourself." Felicissimus tossed the piece to Metellus. The big slave caught the bread with one hand, crammed it into his mouth, and swallowed without even chewing. Felicissimus flipped over the empty chalk bucket and sat down with an exhausted sigh. "I was surprised to find you out and about after the trouble you encountered with the ox. What mischief were you two planning in the Tophet?"

Maggie's eyes darted between the dead mouse and Felicissimus. "We were burying his mother."

"Hush, Maggie," Barek ordered.

Felicissimus considered this information for a moment. "Of course a good son would want his mother properly laid to rest." He picked up a hollowed-out gourd from the water bucket and took a drink. "It is a shame that Aspasius has denied Christians access to their ancestral plots." He rubbed his chin, his eyes narrowed in thought. "My boy, have you pondered what is to become of you now that both of your parents are gone?" Felicissimus emptied the gourd and tossed it back into the bucket.

"My daddy says Barek is like a son to him."

"Maggie, keep quiet."

She crossed her arms to prove that she didn't need his help and aimed her angry stare at the mouse. Barek could boss her around all he wanted, but he was certain she'd do just as she pleased no matter what he said.

"I'm sure the girl is right." Felicissimus flicked dried crumbs from his tunic. "Cyprian is an honorable man. He promised your father he would look after you, and so far the new bishop of Carthage has kept his promise. I don't think you have to worry about Cyprian casting you out." Felicissimus put his hands on his knees and leaned forward. "But what about after Cyprian dies? What's to become of you then? By law, you can own nothing of his, not even his church, unless he makes you his heir." Felicissimus let his gaze slither over Maggie. "Which I doubt he will do now that his real heir has appeared out of nowhere."

Barek followed Felicissimus's line of sight and noticed Maggie drinking from the gourd. "Maggie! No!"

She wiped her mouth with the back of her hand. "I'm thirsty."

"Wait until we get home." Barek took the gourd from her hand, tossed it back in the bucket, and picked her up. He turned his attention back to Felicissimus. "I don't want my father's church," Barek declared. "I'm a free man. I intend to learn a trade or join the imperial navy."

"Admirable." Felicissimus crossed his arms over his belly. "But slaves are either born or made. And you, my boy, are bound to a master as surely as Metellus is bound to me."

Barek let his gaze go to the iron cuff around the black man's ankle and the chain tethering him to the wall. "I told you, I'm a free man."

"So you tell yourself. In effect, your parents sold you into slavery."

Barek bristled. *How dare this slave trader speak ill of my father and mother!* "I've been sold to no one."

"Oh, but you have."

"Who?"

"Christ." Felicissimus chuckled at Barek's shock. "Your end will come as painfully as that of the rest of those who choose to disobey their Roman master . . . unless . . ."

"Unless what?"

"I've made my living judging human flesh and character. From the fire in your eyes, I believe you to be smarter than most, my boy."

"I'm done with Christ."

A crooked smile pushed back the slave trader's jowls. "Then I have good news for you." Felicissimus reached into his pocket and withdrew a crumpled slip of parchment.

"Libellus?" The bold word had been inked across the top by a professional hand. "What's this?"

"Your ticket to freedom." Felicissimus leaned in. "Trust me, this proof of sacrifice will save your life. Believers have more choices than Cyprian would have them know." He rubbed his belly.

"Like what?"

Felicissimus tapped the slip of paper in Barek's hand. "All one has to do is simply pay a clever servant to acquire the necessary vouchers. Then, should their religious loyalties to the gods of Rome ever come into question, they simply show the paper and they are covered."

"Covered?"

"Safe. Declared free to go about their business."

Free? Never to be under Rome's yoke again? "Do you have one?"

He patted his coin purse. "Keep it right here."

"But the Scriptures say you are to have no other gods before the one God."

"I thought you were done with the Scriptures," Felicissimus said with a grin. "It's just a piece of paper, lad. God knows it means nothing to me to bow before a slab of chiseled marble."

Barek turned the slip over before handing it back.

Maggie squeezed his neck. "Let's go."

"No need to run off. I know you're curious. It'll only take a minute to relieve your curiosity." Felicissimus waited. Barek nodded, and the slave trader proceeded. "Believers can buy writs after they visit a temple, or they can bribe a magistrate to lie that they participated in a pagan ceremony when, in fact, they did not. Riskier, but doable."

"Most of the believers are poor. They don't have money for bread, let alone bribes and fancy pieces of paper. And Cyprian would never agree to finance deception."

"That's where you're wrong. He gave me money. Told me to spend it on making things better in this city. What could make things better than to end the persecution of the church?" Felicissimus cupped his mouth, patted the coin bag attached to his belt again, and whispered, "With my help, believers are now able to get their hands upon the protection they need. But since I am the one taking all the risk, I don't think it is too much to ask the recipients to help me spread the blessings around. All I ask is that they find a friend also in need of libellus. Once they convince this friend to convince another friend of the unfortunate necessity of bowing to Rome's gods, the writ is theirs for free. Rome is happy, and the Christians walk away with security in their pockets and perfectly clear consciences."

Barek felt his heart leap. "Walk away?"

Felicissimus smiled and clasped Barek's shoulder. "Or sail away, if they are so inclined." He tucked the writ of libellus into Barek's pocket and gave it a pat.

"Even Cyprian? He could have one and be safe?"

"Especially Cyprian." Felicissimus clasped his hands across his belly. "My boy, this paper offers a freedom like you have never known."

Barek had been so angry at the way Cyprian looked past his mother when Lisbeth arrived. But how ungrateful would he seem if he let Cyprian's desire for his first wife erase all the good the man had done for him, good he was not obligated to do? "I can't pay."

"Oh, I'm sure you won't have to. As Caecilianus's son you have a whole bunch of prospects who know and trust you enough to want in on this rare opportunity. Find one, and the writ is yours. Find two, and I'll locate a centurion willing to give you a commission in the royal navy. Find three, and I'll make certain Aspasius never lays a hand on Cyprian."

"But I don't know anyone willing to pretend they've sacrificed to Roman gods."

"Oh, but you do. They sneak in and out of your house by way of the back gate."

40

THE SOUNDS OF A horse's soft nickering and the splash of water in a trough stirred Lisbeth from a restless sleep. She opened her eyes. High overhead, cobwebs hung from rough-hewn beams. The stink of livestock assaulted her nose. Pale morning rays kissed the fresh straw she was burrowed into. Though the dried grass covering was light, the weight of her burdens pressed so heavily she felt as if she couldn't breathe.

She quickly shook off the straw but not the feeling of being trapped. Shivers dislodged the painful memories of meeting Cyprian in the stable. Hopes of reconciliation had turned into the permanent severance of their relationship.

She pushed up from the wagonbed. "Pontius?"

Startled by her voice, Cyprian's friend wheeled, pitchfork in hand. "Lisbeth? What are you doing here?"

"Good question." She plucked straw from her hair. "I could ask you the same."

"I sleep here." He pointed the sharp prongs toward the loft. "I searched the entire estate for you last night."

"Sorry for your wasted efforts." She stretched the kinks from her neck and rubbed the throbbing place on her shoulder where Felicissimus had pinned her against the fence. Those bruises would heal. The ache in her soul from Cyprian's definitive refusal to let her help him was a wound she would carry always. "What time is it?"

"Time for you to go."

She unfolded her legs. "I'll go when I'm ready."

Even though she and Mama had already laid out the steps of what needed to be done and when, Ruth's absence would leave a big hole in the fight to stamp out these plagues. She would need to train some more help before she could even think about returning to the twenty-first century. Naomi and Junia, perhaps. She would also have to make sure Diona was on the mend and gather as many herbs as possible to restock the makeshift pharmacy.

Lisbeth shoved aside her disappointment in Cyprian's reaction and pushed herself back into action. "I'm going to need medical supplies today, Pontius." She hopped down from the wagon. "Think you could help me scavenge the city after I round?"

Confusion scrunched Pontius's face. "Round?"

"You know, check on Diona and any new patients we may have gotten in last night."

He stabbed his pitchfork into the wet straw he was mucking from the stall. "Cyprian will want to go with you."

That had been her plan all along . . . have her husband want to go far away from here and make a life together. After spending the night alone, she was certain that plan lay in a sodden heap.

"I don't think so." Lisbeth brushed straw from her tunic.

"Cyprian was called by God, you know. His end will be as God wills."

"I envy you, Pontius. Living each day without the fear of tomorrow. It is luxury I will never have."

Lisbeth strode back toward the villa and the aroma of freshly baked bread. Who had taken Ruth's place in the kitchen? "Naomi?" Flour covered the large wooden table and the front of the servant girl's tunic. "What are you doing?"

"Ruth let me help her make the bread sometimes. I wanted to" —tears splashed upon the table's powdery surface, and Naomi dragged a dusty hand across her nose—"do what I could."

"It smells wonderful."

"I knew Barek would be missing his mother, and I just thought . . ."

Lisbeth recognized the signs of unrequited love, and this girl had it bad. Of course, if anyone looked very closely at Lisbeth since her husband had told her to go home, they'd probably find her feelings for Cyprian written all over her face, too. "Well, you know what they say."

"They?"

"The way to a man's heart is through his stomach."

"Who says that?"

"I don't know. But if making bread can bring a guy around to a girl's side, I should have learned how to cook." She kissed Naomi's cheek. "I'm starving. After I check on Mama and our patients I'll come back for a couple of warm slices for me and Maggie."

"I'll take her breakfast."

"That's okay. I won't be that long."

Lisbeth hurried down the typhoid hall. She found Titus pacing like a caged cat while Vivia sat beside Diona, her hands tucked inside her stola and dark circles under her eyes. Neither of these parents had slept much in the past twenty-four hours.

Mama was helping Diona off the chamber pot.

"How's our patient?" Lisbeth asked.

"No more bloody stools," Mama said with a smile.

After Mama's quick recap of Diona's night, she tossed Lisbeth the stethoscope and encouraged her to do her own examination. The only indication of any remaining pain was a slight grimace when Lisbeth applied direct pressure to the operative site. "Appears she doesn't have any complications from surgery. No infection. No sign of pneumonia." She draped the stethoscope around her neck.

"What does that mean?" Vivia asked, her hands twisting wrinkles into her gown.

"It means your daughter is going to live," Lisbeth said. "Now we'll just have to wait at least twenty-one days to see if you or your husband present with symptoms."

Vivia struggled to her feet. "Thank you." She turned to Mama. "Thanks to both of you. I'm sorry we were difficult, Magdalena."

Mama smiled. "All's forgiven." She reached to pat Vivia's shoulder, and to Lisbeth's surprise, the woman didn't shy away. "Besides, we're not always at our best when we're worried about those we love." Her glance slid toward Lisbeth.

"I know, but I shouldn't have . . ." Vivia paused. "How can we ever repay your kindness?"

"Here, take this." Titus undid the coin pouch on his belt. "All of it."

"We don't want your money," Lisbeth said.

Titus thrust the bag into Lisbeth's hands. "Keep it."

"You really should consider his offer quite an honor. Titus is not easily parted from his money, especially when it comes to healers."

Lisbeth gave the money back. "What we really need is some help." She took the chamber pot and held it out to Vivia.

The woman backed up, and her hands disappeared back into the folds of her garment. "Help?"

"We're a little . . . shorthanded."

"I heard about Ruth and the baby." Vivia seemed honestly sad, but still wary of getting too involved in the lives of Christians. "I'm sorry. She was a good woman."

"Yes." Lisbeth bit back tears. "Ruth was a remarkable woman." Selfless, forgiving, and trusting. The kind of woman Lisbeth thought she'd automatically become after she became a Christian.

Instead she continued to forge her own path and look for ways to manipulate outcomes. What had her schemes gained? She hadn't slowed measles. Typhoid could still double the plague's destruction. Her family was more fractured than ever. Cyprian had no interest in coming home with her. And yet, despite her total ineffectiveness, all she could think about was that there had to be a way to turn things around.

"I don't know what I can do to help," Vivia was saying when Lisbeth pulled her attention back to her patients. "I've never changed a bed or emptied a chamber pot. But we're willing to learn, aren't we, Titus?"

Titus's eyes grew wide and shifted beneath his bangs.

"Titus," Vivia warned.

He sighed. "It's the least we can do."

"We'll start by teaching you how to nurse your family back to health." Mama held out the chamber pot. "I'll show you how to properly dispose of the waste and how to disinfect your hands so that you don't contract the sickness."

Vivia's hands slowly came out from beneath her stola. She took a deep breath and grasped hold of the chamber pot and a whole new way of life.

Watching this amazing transformation, Lisbeth felt an idea dawn. A few days ago she was willing to fiddle with time by taking Cyprian away from here. What if she committed to something even more risky? Like staying here and helping him fight evil with good.

41

LISBETH LEFT MAMA WITH the daunting chore of turning the Ciceros into nursing staff while she went in search of Cyprian. Passing the library, she noticed the door ajar. She pushed it open and peeked inside.

Cyprian rifled through scrolls scattered across the desk. Dogs paced nervously around his feet. His hair was wet. Sometime between her failed attempt to save him from himself and her morning rounds, he'd managed to slip to the baths and get cleaned up. He'd changed out of the simple tunic he'd been wearing since her return and donned the dingy, off-white toga Caecilianus had worn to his death. She'd read enough about Roman customs to know what this changing of his dress meant. Cyprian intended to publically demonstrate his sympathy for his fallen leader. If he added Caecilianus to his name, there would be no turning back.

"Cyprian, you shouldn't be in here." The dogs bounded to her outstretched hand.

He looked up from the mess. "It is *my* library." Dark circles under his eyes indicated he hadn't rested any better upon the downy tick he and Ruth had shared than she had upon the lonely boards of the wagonbed.

She held up her palms to deflect his barb. "I only meant it's dangerous for you to be in this part of the house."

"I'll wash my hands." He added another parchment to the stack among the pots of ink and sharpened quills.

She patted the dogs nuzzling her hands. "What are you looking for?"

"Caecilianus's notes." Obviously he was in no mood for more interference from her, but that was too bad.

"On what?"

"Caecilianus worked to acquire one of the finest collections of the early church letters written by the apostles." Cyprian produced a carefully bound scroll. "Paul's personal correspondence to the church at Philippi was one of his favorites."

"Bet that cost a handsome sum."

He fingered the worn parchment. "Worth every piece of silver my old friend convinced me to pay." The loss in his eyes tugged at Lisbeth's heart.

She understood the importance of cherished memories. They'd kept her going through many lonely nights. "Why have you chosen that particular scripture?"

"My feeble attempt to rally the church at their last worship assembly did not go well."

"And you think the right verse will help?"

"Paul was under arrest in Rome when he wrote these words. He knew what it felt like to be afraid." His eyes found hers for the briefest of moments, long enough for understanding to pass between them. Beneath his bravado was a man as anxious as she. "And yet," Cyprian continued, "Paul found the words to encourage that little church to stick together. In their unity they would find joy."

"The church seems perfectly unified to me. Especially in their dislike of patricians." She smiled at his lack of appreciation for her attempt to lighten his mood. "Overall, I was very impressed with how they all worked together and embraced our plan to tackle the problems in the slums."

"They did it for Ruth."

"Oh."

"I didn't mean they weren't glad to help you; it's just . . ." He undid the clasp on the scroll and began to unroll the parchment across his desk. "The church gathers this evening. As their new bishop, I need to offer some sort of encouragement. Some kind of hope now that Ruth is gone."

"Is that why you're wearing Caecilianus's toga?"

"I'm not fit to carry his sandals. It's my attempt to remind them of the man we all loved. The man who brought us together. Give them hope . . ."

"Hope's a good thing." If only hope had been enough to save the last man who wore that garment. Lisbeth stepped in and closed the door. "Especially if it's in Christ and not in the strength of one man."

"Or one woman determined to control the future." He moved from behind the desk and took a step toward her. "Before you go, I think we should talk about what happened or didn't happen last night."

Much as she wished he would make a move to close the gap between them, he did not. He stood his ground, keeping himself an excruciating arm's length away. His drawn expression communicated his contemplation of whether continuing this conversation would result in the undoing of his resolve. If she let this opportunity pass without telling him everything, her own undoing was the only certainty.

Lisbeth took a breath. "You can't imagine what it was like for me to walk the streets of a thriving Roman city for the first time. I'd grown up watching my father reclaim crumbling bits of ancient civilizations from the earth and try to piece them together."

Whether or not it was wise to point out their differences at this critical moment, she believed it foolish to pretend they both weren't fully aware of them. "While Papa carefully catalogued pottery shards, I assigned my own imaginings to the partial remains. I could never have guessed this." She waved her hands to take in the grandeur of his home. "To actually experience something like an occupied villa, or the Colosseum in all its splendor, whole and operational, was breathtaking. To hear the lions roar beneath the floor or to watch gladiators duel to the death . . . all of it was shocking."

She half expected him to say something about how her protest at the games had nearly gotten both of them tossed to the arena floor. But when he didn't interrupt, she took a chance and reached out to lightly touch his arm. "Horrible as that arena experience was, meeting you made it bearable. When I saw your people, dying simply because they refused to recant their faith, and I saw how much you cared, something inside me changed."

His face puzzled. "Changed?"

"Your people became my people. And your God my God."

"How do you know our holy words?"

She waved her hand over the stack of parchments. "In the future, all of these different scrolls, plus a few Caecilianus didn't manage to acquire, get combined into one book, and . . ." She could see that he wasn't grasping the concept. "Anyway, it's all packaged in a handy leather carrying case, so to speak. It's easy to read. Anyone can see for themselves what God has to say."

"Anyone?"

"Anyone."

"Including you?"

"Okay, you caught me. Sue me. Something about all of this *Do unto others as you would have them do unto you* Ruth and Caecilianus not only preached but also lived intrigued me. It didn't make sense. Then I started reading and . . ."

"They lived their life in a way that was hard to ignore." The hard lines etched at the corners of his eyes slackened. "And so?"

In that moment, she wanted him to see her for the generous,

trusting person she was desperately trying to become. "I believed."

His defensive posture melted. "You are a believer?"

"I may not always be the best example of a Christian, but yes, I am."

Her confession did not bring him rushing into her arms as she had always imagined it would. His eyes were once again impossible to read. "Did you become a follower for me?"

"I did it for me." She made a bold move and closed the gap between them, her chest lightly brushing his.

He flinched at the physical contact but did not back away. His quick breaths warmed her cheek. She could feel the thrum of his heart struggling to match hers. In the tense silence, she could hear the sorting of his thoughts.

"I didn't understand how much this church meant to you until . . ." She let her fingers skim the length of his arm, soaking in the heat of him. "I saw how easily you opened your home to them and saw you working with them. I couldn't help but love these people even more." When her hand met his, she felt his fingers relax and slowly take hers in. This small gesture of acquiescence encouraged her to say the hardest part of all. "You've been more than generous. But I don't believe you have to die to prove you love them."

"Don't you think I've asked the Lord if there is any other way?"

"Did it ever occur to you that I may have been sent here to help you find another option? If you let me stay and help you, I think the church can avoid losing you before your time." The emotional boundaries she'd set in place since her arrival disintegrated. With her free hand, she reached into her pocket and fished out the paper. "Let me read this to you." She opened the page. "History records that if you continue on this path, traitors will arrange for your gruesome death. You will be martyred. But you already know that." She pointed at the last paragraph. "What you don't know is what it goes on to say. What the church did after your death, and how successful their actions were at turning the tide of popular opinion. So I was thinking, what if we implemented those tactics earlier rather than later?"

Cyprian extricated his hand from hers and took the paper. He folded it without looking at the paragraph she'd highlighted in yellow. "The difference between us is not a span of time. The difference is that I know we all die. How we die is up to God, and I am resigned to his will. You, on the other hand, live like one who believes if you claim Christ as savior, you can tell him when, where, and what you're willing to die for."

"That's not true. Doctors see deaths every day that they can't stop." Images of the still body of the young mother who'd taken her daughter to Disney World flashed in Lisbeth's mind. "Let me tell you something: there's nothing like staring at a life snuffed out too early to make you come face-to-face with your own mortality. All of us die. Even Aspasius. But I take comfort in knowing that when that jerk leaves this world, he'll go out the same way the rest of us do . . . with nothing." She could still see the wedding ring on that young mother's left hand. Her Disney T-shirt hanging in the tiny hospital closet. Her toddler crying in the hall. All of it had been left behind. "Two thousand years from now, if some archaeologist cracks open the proconsul's tomb, everything that monster has fought so hard to keep will be right where he left it."

Cyprian frowned. "If you know all of this, why do you live like you will do the deciding on when and how death comes to you or to those you love?" He pressed the paper into her hand and closed her fingers around its sharp edges. His breath, although warm against her neck, sent a chill down her spine. "What good is it if we save our own bodies but the church loses its soul?" He released her. "You have your work, and I have mine."

She wasn't the only one who'd returned from exile a changed

person. He was more hardheaded than ever. "I'm saying we can do both. If we join forces, keep the church unified like the early believers in Philippi, we can apply the tactics of the early church and shut Aspasius down." She lifted her hands and smiled. "We both win."

"This is not about winning or losing."

Lisbeth paused. She stood at the crossroads of decision. Was it her knowledge of the future or her need to control outcomes driving this train? Should she keep silent or tell Cyprian the truth? She thought of the cancer rotation she'd done during her internship, how she'd watched each patient's face as the attending broke the devastating diagnosis. *"How long?"* was always the first response. She'd decided then and there that numbered days deserve the truth. While everyone may not know the exact number of their days, she knew Cyprian's days ended on September 14, 258 AD. It was already spring. He had six months at best.

If Cyprian heard nothing else, she wasn't leaving until he heard the whole story.

"Felicissimus is trying to get you killed. If you won't let me help you, the least you can do is cut your ties with him."

"Felicissimus?" His brow crinkled in disbelief. "What does the slave trader have to do with my future?"

"Everything."

"You've held a grudge against him from your first encounter."

"Not easy to love someone who pins your face to the filthy floor of a rank little cell block. But what he did to me is nothing compared to how he has betrayed you and continues to betray you." She hooked Cyprian's arm and kept him from walking off. "Felicissimus was the one who set the trap that day in the market. Ruth and I were the bait; you were the prey."

He stepped back. "And you have proof of his treachery?"

"Am *I* on trial now?" Lisbeth snapped. "No, I don't have proof."

"Then it's your word against his."

"Look, just because I never liked the guy doesn't mean I'd lie about him. On the same day you sailed for exile, I saw Felicissimus sneaking out of Aspasius's office." She could see Cyprian processing, searching his memory for clues, signs of disloyalty he might have overlooked.

"Why would my friend betray me?"

She shook her head. "Why does anyone stick a knife in someone's back? Money. Power. Revenge. Hurt feelings."

Cyprian scowled. "Feelings?"

"Maybe you didn't listen to his ideas, or perhaps he wanted to be in charge, or maybe he's just a greedy son of a gun."

"Gun?"

"Much nicer word than I was thinking."

"When I came back, I was in no shape to take on the leadership of the church. I tried to dump the responsibility in his lap . . . and he refused. Explain that."

"Caecilianus chose you. For Felicissimus to blatantly step in and take over now that you're back from exile could ruffle a lot of feathers. He's smarter than he lets on."

"How could you forget what he did for you? He saved you from Aspasius. If Felicissimus hadn't told me of your arrival on the slave block, we wouldn't be having this conversation."

Lisbeth looked down. She was certain the backstabbing slave trader would carry through on his threats to harm Maggie if she said more. She hesitated for a moment, then boldly went on. "All I know is what this piece of paper says." She swallowed. "The proconsul of Carthage is going to kill you, and I think someone on the inside is helping him."

"Mommy!" Maggie pushed open the door. "Filly saved us."

Felicissimus stood in the doorway.

He had one arm around Barek's shoulders, another around her daughter, and a very pleased smile crawling across his sleazy face.

42

OVERNIGHT, SPRING MELTED INTO summer. Sweltering temperatures matched Lisbeth and Cyprian's steamy attitudes.

It didn't help that hot air had pressed in from the desert and turned the villa into an oven and the sea into a boiling stewpot. The added patrols Rome had sent to quash the "dangerously unruly" Christians had become lethargic in the rising heat. Small patrols sought patches of shade and sat doing nothing while the stench of rotting bodies made it nearly impossible to breathe. It seemed the fly population had doubled since the sun came up. By sundown, their dirty little feet would speed the spread of typhoid across the city. Frightening as fighting two epidemics at once could be, it scared Lisbeth far more to see Cyprian dig in and refuse to believe he had a wolf in the flock.

She watched from the balcony as the harbor gates creaked open. The scarlet sails of the imperial fleet unfurled, and all seaworthy ships lifted anchor. Hundreds of oars slapped the water in a rhythmic cadence that could be heard throughout the city. The royal triremes resumed their patrols of Rome's ever-expanding borders, and in less than an hour, the entire fleet had rowed out to sea.

If she could have been allowed to conduct a cursory inspection of each ship, Lisbeth was certain she would find measles and typhoid stowed away in the bodies of sailors with hacking coughs or upset stomachs. They were too late to shut down the sea routes, and that meant two extremely contagious and deadly diseases would be carried by flies and ships to every nook and cranny of the empire.

Her gaze followed the ships disappearing into the horizon. With the change of the winds, it would be only weeks before Aspasius's ship would return to the harbor without the man they'd been commissioned to retrieve from Curubis. Knowing the day of reckoning loomed near would have filled her with terror if she wasn't certain that day had already come. Felicissimus had too much to gain not to have already alerted Aspasius to Cyprian's current whereabouts.

Lisbeth stepped into the oppressive heat of the measles hall. Naomi waited nervously beside Mama for her first round of medical training. Lisbeth held out a small vial. "Douse your mask with lavender oil. It will help with the smell."

She'd thrown herself into dealing with the two plagues, which was just as well because she was not making any headway with Cyprian. Since the slave trader had saved Cyprian's children, he was now a hero. She suspected Felicissimus had somehow arranged the whole chase scenario through the Tophet so he could swoop in and save the day. Make himself look good in the eyes of Cyprian and the church. Cyprian had given her a look that said Maggie's safe return was all the proof he needed of Felicissimus's trustworthiness. So while Cyprian was thinking the guy deserved a medal, she couldn't help but wonder what treachery Felicissimus planned next. Would he be like Judas and lead the soldiers to their door, then betray Cyprian with a kiss?

Urgent pounding rattled the front door. Low, hostile voices accompanied the scuffle of feet and the authoritative ring of soldered metal.

"I'll get it," Naomi offered. "You two stay out of sight." Naomi cracked the door. "We have the sickness."

The soldiers pushed in, knocking Naomi to the floor. Lisbeth broke free of Mama's death grip.

"Hey, buddy!" Lisbeth shouted, causing the brawny leader with the drawn sword to turn. Wiry red hair peeked from beneath his helmet. Spotty whiskers populated his jutting chin. He was really no more than an oversize boy sent to do a man's job. Had the sickness reduced Rome's military? "Didn't you hear her? This house is filled with measles and typhoid." Lisbeth stepped between the soldier and Naomi, her balled fists upon her hips in hopes of intimidating this boy with ambition written all over his face. "Breathe too long in here, and you'll be begging for relief in a week."

The soldier pointed the tip of his blade at Lisbeth's throat while his worried eyes made a reconnaissance run over the premises. "Are you the healer?"

Her warning had his pimpled friends backing toward the door, but this young foot soldier appeared determined to earn his stripes. She'd have to rein in her galloping heart and work a bit harder to convince him to leave them alone. "Who wants to know?"

"Aspasius Paternus."

Lisbeth gasped.

Mama boldly stepped out from behind a column. "I am the healer you seek."

"No!" Lisbeth placed herself between Mama and the soldiers. "I'm the healer."

Naomi came to stand side by side with them. "I'm the healer."

Confusion sanded the young soldier's bristled bravado. He moved the point of his sword from throat to throat. "We'll take the old one." He thrust the tip toward Mama. "Come with us."

"I'll need my medical bag and help packing it." Mama inched Lisbeth away. "Don't cause a scene," she whispered in English.

"No. You'll come as you are." The soldier reached for Mama. "Aspasius said you were a sly one."

Mama calmly lifted her chin. "Young man, I can assure you the proconsul does not want me without my supplies. I'm assuming he's not well and needs my healing potions, the ones I keep in my medical bag."

The soldier weighed his options. "Stay within sight."

"I just have to step into this room. You're welcome to come, but I must warn you, the sick in this room suffer bloody runs for days and then their bodies convulse and give out." Mama smiled at how quickly the soldier backed down. "Come, Lisbeth."

They hurried into the hall where Vivia was spooning broth into an improving Diona's mouth. "What's wrong? I heard voices."

"Aspasius has discovered my whereabouts." Mama began gathering her surgical equipment. "If he's contracted one of these plagues, Diona's sickness was not a fluke. The plagues are officially moving out of the slums."

"Titus," Vivia roused her husband from his nap. "You must do something."

"No." Mama settled the man struggling to sit up. "There may come a day when I will need the influence of Titus Cicero to save my children. This is not that day."

"When that day comes, he'll be there." Vivia kissed Mama's cheek. "You can count on us."

Lisbeth pulled Mama aside and whispered in English, "If you think I'm going to let those Roman thugs take you without a fight, you've got another thing coming."

"Plague is hardest on those who have lived soft lives. Aspasius will not do well. I, on the other hand, know hardship, and I am not afraid."

Guilt prickled Lisbeth's skin. If she'd somehow prevented Mama from leaving their desert tent years ago, Mama wouldn't have fallen down that blasted hole at the Cave of the Swimmers. Papa would have bagged a few archaeological trinkets, penned an award-winning journal article, and carted them off to a far less dangerous site. None of them would have ever discovered the life-changing secret of time travel. None of them would have suffered the heartbreak they all lived with now.

Shame on her if she allowed Mama to walk into danger again. "I'll go."

Mama dropped third-century operating tools into her bag, refusing to take the modern tools in case Lisbeth needed them. "Trust me. It's best if I go quietly."

"I promised Papa I'd bring you back to him. Don't you want to go home?"

"Yes." Mama stopped her packing and put down her bag. "Very much. But it seems my work here is not yet finished." She took Lisbeth by the shoulders. "Sometimes all you need to be happy is to know that you matter enough that someone would come for you." She cupped Lisbeth's cheek. "And you did, baby. You already did." A tear trickled across the scar carved by the cruel hand of a monster.

"Mama, I—"

"Don't let *your* daughter grow up without her mother." Mama wiped her face and hurriedly crammed tools into a cloth sack. "Promise you will *not* come after me again."

43

SITTING BENEATH THE SHADE of the pergola, Cyprian fingered the limp, worn edges of Caecilianus's felt bishop's hat. Last time he'd tried to encourage the church it had turned out to be a dismal failure. Perhaps he was foolish to think wearing his mentor's head covering could help him replicate the wisdom it once capped. Cyprian set the conical hat upon his head. Until God sent a better candidate for bishop, he was it. He picked up his mentor's favorite scroll and began to dictate his sermon to Pontius.

"Church, I, Caecilianus Cyprianus Thascius, come before you a humbled man."

"Caecilianus?" Pontius looked up from his notes and smiled. "You've added his name to yours?"

"Have I done the right thing, Pontius?"

His friend's suspended pen dripped upon the parchment. "The bishop's name suits you. He and Ruth would be pleased."

"I mean . . . should I have chosen the church?"

"Over Lisbeth?" Pontius freshened his pen in the ram's horn inkwell. "Every man stands before the Lord alone. This is a matter for you and God to settle."

Cyprian shoved the ache of his decision aside. "Ready your pen, my friend."

Pacing the stone tiles, Cyprian waxed long on how the grace of

God had illuminated and strengthened him in the early days of his life as a new convert. He spoke freely of his difficulties conquering the vices of his former life . . . his enjoyment of bawdy theater shows, the hollowness of political aspirations, and the emptiness of his heart.

Emptiness of my heart.

Cyprian paused and turned the phrase over in his mind. "My happiest days were spent listening to Caecilianus tell the stories of the Galilean carpenter. Like the rest of those gathered, I couldn't believe the injustices the son of God suffered." He swallowed. "The day I decided to join this little band and do something to right the wrong was the day the emptiness vanished . . . I'd thought for good."

He gazed at the sea. "But while I was in Curubis, separated from those of like conviction, it felt as if the Lord had deserted me. I was frightened. Not of the dreams, but of dying empty. I know Ruth was right to encourage me to once again cast my lot with the believers. It fills me with purpose to lead them, to serve alongside them in their sacrifice." Cyprian rubbed his chin. "So why do I continue to question my decision to send Lisbeth home without me?"

Cyprian often wondered how different his life would have been had Lisbeth Hastings not appeared from a realm beyond his comprehension. He probably would have journeyed to the marbled halls of Rome in search of a woman positioned to help him win a seat in the council chambers. He never would have opened his home to the sick, let alone allowed himself to become quite so concerned for those under his roof. Caecilianus would not have died. And Cyprianus Thascius, the rich Roman convert, would never have been thrust into the uncomfortable position of marrying a widow who deserved more than he could give, choosing between the wife he adored and taking over a fledgling church.

In the end, had Lisbeth never left Dallas, he would have been a different person.

Cyprian stared at the ships rowing out to sea. Any day the dispatched naval vessel sent to fetch him from exile would return empty-handed. Aspasius would tear this province apart searching for him. Innocent people were sure to die.

He'd been right in insisting that Lisbeth take their daughter to a safer place, hadn't he? Knowing Aspasius would never be able to touch his wife again would make his choice an easier cross to bear. But was the easier path God's path? What if God had a purpose for Lisbeth and Maggie in this time?

"Cyprian?" Pontius's urgent plea snapped Cyprian from his useless ponderings.

He turned to see his deacon's stylus pointing down the beach. Lisbeth sprinted toward the pergola, screaming his name.

"Something's wrong." Cyprian dropped his scroll and ran to her.

When they met, she buried her face in his shoulder. Heaving sobs garbled every word but one: *soldiers.*

"Do they have Maggie?" Heart pounding, he peeled her loose. "Tell me."

Between gasps, she spit out, "Mama . . . Aspasius took Mama." She wiped her nose and lifted her chin. "I need your help."

For reasons he would never understand, just when he'd resigned himself to what he thought was God's purpose for his life, God seemed to reattach his destiny to this woman. Neither his dreams nor her history pages had predicted the course-changing love that would result from this unimaginable collision.

Loving Lisbeth of Dallas had opened up his heart to things beyond rules and honor and expectations. Whatever the consequences, he wanted her—needed her—in his future.

She had risked everything for him. How could he turn his back on her?

"Then let's make Aspasius wish we had never returned." He held her trembling body and whispered into her hair. "I believe we are in need of that crazy plan."

44

STARING INTO THE SUNKEN eyes of the man who'd tormented her for years was harder than Magdalena had anticipated. On the brisk march to the proconsul's palace she'd worked to conquer the churning in her stomach, but when the soldiers dragged her through the front door and she saw the worry on the faces of her old friends she'd immediately felt the need to vomit.

Kardide, a hook-nosed Turk, and Tabari, a brown-bean native, had managed to give her a couple of quick hugs before the soldiers tore them apart and ordered them up against the birdcages. Waxbill finches beat their wings against the gold bars, and ring-necked parrots strutted and squawked their protest.

Neither of her friends said a word. They didn't have to. From the scars on their faces, they'd already suffered for the help they'd given her months ago. She hated that her return might bring a painful end to their lives. Within a few minutes, Iltani emerged from Aspasius's bedroom, grave-faced and motioning Magdalena forward.

With the tip of a soldier's sword in her back, Magdalena now stood at the door of the bedroom she hated more than the naked man shivering on the bed. All she could think of was the sour taste in her mouth.

Pytros perched on the scribe's stool he'd moved beside the

bed. He stopped mopping Aspasius's forehead. "Master, your healer's been found."

A victorious smirk twitched the corners of Aspasius's mouth. There was no end to the creative ways he could make Magdalena and her friends regret the day she slipped free. Had it not been for Iltani, Tabari, and Kardide force-feeding her dying hope with sips of broth, her skeletal body would have aborted the new life she'd carried in her womb. She would have died without knowing the pain of these years, but she also would have missed the joys. She owed her friends a cool head now.

Pytros draped the cloth over his master's brow. "Don't stand there gawking, woman." His screeching reminded her of the ring-necks in the cages, brazen and trapped. "Close the door before our master catches a chill." He lifted a frosty mug from the bowl of snow swift runners had fetched from the slopes of the Atlas Mountains.

She'd never liked Pytros or his sneaky ways. From his condescending tone, the little weasel had full run of the henhouse in her absence. Magdalena did not move. Her nose had detected the sharp, putrid smell of desperation and wet gangrene coming from Aspasius's bed. Life-threatening combination. Pytros was in over his head. He just didn't know it yet.

"Your master stinks."

"He's been unable to visit the baths for several days."

Aspasius's face was flush with fever, and he was sweating profusely. If she was forced to touch him, his skin would surely burn her fingers. He'd always been slow-footed because of his bulk and short leg, but since she'd last seen him, he'd become skeletally thin. Rotting from the inside out. Infection and hatred had withered him to an unrecognizable state. For an instant, she almost felt sorry for him. Almost.

"You're dying, Aspasius," she said bluntly.

He pushed up on his elbows in a shaky show of defiance. "What are you now, a god?"

"I can smell your decomposition from here."

"I allowed a doctor to cut me, and malignant spirits entered my body."

"They've always been there."

"Where do healers come by their arrogance?" Aspasius tried to move his leg and cried out in pain.

"Do something, wench," Pytros ordered.

Magdalena stood rooted to the threshold, unable to move. Somewhere in her head a voice screamed, *"Run! He can't hurt you now."* Another voice quickly countered, *"Put the pillow over his face, and end everyone's misery once and for all."*

A calming whisper silenced the chaos. She recognized the quiet hush, a soft rustle no stronger than the spring breezes that stirred the sea grasses. It was the same serene melody she'd heard all those years ago, the voice that came to her through the pain and darkness, the voice of hope when she didn't think she could live another day. The voice she'd chosen to obey even if it meant her death.

She took a bold step into the room. "I have terms to which you will agree."

"Terms?" Aspasius's labored breaths indicated he was on the verge of pneumonia. "You are my slave. *You* don't issue terms."

"Nothing happens that is not God's purpose. I am *his* slave, and I'm here at the one God's bidding. Not yours."

"Ahhh. The one God." Aspasius fell back upon his pillow. "I'll have you and your *one* God thrown into the arena."

"Save your fool threats for the angel of death."

"These are not threats," he growled through clenched teeth.

"You can kill me"—Magdalena stepped boldly toward the door—"but then who will be left to heal you?"

Pytros puffed himself up like a preening bird. "There is always Galen."

"The vet?" She laughed. "You let that horse doctor cut on you?"

"What's so funny?" Pytros demanded.

She calmed herself and quoted one of the Roman sayings her husband had long ago used to tease her: "He who is born mad cannot be cured in an instant . . . even if his medic is Galen." She chuckled again at the memory of Lawrence's pleased grin whenever his poor attempts at humor got under her skin. "I've always wanted to say those words, just never thought I'd have such a perfect opportunity."

"What do they mean?" Pytros hated when he appeared the fool he was.

"It means I might be able to save your master's leg, but whether or not his mind is salvaged resides with the one whose power he continues to deny."

"What do you want from me, woman?" Aspasius asked, moaning.

So many things. For starters, he could say he was sorry. That he regretted every unspeakable thing he'd done to her. That if he had it to do all over again, he would demonstrate compassion, kindness, and love, not only toward her but especially toward their precious son.

Those were the concessions she wanted, the repentance he would never embrace.

To protect her family, she must let her grudges go. She would ask for things his hard, pagan heart could understand. God would work out the rest. "Running water restored to the tenements. The dead bodies removed from the streets. The highways and harbors closed until this sickness passes."

"Are you trying to destroy my city?"

"Quite the opposite. I'm trying to save it from annihilation. While the rich have marble urinals, the poor live in squalid apartments on crooked streets lined with decaying bodies. Burial outside the city walls is prohibited, but that will soon be inconsequential. Soon no one will have the strength to wheel the bodies beyond the gates."

Magdalena felt her resolve picking up steam. "The bathhouses need to shut down, because they're promoting the spread of the epidemic. For a population to coexist in such close proximity it must have pure water, clean streets, and working sewers. Zymotic diseases flourish in crowds—acute infections transfer from one person to another at the rate of a forest fire, leaping from dry undergrowth to dry timber." She repeated exactly what Lisbeth had told her, letting her own sense of pride at her daughter's brilliance shine through.

She did not give him time to wiggle out from under her demands. "I want Kardide, Iltani, and Tabari spared punishment for my actions." She took a breath. "And most important of all, I want you to grant Cyprian the freedom to do what must be done to save this city."

"Cyprian?" Aspasius struggled to prop himself up with his elbows again. His eyes flickered with a knowing that prickled her skin. "What do you know of that traitor?"

"When he is returned from his exile."

"You used to be such a better liar." He licked his cracked lips. "Do you think I don't know he's in my city? That heretic will die in the arena the moment I'm well enough to enjoy the entertainment."

Her mind raced, putting the pieces into place. Lisbeth's reaction to Felicissimus's appearance at the villa. Her own memory of seeing him leave the palace. "Let me guess . . . Felicissimus told you."

"My business is none of yours."

If Aspasius knew about Cyprian, she was almost certain Felicissimus had told him about Lisbeth, too. She couldn't let herself think of what this could mean for her daughter. For now she had the upper hand on Aspasius, and she intended to use it. "Then you shall die, for I will not set foot into your bedroom." Magdalena recounted her demands. "Running water. Streets cleared. Harbor closed. Kardide, Iltani, and Tabari spared. Cyprian freed. And Felicissimus exposed for the betrayer he is."

Aspasius gnawed on a corner of his chapped lips. "Fine." He fell back and flicked a feeble wave over his leg. "Do something about this dreadful pain."

"Not until you sign off on all you've promised."

"Write it up, Pytros."

"But, master—"

"Now."

Pytros quickly dug through the drawer of the bedside table. He found a scrap of paper, scratched out her demands, and presented the document to Aspasius for signature. The proconsul was too weak to hold the pen.

Magdalena came to his bedside. "Here." She cupped his hand with hers and helped him scribble his mark on the promise. "I'll keep this." She blew across the ink, then folded the paper and slid it into her pocket.

"You should have demanded your freedom," Aspasius croaked.

"You cannot give me what I already have through Christ Jesus." Candlelight shadows created hills and valleys that ran the length of his wasted body. "Open the shutters, Pytros. I need fresh air." She took a moment to enjoy the irritation on Pytros's face, then opened her supply satchel and removed the pair of latex gloves Lisbeth had shoved into her bag at the last minute.

A cursory visual examination of her patient revealed the

source of the fetid odor. The dime-size sore on the bottom of Aspasius's foot had grown to the size of a silver dollar. She lifted the appendage for a closer look. Aspasius howled. The leg wrappings he'd insisted on wearing had dug deep, purple indentations into his bloated limb. Restricted circulation and trapped moisture had created the perfect breeding ground for infection. Three of his toes were black. The rest of his foot was bright red, and his ankle was swollen to twice its normal size. She pressed the yellow blister under his arch. It split open, and purulent discharge oozed out.

"Gangrene." She carefully lowered his foot upon the stack of pillows Pytros had nervously arranged. "Left untreated, the infection will spread through his body. His organs will become septic and throw him into shock."

"What does that mean?" Pytros asked.

She straightened. "The proconsul of Carthage is going to die a slow, painful death."

Pytros wrung his hands. "Oh, dear."

"If I die," Aspasius said with a cough, "she dies."

Magdalena pushed aside the desire to spin on her heels and let nature take its course. If she truly believed in God's timing, then she'd been sent here for a reason. As best as she could tell, the reason seemed to be to save this horrible man. Repulsive as the idea appeared, she continued plowing through her options.

"I could implant live maggots into his festering tissue. They would devour the infection and leave healthy flesh in their wake. The process is slow; it doesn't fix the circulation problem that prevented his healing in the first place; and, most importantly, the risk of infecting him with typhoid is huge."

"Typhoid?" Pytros asked.

"Another log nature has thrown on the fire that is destroying Carthage." She examined the infected limb. "A proper debridement of the wound might give the scanty bit of healthy tissue a chance, but without antibiotics and a hyperbaric oxygen chamber, I'm hesitant to embark on such a risky course of treatment."

To keep from appearing the fool again, Pytros poured Aspasius another round of wine.

"No." She took the cup before it reached the proconsul's lips. "We must keep his belly empty for the next twelve hours."

"But I'm dying of thirst," Aspasius protested.

The quickest and safest option was amputation, but she wasn't quite ready to toss surgery out as an option. She examined the flesh above his knee. Cool and healthy in color. If she removed his leg right below the knee, she could head off the spread of infection and possibly save enough of the joint to support a wooden prosthetic. Fortunately, the infection had ravaged his short leg. Once Aspasius realized he could have a skilled artisan carve a perfect leg, one that would even his gait, he would probably be thrilled. Then again, surgery in these primitive conditions was extremely risky. Blood loss. Infection. Lack of antibiotics. She needed help.

"Pytros, fetch Tabari, Iltani, and Kardide." She emptied out her tools. Now she almost wished she would have agreed to bring Lisbeth and her shiny new saw. "And lots of hot water."

"Why?"

"He has developed a diabetic complication." She continued on, despite the puzzled scowl on Pytros's face. "I'm going to have to operate, and it will take us a while to prepare everything."

"No cutting," Aspasius croaked.

"No worries, my love." She lightly patted his good knee. "I'll be as swift and painless with you as you've always been with me." She ignored his grunt of resignation and addressed Pytros. "I left some important tools at Cyprian's. I'll do my best to stabilize him for now, but at first light, send Tabari to fetch what I need."

45

Barek stood before the apartment door of his fishing buddy, a stack of writs clutched in one hand, a small torch clutched in the other. "I don't think this is a good idea, Felicissimus."

The slave trader hissed in his ear. "Sell one, and protect yourself. Sell two, and you have your commission in the royal navy. Sell three, and—"

"No one gets hurt, right?"

Felicissimus thumped the stack of signed parchments. "These are the only way to save those you love."

Barek stepped up to the apartment door, started to knock, then backed away. "I can't do this."

"You're not selling slaves; you're selling freedom." Felicissimus rapped on the door. "I'll show you how easy it is."

Barek's friend, a short, stocky boy who enjoyed access to Cyprian's private pier as much as he, answered. "Felicissimus?" He looked around the slave trader. "Barek? Is something wrong?"

"Sorry to bother you, Natalis," Barek said.

"Can't fish today. When Mother comes back from the cooking fire we're going to Cyprian's to work a double shift at the hospital."

"He didn't come to ask you to fish." Felicissimus held out the writs. "He came to give you something."

"Barek's family has already given us too much. We wouldn't be well if it hadn't been for his sweet mother, God rest her soul."

"Then you know how much Ruth cared and how hard she worked to keep you well and safe." Felicissimus thrust two sheets at him. "Now that she's gone, she would want you to have these."

"What are they?"

"Protection."

"From what?"

"Soldiers."

Natalis's brow furrowed as he examined the parchment. "Pieces of paper to fend off steel?"

"No. Just show it to them. They are legally required to leave you alone."

"I can't read."

"It says you've sacrificed at the temple."

Natalis's eyes bulged. "But I haven't." He thrust the writs at the slave trader. "And I won't."

"I know. You're a fine young Christian," Felicissimus soothed. "That's what's so wonderful about these certificates of libellus. You don't really have to bow before the pagan gods; just say you did."

"That's lying."

"It's being smart, boy."

Natalis's scornful gaze slid to Barek. "I'm glad your mother isn't here to see this." He gave a disbelieving shake of the head. "It would break her heart." He stepped inside and closed the door.

Felicissimus turned to Barek and shrugged. "Sometimes you have to knock on a lot of doors before you make a sale. Who else is on your list?"

"I'm done."

The slave trader pushed him against the building. "We had a deal." He grabbed Barek by the collar. "There are other fish in the sea, and you will continue to cast your nets until you find them for me."

46

"YOU WERE THERE, LISBETH," Cyprian argued. "You saw the faces of Quinta and Metras when I asked for help moving Diona to the next hall. They wanted no part in caring for a patrician."

Lisbeth crammed her balled fists onto her hips. "Did you or did you not ask me to formulate a plan?" She stepped into his space and squared off. "Are you saying it's okay for Christians to take the bread and shelter of a patrician like yourself but refuse to give a dying patrician like Diona medical care?"

"I'm not trying to kill them!" He held up his hands and took a calming breath. "The majority of the church is poor. It's my obligation to care for the less fortunate. I can afford it." His eyes bore into hers. "But I can't, in good conscience, ask peasants to risk their lives to provide medical care for the ruling class. Not when those in power are the very ones intent on persecuting the lower classes."

She was counting on the same chivalrous inclination that had spurred him to save her from the slave block and bound him to take Ruth as his wife to propel him toward taking another unfathomable action. "That's the point of my plan. Do the absolute opposite of what the pagans would expect. Who empties the bedpans of their enemies or tends their vaporizer tents all night? Can you imagine what would happen if the church repaid evil with good?"

He moved in closer, his breath hot on her cheek. "Believing a few kindnesses could erase the lines of class distinction and sway the populace to pressure Aspasius into doing what is right is not clever thinking . . . it is insanity."

Lisbeth did not back down. "Christ didn't think so, and neither did Ruth." She paused, the sound of rapid heartbeat thrumming in her ears. "Pretending Aspasius won't come for you next . . . that's insanity."

"You could do this? Care for those who pray to their gods for your death?"

"There's only one way to find out."

Cyprian's steady gaze appraised her resolve; her eyes did not waiver. He let out a breath. "You are and have always been a mystery to me." He took her face in his hands and kissed her. "I believe facing the executioner's sword would be less painful than continuing to argue with you. All right, let's see if we can do as Jesus did." He gave a half smile. "It appears I now have a new sermon to write."

Lisbeth hurried through her evening rounds with prayers for Cyprian constantly on her lips. She poured another jug of boiling water into a vaporizer pot. A cloud of scalding steam engulfed her in a blistering reminder that her plan had the potential to burn them all.

She had assured Cyprian that the plan would work, even without the church having the unifying emotional high of Cyprian's martyrdom. But she knew the jury was still out on whether anything they said or did would change the opinions of the ruling class when it came to Christians. Titus Cicero had a favorable opinion of the believers right now, but once Diona was completely recovered, would he stand up in a Senate meeting and tell Aspasius to end their persecution? Or would he forget what had been done for him?

Back home she'd seen scores of grateful patients leave the hospital and never look back. Titus could very easily lose his feelings of goodwill, declare his daughter's right to health care his privilege, and renew his ringside seats at the Colosseum.

Perspiration trickled down Lisbeth's back. The villa had become a sweatbox. She opened the windows and doors to the balconies. Perhaps once she restocked the vaporizer pots in the measles ward, she could grab Maggie and treat them both to a brief respite in the swimming-pool-size tub before the church assembled.

She dumped boiling water into the last vaporizer pot and stirred in crushed eucalyptus leaves. Fragrant steam filled the tent of a small boy covered in the same miserable red rash she'd come to stamp out. He roused and fussed for his mommy. The frail seamstress who'd arrived on Cyprian's doorstep covered in the same rash had died the day before. Now the boy had no one else to comfort him. Lisbeth settled beside his mat. She stroked his head until his coughing subsided and he finally slept.

Stiffly she rose, hoping Maggie was in a mood to tolerate a moment of cuddling, because, frankly, life was too short not to hold those you love.

Lisbeth poked her head into the typhoid hall. Vivia was combing Diona's hair, her free hand tenderly smoothing the blond tresses. So much had changed for this family since Ruth's gracious act of taking them in. Diona had survived with the help of Mama's surgery and Lisbeth's antibiotics. But Mama was right: the best medicine came from a loving touch, a fact she was banking on to change the course of public opinion.

"I'm on my way to the kitchen to check on Maggie. Do you feel like trying to eat something a bit more solid, Diona?"

"Yes. Thank you."

"I'll see what Naomi and the girls have been stirring up all day." Lisbeth headed toward the sound of Maggie and Junia's giggles.

"Mommy, watch." Maggie stood before a flat, iron plate suspended over an open flame. Wheat kernels slid from her funnel-shaped fist and dropped onto the hot skillet. She clomped to the table in Ruth's high heels and reached inside a burlap bag for another fistful of unripe grain. "I'm making popcorn without a microwave."

Maggie let the wheat trickle onto the iron plate. When the kernels began to dance, she stepped back, and Junia took a pot holder and shuffled the red-hot plate over the flame like the Jiffy Pop foil pans Papa's mother used to send to their campsites. When the heads of grain cracked open, Maggie and Junia giggled like they were at a magic show.

Junia lifted the skillet and dumped the fluffy kernels into a bowl.

Maggie sprinkled sea salt over them. "Try it."

"Yum." Lisbeth crammed some into her mouth, suddenly aware that she hadn't eaten all day. "Your g-pa would love this."

"Jaddah would love popcorn, too." Maggie's brow crinkled in deep thought. "She's still coming home with us, right?"

"I'm working on it, baby."

"G-Pa will be so sad if she doesn't."

"We're going to do our best, okay?"

"And pray."

"And pray." Lisbeth kissed Maggie's forehead. "You're warm." She pulled Maggie back from the fire. "It's too hot to be working over an open fire. How about we take a little break and cool down in the bath?"

"Junia, too?"

"Sure, both of you come on. Naomi, Diona feels like eating. I'd appreciate it if you could leave a bowl of that carrot soup at the door of the typhoid hall."

Naomi nodded, and Lisbeth took the girls by the hand to the bath.

Refreshed after a dip in the tub, Lisbeth let Maggie and Junia splash about while she braided her own wet hair. "Careful, girls. Don't swallow any of that water."

Thirty minutes later, two squeaky-clean girls were tucked in next to Laurentius. When she thought of a picture-perfect family, this was almost it.

Lisbeth said prayers and kissed each of the kids. She affectionately ran her fingers down Maggie's cheeks, still rosy from standing too close to the popcorn fire. "'Night, baby."

She closed the cottage door and went to join those gathering in the torch-lit garden.

CYPRIAN WAITED in the center of the dais he'd built for Caecilianus. Wearing his mentor's hat and robe bolstered his courage, for he knew exactly what the old bishop would have had to say about Lisbeth's crazy plan: *"It's about time we were neither slave nor free."*

Serious-faced believers filed through the courtyard gate. Plague, persecution, and the discouragement he feared would follow Ruth's death had shrunk the church's ranks even more since their last meeting. Wary men and women took their seats at the low banquet tables set with baskets of bread and large crocks of wine. They eyed the generous spread, but for some strange reason, they were unusually reluctant to dig in.

Cyprian tightened the belt on Caecilianus's toga. Beneath the weight of the bishop's wool he was not a common man, but a patrician. Without Ruth or Caecilianus to bridge the gap, the divide between the classes was huge. If neither side felt comfortable crossing the lines, this plan would never work.

He surveyed the crowd. Quinta rocked her grandson at one

table. Metras sat on the edge of the fountain, his cane between his legs. Cyprian didn't know whether their expectant faces should make him feel encouraged or even more anxious. Sitting to his right was a bearded quarry worker with the wind-chiseled features of one who hailed from the desert. The man had eagerly volunteered to ash the latrines. Would he be open to this new plan? Tonight the stoneworker had brought his wife, two small children, and a stoic face impossible to read.

Cyprian stepped from the dais and moved toward the stonemason's family. He placed his hands on the man's slumped shoulders. He felt the man flinch, but he did not pull away. Cyprian did not speak until the man slowly raised his eyes. "Tell me your name."

"Tappo."

"Tappo." Cyprian studied the man with dirt under his nails and arms that could split a stone slab with one swing of the hammer. "I appreciate all you've done for Carthage."

The man gave a reserved nod and lifted his younger child on his lap with surprising tenderness.

He and Tappo were men from different backgrounds. They wore different qualities of wool and slept under roofs of far different value. But in truth, they were not so different from one another. Tappo was a father who feared what the future held for his family. Cyprian was a father who knew nearly every gory detail. Tappo was right to fear.

Cyprian glanced around at the group in his garden. All of them were considered misfits and outcasts by those in his social circle. Yet here they were, boldly sneaking through back alleys to worship the same God he worshipped.

Caecilianus and Lisbeth were right. The blood of Christ was the great equalizer, the undeniable commonality that bound them. Every pair of eyes staring back at him belonged to individuals who were equally as frightened as he and equally forgiven.

A newfound empathy for the plight of his fellow believers pressed the tension from Cyprian's shoulders. He reached into a basket, took a hunk of bread, and offered it to the wisp of a girl in Tappo's lap. "Hungry, little one?"

Her eyes devoured the bread, but neither she nor her father made any effort to take the offering.

Lord, help me.

Just as Cyprian was about to raise his voice and announce the plan, Felicissimus strolled in.

The paunchy slave trader paused to survey the situation. "Cyprian!" He shouted congenially from across the garden. "I parted a Roman centurion from this expensive keg of beer." He waved in his slave, Metellus. The big black man came through the gate toting a heavy wooden barrel in his muscular arms. "Where shall I have Metellus crack the seal?"

"Does the centurion who owned the keg follow you to get it back?" Cyprian did not hide his alarm.

"No." Felicissimus chuckled. "I told him we were toasting your appointment as bishop, and he was only too happy to contribute to the celebration."

Cyprian felt the crowd tense. "You alerted Aspasius's soldiers to our gathering?"

"It's a joke, man." The crowd tittered with relief. Felicissimus moved among the people, clapping men on the back and tucking the chins of the children who ran to meet him. Tappo's daughter hopped from his lap and scurried to throw her arms around the slave trader's knees.

Lisbeth was right. The slave trader had charms he'd never recognized before. "Not a very funny joke."

Felicissimus's eyes traveled the length of Cyprian's body. "About as funny as you donning the hat and robe of our dearly departed Caecilianus. What next? Will you assume the old bishop's name as well?" The remark had a sudden and unexpected edge of challenge.

"Actually, yes, I have." The crowd's murmurs did not sway Cyprian from his purpose. "Set the keg by the fountain, Metellus. We'll break open the beer after I've spoken to the church."

Felicissimus scurried through the crowd and pulled Cyprian aside. "So you intend to go through with your promise to rescue Carthage from ruin at the possible cost of all our lives?"

"I do."

"Why won't you listen to me and leave it alone? Have you not enough grief of your own? Has not the church suffered enough, given enough? If there was ever a time, now is when we should turn our focus inward and consider options for escaping the wrath rather than digging our heels in."

"Aspasius has Magdalena."

Felicissimus appeared shocked. "If you persist, he will soon have you as well. There will be nothing I can do."

"Upon my return from exile, I was branded a coward. And in some ways, I have acted a coward. I will be afraid no more. If I place my trust wholeheartedly at the feet of the one God like Caecilianus did, the church will, too."

Felicissimus's lips twitched. "Yours will be the next funeral the church attends."

"So be it." Cyprian returned to the dais. As he prepared to deliver his thoughts, he spotted Barek slipping into the garden, arms crossed and wearing the same snarl he'd had upon his lips since Lisbeth's return. The boy had a lot of growing up to do. In the days to come, Cyprian would do his best to nurture the seeds of goodness Ruth and Caecilianus had planted in their son and help him to one day become the bishop his father would have wanted.

At the table of the young family who'd refused his bread, he noticed Lisbeth had slid in beside Tappo's wife. Lisbeth's smile fortified his courage.

Cyprian took a breath and began. "Like us, the first followers of Christ had reason to fear. Their leader was gone, and they wondered what was to become of them." He left Paul's letter to the Philippians sealed, and unrolled the Apostle John's letter to the church. "They found encouragement in these final words of our Lord."

He cleared his throat and began to read. "'"Dear children, how brief are these moments before I must go away and leave you!"'" He avoided Lisbeth's eyes lest she think he was referring to the fulfillment of her fears. "'"So now I am giving you a new commandment: Love each other. Just as I have loved you, you should love each other. Your love for one another will prove to the world that you are my disciples."'"

He paused, giving the exhortation a moment to impact their hearts. In the flickering torchlight he could see the conviction and resolve that had taken shape in his own heart reflected in their eyes.

Cyprian rolled up the scroll. "Brothers and sisters, Rome has forgotten its founding virtues. Dignity; truth; and, above all, treating each other well." He looked steadily into the eyes of the gathered Christians. "I believe it possible to restore to the citizens of Carthage the attributes that once made our empire great. But the task will not be easy, for it will require that we love without bias, without regard to social standing."

Tappo stood. "Love those who persecute us?"

"Especially those who persecute us," Cyprian said.

"The moment they are well we will suffer their wrath." Tappo began gathering his family.

"Tappo, please. Hear me out. As Christians we have been given not only the privilege of trusting in Christ but also the privilege of suffering for him." He raised his voice above the murmurs. "It is easy to believe those who live in the villas are different from those who live in the tenements. While you believe the rich are without problems, the rich think the poor fortunate for being free to live without obligation. Believe me, Tappo, no one finds this command to love everyone equally more difficult than I do. But if the church is to be the body of Christ, we are neither slave nor free. We are brothers and sisters called to fight together."

"A sickness more deadly than the plague is consuming the entire empire," Tappo said. "Greed. And you want us to help those who would take the clothes from our backs and feed our naked carcasses to the lions for sport?"

"I'm saying those are the very people we must win over."

"How?" Tappo demanded. "Take the bread from my child's mouth and shove it into their fat cheeks?"

"We unite in purpose."

"Rebel against Rome? They will crush us."

"No. Quite the opposite." Cyprian headed off Tappo's growing angst by fleshing out his plan. "I propose we excel in doing good."

"Good?" Quinta said. "What kind of good?"

"We pick up our efforts. Form a stealthy coalition of men to take stretchers not only to the slums but also to the villas of the rich and powerful. Wherever the sick are found, we are there to bring them inside these walls for healing, to care for them like our own whether or not they're one of us. I'm funding a workforce of anyone willing to join in the effort, to transport the sick to our hospital, poor or rich. While you clear the broad avenues of the rich, I shall work in the slums. Who is with me?"

47

GOOSEFLESH RAISED ON LISBETH'S arms as Cyprian spoke to the church. His passion reminded her of Papa's antiquities lectures. Her father didn't have Cyprian's gift of oratory, his intense stare, or his ability to speak without notes, but like Papa's, tonight Cyprian's words came from someplace deep and tender.

He had always been the first to take up a civic cause, especially if he thought the underdog was being mistreated. His noble desire to right the wrongs Rome inflicted on the poor was the very thing Aspasius hated about the solicitor of Carthage. Modern-day politicians would tremble if they had to face Cyprianus Thascius at a debate podium. His unwillingness to back down from a fight was a character trait she admired and one she was grateful Maggie had inherited.

But Lisbeth had never seen this side of her husband. Vulnerable, transparent, and willing to become one of those he considered far below his social standing. His humbling admissions of fear and prejudice drew her in and stirred a fire in her belly. She could spend a lifetime exploring the raw layers he'd just exposed, and it would not be long enough. Until this very moment, she hadn't thought it possible to love this man more than she already did.

She glanced around at the crowd, trying to judge the impact of Cyprian's impassioned argument.

"You'll pay us to care?" Tappo asked.

A flicker of disappointment raised Cyprian's brow. "If that is what it takes to start changing hearts. Talk to Felicissimus. He's handling the hiring for me."

When everyone turned to Felicissimus, he squirmed. "Since Aspasius has forbidden access to our cemeteries, it's been a little difficult to get things started."

"But we will get started, and soon. Right, Felicissimus?"

"Soon enough."

The garden gate flew open. "Soldiers killed my son!" The mother of Natalis panted, her face streaked with tears and her tunic stained with blood.

Cyprian and Lisbeth rushed to her at the same time. Flanking her, they led her to the nearest bench.

"Someone give her wine," Lisbeth called over the gasps of terror and the scramble to gather families together.

"Can you tell me what happened?" Cyprian asked gently.

She refused the cup Lisbeth offered. "I came home from the cooking fires to find them dragging my boy to the street. They put a dagger to his throat and bade him utter blasphemous words. When he refused, they tied him to a hitching post and shot an arrow through his heart." She began to sob. "He bled to death in my arms."

"Natalis should have taken the papers," Tappo murmured.

"What papers?" Cyprian demanded.

Tappo pulled out a slip of parchment. "One of these."

Cyprian's face puzzled. He took the paper and read it out loud. "Let the record show that Tappo from the Egyptian village of Theadelphia has sacrificed and shown reverence to the gods of Rome. As roving commissioner, I do hereby certify that in my presence, this man has poured a libation and sacrificed and eaten some of the sacrificial meat. I, Aurelius Hermas, do hereby certify I saw

Tappo sacrificing." Cyprian slowly raised his eyes. Displeasure plowed furrows in his brow. "You have sacrificed to the pagan gods?"

"No, that's the beauty. This writ of libellus says I did when, in truth, I did not." Tappo grabbed up his younger child. "When the soldiers knock on my door, my family will be safe and my conscience clear. God knows it is nothing but a forgery. Natalis was a fool not to take one for him and his mother."

"Since when is pleasing Romans more important than pleasing the one God?"

"The one God does not have a spear pointed at my girl's head. Rome does."

"And from whom, pray tell, did you acquire this illegal certificate of sacrifice?" Cyprian asked.

"I'm not the only one who's bought protection," Tappo defended as he waved his hand over the crowd. "Show him!"

Cyprian glanced around. Slips of paper fluttered in the hands of most of the crowd. "Quinta? Metras?" The grandmother lifted her writ higher. Old man Metras kept a level gaze and lifted the sheaf in his hand. Cyprian shook the parchment in Tappo's face. "Who sold you this unholy writ?"

Tappo stiffened. "I'm not at liberty to say."

"Who?" Cyprian demanded.

Tappo hesitated before pointing across the garden, his expression hard. "The slave trader."

"Felicissimus?" Cyprian turned slowly, as if a knife in his back had cut him in two. "Felicissimus, is this true?"

Lisbeth jumped to her feet. Her first impulse was to jerk Cyprian away from the pain she'd tried to spare him, but her second impulse, to strangle Felicissimus, won out. "I should have stopped you the moment I returned." She barreled into him. "Tell him!" she shouted at the paunchy weasel. "Let him see what you're really capable of."

"I don't see the harm in purchasing a few pieces of paper if it gives the church a reprieve." Felicissimus smoothed the front of his tunic. "In fact, I think buying these certificates fits well with your plan. I was only trying to help."

"You've been using *my* money to buy a false salvation?"

"Think, Cyprian," Felicissimus purred. "If Christians aren't fretting about the possibility of losing their lives, how much easier would it be for them to do good? The good works you insist will change the feelings of Carthage."

It was as if the smoke suddenly cleared, and Cyprian saw the truth and it sickened him. "What have you done?"

"I've done what you didn't have the courage to do." Naked ambition gleamed in the slave trader's eyes. "I gave these people protection."

"You've given them worthless scraps of paper." Cyprian's nostrils flared, and Lisbeth could see him fighting back the urge to lose it.

"I did what I thought was best for the church!" Felicissimus shouted.

Cyprian's face creased in pain. "Lisbeth was right. You've done nothing but harm." Cyprian sank to the dais. The note of bewilderment in his voice as he scrambled to put the pieces together ripped Lisbeth's heart in two. "It was you who set up the ambush that took Caecilianus from the church and my wife from me." Cyprian shook his head, the anger mounting. "It was you who told Aspasius of Magdalena's presence in my home." His veins throbbed in his noble patrician profile. "And I suspect it is no longer safe for Christians to meet here, because *you* have told Aspasius of my return."

Felicissimus averted his eyes and dry-washed his hands in a brazen show of excusing himself from liability. "I regret you don't see the merit of my actions or the depth of my love for you and the church."

Cyprian grabbed the slave trader by the collar. "When is he coming for me?"

"Don't you see, he doesn't have to now." Felicissimus jerked away. He gathered Metellus, his beer keg, the mother of Natalis, Quinta, and more than half the church. "Without the church, you are already dead to him."

Mama was right. Control was such an illusion. In an instant, everything had changed. Standing with Cyprian, Lisbeth watched helplessly as their hope of altering the world's opinion of the church followed a plump little Judas into the night.

"And what about you, Metras?" Cyprian asked the old man. "Are you going to take your writ and desert the faith, too?"

"Never told a patrician about Jesus before." The old man wadded his paper and threw it in the fountain. "According to those words you just read, once I do, I can't let them sleep on these filthy streets."

48

CLOUDS MUTED THE MOON'S glow on the sand. Lisbeth stood at the top of the stairs leading to the beach, debating her next move. Below her, Cyprian paced ankle-deep in the tumbling waves. Would going to him make things better or worse? And if she went, what could she offer? Another useless plan?

Cyprian was not the only one undone by this debacle. The unraveling of the church had gut-punched her and destroyed her plans to eventually liberate Mama and save her husband's neck.

Cyprian ripped the bishop's hat from his head and threw it into the sea. Unaware she was watching from afar, he stripped out of Caecilianus's toga and left it in a heap on the shore. He shook his fists at the heavens in what looked like a boxing match with God. After a few minutes of wrestling with the wind, Cyprian stood with his muscled back to her. As he stared out at the sea, Lisbeth could see his bare shoulders shake. Broken as he was by Felicissimus's betrayal, he was still a physical specimen of admirable craftsmanship, the man she longed to hold.

As she cupped her hands to her lips to call out to him, he raised his arms above his head, plunged into the foamy waters, and disappeared.

"Cyprian!" Lisbeth gathered her skirts and flew down the steps. Her sandaled feet raced across the sand. At the water's edge she searched the charcoal horizon for any sign of his blond head. As she peeled out of her shoes preparing to dive in after him, Cyprian surfaced with a gasp and began cranking out angry strokes that carried him toward one of the few remaining anchored ships.

"Come back" was all she could manage.

He stopped his thrashing and bobbed in the waves as he searched the shore.

Lisbeth undid her sash and threw it aside. "Don't make me come after you."

"There's only one way to free your mother."

"What? Get yourself killed?"

"Sail for Rome." His voice carried over the water. "Speak to the emperor myself. Tell him of Aspasius's refusal to follow his edict and lift the persecution."

"Before you stow away on a ship likely carrying two plagues, can we at least talk about this?"

"What is there to talk about? It would have taken every hand to accomplish what we planned." He waved her back. "Don't come in the water."

Lisbeth waded in ankle deep. "If you're going to Rome, so am I." She stood in the moonlight, the breeze blowing her hair around her shoulders.

"What about Maggie?"

"We'll take her. She's at least had her shots."

Cyprian stroked toward her. Breathing hard, he came ashore. Although he maintained a distance of a few strides, she could feel the heat radiating off his slick body. "Did you know about the writs of libellus?"

"No."

Strain was etched across his face. Tired, red eyes from sleepless nights of trying to hold everything together. The church. The city he loved. The fractured remains of his family. She knew she looked just as haggard.

"You tried to tell me, but I wouldn't listen. Felicissimus was my right-hand man. I trusted him to administer funds. Supervise the burials. To be my friend. I was a fool. How can the church love those who don't know Christ when we can't even love each other? God forgive me, but when I think that I entrusted Ruth and the church into that weasel's care, I want to kill him."

"I've fought the urge to slap Felicissimus since the moment he removed his boot from my face."

Cyprian slicked his hair back. "They are all fools to think those writs will keep them safe."

She threw Cyprian his toga. "So what are we going to do?"

"What *can* we do?" He slid the heavy fabric over his head. "A few women and an old man with a cane are hardly the army we needed."

Was that regret or blame she heard in his voice? Did he rue the day he'd purchased her off the slave block and started this war with Aspasius?

Beating back her fears, she said, "God's done more with a lot less."

They stood there staring at each other, the wind in their ears and the waves washing across their feet. Angry foam swirled around Lisbeth's ankles, then retreated to the sea with a tug that threatened to pull her under.

Cyprian was the first to speak. "I don't know how long I can keep you and Maggie safe."

Tears clogged the back of her throat. "Nor I you."

His lips twitched. In an instant, his impeccable discipline deserted him, and he reached for her hand. "I never thought you'd come back. I prayed that you would. Dreamed that you had. I saw you everywhere. In the tenements. At the sea. In the boiling water for the vaporizer pots. In your brother's drawings. But I never thought you'd leave the world you knew, the world where you belonged, and return to me."

She held on tightly. "Our daughter needs her father."

"And you?"

"Worse than I need air."

Longing shone in his eyes. He closed the distance between them. Cupping her face in his hands, he lightly brushed away her tears. "It's not death I fear, but losing my faith. God can take my riches, my position, even the church I've come to love." He traced her lips with his salty thumbs. "But it will not be easy to forgive him when the hour comes to send you home. And I'm afraid the time has come."

She took Cyprian's hand. "Follow me." Beneath a velvet sky she led him to the pergola. They stepped into the privacy of the vines. "Remember the last time we were together here?"

He turned to her. "Every time I look out my window." A wistful, worn gaze met hers. "Had I known the future—"

She put a finger to his lips. "We would have missed this moment."

Golden stubble roughened his tense jaw. His eyes reflected the same uncertainty she was feeling. They were once again backed into an impossible corner, one misstep away from destruction. What would they do next? Exactly where did two frightened, weary souls go from here? If they gave in, they might very well shatter any chance of coming out of this intact.

Cyprian's fingers followed the curve of her clavicle. A faint smile lifted the corners of his lips. The aching emptiness she'd carried since their separation grew so large each breath required effort. She wanted to tell him that she loved him, loved him more than her own life, but the words refused to form into a coherent sentence. So she remained as silent as he, willing her eyes to say what her lips could not.

In their need, they reached for each other. One of Cyprian's hands wrapped her waist. The other tangled in her hair and lifted her chin. His breath whispered across her cheek. Desire swirled like fine desert sand, every emotion a tiny granule swept across the peaks and valleys that had been their lives. Every minute that had passed while she was away, hope of them holding each other again grew as distant as the cave portal. Impossible to reach in this life. She wouldn't allow her spinning mind to stop and consider the end of this moment, an end written years ago.

His lips pressed hers, so powerful and intense her mouth opened like that of a little bird demanding to be filled. Her hands traveled the contours of his chest. Fingertips skimming upward, she paused at the rapid pounding of his heart.

The swell of the sea beat against the harbor walls as the years apart fell away. Time shifted. The arrow-straight line connecting past and present faded into a timeless, dreamy circle. Lisbeth pillowed her fears in another dimension and let go.

49

FELICISSIMUS BURST INTO ASPASIUS'S chamber and jolted the proconsul from his slumber. "It's done," Felicissimus said, panting.

Soldiers tumbled into the room behind the slave trader. "We tried to stop him, sir."

Aspasius refused Magdalena's help and pushed himself up in his bed. "Let him speak." He waved a weakened hand. "Offer our guest some refreshment, woman."

Felicissimus came and threw a stack of papers on the bed. "There's nothing left of Cyprian's church."

Magdalena dropped the cup she was filling.

"Well done, little slave trader." Aspasius directed his pleased chuckle toward Magdalena. "There's a small pouch in the dresser drawer. Pay the man."

"I don't want your money or the power you offered anymore," Felicissimus said. "I did what you asked. The church is destroyed, and so is Cyprian. Now you no longer have need to kill him or anyone else. That boy you had executed in the tenements did not have to die. I would have eventually sold him the writs."

"When did you grow a heart?"

"Cyprian *was* my friend."

"I never really put much stock in friendships."

"Neither he nor the Christians are a threat to you now."

"Oh, that's where you're wrong. As long as Cyprian is alive, so is their hope. And hope is far more dangerous than any man." Aspasius waved his hand. "Kill him."

Surprise flashed across Felicissimus's face as a soldier's dagger stabbed him through the back.

50

LISBETH'S EYES FLEW OPEN with a start. Patches of light and shadow freckled the pergola tiles. Cyprian slept curled around her, his arm resting across her stomach. She smiled and inhaled deeply. It was true. Last night was not a dream. They had spent the hours exhausting themselves with apologies and forgiveness.

Lisbeth listened to the deep rhythmic satisfaction of her husband's respirations and suddenly remembered Maggie. She carefully lifted Cyprian's fingers. The sticky sea breeze whisked away the warmth of his touch and this moment of security. Fighting the temptation to stay put and return his palm to her belly, she rose and gathered their scattered clothes, dressed hurriedly, then covered Cyprian with Caecilianus's toga.

Lisbeth retrieved the bishop's hat tumbling in the waves farther downshore. She shook out the sand, returned to the shelter, and placed the limp felt beside Cyprian's peaceful face. No matter how much she wished otherwise, the toga and the hat suited him. As did the office of bishop. Ruth was right. Cyprian was the perfect man to restore the church of Carthage. To ask Cyprian to become anything other than the strong leader the church needed would be like asking her to stop thinking and acting like a doctor.

She couldn't possibly ask him to leave.

* * *

LISBETH WAS fresh from the bath when the door to her chamber banged open. "Tabari?"

Her mother's friend struggled for breath, her eyes urgent and her hands waving. "Magdalena needs the bone saw."

Lisbeth's heart rate quickened. "What has Aspasius done to her?"

Two soldiers stepped from behind the door and shoved Tabari out of the room. "Come with us."

Lisbeth recognized the redheaded one ordering her about as the same soldier who'd taken Mama.

There was no way Lisbeth wanted to help that monster holding her mother captive. On the other hand, there was no way she would miss this unexpected opportunity to rescue Mama. She couldn't believe that God had opened this door and opened it so fast.

"I need my backpack."

"Get it."

She ran to the chest beside the bed and snatched up everything she could cram into her bag. "I need the herbs from the cupboard in the kitchen." There weren't many left, but she'd take what she had just in case.

"No."

"I don't know what's wrong or what I'll need." She added flint to her voice. "You want the proconsul to die because you didn't let me bring the right drugs?"

The redhead weighed her request. "Make it fast."

"If you haven't had measles you might not want to follow me."

"Move it." Their hobnailed boots clicked on the tiles as they trailed her to the kitchen.

Maggie's laughter floated down the hall. Lisbeth panicked. Soldiers dragging her off would scare Maggie to death. That was not the last memory she wanted left in her daughter's mind.

"Wait out here. I don't want to have to explain things."

The redhead grabbed Tabari and held his dagger to her throat. "Try to get away, and she won't be the only one who dies."

"Just give me a minute."

Lisbeth found Maggie and Junia helping Naomi roll out barley rounds.

"Look, Mommy." Maggie held up a circular piece of dough. "If you stab the bread with a fork it doesn't puff up in the oven." Maggie's smile was a deflating prick to Lisbeth's courage. "You look pretty, Mommy."

What if this was a trap? She could be walking into an ambush. Then what would happen to Maggie?

Lisbeth's chest constricted, and for a moment she couldn't breathe.

"You okay, Mommy?"

She moved to block Maggie from seeing the glint of the soldier's blade. Mama wouldn't want her to leave Maggie, no matter what kind of evil Aspasius was inflicting on her. But if Lisbeth didn't go, that ambitious soldier would kill all of them right now and probably be rewarded for it.

Options raced through her mind. The fire poker was the only available weapon. Her attempt to defend them would put Maggie and Naomi directly in harm's way. She could scream. Draw Cyprian into the fight. But without a sword, he'd quickly be cut to bits.

In the end, she conceded, her only option was to give herself up to Aspasius and pray she had the opportunity to beg for Cyprian's life. Lisbeth had been raised by her father. If Cyprian was free, Maggie could be raised by hers. She'd rather have her daughter grow up without a mother than not get the chance to grow up.

"Can I go with you, Mommy?"

"Not this time, baby." Lisbeth pulled her backpack tight to

conceal the cracks forming in her resolve not to snatch her child and run.

She opened the herb cupboard. Besides her backpack and an extra dose of courage, she wasn't sure what she needed. She grabbed a few bundles of eucalyptus and crammed them in her bag. "Naomi, I'm going out for supplies."

Naomi's face puzzled. "Is Cyprian going with you?"

"No." Lisbeth closed the cabinet. "He's busy getting the church back on track and shouldn't be disturbed."

"What about Barek? You shouldn't go alone."

"You need the help here." Steeling herself at the prospect of leaving Maggie, Lisbeth gathered her daughter and held her tightly. "I love you, baby."

"Mommy, I can't breathe."

"I'm so sorry. For everything." Swallowing tears, Lisbeth squeezed one last time. "No matter what, never forget I love you." She kissed her daughter's cheek. "You take care of Daddy, okay?" Lisbeth willed herself out the door without a backward glance.

ASPASIUS HAD doubled the guards throughout the city, but from the eerie silence there was no reason. Corpses left unburied in the streets weren't going to cause any trouble, and the occasional old man crouched in a shady corner wasn't healthy enough to raise a ruckus or rally an uprising. As for the rest, those who weren't covered in rashes or stuck on the latrine were too frightened to come out of their houses.

The soldiers took Lisbeth and Tabari to the front entrance of the palace where a retinue of bored troops entertained themselves with a game, throwing dice carved from the anklebones of goats against the outer courtyard fence. Lisbeth felt their leering gaze.

The redhead shoved them into the atrium. "Remember, we're right outside."

She and Tabari hurried past the birdcages. The click of Lisbeth's sandals, along with the terrifying memories of the last time she was in this place, followed them down the hall. If her mother hadn't risked everything to save her six years ago, she would be the one trapped in Aspasius's bedroom.

Tabari knocked on a heavy oak door. Lisbeth could hear muted voices and the shuffle of feet.

Pytros peered into the hall. When it registered who had come knocking, he threw the door open. "Finally."

For a brief moment, the scene beyond the threshold stood frozen, captured like an old black-and-white photo. Danger magnified Lisbeth's senses. The stench, a primordial soup of bacteria, ammonia, and denatured proteins, hit her nose. The sound of ragged breathing reached her ears. Her eyes lit upon the horrifying sight of a thin, wasted man lying in the middle of the huge ivory bed.

This couldn't be Aspasius. The man who'd taken her hostage after he sent her husband into exile had plump sausage fingers and disgusting jowls that swayed whenever he had a point to make. This man had sunken cheeks and dull gray eyes where coal-black embers had once sizzled. This man was dying. Maybe she had a shot of getting her mother out of here alive after all.

"Lisbeth?" Mama sprang from the couch beside the bed. "Why are you here?"

Pytros peeled back to allow her passing. She ignored the accusation etched in the scribe's stare and went straight to her mother's outstretched arms.

"Mama, are you all right?"

Her mother nodded. "I told Tabari to fetch the saw. Not you."

"The proconsul's soldier boys must have had other orders."

"Felicissimus is dead," Mama whispered in English. Her eyes cut to the body on the floor. "Last night."

Lisbeth's hand flew to her mouth.

"Look what the wind has blown in." Aspasius tried to push up on his elbows but fell back on the pillows. "How nice to have all of my property returned to me."

Lisbeth thrust aside the conflicting emotions of Felicissimus meeting the tragic end he deserved and the possibility that they could shortly meet the same fate. She stepped forward, refusing to be cowed. "This is just a house call. After we do what we can for you, I'm not staying, and neither is my mother." She moved in for a closer examination of the proconsul's swollen leg. Mama had already done a simple incision to encourage drainage and promote healing. The foul odor indicated the necrotized tissue had not been saved. A more aggressive treatment was necessary. "He needs antibiotics and possibly an amputation."

Aspasius coughed. "No cutting." A fevered flush smoldered on his cheeks.

"I think we can get by without your antibiotics." Mama's guarded look warned Lisbeth to agree.

"She has medicine that will save our master?" Pytros moved in beside Mama. "Then you will use it."

His razor-edged threat only served to strengthen Lisbeth's resolve. "After all you've done to us, why should we do anything to save him?" She took her mother's arm.

Pytros lunged for Mama, wrapped his arm around her neck, and put a knife to her throat. "The medicine, or she dies." His eyes were feline, the pupils vertical slits rather than healthy circles. "Now!"

"Don't do it, Lisbeth," Mama said through gritted teeth.

"Mama!"

"Stand back," Pytros threatened. "The medicine, or I kill her."

Lisbeth's eyes flicked from Mama to Aspasius to the knife Pytros pressed against Mama's jugular. Her hand tightened on the backpack strap on her shoulder.

These antibiotics were her backup plan . . . a safety net for her daughter. She'd only packed three rounds for the trip down the portal. Shortsighted for sure, but she hadn't counted on Diona's emergency, which had used up the first round. Giving aid to a stranger. Then, of course, she'd pumped the next round into Ruth without giving it a second thought. She would have given her own blood to save her friend. But to give the last of her security to an enemy? God forgive her, she couldn't do the very thing she'd expected Cyprian and the church to do.

"Give me the medicine!" Pytros shouted.

A trickle of red slid down the olive skin of Mama's neck.

The air thickened in Lisbeth's nostrils. *Lord, help me!*

"This is how they'll know you are my disciples."

God, I can't. What if . . . ?

"Just as I have loved you . . ."

"Okay. Calm down, little man." Lisbeth fumbled with the clasp on the backpack straps. "Let her go, and I'll get you what you want." She struggled out from under the bag's weight and dug out the pills. She shook the package. "I said let her go."

Pytros cocked his head. "Put them on the bed."

"Do as he says," Aspasius whispered.

Lisbeth tossed the pills on the bed, buying her mother's release with a Z-Pak. Pytros stepped back, and she and Mama raced into each other's arms.

"He nicked you."

Mama refused Lisbeth's attempts to stop the bleeding from the tiny gash. "You shouldn't have done this." She gathered the antibiotics.

"Those pills don't come close to repaying all that you've done for me," Lisbeth whispered in English. "You sure you want to operate on him? I don't think he'll make it."

"We could let nature take its course, but neither of us could live with ourselves, could we?"

Lisbeth released a pained sigh. "'This is how they'll know you are my disciples.'"

Mama's eyes glistened.

Lisbeth withdrew the serrated saw from her backpack. "Let's do this." The stainless steel blade sparkled in the sunlight streaming through the shutters.

"Pytros, the pills will not be enough. I'll have to operate," Mama ordered. "I'll need a large, flat surface. Have Kardide clear the office table, and have Iltani boil water. Lots of it."

51

ASPASIUS HATED TO ADMIT the huge relief he felt at having Magdalena once again flank him. Even with the sharp reproof on her lips and a very large knife in her hand, her presence would steady his off-kilter stance and have him back on his feet in no time. Magdalena possessed more than competent skill with healing herbs. She also oozed a bewitching power of discernment and eased his strained mind. This strange, strong-willed woman had cast an unbreakable spell on him.

He would make certain she never left him again. "I need a moment with my scribe."

"Make it quick." Magdalena stepped back. "This infection should have been dealt with days ago. No telling how far it has spread."

Aspasius motioned Pytros to him.

"I'm here." The eager scribe leaned in close, his hands trembling. "How can I serve you further, my lord?"

"Sacrifice to the gods on my behalf and then . . ." Aspasius whispered his brief instructions. Pytros nodded his assent and hurriedly backed from the room.

Aspasius waved Magdalena close, and she returned boldly to his side. He shifted carefully. Despite the pain, he stretched across the span and took her hand.

Though he could tell she preferred they not touch, he couldn't detect so much as a tremble.

Magdalena was the only person in the world who wasn't afraid of him.

His only true friend.

He knew this woman. And most importantly, he knew of the son she'd hidden from him all of these years. That she had saved the imperfect result of their union was the very reason he knew she could do him no real harm. On more than one occasion, she'd had ample opportunity to add something fatal to his sleeping potions. He'd always awakened. It wasn't in her nature to cause harm. Magdalena was a healer. And though she may hate him, the point of her blade would be well placed, and her hand would remain steady. This woman would do everything within her power to see that he lived.

Aspasius raised her hand to his lips. "Thank you."

Magdalena's mouth opened, then closed.

He'd always loved the thrill of sending a shocking blow through her body. His unexpected words of kindness hit her harder than his hand ever could. For once, she had nothing to say, and he found her stunned silence deliciously arousing.

His enjoyment of the moment was interrupted by the beautiful young healer pushing up to the table. "What did he say?"

"Thank you," Magdalena whispered. She withdrew her hand and stepped back. "He said thank you."

Lisbeth's perfect brow creased. "Did you already give him something for pain?"

It was all Aspasius could do not to laugh out loud. These two were so much alike.

Magdalena shook her head, never taking her eyes off of him. "No."

Aspasius chuckled low and to himself. With his healer's confusion seared into his memory, he closed his eyes in peace. The proconsul of Carthage would wake up a well man.

"I DON'T understand why you insisted we operate in his office." Lisbeth helped Kardide pour scalding water across the top of Aspasius's giant desk, taking a bit of sadistic pleasure in watching the finish on the burled mahogany warp. "The last time I was in this room I was forced to stand naked before the entire Senate."

"Trust me in this, Lisbeth." Mama directed the soldiers carrying the proconsul on a sheet. "Set him down carefully."

Though the room was large, Lisbeth felt compressed between the floor-to-ceiling bookshelves and the wall mural of a chariot racer whipping his frightened horse. "Mind if I open the shutters?"

"We don't need the flies." Mama handed their patient antibiotics.

Aspasius greedily washed down Lisbeth's last line of defense with an herbal sleeping cocktail. *What have I done*? She gripped the edge of the desk to keep from stuffing her hand down his throat and taking back what was hers.

It didn't take long for the proconsul's eyes to cloud over. Once he drifted off, she and Mama rolled up their sleeves, scrubbed in, and gloved up. While Mama arranged her freshly sterilized instruments, Lisbeth made a mental list of all the things making her nervous. So many obstacles were stacked against their success. Aspasius was not a healthy man. Even if he was, he could suffer a heart attack, heart failure, or blood clots during or after the excruciating procedure.

Say, by some impossible miracle, Aspasius survived the surgery, one Z-Pak was slim protection against possible infection at the operative site, pneumonia, or the need for further limb reduction if this initial tissue removal didn't arrest the gangrene. Lisbeth lifted the proconsul's gown out of Mama's way. The outline of his ribs was shockingly pronounced. Lisbeth plugged the stethoscope into her ears and listened to the rise and fall of his chest. Lungs a bit congested. Heartbeat slightly irregular. If he lived through this gruesome ordeal, there was no way he would survive another round of surgical trauma and blood loss.

Lisbeth draped the stethoscope around her neck and stated her biggest fear of all, "If he dies on the table, we won't make it out of here."

"If we do nothing, he'll die in his bed." Mama glanced at the soldiers stationed at the door. "You saw him whispering to Pytros. How far do you think he'd let us get?" Her face transmitted a determined calm Lisbeth didn't understand. "Either way, we're in too deep to jump ship now."

"We were in too deep the day we fell through that hole." Truth was, the secret of the Cave of the Swimmers had destroyed any chance of a normal life, and they both knew it.

Mama whispered a prayer, pressed her feet solidly to the floor, then leaned in to the task. Lisbeth helped her cinch a tourniquet high on his thigh. Mama cleansed the wound site with an antiseptic wash of ground leaves and barks.

While comparing the appearance of Aspasius's diseased limb to his other leg, Mama discussed with her the best place to cut. Determined to maintain as much of a functional stump as possible, Mama opted to saw below the knee. First, the tedious task of removing most of the dead tissue. Within seconds, the office smelled like a stagnant pond. The soldiers standing guard clamped hands over their noses and fled while Kardide and Iltani stood fast. Sometime during the transfer of Aspasius to his office Pytros had decided to make himself scarce. It was just as well. The scribe's all-seeing eyes made Lisbeth's skin crawl.

Mama set her jaw, lifted the saw, and gave Lisbeth a curt nod.

Other than moral support, Lisbeth didn't feel she had much to offer. She was an epidemiologist, not a surgeon or an anesthesiologist. If Mama's patient crashed, Lisbeth didn't know how much she could help past performing CPR. Her gaze ping-ponged between Aspasius and the sheer strength Mama was expending to carve through bone. No wonder most ortho surgeons were the size of linebackers.

"I can take a turn on the saw, Mama."

Her mother used her forearm to brush hair from her sweaty forehead. "I've about got it." She straightened her back, twisted the exhaustion from her shoulders, then put her weight behind the dulling blade.

As the minutes dragged by, Mama continued her precise back-and-forth movements until the leg had been completely severed below the knee.

While her mother tied off veins, Lisbeth fought the sour taste in her mouth. Caring for her enemy was ten times harder than caring for the strangers who came through the doors of the county hospital.

When the last bleeder had been sutured, awareness that she and Mama had done the impossible drained the adrenaline from Lisbeth's limbs. Only one thing could explain their success. For some reason God wanted this monster to live.

52

BAREK BROUGHT IN THE load of driftwood he'd scavenged after spending the night weeping for Natalis at their favorite fishing pier. He'd tried and failed to find the slave trader who'd shackled him to his treachery. Which was just as well, since he was the one who deserved to be beaten. Today he would pack a few things, tell Cyprian the truth, and cast himself into exile.

He closed the door to the kitchen with his foot and dumped the sun-bleached sticks next to the oven. The wad of parchments Felicissimus had given him slipped from his pocket and fell to the floor. He hurriedly gathered them, but not before Naomi turned from her bread making.

"Where have you been?" The doe-eyed servant girl wiped flour from her hands.

"Out."

"You left with those who broke Cyprian's heart."

He didn't appreciate the way Naomi kept tabs on him or the way she looked at him now. "I needed air."

It was like she'd somehow discovered what he'd done and didn't approve. He didn't need her judgment to make him feel bad. He already felt lower than a sand viper. If he would have taken the time to think things through a little better, he would never have agreed to help Felicissimus. His anger over his mother's death had blinded him. Made him a fool.

A naval commission on the first ship out of here was not worth destroying Cyprian, the church his parents had died for, and his best friend. Once again, he'd let down the people he loved the most.

Barek stuffed his guilt and tucked the pieces of paper back into his pocket. "Where's Cyprian?" He cut his eyes at Maggie. She stood on a stool scrubbing vegetables with Junia and eyeing him with that evil little stare of hers. "I need to talk to him."

"He's been praying and poring over your father's scrolls all day." Naomi lifted the lid on a pot over the fire. "I've kept the soup warm."

"I'm not hungry."

"If you ate dinner you might not be so cranky." Maggie pointed a carrot at him. "When are we going back for Ruth?"

He didn't want to admit spending a good part of the morning searching through the burial crocks in the Tophet. Since the day he and Maggie had left his mother's urn, a hundred more had been added. He couldn't find the jar with Maggie's charcoal drawing. "*We* aren't going anywhere."

"You can't just leave Ruth in that cave." Maggie tossed a clean vegetable into a bowl. "When my mommy gets home, she'll take us there."

Barek didn't like all their eyes on him. "It's not a cave, and it's not your business." He grabbed a piece of bread and jabbed it in Maggie's direction. "I'll worry about my mother; you worry about yours."

She lifted her chin in that defiant way of hers. "You're not my boss."

He started to say he was glad of that, then stopped cold when he saw a dark red trickle dripping from her nose. "You're bleeding."

"No, I'm not," Maggie argued.

Naomi gasped. "He's right." She grabbed a towel. "You are." She pressed the cloth to Maggie's nose, then pulled it away. "See?"

Maggie's eyes expanded to the size of two huge sapphires. "I don't feel good." She rubbed her stomach. "I need the bathroom."

Barek snatched her off the stool. "Come on."

He ran down the hall with her pressed to his chest. He could feel her hot skin through his tunic. He remembered how hot his mother had felt when she had the measles. He raced to the latrine, praying Maggie's drink from the bucket at Felicissimus's slave cell hadn't made her sick. He shouldn't have let her go with him to the Tophet. If she was sick, it was all his fault.

Another failing to add to his growing list.

He gently set Maggie down before the hole in the marble slab.

Her face was bright red. "My head hurts."

"You're going to be fine." How could somebody be so mouthy one minute and so sick the next? Why hadn't he told Lisbeth about Maggie drinking out of the bucket? Maybe she could have done something. Given her some of the fancy medicine she kept in her strange bag.

Maggie swiped her hand across her nose and smeared blood across her cheeks. "Wait outside."

"Are you sure?"

"You're a boy." She looked so little and helpless. She was getting sicker by the minute.

"I shouldn't leave you."

"Go."

"If you need me, shout and I'll come running." He stepped into the hall.

Naomi and Junia had gathered clean towels and a fresh tunic. Junia stayed with him while Naomi went in to check on Maggie. He could hear Maggie moaning and crying.

Barek paced. "I should go find Lisbeth."

"Wait." Naomi emerged with Maggie in her arms. "She has diarrhea and a rash on her chest. We need to get her to the typhoid hall."

Barek held out his arms, and Naomi deposited Maggie into his hold. He cradled her close. "I'm so sorry, Maggie."

She opened her eyes. "I want my mommy."

53

"WHATEVER THE PAST BEQUEATHS to us, know this: God is the one with the ultimate control of the future." Tears brimmed in Mama's eyes as she tucked a note into Lisbeth's hand. "Cyprian is safe now."

"I won't go without you."

"That was the deal. I stay, and everyone I love is free."

The eager click of Pytros's shoes sounded outside the office door. Before he'd stepped out to run a quick errand, he'd stationed the redheaded soldier outside the door. The sharp-eyed scribe would expect two doctors to be attending his master when he stepped back in.

"Mama, don't do this," Lisbeth whispered in English. "Come with me. Please."

"I'm so proud of the woman you've become." Mama hurriedly kissed her cheek. "Run to your family, and don't look back."

Pytros breezed into the room. "Well, how is he?"

"Sleeping." Mama took Pytros by the arm and wheeled him back out the door. "You know how irritable our master can be if he's awakened. Let's discuss the best ways to keep him comfortable."

While her mother chatted Pytros to distraction in the hall, Kardide and Iltani positioned themselves between Lisbeth and the closed door.

"Do like your mother says," Kardide ordered.

Lisbeth grabbed her backpack, activated the lever on the secret wall panel, and stepped into the tunnel that ran beneath the palace. The stones slid shut. Forever cut off from her mother, Lisbeth fought panic. She struck the flint. The flame glowed in the stifling emptiness.

She'd journeyed to this world prepared to win. To take control of the situation and turn things around. She'd studied Roman history. Worked to become an expert on controlling infectious diseases. Memorized botany charts and different herbal recipes. She'd given a great deal of thought to the supplies she packed in her medical bag. Granted she regretted not obtaining more antibiotics for the trip, but for the most part she'd had what she needed. Yet, when it came time to save her own mother, her plans were as useless as her cell phone.

If she'd learned anything in the past two weeks, it was that control did not inoculate someone from disappointment, heartbreak, or catastrophe. The past pursued the future with the specific intent of creating chaos.

Lisbeth choked back sobs and thrust the tiny oil lamp into the musty darkness. Rats squealed and scattered. Clawing her way back to Mama was useless. Mama had chosen to operate in Aspasius's office with the express purpose of pushing Lisbeth to safety at her first opportunity. It shouldn't have surprised her that Mama had chosen to secure her daughter's freedom at the cost of her own life for the second time. Tempting as it was to cry foul, Lisbeth had done the very same thing to save Maggie.

Lisbeth descended into ankle-deep water. As she stepped away from the mother she'd longed for her whole life, the dream of reuniting her whole family sank into the sludge.

She slogged through the tunnel, her hand cupped around the flickering light. One wrong turn could alter her course, and she might never find the exit. Wandering aimlessly through the inky blackness was a lot like time travel. She'd thought doing her homework would give her an advantage this time around. But hindsight was not the twenty-twenty panacea everyone claimed. Knowing what was coming had distracted her and stripped away the ability to find joy in the moment.

She pressed forward. Sweating and weak-kneed, she emerged worse for the wear. She snuffed the lamp and slipped through the opening in the stone wall. Blood, perspiration, and muddy water soiled her tunic. Sticking to the tenement alleyways, she set off toward Cyprian's villa.

The acidic bite of urine and the stench of decomposing bodies overwhelmed the heart of the city. Carthage, like Aspasius, was rotting from the inside out.

The deserted market offered the perfect shortcut. She headed for a gate swinging on rusty hinges. The flutter of parchment, an announcement of some sort, caught her attention. She rose on her tiptoes and ripped the paper from the peg:

BY ORDER OF THE PROCONSUL OF CARTHAGE!
CURSES ON CYPRIANUS THASCIUS.
A CHRISTIAN AND TREASONOUS HERETIC.
MAY HE BECOME LIQUID AS WATER AND
DISAPPEAR INTO THE EARTH FOREVER.
A REWARD OF FIVE GOLD PIECES IS HEREBY
OFFERED TO THE MAN WHO BRINGS
CYPRIANUS THASCIUS BEFORE THE THRONE OF JUSTICE.

Hands shaking, Lisbeth glanced around the square. Copies of the curse fluttered from every post and pillar. So was this the errand Aspasius had sent Pytros on? While she and Mama were saving their enemy, he was having his sorry little scribe paper the city with what was basically a Most Wanted notice, a death warrant for her husband. Aspasius had lied, and she'd helped him live long enough to get away with it.

Blood boiling, she marched around the square, ripping each piece from its nail. She wanted to toss the wadded lot of them into the disgusting gutter where they belonged. Instead, she clutched them tight.

Lisbeth sprinted the avenue snaking along the coastline. The late afternoon sun had set the sky ablaze and turned the crystal sea bloodred. She ran faster. Aspasius was sending his men for Cyprian.

She burst into the villa.

Cyprian paced the atrium, his face grim. "Thank God you're here."

Had he heard of the bounty on his head? "Aspasius lied." She pulled the note from her pocket. "He signed this agreement to leave you alone, and yet I found these . . . " She stopped midsentence. "Wait. What's going on? Tell me."

"Maggie's sick," he managed before his voice broke.

"Where is she?" Her gaze followed the movement of his hand toward the hall where Diona Cicero convalesced. A shudder shook the support pillars deep inside Lisbeth's body, the resounding blow she deserved for giving away the last of her antibiotics. "No!" She shoved the papers into Cyprian's hand and pushed past him.

"It's my fault she's sick!" Barek called after her.

Lisbeth skidded to a halt. "What?"

"I let her drink from a bucket in Felicissimus's slave cell," Barek explained. "I turned my back for a second, and next thing I knew she was guzzling water from a filthy gourd."

Typhoid needed a minimum of seven to twenty-one days to incubate. Maggie had taken that drink in Felicissimus's slave cell no more than three days ago. As much as she'd love to blame the slave trader, the source of her daughter's exposure was not that bucket. The third-century cistern was the most likely culprit. The same cistern where she and Maggie had surfaced three weeks ago to the day. During their entry, Maggie had swallowed so much stagnant water she'd nearly drowned.

"If Maggie has typhoid, it's not your fault, Barek."

"Can't you give her the same medicine you gave Diona?" Cyprian asked.

Lisbeth had meant to give a precautionary round of antibiotics the moment they'd arrived at Cyprian's, but in the shock of discovering her husband remarried she'd completely forgotten. If her daughter was sick, she had no one to blame but herself. She was the one who'd made it possible for her daughter to jump into a world of killer epidemics.

As if her malpractice as a mother weren't bad enough, she'd just given her daughter's hope to the vilest man in all of history.

"I gave it to Aspasius." She wheeled and raced toward her daughter. "I'm coming, baby!"

When she reached the hall, Vivia sat beside Maggie's mat, twisting water from a cloth. "I'm trying to get her fever down."

Lisbeth dropped to her knees at the head of Maggie's bed. She ran a trembling hand over her child's sweaty brow. Maggie was burning up and unresponsive. "Baby, Mommy's here." What to do next jumbled in Lisbeth's mind. She looked helplessly to Vivia.

Vivia's eye widened. "I've offered Magdalena's special mixture of salt and fruit juice whenever she wakes, but she refuses and complains of belly pain. Maybe she's just picked up one of those passing sicknesses children get from time to time."

Lisbeth ignored Vivia's doubtful expression and lifted Maggie's tunic. The flat splotches on her tiny chest were undeniable. Lisbeth ran her shaky fingers along Maggie's abdomen. When she approached the lower right quadrant, Maggie winced and opened her eyes.

"Mommy, it hurts." Maggie's raw voice croaked from chapped lips.

"I know, baby. I'm sorry. So sorry." Lisbeth lowered Maggie's gown and kissed her forehead. "Mommy's going to make it all better." She had to look away before her daughter saw beneath her tears and guessed that she had no way of pulling such a miracle out of thin air.

54

BAREK WAS IN THE middle of apologizing to Cyprian for siding with Felicissimus, for taking Maggie to the slave blocks, and for everything else he'd done to disappoint his family when burly soldiers brandishing swords stormed the atrium.

Before either of them could react, angry-faced troops swept through the measles hall. They turned over mats and destroyed vaporizer tents, then planted their hobnail boots in the backs of patients too weak to run.

"Stop. This is a private residence!" Cyprian commanded authoritatively. "You've no right."

"What are we to do with them?" one of the soldiers asked the commander.

"Slit their throats."

"No!" Lisbeth emerged from the typhoid hall and threw herself between the little boy whose mother had died and the redheaded soldier.

The soldier's boot landed in Lisbeth's belly and sent her flying into a wall. She groaned and put her hand to her head. It came away red with blood, but she scrambled to her feet. "Leave them alone."

Cyprian snagged her arm. "No."

Barek ripped his sword from his belt and yelled at Cyprian, "Take her and go!"

"No! I'm not leaving!" Lisbeth screamed as Cyprian snatched her up and navigated his way across the mangled landscape. "Barek, no!"

55

LISBETH CLAWED AND KICKED all the way back to the typhoid hall. By the time Cyprian set her down she was beyond consolation. "I won't go."

Titus had Maggie in his arms. "You must." He thrust the child at Cyprian.

"But I won't leave Laurentius and Junia," Lisbeth said.

Vivia crammed the backpack into Lisbeth's hands. "The day has come for Titus Cicero to defend the children of Magdalena. They will be safe with us."

Cyprian shouted, "Come now, Lisbeth!" He raced toward the back gate. Lisbeth had no choice but to follow.

The three of them arrived at the well, breathless and frightened as cornered prey.

"But I promised Mama I wouldn't leave Laurentius or Junia. And what about Barek? We can't leave Ruth's son."

"I'm going back for them," Cyprian said between labored breaths.

"But Aspasius . . . his soldiers are coming for you."

Cyprian held Maggie's limp body close to his chest. "We have come to the end of things."

Lisbeth placed her palm on Maggie's forehead. Typhoid's heat seared her hand. Far down the alley, hobnailed boots marched for Cyprian.

If she saved her daughter she would lose her husband. Maggie would receive lifesaving drugs, and Cyprian would kneel before the executioner's sword. The past would forever carry the stain of his selfless blood so that somewhere in the future, a young woman would learn the truth of her father's sacrifice and weep in appreciation.

"I shouldn't have given Aspasius the medicine."

"You lived what I have only had the courage to preach."

"I didn't do it out of love. Pytros had a knife to Mama's throat."

"Fear may have been a factor, Lisbeth, but in the end you chose to love someone who did not deserve your sacrifice." He stroked her cheek. "Promise me you'll teach our daughter this beautifully illogical love."

"You're not coming with us, are you?"

He didn't answer. He didn't have to. His love for a group of people who did not deserve his sacrifice would allow him to do nothing less.

She withdrew nose plugs from her backpack, and clamped Maggie's nose. Their daughter was the perfect sum of the best parts of him and the best parts of her. Two completely different sets of DNA woven into an intricate little being time and distance could never separate. No matter how long the time or how far the distance, Maggie's father was forever captured in Maggie's regal features, unruly curls, eyes blue as the Mediterranean, and selfless heart.

"We must be quick." Cyprian deposited Maggie into Lisbeth's arms. He removed his sash and lashed Lisbeth's wrist to Maggie's. "So you do not become separated."

This was it. The moment she'd fought since her arrival. And she was not afraid.

All this time, she'd believed the reason for her travels into this harsh world a simple one: she was meant to rewrite history. But now she knew she'd been dropped into the middle of these struggles so the past could rewrite her.

She gazed into Cyprian's eyes and caught a glimpse of his future, a portion that had been hidden from her until now. Her breath snagged on the clarity. He, too, was not afraid.

No matter what happened in the next few minutes, Cyprian would follow his destiny. She must follow hers.

Lisbeth shifted Maggie over her shoulder and took her first deep breath in six years. "I love you."

Cyprian took Lisbeth's face in his hands. "Promise me you will never come back."

She could only nod.

He gently brought his lips to hers. When at last he withdrew, the bittersweet tang of their mingled tears lingered. He kissed the top of Maggie's head, never taking his eyes off Lisbeth. "I know you will love our daughter enough for the both of us."

She did her best to smile, then opened his hand. She pressed his palm against the tiny swimmer painted on the side of the well. "Send us home, my love."

Epilogue

Cyprian felt his heart sink along with his wife and child in the dark cistern waters. The fast-approaching double time of armed men denied him even a moment to mourn. He wheeled from the time portal and ran in the opposite direction. He cut through the tenement alleys, putting multiple turns and as much distance as possible between him and the sounds of soldiers' boots. Huffing, he scrambled through the deserted market, veered onto one of the major avenues, and raced toward his villa.

"Barek!" he called as he burst through the door. Overturned mats, smashed pottery, broken vaporizer tents, and the still bodies of Lisbeth's patients littered the atrium. "Barek!" His calls went unheeded. His anxiety growing, Cyprian picked his way through the mess and sprinted to the gardener's cottage.

The door stood ajar.

Heart pounding, he slowly pushed the weathered wood. "Barek!" Ruth's son stood with his back to the corner, dagger drawn, his eyes wide and his face ghostly pale. Cyprian held up his palms. "Barek, it's me. Where are Junia and Laurentius?"

Barek shook his head as if he didn't understand Cyprian's question.

"Where are they, boy?"

Barek stepped aside. Laurentius had his face buried in Junia's shoulder, and she had her arms wrapped tightly around him.

"Is everyone all right?" Cyprian rushed to the little huddle. "What about Naomi and the Ciceros?"

Barek pointed, and Cyprian turned to see them hiding behind the door.

Junia was the first to snap from their terrified trance. "Aspasius is dead."

Cyprian dropped to his knees. "What? How? When?"

"Aspasius is dead," Barek repeated. "And Magdalena has been arrested for his murder."

Acknowledgments

AS WITH ANY WORK of fiction, it takes a lot of real people to transfer the story from an author's head into the hands of faithful readers like you.

A special thanks to the young doctor who diligently pores over my attempts to practice twenty-first-century medicine with only a stethoscope and a bag of herbs. My blatant malpractice for the sake of story drives her crazy.

Writing about the early church would be difficult without the help of the young theologian who constantly sends interesting pieces of sound research my way.

Keeping the time travel rules straight would be impossible without my time travel consultants. You know who you are. Even though you do seem a bit confused about what century you actually belong in, I'm grateful you're willing to make this journey with me.

I'm grateful to Graham Ellis, a high school student wise beyond his years, for his invaluable help with the typhoid research.

My incredible Street Team continues to tell everyone they know about this series. Their enthusiastic support and continual prayers are constant sources of encouragement. Thanks, girls.

I am blessed to be part of a group of writers who meet every Tuesday. These dear friends motivate me to be a better storyteller.

Then there's my writing partner, Kellie Coates Gilbert. On the days when I wearied of slogging through, she would put her foot in my back and not let up until I had finally pushed through. A friend who won't let you settle for less than you can be is a true friend.

To my wonderful family I pray my work will make you as proud of me as I am of each one of you.

My publishing team at Howard is top-notch. Beautiful cover and layout designers. Stellar sales, marketing, and publicity gurus. Brilliant editors such as Jessica Wong. This woman knows how to polish a story without dulling the spirit of the creative types she shepherds.

And finally, all praise, honor, and glory to a God whose perfect love compelled him to come to this sick and dying world and dwell among us.

A Howard Reading Group Guide

RETURN *to* EXILE

Lynne Gentry

Introduction

LISBETH HASTINGS, A TWENTY-FIRST-CENTURY doctor, travels back in time to third-century Roman Carthage once again to rescue her husband from martyrdom, but the arrival of a second epidemic forces her to make the impossible choice: save her husband or save her daughter?

Topics and Questions for Discussion

1. As the book opens, Aspasius is rotting from the inside out (p. 1), and in an effort to cover his decay, he douses himself in expensive nard. We often go to great lengths to mask what is eating at us. What are some ways you hide your secrets? What are the dangers of letting those struggles fester?

2. While Cyprian wastes away in exile, he continually replays his last conversation with Lisbeth (p. 11). When unexpected tragedy strikes, those final conversations can plague us, especially conversations we regret. Does hindsight clarify or cloud the ability to move forward? Why?

3. Cyprian's refusal to reconcile his current life situation with the life situation he'd hoped for almost leads to his arrest (p. 42). His anger rises again when he realizes he is "a man uncertain of where to place his feet" (p. 66). How do you think his disappointment plays into his crisis of faith? What do you do when your expectations and reality do not match?

4. Cyprian was raised in the social-class traditions of Rome. When he converted to Christianity, embracing equality was difficult. What are some struggles new Christians face today? How can the church aid these difficult transitions?

5. Based on her past experience, Lisbeth intends to return to the third century armed with the knowledge and supplies she will need. However, despite Lisbeth's best preparations, she dis-

covers that she has underestimated everything (p. 104). What is the value of being prepared? How do you handle it when life throws you a change of plans?

6. As Lisbeth works to reconcile her decision to meddle in the past with God's purpose for today, she digs into the Bible for any clues about time (p. 86). If you could time-travel, would you change something you regret? What would that be? If you could successfully alter the past, would you be a different person today?

7. Like many who desire to do it all and get it all right, Lisbeth struggles with control. In the end, she realizes control is an illusion. Name some things over which you have no control. Name some things you can control.

8. Barek questions the church not raising arms against people doing wrong. "*'Turn the other cheek,' his father's voice rang in his head. In truth, he knew full well he was turning a blind eye to their suffering, and he hated how the teachings of the church had turned him into a coward*" (p. 256). What's the difference between turning the other cheek and ignoring a situation? In your opinion, is turning the other cheek bravery or cowardice?

9. Cyprian struggles with the idea that someone in the church could betray him, especially after he's done so much for them. How does Felicissimus's relationship with Cyprian parallel our relationship with God? Do you think God wearies of our ingratitude? Discuss how we sometimes betray that relationship.

10. Lisbeth is struck by the fact that we take nothing with us when we die. Everything we hold dear in this life will be left behind in the next. What we can leave behind is our legacy. How will people in the future remember you?

Enhance Your Book Club

1. Maggie fears tight spaces, and Lisbeth fears losing control. Cyprian fears failing those who are depending on him. How did fear cripple these characters? Share as a group about what fears you would overcome if you could each choose one, and schedule a time to take a step of faith together.

2. In Ruth's discussion with her teenage son, she tells him, "In the end, service changes not those who are served but those doing the serving." (p. 163). What do you think she meant? Share a time when doing something for someone else changed your life. Discuss ideas of how your group can serve the community together, and put it on the calendar for your next group outing.

3. People walk away from faith for many reasons. Compile a list of some of those reasons and think of people in your life who have left or are struggling with their faith. Discuss together what you can do to show the love of Christ. Then choose at least one person to encourage.

A Conversation with Lynne Gentry

***Healer of Carthage* ended with such a cliff-hanger. Did you know even as you were writing the first book what would happen in the second?**

Return to Exile *is the middle of what was originally one story. So yes, I knew some of the things that had to happen. However, I love experiencing the story along with the characters, which means I'm often surprised. For example, I had originally planned for Lisbeth and Maggie to get separated because Maggie refused to enter the time portal. I was writing along, and all of a sudden that little sprite ran and jumped in after her mother. I literally screamed, "Noooooo!" And then I thought,* Now what? *Having Maggie in the third century changed the whole story in ways I never planned but absolutely love.*

How did you work on developing already familiar characters even more in this second installment? How do you see the difference between their growth in the first book and this one?

Life never goes exactly as planned. Unexpected twists and turns can create hard times that test the mettle of a person. According to Cyprian's own words, he struggled with his faith. Leaving his pagan beliefs behind was difficult, especially when it seemed that this new God he'd chosen had forgotten him. This was shocking to me. Here was this man who changed the world, and he wrestled with his faith. Just like me. So Cyprian was easy. I just put myself in his shoes and asked God, "Why me?" Lisbeth was a little bit harder. In the first book she is this headstrong heroine who thinks only of herself until the very end. Now that she's a mother, and wants to be a good one, she no longer has that luxury. But her character arc started coming together when I realized good intentions don't always bury selfish desires.

We meet and get to know the church more in this book as we're introduced to various characters such as Quinta, Metras, and Natalis. Did you have a favorite of all these new characters?
All of these people represent different stages of faith. Natalis's faith is young and unscarred by trials. Quinta's faith is in the midst of storm. Metras's faith has weathered hard times and made him a better person. My faith has undergone all of these stages. I would have to say Metras's faith journey gives me hope. In the end, I want my struggles to shape me into the image of Christ.

You write from a lot of different points of view. Was that very difficult to do? Did you ever get confused switching back and forth?
Managing a large cast on the page is a lot like managing one on the stage. I love that. To me, it is exciting to pop into someone's shoes and look at the world from their eyes. Whenever similar phrases in narrative or dialogue sneak in, I realize those came from me, not the character. Writers can't help but bring their past experiences to their characters. The challenge is to spread our junk around so that we create cast members capable of standing on their own.

As you were writing about the choice Christians made between obtaining a writ of libellus for their own safety or defying the Roman edict, were you thinking about the similarity between that and the situations people have been in more recently, such as German Christians during the Nazi regime or the persecuted church in China?
When it comes to defending my faith I would like to think I would have the same courage many believers have demonstrated throughout history. But I confess, there's a bit of cowardice in me. The thing that

struck me during this research process was how much Christians have suffered for their choices. According to a recent survey at least 75 percent of religious persecution around the world is directed at people of the Christian faith. I believe the day is fast approaching when the church will find itself backed against the wall. I pray that when that day comes, I will have the courage to join the ranks of those who stared down arena cats, the guns of Hitler, or the imprisonment of the Chinese.

Tell us a little about the research you had to do while writing *Return to Exile*. Was there anything you found that surprised you?

Research is one of my favorite parts of the writing process. I start out looking for one thing, and that always leads to another and another and another. I think the discovery that surprised me the most was the personal struggle of Cyprian. His extensive writings gave me a glimpse into a flawed man. Realizing that God used Cyprian despite his imperfections gives me a great deal of hope.

What do you want readers to take away from this novel as opposed to *Healer of Carthage*?

Like many people, fear of failure has held me hostage. It has only been through the perfect love of Jesus Christ that I have found the courage to accept my imperfections. If the struggles Lisbeth and Cyprian faced encourages one reader to cast aside fear, I know there will be singing in heaven.

Can you give us any hints about what's coming next as you conclude The Carthage Chronicles?

I guess what you're really asking is will Lisbeth and Cyprian be reunited? Will Cyprian face the chopping block? If I told you, then you wouldn't need to buy the third book. I do know this: there's a new guy in town. If you thought things were bad in Return to Exile, *they get a whole lot worse before they get better in* Valley of Decision.

Keep reading for an excerpt from
Valley of Decision,
the exciting conclusion to
The Carthage Chronicles!

1

DR. LISBETH HASTINGS CHECKED her watch as she fished her buzzing cell phone from the pocket of her white coat. "Make it quick, Papa. I have a department meeting in five."

"Maggie's gone," he blurted.

Lisbeth set a stack of charts on her desk. "Slow down."

"That fancy art college called." Panic expanded the fault line in his voice. "She's not been to a single class since we hauled her to Rhode Island."

"I talked to her on her birthday."

"That was almost a week ago."

Lisbeth glanced at the framed photo of Maggie standing outside her freshman dorm with one arm draped around her, the other around Papa. "She was excited about turning eighteen and being able to make her own decisions."

"What did you say to that?"

"When you start paying your own bills, kiddo."

"Could she possibly gain access to the inheritance your grandfather left?"

"I just set her up with an account that automatically transfers money once a month." Lisbeth could feel her heart rate increasing. "Give me a second." A few furious clicks on the computer and Maggie's account transactions appeared.

$1,279. Tunisair. Charged at 12:02 a.m. Six days ago. The day Maggie turned eighteen.

Lisbeth's body prepared to run. "Grab my emergency bag and passport. I'll meet you at DFW."

"Where is she?"

"Where I *never* wanted her to go again."

Twenty nail-biting hours later, Lisbeth and Papa set foot on African soil for the first time in more than twelve years.

"Maybe we can catch her before she finds someone to take her to the desert." She threaded her arm through her father's. None of her arguments had convinced him to stay behind, and this time she was grateful. "I'm going to try calling Nigel again."

Inside the stuffy cinder-block terminal a cacophony of French, Arabic, German, and heavy British drowned out the live Tunisian band of Berber drums, sitars, and flutes. In the gray haze of cigarette smoke, Lisbeth rotated like a weather vane, listening to her cell phone dialing while she searched for the sugary Texas twang of a strong-willed blonde in big trouble.

She clicked off her phone. "You don't think he took her to the cave, do you?"

"Maggie can be mighty persuasive, and Nigel's a softie."

"But she's just a kid."

"He took *you* there, didn't he?"

"I was twenty-eight, and it was an emergency." She crammed the phone into her duffel. "Go ahead and say it. This would not be happening if I'd taken your advice and brought Maggie to Tunis the moment she started pressing for answers." She hefted her bag onto the customs inspection counter. "You were right. I should have walked her through the ruins. Helped her find closure. Put the past to bed once and for all."

"You can't ask her to do something you haven't done yourself." His blue eyes drilled her. "It's forgiveness that girl craves. And I don't mean from you."

The customs official studied her and Papa suspiciously. "Coming into the country for business or pleasure?"

"Business." Papa scooped up their stamped passports. "Very unfortunate business." He took Lisbeth's elbow and led her around a group of retired Americans on vacation. Flowered shirts, straw hats, and sensible shoes gave away their plans to spend their vacation tramping the sunbaked remains of a forgotten civilization.

The presence of so many tourists shamed her. Tunis was not the volatile hotbed she'd claimed every time Maggie broached the subject of returning. Truth squeezed Lisbeth's conscience like the crowds pressing in from all sides. Political unrest wasn't the real source of her reluctance to bringing her daughter to Africa.

She'd made a promise. Until the cost versus the gains of breaking that promise was settled in her mind she couldn't do anything.

"This way." Papa pushed past the luxury shops, cafés, and beauty salons. "I've got us a ride."

Intrusive taxi drivers rushed them the moment they stepped into the sticky air.

A snaggletoothed man leaped in front of her. "Thirty dinars to Old Carthage."

"Twenty to the Bardo." Another driver hugged her left side.

A man who smelled like a goat moved in on the right. "Fifteen and a guided tour of the Tophet."

"Camel rides only ten dinars, pretty lady!" shouted a young Bedouin elbowing into the cluster, the reins of two saddled beasts of burden clutched in his hand.

"How did Maggie navigate this?" Lisbeth asked.

"She's a smart girl." Papa squeezed her arm tighter. "Like her mother."

"That's what scares me."

"Doctors Hastings!" Across the parking lot Aisa, her father's faithful fry cook, paced the wind-sanded hood of an old Land Rover. His cream-colored tunic stood out against the black smoke pouring from the exhaust pipe of a nearby bus. He waved his hands and shouted, "Come!"

They hurriedly wove their way through the honking cars and heavy foot traffic. Aisa scrambled down from the vehicle with surprising agility for a man she guessed to be nearly seventy.

Lisbeth threw her arms around the wiry-thin Arab. "Aisa!" Her nose immediately detected the comforting scent of lamb roasted over an open fire. "New glasses?"

"And new teeth." Shiny white dentures peered out from beneath the bush of Aisa's graying facial hair.

"Nice." She pointed at his glasses. "I kinda miss the duct tape."

"Nothing stays the same." He took Lisbeth's duffel. "Come. We'll get some food into your bellies and a plan into our heads for what we should do next."

"We?"

"Isn't that what friends are for?"

He loaded their gear into the SUV, then hopped in and floored the gas. The Rover shot into traffic. Lisbeth gripped the dash. Their chauffeur dodged parked cars and bicycles that clogged the streets leading away from the airport. Once clear of the traffic, they flew along the paved coastal road connecting Tunis and Old Carthage, windows down and the salty breeze kinking Lisbeth's hair and anxious nerves into knots. As they neared the older part of the city, Aisa was once again forced to slow down. The narrow avenues crawled with street vendors hawking aromatic oils, brightly colored fabrics, and pottery in every imaginable shade of blue.

Aisa laid on the horn and shook his fist. "Hang on."

At the huge clock tower, their aggressive cabbie abruptly

turned east. He zipped through quiet residential streets lined with whitewashed houses trimmed in the same cobalt blue as much of the pottery. Leafy trees heavy with ripening oranges filled the yards. Here and there, ancient stone columns converted into streetlamps embellished the neighborhoods only the very rich could afford. Grand estates like the one her mother's father had left to Lisbeth when he died.

Aisa whipped into a drive blocked by a massive wrought-iron gate. "Here we are."

"Here?" Lisbeth stared at the familiar gate. "This house belonged to my grandfather." She'd sold her *jiddo*'s estate through a third-party transaction to finance Maggie's steep college tuition. She had no idea the buyer had been her father's camp cook. "You live *here*?"

"Yes." Aisa's toothy grin showed his delight at her surprise. "The good professor is not the only one who knows how to turn sand into treasure."

Lisbeth shifted in her seat. "You sold recovered artifacts?"

Aisa lifted his chin proudly. "My recipe for fried dough."

"To whom?"

"An American food chain." He pressed the remote control attached to his visor, and the gate swung open.

In the distance, Lisbeth could see the hill where the Roman acropolis had once stood. The French had built a huge cathedral. All around her, the palm trees had grown bigger and had acquired multiple rings of thick bark. Beside her sat a wealthy souk vendor who used to be a man who just barely eked out a living frying bread dough on an oil drum.

Nothing stays the same.

The power of time and its ability to change everything had tugged at her since the moment she set foot back in Tunisia. The port that had once been the spear pointed at the rest of the world was now an accusing dagger aimed at her. She'd abandoned Carthage in its hour of need. She could take no credit for its survival. For some unknown reason, its modern progress made her very sad.

Aisa settled Lisbeth in the room where she'd stayed during their rare supply runs to Carthage. She and Papa didn't come often, because things were always so tense between her jiddo and her father. The two men had never had a good relationship, but after Mama's disappearance it was easier to beat each other up than themselves.

Lisbeth showered quickly, slipped into the simple tunic she found laid out on the massive burled mahogany bed, then followed the enticing smell of roasting meat to the large, wraparound terrace with a stunning view of the port. Over by the fire pit, she spotted Papa. He was dressed in a woolen tunic that hit him midcalf. His fry cook was whacking fist-size dough balls with a tire iron and wearing Papa's faded chambray shirt and dungarees.

"Hate to interrupt this touching reunion, but, Papa, why did you and Aisa switch clothes?"

Her father handed Aisa another dough ball. "I thought I'd better dress appropriately for our journey into the third century."

"Oh, no you don't. I let you come to Tunis, but I did *not* agree to letting you go back in time. Plus, Maggie may still be in the twenty-first century."

"You haven't been able to get Nigel on the phone. Either he's dead, or he took Maggie to the desert already." Papa eyed Lisbeth carefully. "I'm current on all my shots."

"That's the least of my worries."

"Well then, if things are as bad back there as you've always said, you'll need my help. And I can tell you right now, it's going to take both of us to wrestle Maggie Hastings back down the rabbit hole."

"I don't suppose your willingness to fling yourself into a waterslide has anything to do with finding Mama?"

"I intend to bring my wife home along with the rest of my family."

Lisbeth thought for a moment and then held up her palms. "We'll have to hire a jeep."

"I checked with customs, and the borders into Egypt are closed to vehicular travel," Papa said.

Lisbeth's stomach clenched. "So as of right now, neither one of us has a way to get to that cave."

"The bald Irishman is not the only one with a plane." Aisa glowed at their shock. "Came with the estate."

She hugged Aisa and kissed his sun-weathered cheek. "Then we've got work to do."

After a quick meal of lamb and fried dough, the three of them set out to prepare for Lisbeth and Papa's entrance into the past. Flashlight in hand, Lisbeth hurried down the steps that led to the cisterns in the oldest section of Carthage. Lizards skittered over the broken blocks of masonry that littered the path. Papa and Aisa followed close behind, heavy ropes slung over their shoulders.

This crazy plan she had might not work at all, but she didn't know what else to do. She couldn't count on Barek being at the well or the small chance that he'd be willing to haul them into the third century again if he was.

Shining her light around the stone base of each cistern, Lisbeth searched for the faded painting of the swimmer family. "I found them."

Papa rushed over. "Look, Aisa. It's the Hastingses."

"Don't touch it, Papa. Let's just do what we need to do and get out of here."

"Seems to me it would be a lot easier just to go from here," Papa said.

"Who knows where we'd end up? I can't take that chance." She kept her light on the tiny figures that had guarded this portal for centuries. "Finding Maggie means we're going to have to take the same route she did. And she only knows how to get to the third century via the Cave of the Swimmers."

Fifteen minutes later they had one end of the rope tied to a stone and the other dangling inches above the dark water. A lifeline she prayed would somehow miraculously be there when they arrived in the third century.

"Now what about those antibiotics?" She turned the beam of light on Aisa. "I don't suppose you were successful in finding a local doc who'd write me some scrips."

The cook's teeth glowed white. "No one can resist my fried bread."

DON'T MISS THE BEGINNING OF THE ADVENTURE!

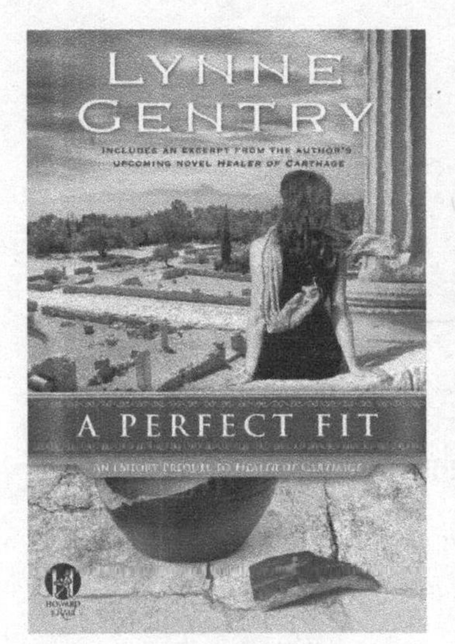

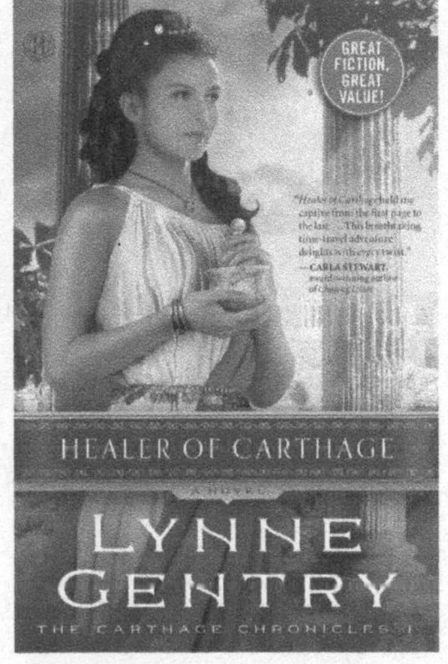

"Lynne Gentry's authentic voice and rich detail in this breathtaking time-travel adventure delight with every twist. Highly recommended!"

—Carla Stewart,
award-winning author of *Chasing Lilacs*

Available wherever books are sold or at www.SimonandSchuster.com